A Monstrous Regiment of Women

"As audacious as it is entertaining and moving."
—*Chicago Tribune*

A Letter of Mary

"A lively adventure in the very best of intellectual company."—*The New York Times Book Review*

"The great marvel of King's series is that she's managed to preserve the integrity of Holmes's character and yet somehow conjure up a woman astute, edgy, and compelling enough to be the partner of his mind as well as his heart. . . . Superb."
—*The Washington Post Book World*

The Moor

"Erudite, fascinating . . . by all odds the most successful recreation of the famous inhabitant of 221B Baker Street ever attempted."—*Houston Chronicle*

A
DARKER
PLACE

LAURIE R. KING

BANTAM BOOKS

New York   Toronto   London   Sydney   Auckland

This edition contains the complete text
of the original hardcover edition.
NOT ONE WORD HAS BEEN OMITTED.

A DARKER PLACE

A Bantam Book

PUBLISHING HISTORY

Bantam hardcover edition published February 1999
Bantam export edition / September 1999
Bantam paperback edition / December 1999

Grateful acknowledgment for permission to reprint artwork on page 154
from *VW Transporter 1961–1979 Shop Manual, 6th edition.* Copyright ©
1981 by Clymer Publications.

ISBN 0-553-57824-3

Published simultaneously in the United States and Canada

Bantam Books are published by Bantam Books, a division of Random
House, Inc. Its trademark, consisting of the words "Bantam Books" and
the portrayal of a rooster, is Registered in U.S. Patent and Trademark
Office and in other countries. Marca Registrada. Bantam Books, 1540
Broadway, New York, New York 10036.

PRINTED IN THE UNITED STATES OF AMERICA

OPM   10 9 8 7

This one is for
Ken and Susan Orrett,
with love

With thanks to Jane-Marie Harrison
and Paul Harrison, Bronwen Buckley,
Jack from Freedom Independent Service,
Alverda Orlando, and Mark Jacobs
from Intertec Publishing.
And particular gratitude for the clever hands
and eyes of Ken Orrett and Nathanael King,
who brought to life the vision of Anne
Waverly and Jason Delgado.

Section headings are taken from *The Compound of Alchymie* by Sir George Ripley, collected in *Theatrum Chemicum Brittanicum* by Elias Ashmole in 1652. Some of the archaic spelling has been modernized by the current author.

Section definitions are from *Webster's Ninth New Collegiate Dictionary*.

1.
PRAEPARATIO

prepare *(vb)* the action or process of making something ready for use or of getting ready for some occasion, test, or duty.

O Power, O Wisdom, O Goodness inexplicable;

Support me, Teach me, and be my Governor,

That never my living be to thee despicable . . .

Grant well that I may my intent fulfill.

CHAPTER 1

In this country, we have the right to religious freedom. The nation was given its form by men and women who came here to escape religious persecution. When their descendents joined together in independence to frame a constitution, they recognized the right to freedom of religion as the very backbone of the nation: take it away, define just what a religion is permitted to look like and how the people may worship, and the entire basis of constitutional government is threatened. Argue as we might with Satanists or witches, followers of disagreeable mullahs or believers in the efficacy of comets to conceal alien spacecraft, from the beginning it has been made clear that, so long as the doctrine involved does not interfere with the country's legal system, a religious community has the right to define its own beliefs: In this country, heresy is not a concern of governmental agencies. Madness may even, at times, be a relative definition; after all, two thousand years ago the Roman government and the Jewish authorities judged a middle-aged rabbi to be criminally insane.

Still, laws must be obeyed, and the dance of what may and what may not be allowed keeps the courts very busy and law enforcement agencies torn between the need to intervene in a community that is behaving in an unlawful manner and the need to preserve the rights of individuals to act out their beliefs in any way short of the unlawful. For example, a community has the right to treat its children as adults when it comes to matters of worship and the determination of authority; it does not have the right to violate the state's child labor laws or treat minors as adults in matters of sexuality.

In investigating the legality of a community, the key element is information, accurately obtained and accurately interpreted. We have all seen the tragedies that occur when law enforcement personnel simply do not share a common language with a group of believers; the only choice in that situation is

From the notes of Professor Anne Waverly

The woman at the focal point of the tiered rows of red and blue seats in the lecture hall did not at first glance seem the type to hold the attention of two hundred and fifty undergraduates at the slump time of three in the afternoon. She was small and her hair was going gray, and her figure, though slim, was long past the litheness of youth. Her voice was quiet and deliberate, which in another speaker would have lulled the back rows to sleep, and the subject of her lecture was more cerebral than kept the average twenty-year-old on the edge of his chair.

The number of sleepers was few, however, and the percentage of spines inclined forward over the tiny writing surfaces attached to the chairs was high. There was an intensity in her that proved contagious, a vivid urgency in her voice and her body that overcame her undistinguished appearance and the torpor of the unseasonably early warmth of the day, transforming her limp into the stately pace of a sage and the wooden cane she leaned on into the staff of a prophetess.

In the eyes of her undergraduates, at any rate.

"What the hell is she talking about?" whispered the woman standing high up at the back of the hall, speaking to the man at her side. The two were not undergraduates; even if their age had not disqualified them, her skirt and blazer and his gray suit made them stand out in the denim-clad crowd.

The man gestured for her to be quiet, but it was too late; they had been noticed. A nearby girl glanced over her shoulder at them, then openly stared, and turned to nudge the boy next to her. The woman saw the girl's mouth form the word "narcs," and then she felt her temporary partner's hand on her elbow, pulling her out the door and out of the lecture hall. Professor Anne Waverly's voice followed them, saying, "In fourth-century Israel this concept of a personal experience of God came together with the political—" before her words were cut off by the doors, and then the police officer and the FBI agent were back out in the watery sunlight.

In truth, neither was a narcotics officer, although both had worked narcotics cases in the past. Glen McCarthy made for a bench just outside the building and dropped into it. Birdsong came, and voices of students walking past; in the distance the freeway growled to itself.

"Did you understand what she was talking about?" Gillian Farmer asked idly, examining the bench closely before she committed the back of her skirt to it.

"*Merkabah* mysticism as one of the bases for early Christian heresies," Glen answered absently.

She shot him a dubious glance and settled onto the edge of the bench.

"And what is mer-whatever mysticism?" she asked, although she was less interested in the question than in the underlying one of how he came by his easy familiarity with the subject of Professor Anne Waverly's arcane lecture. She listened with half an ear as he explained about the Jewish idea of the *merkabah,* or chariot, mystical experience, the "lifting up" of the devotee to the divine presence. The scattering of early flowers and one lethargic bee held more of her attention than his words, and he either saw this or had little to say on the subject, because he kept the lecture brief.

After a moment's silence, the bee stumbled off and the subject Gillian really wanted to talk about worked its way to the surface.

"This whole thing has got to be unconventional, at least," she said finally.

"I suppose it looks that way."

The mildness of his answer irritated her. "You don't think that hauling a middle-aged professor of religion out of her ivory tower and into the field to investigate a cult is a little unusual?"

"I wouldn't use the word 'cult' in her hearing if I were you," Glen suggested. "Not unless you're interested in a twenty-minute lecture on the difference between cult, sect, and new religious movement."

Gillian Farmer was not to be diverted. "It still sounds like something out of an Indiana Jones movie, not at all like a setup the FBI would come within a mile of."

"The bureau has changed since the days of J. Edgar. Now we do whatever works."

"And you think this will work?"

"It has three times before."

"And, as I understand it, once it didn't. People died."

"We were too late there—the final stages were already in motion before Anne could work her way in. I don't think even she can still feel much guilt about that one."

"Why on earth does she do it?" Gillian asked after a while. "Undercover work has got to be the most nerve-racking job in the world, and she's not even a cop."

But the man from the FBI was not yet ready to answer that question.

Seven minutes later, the double doors burst open and the first students tumbled out into the spring air, heading for the coffeehouse. After a pause, they were followed by the main body of participants, walking more thoughtfully and talking among themselves. When this larger group began to thin out, Glen got to his feet and turned to face the hall, pausing to run his palms over his hair and straighten his necktie. This was the first sign of nerves Gillian had seen in him, and it surprised her; since they had met ten days before, she had found McCarthy more idiosyncratic than the caricature of the FBI man, but every bit as cold and competent as the most stiff-necked of them.

Agent and police detective walked back through the double glass doors and down the hallway to the big lecture hall, where they again took up positions on the flat walkway that circled the top tier of seats. Gillian was seething with impatience; she did not at all like the feeling of being kept in the dark. McCarthy had his hands in his pockets, his feet set apart and his head drooping as he gazed down the length of the hall at Anne Waverly, who was now discussing papers, projects, and reading material with the six or eight remaining students.

She put off noticing the intruders for as long as she could—until, in fact, one of the students touched her arm and leaned forward to speak into her ear. She stood very still for three long seconds, then with great deliberation pulled off her reading glasses and slowly raised her eyes to the two figures on the high ground at the back of her lecture hall.

Her expression did not change, but even from on high Gillian Farmer could feel the impact their presence had on her. When the woman bent her head again and slid the glasses back onto her nose, she still looked strong, but she seemed older, somewhat flattened, and her uncharacteristic distraction from the words of her students was obvious. The young men and women knew that something was up and grew taut with a curiosity that verged on alarm; however, when eventually she wished them a good week, they could only disperse, reluctantly, and make their slow and suspicious way up the stairs and past the two intruders.

One boy, however, found retreat more than he could bear. He scowled at Glen as he went by, and then turned back to the podium to ask loudly, "Do you want some help, Dr. W?" His stance even more than his words made it obvious that he was offering an assistance considerably more physical than merely carrying her books, but McCarthy was careful not to smile, and Gillian Farmer merely glanced at the boy.

The woman he had called "Dr. W" did smile. "Thank you, Josh, I'll be fine."

Their protests unvoiced, the students left, with a furtive rush of low conversation that was cut off when the glass doors shut behind them. The lecturer turned her back on McCarthy and Farmer, gathering up her papers from the table and pushing them into an old leather briefcase. She buckled the case, took it up in her right hand and the cane in her left, and started for the steps, her very posture vibrating with displeasure.

Each stair was deep enough for two short footsteps, which was how she took them, leading with her right, bringing her left foot up, and taking another step with her right foot. She seemed to depend on the cane more for balance than sheer support, Gillian decided while watching the professor's slow approach. And it was the knee, she thought, rather than the hip, that was weak. Other than that, she was in good shape for a woman in her mid-forties, perhaps a vigorous fifty. Her back was straight, her graying hair worn as loose as that of her students, curling softly down on her shoulders. Her clothing, though, was far from a student's uniform of jeans and T-shirt. She was dressed in the sort of professional clothing a woman wears who does not care for dresses: khaki trousers, sturdy shoes that were almost boots, a light green linen shirt that seemed remarkably free of creases for the tail end of a day, and a dark green blazer shot through with blue threads. The clothes seemed a great deal more formal than those of the other adult women on the campus, Gillian thought, and found herself wondering about the professor's status in the tenure stakes.

At the top of the stairs, the woman neither paused nor looked up, but merely said to the carpeting, "Come to my office, please."

They followed obediently, submitting to the hard looks of the handful of students who hovered in the distance to be quite sure their professor did not need assistance. She ignored them, as did McCarthy. Farmer tried to avoid looking as though she was escorting a prisoner, with limited success.

They went down the paved path through some winter-bare trees and past a small patch of lawn, and into another building designed by the same architect as the hall. The lecturer unlocked a door and they followed her in, and Gillian revised her speculations: If her recollection of academia was correct, this was not the office of a woman with reason to fear a lack of tenure. The room looked, in fact, like that of a high administrator or department chair, a corner office complete with Oriental carpet and wooden desk—although surely an administrator would not be surrounded by shelves sagging under the weight of books and piled high with untidy heaps of journals and loose manuscripts. The professor slammed her briefcase on the desk, dropped the keys she had just used into her jacket pocket, hooked her cane over the edge of the desk, and sat down.

"Close the door, Glen."

McCarthy shut the door and settled into one of the three chairs arrayed in front of the desk. Gillian Farmer tucked the strap of her shoulder bag over the back of one of the other chairs, hesitated, and took a step forward with her hand out.

"Gillian Farmer," she said. "San Francisco Police Department."

The professor looked at the hand for a moment before reaching out to take it with her own. "Anne Waverly, Duncan Point University. And occasionally FBI. Glen, what are you doing here? I thought I was finished with you."

He did not say a word, but without taking his eyes from hers he reached inside his jacket and withdrew a thick, oversized manila envelope. This he laid softly on the wooden surface between them, allowing his fingers to remain for some seconds on the buff paper before he pulled his hand back. Anne Waverly tore her gaze away from his and stared at the envelope as if it might sprout scaly skin and rear up to strike her. When eventually she looked back at him, for the first time since she had seen them standing at the back of her lecture hall she gave them an expression, one that lay somewhere between exhaustion and loathing.

"Get out of here, Glen."

He immediately stood up. "My cell phone number's in there. Don't wait too long to call—Farmer here has to get back to her caseload."

The two intruders left the office. McCarthy closed the door quietly behind them and strode off down the hallway.

"So much for 'whatever works,'" Gillian Farmer said when she caught up to him. Her mind was already moving toward what she could do next, now that Anne Waverly had turned them down. She did not have many options left: The thought of being forced to do nothing filled her with deep apprehension.

"She'll do it." McCarthy sounded completely sure of himself.

"For Christ sake, Glen, she threw us out of her office."

"She won't be able to keep away."

"Oh, right," she said sarcastically. "She sounded so enthusiastic."

"I didn't say she'd want to do it. I said she wouldn't be able to help herself."

2.
FIXATIO

fix *(vb)* To make firm, stable, or stationary.

In which our Bodies eclipsed begin to fight . . .
One in Gender they be and in Number not so,
Whose Father the Son, the Moone truly is Mother.

CHAPTER 2

From the journal of Anne Waverly (aka Ana Wakefield)

In the silence of their absence, Anne Waverly sat listening to the inner reverberations of the sound the envelope made sliding onto the surface of her desk. She had heard that ominous whisper before. Three times, in fact: twice when Glen had stood before her and put identical envelopes on this same desk, and once out in the desert when she had been sitting on a boulder and looked down to see a rattlesnake glide over the grit-covered rock inches below her boots. Anne's hand reached down and, of its own accord, began to massage away the eternal ache in her knee.

After some time, a soft rapping came from the door —a tentative noise, since all her students knew that Anne never closed her office door when she was inside. She took a deep breath, and her hand came back up to rest on the desk.

"Come on in," she called, and constructed a smile for the girl who appeared in the doorway. "Hello, Monica. What can I do for you?"

Two hours later, Anne's office hours were long over. The last students left, the last telephone calls were made, and around her she could feel the busy building settling into the doldrums of the dinner hour. Time to go home.

Papers and a book for review went into the briefcase. Three folders were set aside to leave at the steno pool for typing. Anne got tiredly to her feet, took the thick woolen coat from the wooden hanger on the back of the door, and drew it on. She switched off the reading lamp on her desk, folded her glasses into their case and put it into her briefcase, and finally picked up the manila envelope that had waited at her elbow all afternoon.

She stood with it in her hand, a study in indecision;

she even went so far as to turn back to the door and lock it, preparatory to opening the envelope, but she changed her mind and dropped Glen's offering into the briefcase with everything else, fastening the buckles over the case's bulging sides. She tucked the folders under her arm, took up cane and briefcase, clicked off the overhead light as she went out, and locked the door. On her way out to the parking lot she detoured past the steno pool, where she left the folders of typing for the secretaries to do the next day.

Then she went home.

It was dark when her headlights hit the tubular steel gate at the foot of her drive, despite the lengthening daylight hours of early spring. She put the ancient green Land Rover into neutral while she got out and unlocked the gate, then drove through and got out a second time to lock it up. The road just inside the gate was viciously rutted, and she picked her way with care as far as the first bend, where the surface became miraculously smooth and she could shift up into second gear for the long climb to the top.

A trio of floodlights came on when the car breasted the hill and a light shone from inside the log house, but these signs of life and welcome were purely mechanical, a matter of motion sensors and timer switches rather than human hands. Anne Waverly lived alone; she had done so for the past seventeen years.

There were the dogs, of course: In them lay life and welcome, and there was Stan now, ecstatic at her return, pushing his nose at the opening of the car door, bumping gently against her as she climbed out. His flat boxer face grinned at her, his hard body wriggled with the effort of wagging the ridiculous stump of his tail, he slobbered and whined and practically pissed himself in pleasure, and Anne allowed herself to be distracted by him. She thumped him and spoke nonsense to him and threw a stick before she picked up her things from the front seat to follow him into the house.

She went in through the unlocked back door, dumping her briefcase on the kitchen table, and then walked quickly into the small side room, once a pantry, that she had given over as a nursery. Away from the university, she did not seem to need her cane as much.

The boxer bitch got up to greet her, spilling pups in all directions, and then immediately looked worried at the tiny mewling protests that her movement had raised. Anne ran her hands along Livy's sleek sides and up her neck, and lowered her head to rest against the dog's hard forehead. The words "animal comfort" came into her mind, the sheer, primitive comfort of touch, she thought; another living body making contact.

With that, Livy backed away apologetically to wade back among the pups and settle down to their tiny howls. The sightless grubs went for her as if she'd been away for hours, and Anne laughed quietly at her own abandonment. Oh, well, she thought, there's always Stan.

The dog was quite happy to leave his preoccupied mate and join Anne for a brief moonlight hike up the mountain. This was a common ritual, just the sort of regular activity that Anne had been told not to establish, years ago, when the possibility of threat and retribution in her life had seemed real. Some of the precautions she had maintained until they were habit; others were difficult: How was she supposed to get in her road without climbing out of the car twice? How could she teach without showing up in predictable places at the posted times? Besides, all that covert mumbo jumbo was over and done with, she had thought. She had thought.

A close observer familiar with her habits would have noticed nothing out of the ordinary about her actions during that evening—or, rather, would have seen only minor things: the way Stan had to bark to catch her attention when shoving against her leg and drooling all over her hand failed; the length of time she held one of the blind puppies against her cheek, cupped in both hands, her own eyes tightly shut; the way she twice forgot to use the cane, walking back to get it with only a mild limp; how she cooked a large meal and ended up putting most of it into the refrigerator; and finally the way she got out of her bed after a couple of hours to sit in the small screened-in porch, wrapped in blankets and listening to the night sounds of the early mosquitoes and the bats and the pair of horned owls that lived nearby. She drank, first from a glass and later from a teacup, and let her hand rest on the back of the dog whenever he came and settled for a time beside her chair. She was still in the porch chair at dawn.

When the sun was up, she got to her feet. Stiff with discomfort and limping heavily at first, she went down the rough-hewn wooden stairs to the main room of the house that served her as study and living room and retreat from the world. She laid several split logs on the coals in the cast-iron stove and opened the dampers full, and then made a restless circuit around the big wood-paneled room filled with comfortable furniture and bookshelves and dark rich colors of orange and red before she eventually fetched up at the heavy desk where she had left her briefcase the night before. She sat down in her chair and took the manila envelope from the bag, only to sit listening to the crackle and hiss from the stove with Glen's next worrisome community unopened in her hand.

Three times I've gone into the belly of the whale for Glen McCarthy, she thought; three times for him, and once for myself. More than any one person owed her fellow human beings, and a greater slice of her life, her sanity, and certainly her health than she could readily afford to give. She was tired now, she felt thick and damaged and middle-aged, and she wanted nothing but to dedicate herself to simple things like work and friendships and growing things.

In the beginning, she thought, I worked for Glen because doing so was the only thing that might justify my continued existence, a payback for the lethal blend of arrogance and blindness that killed Abby. Suicide would have been a relief and a coward's way out, so I gave myself over to Glen and his crazy schemes.

And on the whole, her work for Glen had been worth it. There was no bringing Abby back, but she had at least saved other mothers' children. Maybe only a few; perhaps as many as sixty-eight, all the children salvaged from the four communities she had interfered with. No matter the numbers, she had begun to feel a semblance of equilibrium, that she had done her penance and might be allowed to move on.

How long, Abby? she whispered into the still air. How many more weeks of acting stupid and serene while my bowels go loose with shitting out the terror? How many more times do I ritually pollute myself with that man, whom I don't know if I love or hate? How long until a great wave of tiredness overtakes me at some crucial moment, and I blurt out something that triggers a madman's paranoia? *Oh God; how many more times can I do this?*

Anne had not realized that she was taking Abby's photograph from its resting place in the drawer until she found herself sitting back in the chair studying her daughter's face. She kept the picture hidden for fear that it would become familiar and lose its ability to reach her. Time, however, and the first faint distortions of color on the paper had conspired to make the child a bit of a stranger.

Abby had not been beautiful; Anne had known that even when she was alive. She was an ordinarily lovely child with a wild mop of curly, almost kinky black hair —Aaron's impossible hair—dark brown eyes, and a dimple in her right cheek. Her teeth would have required braces had she lived long enough, but at the age the photograph was taken, just after her seventh birthday, their crookedness was merely charming.

Aaron had taken the picture, unusually enough, although Anne had still been there on the Farm. In the early years of gazing at the photo she had thought that the faint blur on the far right border was her own arm, because she remembered Abby grinning just that way, on the picnic lunch two days before Anne had left, and she wanted very badly to be in the picture with her daughter.

Print it how they might, though, the photo labs had been able only to raise a blur. It might possibly have been Anne's elbow; more probably it was the tail of one of the Farm dogs.

Two days before Anne had driven away in their Volkswagen camper van, the aperture of Aaron's camera had opened and allowed Abby's face and her living body to be imprinted onto the emulsion of the film. Two days after the picture was taken, Abby's mother had abandoned her, driving off to try and "find herself" (a phrase that still had the power to set Anne shaking with an intensity of fury and detestation, on the rare occasions when a student or a friend chanced to use it in her hearing). She drove off to find herself, and eight days later drove home to find instead the remote dirt road clogged with the pulsing lights of a hundred strange vehicles, sheriff and newsmen, ambulance and coroner's vans, disturbed neighbors and frightened relatives, and at the core of it, when she had finally clawed her frantic way through to the cloying miasma of death that lay over the farmhouse and barn complex, a dozen or more invisible, unmarked, and distinctive late-model cars of American manufacture, driven by men like Glen McCarthy.

The film in Aaron's camera had been developed by one of the government agencies as an automatic part of the investigation, and returned to her many months later along with Abby's shoes and teddy bear and several cartons of Aaron's books. More than three years later, during the final stages of her Ph.D., she had been moving apartments and come across the few things of theirs that she had kept, and she made the mistake of taking the developed strips of negatives in to be printed. There had been only seven pictures on the roll, three blurry shots of a new foal that Abby had wanted to take, a couple of the hills around the farm, green with the spring rains, one odd and accidental picture of (she thought) Aaron's boots, and this one of Abby.

It had been a bad mistake, a nearly disastrous one. The life she had built up for herself, the competent persona she had constructed so painstakingly, had proven more fragile than she could have suspected. That one photograph had acted like the carefully set charges of a demolitions expert taking down a high-rise; when she slid it from the photo-lab wallet, sitting behind the wheel of her car outside the shop, she had felt the shudder immediately, and succeeded only in making it to the safety of her apartment before her mind fell in on itself.

Once home, she had collapsed into bed and spent a week there, alternately crying and lying in a sleep so deep it felt closer to a coma, before she was dragged out of it by her insistent doorbell with Glen McCarthy's finger on it. His request for assistance, from someone with not only professional training but personal experience as well in the mechanics of religious aberrations, had literally hauled her back to life. Whether or not this was for the best she had never decided, but it had at least provided a focal point for her life, some sort of purpose to the random motions of eating and thinking. For that, at any rate, she supposed she was grateful.

Now, though, she was surprised to realize that the momentum of daily life had become a purpose in itself. There was an interest and a savor to her interactions at the university, and she had lately been anticipating the rich smell of warm, freshly turned spring soil as her digging fork sank into the overgrown vegetable patch and the amusement and satisfaction of seeing six boxer puppies learn to run and leap. She had even thought vaguely of taking a trip somewhere, for no reason other than pleasure. *How long, Abby?*

Abby looked back at her from the glossy rectangle in her hand, a smiling young face with a faint worry line between her brows as if in foreknowledge of the death that awaited her in her mother's absence, and did not answer. After a while, Anne Waverly closed the photograph of her long-dead only child away in the drawer and reached again for the manila envelope. She carried it into the kitchen, made herself a pot of strong coffee, and sat down at the table to read.

It was not a terribly thick file, as McCarthy offerings went, and Anne had read it through twice before the coffeepot was empty. She felt somewhat better about this one; indeed, the symptoms were so mild she had to wonder if Glen wasn't getting a bit fixated. Still, some signs of impending loss of balance within this remote religious community were there, and it was certainly worth taking a closer look from the inside.

They called themselves Change, and the leader of the Arizona branch, born Steven Chance, was now named Steven Change.

Twelve years ago Steven and two friends had taken a

trip to India and returned, as had countless others, transformed.

Steven Chance was an American, a young chemist who had been born into a conservative Christian family in the Midwest, put himself through university on a full scholarship, graduated with a degree in chemical engineering, and then gone to work for the English branch of a huge chemical conglomerate. Thomas Mallory was a friend from university with whom Chance had kept in touch, who dropped his job in his father's contracting business to join Steven on the trip. With them went a brilliant and independently wealthy research physicist with an interest in metallurgy whom Steven had met in England, a man seven years older than Steven, named Jonas Fairweather.

Something had caused Chance and Fairweather, these two members of levelheaded disciplines, to throw down their lab coats and turn to esoteric doctrines. They quit their jobs—Fairweather not even bothering to resign formally, simply walking away from his desk and his ongoing projects, to the confusion and indignation of his former employers—and sold their cars and furniture, and left.

In India, they met a young Canadian named Samantha Dooley, who had dropped out of her sophomore year at Harvard at the age of seventeen and a half and gone to live responsibly on the earth on a commune near Pune, where she was quietly starving, when she met the three travelers. The four Westerners joined up, moved on to Bombay for a while, and eventually worked their way back to Fairweather's native England, where they used his considerable inheritance to buy a run-down estate. There they established a doctrine and a community called Change, which attracted a growing number of followers over the years. Steven and Jonas changed their names, Fairweather becoming Jonas Seraph, although Mallory and Samantha Dooley retained theirs.

Eight years after returning from India, the original four divided: Steven and Mallory to concentrate on their new site in Arizona, which drew heavily from the San Francisco and Los Angeles branches, while Jonas and Samantha Dooley continued their efforts in rural England. Both enterprises flourished, and although the San Francisco branch was being shut down, there were still smaller branches in Boston, Los Angeles, southern France, Germany, and two in Japan. There were now nearly eight hundred members.

On the surface, there seemed little to draw the attention of Glen McCarthy's project to Change. One of the things working against a possible diagnosis of coming disaster was the far-flung nature of this particular group. Most problematic communal entities—the kinds of groups that were dubbed "cults" by the media and which tended to flash into an orgy of violence, either self-directed or against a perceived enemy—were close-knit, closemouthed little communities obsessively focused on one individual, a person whose irrationality and fears were in turn nourished by the attentions of his (or occasionally her) followers. In this case, although each branch had its leader, they were scattered. Members of the different groups were constantly in and out—Steven to England, the Japanese leaders to Arizona, families and kids moving from one house to another—not characteristic behavior from threatened communities.

Another interesting oddity was the Arizona branch. Within months of its founding it had begun a school, a large portion of its students being kids who had been thrown out of other schools, were on parole, or had been remanded from one of the state's youth facilities. "Troubled youth," formerly called delinquents, were an odd choice for a religious community, but well established within Change: All three men of the original leaders had brushed up against the law in some way, Steven as part of a high school drunken spree with several friends (so much for sealed juvenile records, Anne noted disapprovingly) and Jonas Fairweather in England for a series of nuisance crimes that boiled down to ignoring rules rather than deliberately flouting them. Thomas Mallory had the most serious history, having spent six months in jail at the age of nineteen for threatening a neighbor with a gun and blowing holes in the man's television set. This was during university finals week, and although it marked the end of Mallory's university career, Anne could feel a twinge of sympathy for the man's desperate action. Mallory had also been fingered as instrumental in an investigation into illegal arms possession and sales in the Los Angeles branch of Change three years before, where he had gone to assume an apparently temporary leadership for a couple of months, but charges against him were dropped for lack of evidence. Beyond the three of them, the Change leader in Boston had a record as well, for drunk driving and drunk-and-disorderly, and one of the Japanese leaders had a history of "political crimes," whatever that might be. Passing out leaflets at an antigovernment demonstration, no doubt.

It was the presence of the "troubled youth" in Arizona that had first sparked Glen's interest, even though there were no official complaints, no firm evidence from the periodic medical checkups or the social workers' visits aside from one report that some of the older boys had seemed "unnaturally subdued."

Looking through the material the second time, Anne decided that it was probably Steven Chance's background in chemistry that had originally pressed an alarm button somewhere in the FBI's corporate mind. A small religious group led by a man who could construct a bomb was a group the government wanted to keep under observation.

The material she'd been given was detailed but hardly complete—another indication that Glen wasn't absolutely convinced that there was a problem, or if he himself was, he hadn't managed to bring his superiors around to his point of view. There was an elaborate chart comparing purchases of the various groups, but no conclusions had been drawn concerning the relatively high consumption of rice and fish by the Japanese compared with the Germans; the high demand for concrete mix and heavy lifting equipment in Arizona, currently under construction; or the large orders for chemical fertilizer, garden equipment, and chain saws by the English branch, which was busy restoring a large garden.

She put the purchase records to one side and returned to Glen's personal analysis, which was based largely on a visit he had made to Steven Chance's compound in the Arizona desert. What it boiled down to was that a) the children were too well behaved, b) Steven's speech was heavily laced with references to the Book of Revelation and the cleansing nature of fire, and c) Thomas Mallory's history of guns.

Anne thought it all sounded very thin, although she had to admit that Glen's judgment in these matters had in the past been extraordinarily good.

And in the Arizona community alone, there were one hundred and three children.

At eight-thirty she reached behind her and took the kitchen phone down from the wall. The departmental secretary answered.

"Morning, Tazzie," Anne said. "I'm going to need half an hour with Antony today. Any chance?"

"He's really busy. Is it important?"

"Yes," Anne said flatly. There was a pause while Tazzie thought about this, and then Anne could hear the rustling of papers and a strange humming noise, Tazzie's habit while she was thinking. In a minute the secretary came back on the line.

"I can cancel a couple of things. Two-thirty do you?"

"I have a two o'clock lecture," Anne said apologetically.

"Of course you do, stupid me. Four-thirty, then. I'll cancel Himself."

"Don't do that," Anne said in alarm. "Himself" was the royal reference to the pompous academic vice-chancellor. "I could wait until tomorrow."

"Himself has canceled on us twice, it would be a pleasure to return the honor. Are you okay? You don't sound yourself."

"I'm a bit tired."

"All those babies keeping you awake? Don't get too run-down. There's a nasty bug going around, and you wouldn't want it just before finals."

Anne's laughter was more hysterical than the remark called for: With all the things on her mind, a viral infection might prove a welcome distraction. Perhaps a nice bout of pneumonia would stick her in the hospital and give her an excuse to step aside.

When she had hung up, she hesitated over the phone. She ought to make this next contact in person, but perhaps for the preliminary stages, she could be a coward. She picked up the phone and dialed another number.

"Hello, Alice, could I speak with Eliot, please? Sure, I can wait." An interminable five minutes later, Alice Featherstone's flat-voiced monologue on the problems of raising chickens faded suddenly in midsentence, to be replaced by the taciturn young voice of her son Eliot, grunting a query into Anne's harassed eardrum. "Eliot," she said in relief. "Look, I just found out that I'm going to have to go away for a while. Are you available?" She knew that he would be, and that he would be overjoyed, in his completely undemonstrative way, at the chance to be away from his mother and the rest of the world. It was, nonetheless, only polite to make a question out of it.

"When?" he asked.

"As soon as I get the final grades in, a little under three weeks. I may be away till summer, I'm afraid. Maybe longer."

"The puppies?"

"Yes, we'll have to think about them. Could you come by one day and we'll talk?"

Eliot grunted an assent.

"Over the weekend?"

He grunted again. She thanked him and heard the telephone go dead in her ear. She put her own phone on its rest and then leaned forward, her elbows on the table and her hands buried in her hair.

Her hair smelled warm, faintly of coconut from the shampoo she used. It felt soft and thick to her fingers, a luxuriant, well-styled, and well-cared-for head of hair. She bent her head further forward until the wavy mass tumbled down onto the table, forming a cave around her face. This is the longest it's been in seventeen years, she thought; almost five years' worth of hair, smooth, thick, and alive. She pulled a handful around and pressed it against her face, inhaling the smell. She thought, it's no wonder hair has been such an issue and a symbol over the centuries. The tactile glory of the stuff.

I will miss it, she thought.

CHAPTER 3

Final Exam
Religious Studies 204, The Prophet and Prophetic Speech
Prof Anne Waverly

Choose three of the following questions. As you should know by now,
having been in this class all term, there are often no right or wrong answers,
simply arguments to be explored. You will be expected to support any
opinions or statements with chapter and verse or specific references. Extra
points will be given for the use of extra-canonical writings.

1. What was the role of the prophet in ancient Israel? Give an example of a
twentieth century prophet, and explore the similarities and differences.
2. Trace the development of the prophetic idea of "speaking with God."
3. What are the essential differences in world view between First Isaiah and
Third Isaiah? Can we determine what influenced these differences, and can
we say how they affect the two concepts of God?
4. To what extent did Old Testament prophecy correspond to what we would
now describe as mental illness? Choose two specific examples.
5. Describe some of the differences between prophet and messiah in first
century Jewish thought.
6. Was Jesus a prophet? Was Paul? Why?
7. If Jesus were born today, how would he live and who would his followers
be?

From the notes of Professor Anne Waverly

At four-thirty, the departmental secretary was just getting ready to leave for the day.

"Hello, Tazzie. Have I managed to catch Antony?"

"He called to say he'd be five minutes late, but better give him ten. You know, you really don't look too hot."

"Just tired, Tazzie."

"Don't get sick, honey. Anything I can get for you?"

"No, you run along."

"I think I will. I have to pop into the store and pick up some things for dinner."

"Hot date?"

"Warm, anyway. When can I come out and look at the pups?" Tazzie was on her feet, turning off the computer and retrieving her purse from a drawer.

"Give it another week or two. But really, Tazzie, you don't want a dog when you have a full-time job."

"Actually, I was thinking of my brother. His wife wants a puppy, and she's home with the kids all day."

"Have her come and look at them, then."

"A couple of weeks?"

"Good. They ought to have individual personalities by then."

Anne thought she was going to have to eject the woman out the door by force, but eventually she left, with one last warning about stray viruses. When she had gone, Anne went into Antony Makepeace's office and lowered herself into one of his tatty, overstuffed chairs to wait for him. She eased her bad leg out in front of her and leaned her head back to rest on the chair.

The office had not changed much since she had first seen it nearly eighteen years before, five months after losing her family. She had come in that door a shell-shocked, bereft young woman one narrow step from suicide, but this office had somehow made an impression on her. Antony had been missing that time, too, she remembered now, and she had sat in this same chair, waiting for him in the silence and the smell of books, looking at the leaves of the tree that grew outside one window and at the small birds that came and squabbled on the feeding tray at the other. She had fallen asleep, slipped into the easiest sleep for months, and woke an hour later to find Professor Antony James Makepeace, half-glasses on his nose and pen in his hand, matter-of-factly going about his work of grading papers, ten feet from where she slept.

She wasn't far from dozing off this time when he returned. He was grayer than he had been eighteen years earlier, and a little thinner, but still big and shambolic with the same warm, welcoming, and patient expression on his long face and an identical pair of half-glasses tucked into his breast pocket.

Instead of holding out his hand, though, this time he leaned down and kissed her cheek. "Don't get up, Anne. You look comfortable. Let me fix a cup of tea and I'll sit with you. Like a cup?"

"Thanks, I would."

"Not Earl Grey." His broad back was to her but his voice smiled.

"Flowery rubbish. You'll never convert me, Antony."

"I live in hope. How are the puppies getting on?"

They talked of her dogs and his cats while the electric kettle boiled and the tea was made, and he brought two mugs and a once-colorful cookie tin, now dented and worn down to bare metal at the edges, over to the arrangement of chairs and sat down with a sigh. The age of compulsory retirement had been done away with some years before, or he would not be here, but he had begun to make tentative noises about retiring, and had firmly said this would be his last turn as department chair.

The two old friends drank their tea and ate the cookies his wife made every week, and when the bottom of his cup was reached, Makepeace dusted off his fingers and said, "Now tell me, my dear, what I can do for you."

"I'm really sorry about the short notice," she replied, "but I'm going to have to ask you to get someone to take my classes for the coming quarter."

Surprise and administrative concern gave way almost instantly to a deeper, more immediate anxiety.

"Tazzie said you sounded tired . . ." he ventured.

Anne shook her head. "It's nothing like that. Glen McCarthy showed up yesterday."

He reared back in the armchair looking stricken, almost angry.

"No, Anne. Oh, no. Not again."

"I'm afraid so."

"I thought you were finished with that nonsense."

"So did I."

"Let someone else do it."

"They don't have anyone else."

"Make them find someone."

"Antony, I have to do it. It's the only reason I'm here."

"My dear Anne, you cannot continue to feel responsible for the world's actions. You have done your part—more than your part—and at great cost. Let it go."

"I can't, Tonio. I thought I could when I saw him yesterday. I tried all night to pick up the phone and tell him to go to hell, but I couldn't." She said nothing about her sure conviction that Glen McCarthy had handled her with his usual Machiavellian skill, putting her off balance from the beginning by deliberately appearing without warning and in the one place where she could not scream at him to fuck off—and by bringing the young policewoman along to distract Anne and keep her polite. He had even taken care to put his telephone number on the inside of the manila envelope, so she would be forced to open it and handle the papers even if she had already decided to refuse the case. From any other man, she might have thought the actions accidental, but not McCarthy: He was quite subtle enough to have planned his attack meticulously. And, he was very determined.

Makepeace did not know this, of course, and although the knowledge of the FBI man's manipulation might have armed him for another round of argument, all he heard was the flat commitment in her voice and the affectionate use of his nickname. He looked into his mug for a while, then rose to brew another of his endless cups of Earl Grey.

"You don't have to go immediately? It's usually a drop-everything rush when Agent McCarthy shows up."

"Two weeks won't matter one way or another—or if they do, then the thing was moving too fast for me to interfere with anyway. I'll finish up the quarter, hand in my grades. I will tell the students there's an extra ten points for getting their final projects in on Monday. That should help."

"But you don't think you'll be finished with this . . . what do you call it, anyway?" His burst of mild irritation would be another man's fury.

"Case, investigation, mess, disaster, bit of primal chaos—whatever you like. No, it'll take at least two or three months."

"You will be back by September, though?"

"I hope so, but it's best not to count on me."

"God, Anne. I don't know what to say."

" 'Good luck,' maybe?"

"I will pray for you every day."

Anne had to smile. "Antony, when will you learn

that professors of religion are not supposed to actually believe in it?"

"When you learn to enjoy Earl Grey tea, I suppose. But seriously, Anne. You can't allow them to use you forever. And they will if you permit it, you know that. Do it this time if you must, but tell them it's the last."

"When I can't face it anymore, Antony, they'll be the first to know."

Makepeace had to be satisfied with that. The talk turned to mundane matters, of replacement lecturers for one of the classes and the probable cancellation of the other, arranging for Antony to take over her three graduate thesis projects, the choice between leave-without-pay or trying for a last-minute paid sabbatical. Finally, Anne made a move toward gathering her things.

"Come home for dinner," Makepeace offered suddenly. "Marla would love to see you."

"I can't, Antony. I have to get home for the dogs."

"Another night, then. Before you go."

"I'd love to." She put on her coat and pulled a pair of gloves out of the pocket, and then she looked up with a faint trace of mischief in her eyes. "Oh, and I should warn you, rumors may start up when I fail to appear next quarter. Glen and his policewoman made quite an impression on some of the students. They'll probably work it up into an arrest for drug smuggling or white slavery."

"Agent McCarthy is fairly unmistakable, isn't he? I can't imagine *him* doing undercover work."

She heard a clear note of rather catty pride that she should be better at the wicked and dangerous job he so disapproved of than the hateful man who dragged her into it, but she hid her amusement. "He's actually not bad at it, given time to grow his hair out a bit."

Makepeace shot a glance at Anne's own thick hair,

but did not say anything. He let her go and prepared to leave himself.

It was only much later that evening, as he sat in front of a dying fire brooding over their conversation, that it struck him there might be a second, darker meaning to Anne's not being able to face it anymore.

For two days Agent McCarthy and Inspector Farmer cooled their heels, Farmer impatiently, McCarthy with the resignation of a man who had done this before. On Thursday afternoon, McCarthy was seated on a park bench, his arms spread out along its back and his face lifted to the weak sun, while Gillian Farmer paced up and down on the gravel pathways between rows of brutally pruned roses. As chance would have it, she was at the farthest point in her circuit when McCarthy's cellular phone chirped in his pocket, and she did not hear it. She saw it in his hand, however, the moment she turned, and broke into a trot in her eagerness to get back to him.

It was a very brief conversation; McCarthy was folding the telephone before she reached the bench. He stood, putting the phone back in his pocket.

"Was that her?"

"It was."

"Christ. About time."

McCarthy glanced at her sharply, but he did not speak until they were in the car and on the freeway out of town.

"Anne doesn't have to do this, you know. She's under no obligation; she doesn't even take a salary beyond expenses."

"So why does she?" Farmer demanded, still impatient. Three days was far too long, and her department had begun pressing for her return after the second.

"Eighteen years ago, Anne Waverly's seven-year-old

daughter and thirty-one-year-old husband died in a mass suicide in northern Texas. The child drank a glass of cyanide-laced fruit juice, probably given to her by her father. You may have heard about it—they called it Ezekiel's Farm—but it was only in the news for a couple of days because there was a plane crash and then some enormous political scandal just after they were found that knocked them off the front pages. A lot of comparisons were made to the People's Temple suicide in Guyana two years before, and I suppose their reasons were much the same although there were only forty-seven people instead of nine-hundred-and-some. The bodies were not found for nearly a week. In early summer. You can imagine what they looked like."

Gillian grimaced; she had been a cop long enough to know.

"Anne herself was a member of the group, but she had begun to question the methods and beliefs of the community. Her doubts were serious enough for her to take a leave of absence, as it were, to go away and think about things for a few days. She left the child, Abby, with her husband. Three days later the leader Ezekiel had a final revelation, and broke out the cyanide."

"Christ."

He added in an unemotional voice, "Anne believes that her departure triggered the suicides. It is quite possible that she is right."

They drove in silence for a long time, until Gillian stirred and asked, "So this is, what, some kind of penance? Or revenge?"

"Neither, as far as I can tell. I believe it's her own form of suicide."

"You mean she goes into these situations with a death wish? Jesus, McCarthy, how could you possibly allow—"

"Not a death wish, no. She's sensible and cautious, and she does her part very, very well. She goes in, she looks around, she comes out and tells us what the community looks like and gives us her opinion concerning its internal stability. It's just that on a very deep level, she's made her peace with death, and she doesn't really care if she comes home or not. A lot of people who do long-term undercover work have it to some degree, and with Anne it's never interfered with getting the job done. Up to now, that is."

"What do you mean?"

"Probably nothing. It's just that her reaction to me this time was different. She was angry."

"Pretty normal reaction, I'd say."

"That's exactly it. She seems to have gotten used to the idea of living again."

Their rental car had problems with the first section of Anne Waverly's road, but at the end of it—up the rutted gravel track, through the gate, and around a mile or more of narrow twists and turns—she was waiting for them. She watched them get out of the car, saw the woman, Farmer, look around her with a sudden delight in the dappled sun and the clean silence that followed the laboring engine sounds of the last ten minutes, and waited with neither movement nor expression while her guests metaphorically brushed off the dust of their journey and came toward her.

They stopped when they saw Stan at her knee, then Glen came on with Gillian Farmer following cautiously. Ten feet away Glen stopped and spoke to the dog. "Hello there, Stan. It is Stan, isn't it?"

"That's right," Anne said.

"C'mere, boy." McCarthy dropped to his heels and held out a hand. "You remember me. I'm a friend, right?"

The dog shot his mistress a glance, and at her gesture

went forward to snuffle with his flat nose at the man's hand. Something tickled his memory, because his tail wagged briefly before he turned his attention to Gillian. With dignity he walked up to her and examined her feet and the hand she ventured out; then, without expressing an opinion, he returned to Anne.

The incident with the dog confirmed Gillian's suspicions that McCarthy knew Anne Waverly as something more than just an occasional colleague. His intimate acquaintance with the road had been obvious from the time they left the blacktop, for one thing. He knew the dog, knew that the door they would enter was not the one behind Anne Waverly but the kitchen door around the side of the house. He seemed unsurprised by the sharp difference between the dusty, rustic log exterior and the rich simplicity inside, and when he sniffed the air, it was more with the welcome of homecoming than puzzlement at the peculiar combination of the rich, yeasty odor emanating from two pans on the sideboard underlaid with the raw bite of cordite. The cap was put on her confirmation by his first words to Anne.

"Target practice?"

"I thought it might be a good idea," she said. "I was getting rusty." She walked past them and pulled shut a narrow door to what looked like a pantry.

"You shoot indoors?" Gillian asked in disbelief.

McCarthy laughed—actually laughed. She hadn't thought him capable of anything beyond a rueful chuckle. "Like Sherlock Holmes picking out the Queen's initials on the wall?" he asked, which reference meant nothing to Gillian. He looked at Anne and asked, "May I show her?" When she nodded, he went to another door and started down the open wooden stairs heading into a basement.

The bare bulb lit only the immediate area, but McCarthy reached over and flipped a series of switches, and to her amazement Gillian found herself at one end of what could only be called an indoor shooting range, complete with a man-shaped paper target hanging at the far end.

It was also, incongruously, a farmhouse cellar lined with cupboards and shelves, bearing canned goods, economy-sized packages of toilet paper and soap powder, odd shapes wrapped in black plastic garbage bags, and an array of hand tools and power saws—all the necessities of life in the woods. McCarthy called her over to a low table on which lay a pair of ear protectors, an automatic pistol, and the equipment for cleaning it. Standing next to him, she surveyed the panorama of bottled foodstuffs, the fruit on the top shelf, red tomato sauce below, a neat display of jams and preserves and shelled nuts that ended three-quarters of the way down the room at an arrangement of hay bales, tightly laid up to the ceiling. They were tired and dusty-looking, and no longer gave out enough odor to stand up to the gunpowder; they had been in place for years.

Bemused, Gillian studied the odd juxtaposition of home canning and the hanging target with the cluster of shots in its center until she realized that the FBI man seemed to expect a reaction.

"Wouldn't want a ricochet to smash your peaches, I suppose," she commented.

He looked a little disappointed at her lack of amusement, but personally she thought it a bit crazy. The woman lived in the middle of nowhere; why not shoot outside, where she could practice at distances of more than twenty yards? Or at a proper shooting range?

"Bring up a bottle of tomatoes when you come, would you, Glen?" the voice at the top of the stairs asked prosaically. "And don't forget to shut off the lights."

Back in the kitchen, they found Anne Waverly at the stove, lighting the gas under a big saucepan. McCarthy

closed the basement door, put the quart bottle of tomatoes on the counter, and took a chair at the wooden table.
He sat watching Anne Waverly's back, strong and
straight with the lovely graying hair, caught up in a clip,
that hung down between her shoulder blades, and Gillian abruptly realized what the two of them reminded
her of: her sister Kathleen and Kathy's ex-husband when
they were forced to be together at some family function.
Between them was lingering affection, a heavy residue of
physical attraction, and a lot of emotional scar tissue, and
although they were polite for the sake of the children,
there was also the mutual awareness that if they ever
relaxed, blood would flow.

Glen McCarthy and Anne Waverly had been lovers,
Gillian was sure of that.

She was also quite certain that whereas the professor
might be finished with the FBI man, he was afraid that
he was not through with her. Gillian Farmer was
enough of a cop to disapprove of sex cluttering up a
professional relationship, enough of a woman to find it
both troubling and mildly amusing. She cleared her
throat. "Can I help with anything?"

"No thank you, Inspector Farmer. I'll just dump this
together and we can eat when the rolls are done." Anne
swept a handful of finely chopped onions and a heap of
other vegetables into the seething pot, poured in the bottle of tomatoes and a generous amount of red wine, took
a hefty pinch of dried herbs from a pottery jar and sprinkled it over, dropped the top on the pan, and turned the
heat down.

"Coffee, tea, or wine?" she asked.

Over coffee, she finally joined them at the table, and
Gillian began her side of the report.

It did not take long, or the hint of several culinary
interruptions, for Gillian to see that Anne Waverly was
not very interested in the events that had brought the

group calling itself Change to the attention of the San Francisco Police Department. Missing persons reports and complaints of financial chicanery from swindled relatives were, her attitude seemed to say, only to be expected. She came alert only when Farmer started to talk about the emigration of Change members from their former urban setting into the Arizona high desert. Then she wanted to know precisely when the members had sold the houses they owned, how big the houses were, the physical state they had been left in by the former owners, what had been left behind, and a dozen other equally meaningless questions. Prepared as she was, Gillian had to admit that most of these things she could not answer. She told the professor that she would find out.

This seemed to signal a hiatus in the evening's program. Anne stood up and limped back to the sink, where she fished a head of garlic out of a pot on the windowsill and began to skin some cloves and squeeze them through a press into a small bowl.

"Dinner in ten minutes," she said. "Glen, show Inspector Farmer where the bathroom is—"

"Please, call me Gillian."

"And I'm Anne. And then if you'd choose a bottle of wine, Glen, and get a tablecloth from the drawer under the oven. Gillian, the silver is in that drawer, we'll need soup spoons. Plates and bowls are on that shelf."

The plates were handmade stoneware, the tablecloth looked as if it belonged in a prosperous farmhouse in Avignon, the silver was silver, and heavy, and the dinner was an intensely flavored stew with olives and vegetables and some unidentifiable meat, with a simple green salad, bread rolls hot from the oven with herbed garlic butter to slather on, and deep red wine that had just enough of an edge to hold its own.

Respectful silence held, until Gillian spoke up.

"What kind of meat is this?" she asked.

"Bambi," Glen answered, his mouth full.

"Venison," Anne corrected him. "My neighbor gives me a haunch every year and it takes me months to get through it. I'm trying to clear out the freezer before I go."

"So, how is dear Eliot?" Glen asked. "Talkative as ever?" He was concentrating on the application of garlic butter to hot bread. Gillian glanced at him curiously, and Anne seemed amused at the asperity of his question.

"Eliot is eternal; he changes not. He's going to—" Anne broke off at a scratching sound that startled Gillian, followed by a low whine. Anne put down her napkin on the table and went to open the narrow door that she had shut when they first arrived.

The mother of six stopped halfway through the doorway, torn by her need to go out and the protective drives of her hormones. Anne solved her dilemma by taking up the loose skin at the scruff of her neck, walking her to the outside door, and pushing her through it. Normally she would have scolded Livy for passing through the kitchen with lifted lip and a rumble in her chest, but then normally Livy would not have growled at visitors.

"She's had puppies," Glen exclaimed at the sight of the bitch's sagging belly. "I didn't know you were having puppies."

"Good Lord, something the FBI doesn't know," Anne said, dry to the point of sarcasm. The rest of the meal passed with brief and desultory conversation, although Gillian was the only one who seemed to feel the least uncomfortable. The other two merely ate, engrossed in the food and their own thoughts.

Eventually, with second helpings distributed and polished off, Anne got to her feet and began to clear the dishes. "There's an apple pie that Eliot's mother made for dessert. I hope you'll help me eat it, or I'll be living on it for a week."

"Gillian and I will wash the dishes first, and let the food settle a bit."

How very homey, Gillian Farmer thought. Who would believe that an FBI investigation could start with venison stew and a sink full of soapsuds?

While her two guests washed and dried, Anne made more coffee, put the pie in the oven to warm, carried two bowls of dog food outside, and took the opportunity to change the bedding under Livy's pups. She looked up from this last job to see Glen at the door.

"I think she wants back in," he said, and then asked, "Can I see them first?"

"Sure." He stepped into the tight space without even wrinkling his nose at the earthy smells of milk and blood and infant fecal matter, and squatted to look at the mound of fawn bodies. Gillian, too, came over, and Anne slipped out with her armful of laundry so the two hardened law enforcement personnel could coo over the grubs and argue over which one's eyes were closest to being open. She gave them five minutes, then called, "Sorry, but if I don't let Livy back in she'll have the door off its hinges."

Reluctantly, they emerged, and Anne went to let one highly suspicious dog inside. This time she left the pantry door halfway open; time for socialization to begin.

Over the crumbly, sweet pie and strong coffee, Anne began to set out her requests to Gillian Farmer.

"The things I need to know may seem peripheral, and in a way, they are. Normally in a criminal investigation into embezzlement, for example, you're not looking for signs of child abuse." She saw Gillian begin to react, and held up her hand. "I'm not saying there is child abuse here, don't misunderstand me. There very probably is not, at least not the sort of abuse that the law can concern itself with. But children will act out the problems within their family, in symptomatic behavior.

"I need you to talk to their former teachers, or if they had a private school, the district liaison for home schooling. See if you can find any of the kids' work, written materials or drawings. You might try the relatives for that, the grandmothers and aunts—they may have been sent pictures to put on their refrigerators. And it would be helpful if the age and sex of each child was on the piece, and roughly the date it was made—not the names, though; I don't want to know their names. It distracts me when I meet them.

"Talk to the ex-neighbors again. Any problems or oddities, from vandalism to too-perfect behavior? What hours did the families keep, any odd sounds or smells coming from the houses, what vehicles did they have, what jobs?

"Bank accounts and credit references are probably best retrieved by Glen, but Steven in Arizona seems to have come from your town originally, Gillian, and so did the leaders of the smaller branches in Boston and L.A. See what you can find out about their histories—families, education, jobs, all that."

"Can I have those names?" Gillian asked, her pen poised.

Anne closed her eyes, took a deep breath, then opened them, and Gillian was surprised to see her look at Glen with real anger. "The old 'need-to-know' bullshit again, eh, Glen?"

"You know I—"

"You give her the information, or I will."

"I don't think I can get approval on—"

"I don't negotiate, Glen. You know that. We do it my way, or we don't do it."

McCarthy's eyes wavered and fell, and he threw up his hands in surrender. "Okay. She'll see the file."

"You will copy the file and give it to her. No crap about coming to a secure room to read it."

"Jesus, Anne."

"If you don't have the authority to run the photocopier, Glen," she said softly, "let me know as soon as you find someone who does. We'll resume then."

"Okay, okay. She'll get the file."

She leaned forward across the table with no sign now of the warm and encouraging teacher she was at the university. Her eyes glittered. "If you don't trust her, Glen, how can I trust you?"

Not knowing their past, there was no way Gillian could evaluate the depths to that bald question. She could see, though, that it hit McCarthy hard: His jaw tensed all the way down to his collar, and though he reared his head away, his eyes remained locked on those of Anne Waverly. After a long moment, the professor let him go and returned her gaze to Gillian.

"You'll find the names in the file. If there's anything else you notice, in its presence or its absence, please speak up. Even if it seems unimportant. You're going back to San Francisco soon?"

"Tomorrow, I guess."

"I'm sorry to have kept you here so long, but it was not an easy decision for me to make."

The last vestiges of Gillian Farmer's annoyance with this woman vanished, and she began to see why those students loved and respected her.

"I understand," she said.

Anne went into the next room, returning with a card that she handed to Gillian. "There's my phone number, my e-mail address, and my home fax number, which works fine if no more than two of my neighbors are using their phones at the same time. I'll be here for two weeks, and after that you'll have to go through Glen. Keep in touch."

•   •   •

Neither of Anne's visitors spoke on their way back down the hill. Gillian got out at the bottom to let Glen drive through the gate, then she shut the gate and locked the padlock through the chain. Back in the car she turned up the heat controls and sat watching the headlights illuminate the passing trees and gates and rural mailboxes.

"I tried to read one of her books," she told him. "I didn't get very far—it might as well have been written in German."

"Was that *Modern Religious Expression*? Big thick thing?"

"Yeah."

"That's an expansion of her doctoral thesis. You should take a look at *Cults Among Us*—a title she hates, by the way. It's much the same material, only rewritten for a general audience. I'll send you a copy if you can't find it."

"You know," Gillian said after a while, "I just can't see that woman living in a commune. She'd stick out like a sore thumb, she's so . . ."

"Cerebral?" Glen suggested.

"Professorial," she supplied.

"She's superb," he said flatly. "It's like putting a chameleon on a leaf: She just becomes a different person. Her posture changes, her voice softens, her vocabulary shifts, her eyes go wide. It's not even an act—if anything, the person you saw is the artificial construct. She opens up and just sucks in the community, lock, stock, and Bible."

"Hmm," she grunted. "Well, most good undercover cops are people I wouldn't exactly trust with my wallet."

"In her case it's even more radical than that. Sure, sometimes the only difference between the cop and the criminal is a badge, but when Anne Waverly plays a person, she isn't just making a shift in emphasis; she turns herself inside out. She becomes . . . earnest. Accepting. Completely unconscious and nonjudgmental. And absolutely fearless. And it really isn't an act." This conundrum of the empty-headed professor was obviously something that Glen had long dwelt on in the privacy of his mind; Gillian had never heard so many words in a row from him, and so nearly lyrical. "Anne let slip during her second debriefing that what she experiences is a freedom born of terror, and she suggested I read Solzhenitsyn. In real life—or in her Waverly life, anyway—she's jumpy underneath that calm, she has panic attacks on airplanes, she only recently got off tranks and sleeping pills. She still sees a therapist regularly—her boss's wife, in fact."

"You ever try and get her psych records? They'd make for interesting reading."

"God, no!" Glen's face twisted in the dim light, perhaps from disapproval, although it looked more like revulsion. "The last thing I want to know is what's going on in that woman's head."

"Really? I thought she was fascinating."

"She's one of the most disturbing creatures I've ever met," he said, and firmly changed the subject.

CHAPTER 4

צוֹרֵף   צָרַף‎   1) refine 2) purify 3) to try
                                prove
                                    (Da 11:35

צֹרְפִי‎ = pr. name   Ne 3:31
צָרְפַת‎ = a town bet Tyre & Zidon
צָרוּף‎ = purified, pure

tsorēf

                              14:29, 30:6

serafim   שְׂרָפִים‎   Isaiah 6:2-6
שָׂרָף‎ = a species of venemous serpent – Num 21:8
                                       & DT 8:15
                                     (ie.– Poss. winged
                                           serpents)

שָׂרַף‎ = to burn, consume – lamps for the dead,
                                 2 Ch. 16:14, Je 34:5
     = to burn or bake bricks ge 11:3
                                    Je 10:16

      s = samek   ס
        = sadeh   צ
        = sin / shin   שׂ / שׁ

      Seraph = a desc. of Judah   1Ch 4:22
      (RSV – based on <u>vulgate</u>
      HB is unintelligible …

For the next two weeks, it was chaos upon chaos as Professor Anne Waverly coaxed and goaded her students into their exams and final papers, as homeowner Anne Waverly scrambled to make arrangements so that her lawyer, her neighbor Eliot, and her friend Antony Makepeace among them could keep her creditors happy and her roof standing, as the FBI's consultant on cultic behavior Dr. Anne Waverly embarked on the necessary research into the Change movement, and as the newly incarnated Seeker-after-Truth Ana Wakefield began to take form.

After two days, Anne decided that the easiest thing would be just to give up sleeping, and to all intents and purposes that was what she did, napping at odd moments when she could no longer keep her eyelids up. Several nights she did not make it home, camping out instead in her office under the vastly disapproving eyes of Tazzie and her boss.

Still, the work seemed to get itself done. Three hundred exams were farmed out to grad students for grading, leaving Anne with some three thousand written pages to evaluate. Her own writing—two articles, a review, and the proposal for a book—was simply canceled or put off, with apologies. A replacement instructor for her big spring class was found, a casual, bearded young Ph.D. about whom Anne had grave doubts as she tried to impress on him her reading list and curriculum. It seemed, as she complained to Antony, that he preferred to "let it flow" rather than commit himself to too rigid a structure. How did he expect the campus bookstore to conjure up two hundred twenty-five copies of a book he might not decide upon until the seventh week of the ten-week quarter? she demanded. Antony shook his head and patted her shoulder and took her home to his wife for dinner.

Anne's lawyer, on the other hand, was none too pleased with a proposal that the taciturn and unworldly Eliot be given any authority at all over Anne's financial affairs. Anne eventually had to admit that a man who had never owned a credit card and who wrote perhaps as few as three checks a year off the bank account he shared with his mother, brilliant as he was with machines and dogs and roof repairs, might be less than ideal as a custodian of her business matters. She appealed again to Antony. He patiently agreed to act as signator of checks and liaison between Eliot's inarticulate requests for occasional repair and maintenance funds and the lawyer's overall supervision.

Then there were the numerous visits to the specialist about her knee, first to convince her that Anne did indeed intend to mistreat it, then to come to an agreement about what therapy would make that possible, and finally to have several fittings for a new, high-tech brace, invisible under any but the tightest of trousers and guaranteed never to give off the faint but maddening squeaks the old one had developed.

Another specialist, too, agreed to several sessions in the short time before Anne had to leave. Anne's psychotherapy with Antony's wife, Marla, had tapered off over the last year or so, but halfway through the first week following Glen's reappearance, Anne knew she would never make it without committing murder if she could not talk with Marla, who was friend as well as therapist. Anne phoned her at home.

"Marla? Anne here. I wonder if you could fit me in for a couple of hours, soon."

"Of course. I hoped you would call. I was going to wait another day or two and then call you."

"Antony told you, then?" The lines between the professions were firm but flexible; of course Antony would have told his wife, Anne's friend, that she was suddenly leaving, although to his wife the psychiatrist he would only have hinted gently at the reason.

"You don't mind?"

"Certainly not. But, Marla? We're not going to be discussing whether or not I want to do this. I'm going, and I can't afford doubts."

"If you didn't have them already, you would not be concerned about them," Marla pointed out. "I can't promise to help you strengthen your resolve, Anne, just to understand it."

"I'll take the chance," Anne said with a smile, and went back to her work.

There were also, inevitably, the students, not only the regular end-of-term crush, but also the handful of independent study supervisions and the fragile few in need of babying as they went through times of personal trauma or entered the delicate phases of their thesis projects.

Meanwhile, in her role of sometime agent of the FBI, Anne was finding Gillian Farmer all she might have asked for in a research assistant. Faxes spilled daily into Anne's home machine, e-mail dinged merrily whenever she logged on to her computer, and three parcels arrived containing photographs and color reproductions of children's drawings. Anne spent hours poring over the material, particularly the drawings, and took long walks thinking about them.

She also looked at the odd details, the minutiae that comprised this unique organism that called itself Change. The Web site they had set up was remarkably down-to-earth, as such things go, and although Anne could see Steven's interest in what Glen had called "the cleansing nature of fire," the texts Steven (or whoever had drawn up the Web site) used were not taken exclusively from apocalyptic material, and indeed were often not even biblical. The quotations given ran the gamut from Aboriginal teaching stories to Zoroastrian writings, in what Anne could only assume was an attempt to prove the universality of the doctrine of Change—which doctrine, however, was remarkably unclear. There were small, tantalizing clues in the material Glen and Gillian sent her that set the scholar in her tingling; unfortunately, small and tantalizing they remained.

Former members of a religious movement were a valuable if dangerous source of information—valuable because they were usually as eager as ex-spouses to spill all the dark and misshapen beans of their former relationship, and a hazard because the negative was often the only information they were interested in giving. In this case, though, the only disgruntled exes they had found were four women and two men who had been involved in Change for only an average of four and a half months, with the longest stay just short of eight. Samantha Dooley, who had been with the movement from its beginning and would have been the most important informant they could have found, had apparently left Change some months before and was now hidden within an extremely withdrawn, even xenophobic, women's commune in Canada, flat-out refusing to talk to Glen's men about her time with Change. Anne didn't even think they had been allowed to speak with her directly, and suggested that he send a woman to try.

Anne was forced to fossick through the pages of information for the odd trace of gold, though when she found a gleam, she had to admit that she could not be sure it wasn't mere pyrite instead.

Take the names of the two men who seemed to be joint heads of the movement: Steven Chance had become Steven Change when he and the others came out of In-

dia, but what of Jonas Fairweather, whose legal name
was now Jonas Seraph?

Names have meanings, and a name deliberately chosen by an adult could only vibrate with resolve and a
new identity. Jonas, like Steven, had kept his first name,
but what did he mean by Seraph?

Anne spent a couple of hours late one night at the
desk in her home study, deep in Hebrew dictionaries,
biblical concordances, and a selection of commentaries,
which told her that a *seraph* was, in Numbers 21 and
Deuteronomy 8, a kind of venomous serpent. Whether
or not this was related to the verb *seraph,* which meant to
burn or consume in flames, was debatable, and one could
only speculate about Isaiah's use of the plural *seraphim*
when talking about angelic beings, and suggest that he
may possibly have been visualizing winged serpents
wreathed in fire.

Interestingly, a second Hebrew word with a completely different spelling but with an identical spelling
when transliterated into English was *tsaraf,* which also
had to do with purifying fires. That verb meant refining,
purifying, with an overtone of testing a substance, putting it to the proof to determine its purity.

There were proper names spelled with some variation of the Hebrew roots *srf,* in Nehemiah and I Chroni-
cles, but on the whole Anne wondered if she was not
crediting the man with more subtlety than he possessed,
and that the name Fairweather had taken wasn't simply
a reference to Isaiah's fiery messengers.

Anne looked over the stacked chaos of books and
scribbles, and shook her head. Speculation and word
studies were all very well and good, but it was now two-
fifteen in the morning when she had a lecture in eight
hours. Tantalizing or not, she had to admit that she simply did not know enough to determine what the English-
man meant by his name change.

Quit playing with your books, Dr. Waverly, she told herself sternly. Go to bed.

And while all this was going on, while the householder's legal arrangements and professorial demands vied for her limited hours and Gillian Farmer's faxes spilled their stories into her home, all the while, on the edges of her vision, there moved the ominous presence of Glen McCarthy, solicitous as a wooing suitor, insistent as a slave owner, crowding her and driving her to fits of nervous petulance when they were due to meet. She found his unremitting cheerfulness, now that he had his way, foreboding, almost menacing, and she found it difficult not to take it out on her students. The phone messages and letters (the latter well sealed and marked with a large "Personal") began to provoke gently ribald comments from the steno pool, causing Anne no little humiliation until finally she blew up at McCarthy, heaping on him her accumulation of burdens and tensions and telling him to leave her alone if he expected her to continue. For two days he remained silent and invisible. For some perverse reason, this made her even more furious, until the Friday afternoon she telephoned his message number and said that he should come to her house at midday Saturday.

That night she dreamed of Glen, dressed in a black turtleneck, black jeans, and black, steel-toed work boots, storming into her lecture hall in a terrible rage and thundering at her, "I, the Lord thy God, am a jealous God."

She woke up laughing, a sound that rang through the silent house and startled the dogs into a barking fit.

Marla Makepeace had been Anne's therapist for years, beginning as a friend who helped put her together after the breakdown set off by Abby's photograph and continuing over the years. Anne, Marla, and Antony made for an odd friendship, one that should not have worked for any number of reasons, not the least of which was Anne's oft-stated preference not to inquire too closely into the darker places of her mind, a firm conviction that it was at times better to let sleeping Minotaurs lie rather than continually offering up virginal portions of herself to be devoured by them. Beyond this attitude, unacceptable to a believer in the psychotherapeutic method, there was the objection that a therapist and her client should never have a relationship outside the therapy room, any more than a grad-student-turned-employee ought to befriend her adviser-turned-boss, and as for a married couple who had to create a line between talking about Anne their friend and professional indiscretions about Anne the client— All things considered, their friendship shouldn't have worked, but it did, quite smoothly.

She sat in Marla's comfortable chair in the quiet, fragrant, plant-filled room and told her about her dream of Glen the jealous God. Marla chuckled, as Anne had known she would, but she then went on, to Anne's dismay, to ask about the dream's meaning. Anne shook her head ruefully.

"What is it?" Marla asked.

"Oh, the mind is such an amazing thing. I tell you about a funny dream in order to make you laugh, but I manage to overlook the fact that you're going to make me dig beneath the surface and see things I don't want to see."

"Would you not have told me if you'd stopped to think about the consequences?"

"Oh, I probably would have. But it wouldn't have been funny."

"Perhaps that's why your mind chose selective blindness: in order to allow me the humor before the content."

The two women smiled at each other with affection, and the smile was still in Marla's eyes when she asked gently, "You are concerned about this upcoming investigation, aren't you?"

"I am."

"Tell me how you feel about Glen."

"He frightens me," Anne said immediately. "He's so utterly fixed on what he's doing, everyone else is just a tool. You have to shout just to make him aware of you as a person. He's inhuman, and he's not even aware of it."

"So why submit yourself to that treatment again?"

Anne tried to laugh, but it was a poor, twisted thing. "He may not be much of a god, but he's mine. No, of course I don't mean that I worship him or anything, but I suppose you could say that he created me in his image. I was thinking the other day about that time fifteen years ago. You know, I still think I would have killed myself in another day or two if Glen hadn't barged in and just swept it all away because he needed me to help him and he didn't have time for my problems. And with him there, I never stopped to think, never had the time or the energy to stand back and look at what it was I wanted to do, until—oh, maybe the last year or so. And now again he's just blindsided me and swept me along."

"Would you have agreed to help Glen this time if you had been forewarned that he was going to ask?"

"I wonder. Yes, I think so."

"Why?"

"Because it's what I do, who I am. I was dead for three years after Aaron and Abby were killed. I would have committed suicide at the time except I felt it would be the ultimate betrayal of their deaths. So instead I went dead. For three years after I came here, the only person I talked to was Antony. And I began to take stupid risks. I started walking around campus at night during that time we had the rapist attacks. One winter I kept forgetting to replace the tires on my car even though they were almost bald, and I couldn't stand to have the seat belt around me. Stupid, suicidal things."

"Guilt is an insidious force."

"I'd sometimes wake up in the morning and need an hour before I could bear to get on my feet, it was like I was under half a dozen of those lead blankets they lay over you when you have an X ray. Everything was just so much work."

"And then Glen came." The story was familiar to both of them, like reciting a litany.

"And then I collapsed under the weight of Abby's picture, and then Glen came and offered me a way out. And it was so . . . easy. I knew it was dangerous. Glen tried to convince himself and me that it wasn't, but I knew otherwise, and I was glad. Because if it killed me, at least the weight would be off me. And as soon as I left, as soon as I walked off the plane in North Dakota, I wasn't even frightened anymore."

"Surely you must have been, to some degree."

"Oh I was, scared shitless about the whole setup and my inexperience and not knowing how I'd react, but at the same time I could push that person away and be just stupid, wide-eyed Anita Walls bumbling her way into an armed camp. It was intensely liberating. The three months flew by, and I never made a mistake, never showed any fear. It was like jittery old Anne Waverly was locked up inside a glass ball, looking over my shoulder."

"And then you came back."

"Christ, yes. I came out and was taken away for debriefing, and it left me so depressed, I couldn't eat. But I'm sure you remember that."

"I remember."

"It must have been fun to have one of Antony's flaky

grad students move in on you and spend a couple of weeks staring at the walls."

"It was not that long, and you didn't stare at the walls. You were charming, in a quiet way."

"I'll bet. But the whole business in North Dakota helped. And once the postpartum depression lifted, the weight I woke up to every morning didn't seem quite so heavy."

"Let's talk about guilt."

" 'Survivor's guilt,' " Anne said wryly.

"It wasn't quite that simple, was it?"

"No." Anne took a deep breath and let it out. "No, it wasn't. Still isn't. I did have something to do with Abby and Aaron's deaths. With all the Farm deaths."

"So you have told me."

"My leaving the Farm set Ezekiel off. Look, even then I had enough training, enough *experience* to know how dangerous it would be to cross a man in his mental state, but I went ahead. I should have known. I did know—but I took off anyway."

They had stepped off the familiar path of the litany, and Marla watched her carefully.

"Why?"

"Why? Because I was selfish. I was stupid and greedy—I was *bored* with life on the Farm. I wanted to get back to grad school, where people valued what I did instead of telling me how bad I was at milking cows and how unfocused and disruptive I was getting."

"You are saying that your desire for self-fulfillment led to their deaths."

"My impatience, my self-importance, my . . . my . . . inability to get along with the father of my child."

"You and Aaron were having arguments," Marla said quietly.

"We had a huge fight about going back to Berkeley

and I got in the car and drove away. He didn't want me to take Abby, and I didn't want her with me. And that was the end."

"But not for you."

"Yes, for me. Annie died, too, and Anne was built up on the wreckage, poor old battered Anne with her limp and her dogs. And every so often Anne goes away and Anita or Ana or whoever comes to life instead."

"So why are you concerned about this investigation, Anne? Why have you come to me?"

"I'm worried that I can't do it this time. That Ana won't, you know, take over."

"Is this different, the feeling this time?"

"Yes. No. I don't know. I know it sounds crazy, but I'm afraid that I'm not frightened enough."

"You need to be frightened?"

"You know I do," Anne said, growing angry with the slow repetition of the therapist.

"Tell me again," Marla said, meaning, Remind yourself how it works.

"Fear is the force that drives Anne into her corner. Fear's like pain—it can be overwhelming at first, but if you live with it long enough, it can be shaped and molded, and it can be walled away to give you just a little space of your own where it isn't. And that's where Ana and the others live and breathe."

"And you wish to undertake yet another enterprise that will require you to break open your half-healed wounds and encourages you to split into a dual personality."

"You're exaggerating, Marla."

"Am I? Listen to your own words."

"That's just a way of talking about a mental process. A shorthand."

"I don't know that it is."

"Marla, I can't afford this," Anne snapped, and began

to gather herself to go. "I can't risk anything getting in the way. You don't know what you're asking."

"Anne, sit down." Marla waited for her client to subside warily into the chair. "Anne, I cannot encourage self-deception, I cannot countenance actions that are so antithetical to the healing process. You knew this when you came here with your dream about Glen."

"Marla, sometimes you have to work beyond the immediate good to see the long-term picture."

"You are saying you need to do this work for Glen for your own state of health?" Marla asked dubiously.

"I'm saying there's unfinished business."

"I thought the last case, the one that you took to Glen, was meant to settle unfinished business."

"It was. But." Anne thought for a moment and then said slowly, "When I volunteered to go into Kansas, I was deliberately going after Martin Cranmer as a way to balance the disaster of the previous case in Utah. Kansas did that. Now it's a matter of reaching back to the beginning of the circle again, back to when Glen first took control of my life."

"The creature has to stand up to the creator?"

"Something like that."

"You and Glen have been very close from time to time. Tell me this, Anne: Do you love Glen?"

"I detest him," Anne said without thinking. "No, I suppose it's not that simple. I feel . . . God, what *don't* I feel when it comes to Glen McCarthy? It's like every emotion put together, all the contradictory drives at once. Maybe that's why he was wearing black in the dream— don't they say that when you mix all the colors together, you come up with black? That's Glen, the black hole of my emotions."

"He declared himself God."

"And was dressed as the devil."

"So tell me, Anne: How does Glen feel about you?"

"I think I make him nervous." There was a degree of satisfaction in her voice that neither of them missed.

"Why would that be?"

"He thinks he controls me but he's afraid he doesn't. He thinks he understands me, and he does on one level, better than anyone else in the world, but not on another. He respects and admires me, to the extent that he has an inflated sense of my abilities, but he also, without realizing it, hopes that I will fail."

Marla had been a therapist for a long time, but even so it took her two or three seconds to wipe all trace of the shock and concern she felt out of her voice so she could ask evenly, "Why would Glen hope that you will fail?"

"Oh, he's not about to set me up for a fall. If I screwed up again, it would mean his job. I just meant that deep down he has to feel some resentment that he's so dependent on me. I mean, really: Don't all men secretly want to be the one to come riding on the white stallion to the rescue?"

Marla chuckled again at that, but Anne decided against any further revelations in the Glen department. If Marla, friend and therapist, was already worrying about Glen's motivations, it would only muddy the waters further if Anne were to voice her growing suspicion that Glen, deep in a hidden place within that smooth, whole, and completely unscarred skin of his, held a certain dark fascination with the scars and injuries that his job had inflicted on her body and mind.

No, they both had enough to think about; besides, her hour was up.

The term ended, the grade sheets were turned in, she had a final appointment with her lawyer, a farewell dinner with Antony and Marla, and a relatively full night's sleep. Two days, and she would be gone.

The next day she brought out the old Volkswagen bus named Rocinante from its resting place in the barn. Eliot had spent the better part of one enraptured week stripping down the engine and servicing it from roof to road, and it now had nearly new tires, completely new brakes, a more powerful electrical system, a rearview mirror that actually reflected the road behind her, and it had seen the occasional and disconcerting loss of power during acceleration cured by a radical revamping of the entire fuel system. The old lady was set to tackle mountains and deserts again, albeit at her own placid speed.

Glen McCarthy's men had also had their hands on the bus, adding a new and very well concealed compartment for her gun and the supply of cortisone and needles for her knee as well as an emergency call transmitter that would be discovered only if the entire body of the vehicle were torn away. Even if a cellular phone would go with her persona (which it would not), it would be useless away from the cities.

Now the bus was Anne's again. She sat in the driver's seat and breathed in the musty odor of old upholstery and traces of mildew, a scent that always reminded her of her grandfather's old Chevy with its wide horsehair seats and soft cloth roof lining. She sniffed, wondering if any of it was the smell of ancient blood that Glen's men had missed after the Utah shootout. (Such a melodramatic word, that, and inaccurate as well: She'd been far too busy negotiating an escape to try to return fire.)

She shook herself out of her macabre reveries and got out of the bus to begin her own renovations. She began by pulling the inside furnishings apart and scrubbing every corner and surface, then giving the bus back its personality. New curtains, a cheerful batik fabric with heavy lining to keep out the light, went up on the rods over the windows, along with new covers for the cushions. She filled the water reservoir and checked the propane tank, stocked the tight little drawers and cupboards with sheets and blankets, a quilt and a towel, foodstuffs and pans, and a wardrobe of jeans and flannel shirts that would have surprised her students. Hiking boots and a pair of sandals, heavy wool sweaters and an old but sturdy rain poncho, Dr. Bronner's liquid almond soap (good for body, hair, and light reading matter), a first aid kit, a couple of coffee mugs with humorous pictures on them, some cones of pine-scented incense, and a myriad of colorful necessities went into the camper van that was to be occupied by the woman Ana Wakefield. She ended by hanging a small, well-balanced mobile of varicolored crystals that she had bought in the local alternative bookstore over the table that converted into a bed and then mounting a Navajo dream-catcher on the cabinet over the one-burner stove, where the spiderweb shape would be set off by the white paint. Finally she arranged the smooth leather cord of a tiny, fringed buckskin bag from the rearview mirror. This, her medicine pouch, was lumpy with bits of rock from the stream in back of her house, tiny thread-wrapped tufts of hair from each of the dogs, some bits of bee pollen she had bought at a health food store, and one red bead from Abby's favorite necklace.

It should have been a relaxing day, with the relief of physical work and the blessed simplicity of concentrating on one thing, but in truth it was nearly unbearable. Anne wanted only to climb into Rocinante and drive off, leaving Glen McCarthy to run after her and fling all the last-minute business into her lap without speaking, allowing her to sort out her new identity and purpose unimpeded.

Instead, he phoned that evening as she was sitting with her stomach in a knot, pushing lumps of food around on her plate, to say that one of her credit cards had not yet arrived and he thought they ought to wait for it. Did she mind putting off her departure for another twenty-four hours?

Oddly enough, she did not mind; in fact, the rush of relief left her light-headed. No, she managed to say calmly, that was fine, she actually had a number of things left undone here anyway. It was a lie, but Glen would not know that, and he said he would be up in the late afternoon tomorrow.

Giddy with an entirely unwarranted sense of freedom, Anne ate her meal and had another glass of wine, chose a handful of improving books to take with her in the bus, and sank gratefully into ten hours of sleep.

The next morning she took a last look at the now-thick dossier that she had compiled from the things Glen and Gillian had sent her. She was careful not to see the details—Glen's material even had the names of the Change members blacked out, at her request—but she leafed through, letting her attention roam.

The last set of drawings Gillian had sent her held her gaze for several minutes. This was the abandoned drawing pad of a child who had stayed with his grandmother for several days when the boy's mother had taken ill on a visit home. The sketchbook began with stiff, clichéd drawings of houses and figures, but as the days passed, so did the artist's reticence, until the pages flowed with snakes and rocks, horses in a paddock, two distinctive cats, and a very lifelike scorpion that had obviously made a deep impression on the child.

Then toward the end, the second-from-the-last drawing in fact, there appeared an odd image of what looked like a stick figure of a bearded man trapped inside a giant raindrop. On either side hung two huge monsters, all gaping teeth and red eyes, looking as if they were about to bite into the pear-shaped raindrop and the man inside.

The details were difficult to make out because the

child had drawn over it when it was finished, brief but furious swings of the red crayon across the image, and then quickly gone on to the next page and drawn a cheerful rainbow in primary colors, arched over a grassy field with bright flowers.

Then he had closed the sketchbook and left it behind.

The drawing troubled Anne. She studied it for a long time, wondering what it could mean. Finally she closed the folder, put it into the box where she kept all the other Change material, and went to make herself a Spanish omelet for breakfast. She chopped the peppers and tomatoes and onions with great attention to their size and consistency and she ate the food slowly. She then washed and dried the dishes and pans, retrieved her hiking boots from Rocinante, strapped on the new knee brace, put on her heavy jacket, and set off up the mountain.

For the first hour, Stan was hard put to keep up with her. She walked fast, leaning into the cold wind, taking little notice of her surroundings, aware only of the need to get out, away, free. For the past two weeks she had felt as if fifty radio stations had been blaring in competition inside her brain, a cacophony of sounds and conversations and images, none of them strong enough to override the others for more than a few seconds. The truncated plan for next quarter's class on New Religious Movements, arrangements to find homes for the puppies, anger at Glen, concern about Antony, the nag of her unwritten book dying away in the back of her mind, details from the thick dossier on the Change community catching at her, the damage she might do her knee by forcing it to act normally, reminding herself to remind Eliot to clean out the water tank and replace two of the window screens and keep an eye on that place in the roof that seemed to need patching, and resentment at Glen and worry about one of her more troubled students and a book that InterLibrary Loan had recalled and Anne couldn't find and—

And then below that lay the anger, a wild irrationality that was the only sane response to the idea of walking calmly into the camp of a mortal enemy and pretending to be his friend.

And below the anger and the confusion and the craziness, underlying it all, she could feel the disturbing roil of her old, tired guilt, as worn and dull as a river rock from all the long years of handling. She was asking it now to support and energize yet another hard slog through the most distressing times of her past, a past that she thought she had earned the right not to forget, but perhaps not to dwell on quite so much. The dreams she had were no longer so utterly devastating, the flashbacks she experienced no longer galvanizing; the memories had become, at long last, a part of the vocabulary of her inner life.

She'd been spoiled by complacency and resented being forced to face herself again. Very well: She would be manipulated. But only so far. And not again.

In the cold spring wind and the brush of damp, fragrant branches against her jacket and her face, the cacophony of voices began to fade. The confusion and resentment receded somewhat, the opposing pulls made an effort to sort themselves out, and the fluttering thrill and dread she always felt on these last nights screwed themselves down into a semblance of calm anticipation. At the same time, walking among the trees and hills with only Stan and the wind for company, she came to the decision that this would be the last time. Never again would she submit to Glen McCarthy, become a part of the machinations of federal justice and the personal manipulations of the man himself. Dues paid endlessly became tribute to an extortionist, and with this last operation, Glen had revealed himself as perilously close to a blackmailer.

Clearheaded and satisfactorily aching, her bad knee only one sharper twinge among the pangs of middle-aged exertion, Anne walked back down the hill to her home. She showered and washed her thick hair with slow attention, put a pot of lentils and sausages on the stove, and went outside to split firewood until she heard the sound of Glen McCarthy's government car dragging its inadequate transmission up her hill. So much warning did it give her that she had all the wood neatly stacked before he arrived.

As his overheated car pulled up onto the flat before her house, Glen saw her, standing next to the woodpile with an ax in her hand. She watched him park and heard the engine die, and then she half turned to sink the ax, one-handed, deep into the chopping block before stooping to gather the kindling and carry it in through the kitchen door. Glen sat for a long moment looking at the door before he reluctantly set the brake and got out. It must have been a trick of the light, he told himself, the approaching dusk and the overhang of her roofed-over woodpile, but when she had so easily driven the hand ax into the stump, there had seemed to be a very odd expression on her face, a sort of grim pleasure, almost of malice.

Not Anne, he told himself, closing the car door. It was the light. He said hello to Stan, who sat on the porch as aloof as always despite all Glen's friendly overtures, and then went in to see what Anne had on the stove.

Anne was calm over dinner, Glen was relieved to see. Quiet perhaps, but without the jitters he had been faced with at previous times. She seemed watchful, however, and smiled to herself at odd times. She also drank more than he'd seen her drink before, glass after glass of the heavy red wine that seemed to have no effect on her, and as time went on her strangeness began to worry him and inflict him with a compensatory anxiety, until he almost felt as if he were the one about to set forth in the morning.

It seemed odd to Glen that he did not know Anne well enough to tell what her behavior meant. On one level, he knew her better than he knew anyone else in the world. He was intimate with her physical history, her psychological profile, her finances, training, and personal history, her family and friends, her strengths and her weaknesses. He knew what size shoe she wore and what kind of blouses she liked, her taste in cosmetics and where she bought her furniture. He knew in general what men she had relationships with, and could, if he wanted to, find out a great deal more about them. He even knew why she liked men of their particular physical type, big and strong and preferably hairy, since he had seen pictures of her husband.

On another level, though, Anne was as much of an enigma to him as she had been the first day he had sought her out fifteen years before. How could he know, really know, what essential shifts would be made when a mother saw her own beloved daughter laid out on the ground beside a row of other children? How could he even begin to guess at the dark areas she hid so efficiently inside her? Nothing truly bad had ever happened to him personally—hell, both his parents were even still alive. He understood how Anne worked well enough to make use of her, but he could not say that he knew her. He did not even think that he wanted to.

When the table was clear and the dishes stacked by the sink, Glen brought out his briefcase and gave Anne her identity. She studied the California driver's license with its address in a town where she had actually lived, if briefly and many years before. The photograph on her passport was a different one, more recent than that on the license, with an issue date three years earlier and a smattering of European and Asian stamps on the pages—again, all countries she had at least visited in the past.

She now possessed a checking account, two credit cards, a telephone card, an assortment of memberships to video rental places she had never heard of, an REI sporting goods member number, and three library cards (two of which were expired) from far-flung towns. He also gave her half a dozen letters and communications from mythical relatives and an insurance company, bearing forwarding labels to "general address" at a number of post offices up and down the West Coast. Ana Wakefield had kept an account with a mailbox service in Boise, Idaho, for the last four years, set up automatically when Anne had ceased being the last identity, Annette Watson. Glen had apparently thought it worth maintaining a new name for her even though she had made it clear at the time that she would not work for him again. Well, she had been wrong, and he had been right, and here was Ana Wakefield with a history ready to slip into. She pushed away the bundle of old letters, unable to face the new relatives and the paperwork from a minor accident Ana had had in Seattle. Glen drilled her on the methods of getting in touch, ranging from postcards addressed to her imaginary Uncle Abner to the extreme use of the panic alarm that was wired into Rocinante's chassis. Although they had been over this already, he decided that they had to review it again and check on the gun safe, so Anne turned on the floodlights and they went out to the barn.

She watched in silence while Glen fussed with the gun's compartment, which was indeed invisible and which did work perfectly, but when he stretched out on the floor and began to prod at the panel that hid the transmitter, she studied his legs for a minute and then withdrew to go back out to the woodpile. The crash of an armful of split logs dropping into the wire cage on the back of the bus, a device she had asked Eliot to weld on over the engine panel, brought Glen to investigate.

After a minute, he asked, "Doesn't the wood get pretty wet out there?"

"Last time out, I woke up one morning to find a nest of baby black widow spiders hatching out from a log I had stored under the front seat. I don't bring wood inside anymore." She eased herself down to examine the welds, and then to look under the back fender at the exhaust pipe.

Staring down at the top of her head, the curve of her spine, and the jeans tight over her butt, Glen took a sudden step back and said abruptly, "I'm engaged, Anne. I'm going to get married in the summer."

"Good for you." Her voice was so lacking in interest that for a moment he wondered if she had heard him.

"Her name is Lisa. She's a—"

"I don't give a damn, Glen." Anne got to her feet and fastened the wire catch that kept the firewood from bouncing out onto the road.

"Anne, I'm serious. I can't—"

"Yes you can, Glen."

"Anne, no."

She whirled, and he took another step back. "No changes, Glen. No negotiations, no changes, not if you want me to drive away tomorrow. I'd be more than happy to stay here and teach my kids and never see you again. It's up to you."

"Jesus, Anne, why?" It was a question he had never asked her before, though he had certainly asked it of himself. "Why do you . . . do it?"

"Don't ask, Glen. You wouldn't like the answer."

She did not move, did not bring up her hands to undo the buttons of her shirt or cock her hip in coy seduction or even pout her lips, but as he stared at her, angry and disturbed, he began to feel something growing along with the anger, something dark and strong and not very civilized but oh, very, very tasty. She felt the change, and a smile grew behind her eyes. He swallowed, put on a crooked smile of his own, and moved forward.

"God," he murmured, sinking his fingers into her thick hair and pulling her face up to his. "The things I do for my country."

Eight—no, nine times, over a period of twelve years, and sex with Anne Waverly had never been remotely the same twice. Breathless one time, funny the next, concentrated and athletic and even—terrible word but quite an experience—nurturing, and never once a repeat.

This time it was brutal.

They started there in the barn, nothing gentle about her mouth on his, her arms half fighting against his own, their two bodies grinding against each other. Their teeth scraped and then Anne's mouth opened and Glen's tongue was free to explore the vividly remembered and weirdly erotic plate of the dental appliance that held in place the two front teeth lost in the Utah disaster. Their breathing quickened. Glen's hands moved up and down over Anne's clothes until she pulled away slightly, buried her head in Glen's neck, and bit down hard.

He yelped in surprise and real pain, shoving her away so that her bad knee would have failed to hold her had Rocinante not been there. She said nothing, just turned and walked off in the direction of the house. He followed more slowly, pausing to loosen his collar and crane his neck to see the tooth marks, touching the welt gingerly. He was examining his fingertips in the floodlight

over the barn door for signs of blood and thinking ruefully that he would certainly have to stay away from Lisa
for a couple of weeks, when the lights went off, leaving
him to pick his way, stumbling and cursing, through the
obstacle-strewn woodyard and up the steps to the
kitchen.

He half expected the door to be locked, but it was
not. He flung it open and was drawing breath to bellow
a furious protest at the woman inside when he saw Stan,
feet braced, head down, and ready to do battle. Glen
strangled on the angry words and forced out a soothing
prattle while he inched past the dog. Stan allowed him to
pass, and in relief Glen slipped through the door to the
living room and slammed it. He then turned, fuming, for
the stairs. He didn't know if this was rejection or
foreplay, but he wasn't about to get in the car and drive
meekly away without knowing for sure.

He found her in the bedroom, and took the fact that
she was rapidly throwing off her clothes as a sign that
she did not intend him to leave. He watched her push
her thumbs into the waist of her jeans and peel them
down, and when she stood naked before him, strong and
middle-aged and bearing the scars he had given her, he
took a shaky breath and decided to make a joke out of
the past five minutes.

"Look, Anne, if you're still hungry, I'd be happy to
bring you something from the fridge, but try not to bite
any more pieces out of—"

Only his training saved him from a split lip, if not a
concussion. He caught her arm as it came toward him,
and then nearly fell victim to her knee. He was bigger,
he was stronger, he was eight years younger, and he was
trained, but she was wild and fast and she wanted seriously to hurt him, and all he could do was to wrap
himself hard around her like a human straitjacket and
ride out whatever storm had hold of her. It took an age

to pass, and his arms were aching and his mind was torn between the wish simply to slap her hard to stop her from trying to bite him through his padded coat and the growing and genuine alarm for her sanity, when between one moment and the next she went limp and stopped struggling against him. He held her, fully clothed against her nakedness, and rocked her gently until he was sure it was not a feint. When her arms moved to free themselves, he allowed her to reach up and pull his mouth down to hers.

Still, the skirmish was not over. The outright violence turned to a slow struggle, with Glen gradually realizing that her arms were content only when they were pinned down, her body free to respond only when it was hedged around and wrapped by his. Putting on the damn condom one-handed while he was lying across her, the other hand clasping both of her wrists together behind her back and his legs wrapped around hers holding her down, was one of the most difficult and grimly ridiculous things he had ever done. When he finally had it on, he was aroused in more ways than the one. He bruised her mouth with his, grabbed her and pinned her down, and finally entered her with no more thought of lubrication than a drunken teenager. He held her down and thrust against her, knowing that he had to be hurting her, wanting to make her ask him to stop. She did not ask, but eventually, finally, she arched herself away from his restraining hands and gave a brief shuddering cry like a sob. He shouted his relief into the hollow of her throat, moved against her slowly two or three more times, and collapsed.

He lay with his chest heaving, wondering what the hell had gotten into him, hurting her like that, and wondering how the hell he was going to begin to apologize, when to his astonishment he felt her arms go around him and he felt her mouth kiss his hair in an unprecedented gesture of affection.

He turned his head, heavy and damp with sweat, to rest against her breast. "Next time you want to do that," he gasped, "give me a little warning so I can bring along my cuffs and some rope."

"Duct tape," she said indistinctly, and he snorted in astonishment. Then, to his even greater disbelief, he heard her say, very clearly, a thing she had never told him before. "Thank you, Glen."

He buried his face into her body and lay there. He listened to her heart slow, and heard her breath return to normal, and gradually he fell asleep.

CHAPTER 5

case an individual can achieve results that a concerted effort cannot. Small, niggling, low-key intrusions by an intensively trained individual, who always has at the top of his or her priorities the need to keep a low profile and avoid escalation of the situation's tension, can result in the slow collapse of the group's structure.

Some of you may remember the case of the separatists in White Rock, Illinois a few years ago. I say some of you because it is a textbook example of how a tense religious situation--a "cult"--is defused. In this case, the early signs of problems were caught, an undercover investigator sent in for several weeks, and the result of that investigation closely analyzed. As a result, one of your men dressed up as a fussy, bespectacled housing inspector in an ill-fitting suit, clutching his clip-board in his hand, utterly reasonable, terribly sympathetic, but determined to carry out his job for the housing department. [laughter] I see a number of you recognize the agent involved, particularly as he has now turned bright red, although I doubt you would have recognized him at the time. Anyway, he went in and spent a number of weeks slowly splitting the community down the middle--literally, as it turned out, by changing the tight living arrangements that had allowed the three leaders to control the rest, as well as figuratively, by sowing seeds of discontent and contributing brief and "accidental" glowing reminders of outside life.

It was a spectacular triumph, but was never acknowledged as such simply because it remained low key. The media were led astray, which avoided the intense pressures of the citizenry and their elected officials toward action, the community never felt threatened enough to resort to violence (particularly as the agent involved always offered to help them fill out all the forms he brought). [laughter] Tear gas was never even

Excerpt from the transcription of a lecture by Dr. Anne Waverly to the FBI Cult Response Team, April 27, 1994

When Glen woke, it was not yet light, although it seemed to him that the pale square of the window indicated dawn rather than moonlight. Too early to wake Anne, who had a long day ahead of her, although he felt a stir between his legs at the prospect of turning over and fitting himself against her warm and sleepy body. Instead, he thought about sex with Anne Waverly.

The first time—ten? No, twelve years before—had taken him completely by surprise. He had, then as now, been dismayed by the sheer unprofessionalism of it, and had long since convinced himself that the fear that she was about to back out of the project he had fought so long to set up was all that had kept him from standing up and walking out.

She had been terrified that night, so afraid at the idea of putting herself into the North Dakota community under investigation that her hands had been like ice, and she had turned to him impulsively in her apartment in town, where they were working late to complete the briefing, reached for him as the only warm thing in the world. Pity and compassion and the cold-blooded snap decision that a good screw tonight might be the only thing that got her through to the next day had stopped him from gently pushing her away; the intensity of her response had quickly overwhelmed rational decision, and had made the next morning's slow, languorous follow-up an experience that had not faded in memory in all the years and the various women since then—including his fiancée.

He wasn't sure what it was about her that made her so difficult to push from his mind. Physically, she had nowhere near the attraction of most of the women he slept with, and certainly nothing of Lisa's hard, sports-club-tuned body. Anne was fit, but it was the seasonal fitness of someone who went soft over the winter, and her skin was frankly wrinkled and stained with too many years in the sun. She was too old for him, she often made him more uncomfortable than attracted, and she had a knack of making him feel even younger than he was and considerably more incompetent. But he could not forget her and did not really regret whatever quirk it was that made her want to begin a case by sleeping with him. He had finally dismissed his discomfort by classifying their attraction as some mysterious form of "chemistry."

After that first time, three years went by before he had slept with her again, the night before she was to fly to Miami to look at a group of rumored Satanists. It had been a more clear-cut case, less personal to her and more professional, and her nervousness had been less intense. Still, when he had gotten to his feet to leave this house and drive down the hill to town, her cold hand had stopped him, and he had ended up in this same bed, with a vigorous and intense night followed by a slow and climactic morning.

The third session had also been here, eighteen months after the second, just before she left for Jeremiah Cotton's armed camp in Utah. That had been a light-hearted night, punctuated by laughter and the electrifying sensation of Anne seized by giggles while he was deep inside her, and she had turned to him in the morning with a sort of farewell affection. She had bought and restored the old Volkswagen bus by then, and as he stood next to his government sedan he'd seen her arm pop out of the driver's window and wave merrily before the lovingly revived old chatterbox of a vehicle dipped behind the trees and the distinctive rattle of the VW engine faded into the quiet morning sounds of the woods and the distant growl of a neighbor's chain saw.

Only twenty-nine days went by before Glen saw the bus again. He thought he was ready for the sight, having just come from the hospital bed of its owner, but the appearance of the old vehicle by the roadway had been chilling: spattered with mud, most of the paint gone along one side and a fender torn half away, two tires flat and all the front windows shattered by a continuation of the neat line of holes punched up the driver's side door. Inside, the bright cotton Mexican blanket covering the driver's seat was stiff with dried blood.

Anne was in intensive care for a week and in and out of half a dozen hospitals for the next year while they attempted to rebuild her knee. The fiasco aged her badly, and when Glen had last seen her, in a Bethesda surgical ward, she would not meet his eyes.

She disappeared for some months after that, and although the following September Glen had been relieved to get word that she was teaching again, he stayed away from her. Some bizarre impulse had prompted him to send her a Christmas card, but she had not answered it, and he had removed her from his mental list of potential colleagues. Someday, he thought, he would drop in and see her: But somehow whenever business took him to the Northwest, there was never quite enough time for a visit.

Three years went by after that last cold hospital conversation, three years and seven months before the Friday afternoon when he picked up a letter from his desk and saw, in the instantly familiar handwriting, the terse message off the fax machine:

Glen—I must talk to you.
Anne

He did not hesitate—or at least not more than an hour or two. She was not at home or in her office, but when he reached the departmental steno pool, the secretary said she was around, and indeed, twenty minutes later he picked up his phone to hear her voice, tight and low.

"Glen, I have to see you."

"That's what your note said. What's it about?" He was pleased to hear that his voice sounded calm, professional, normal.

"Not over the phone. Are you free this weekend?"

He had not expected this. After a minute he said, "I am, but I have to stay available for an investigation I'm coordinating. I can't leave town."

"I'll come out," she said immediately. "Shall we say five o'clock tomorrow? Where shall we meet?"

Glen offered the name of a restaurant where they had eaten before, but she rejected it.

"I don't want to talk in front of waiters. Your office?"

"How about if I meet you at the airport and we can decide on the way in?"

She agreed, and called back half an hour later with the flight information, her voice still tight with inexplicable tension. That tension and her refusal to say what it was about had given him a sleepless night, as a parade of possibilities marched through his head, ranging from a bone cancer induced by the injuries to the revelation of a four-year-old child resulting from one of the dusty packets of condoms she had taken from her bedside table.

This last irrational thought had sent him angrily for the rarely used bottle of scotch, and he gulped down the dose like medicine. No pregnancy could have been concealed during those months of intense medical care, he told himself, and went with spinning head back to bed.

Her flight was due into Kennedy at three forty-five. At two-thirty, something came up that demanded his

attention, or seemed to, and so he sent a driver to meet
the plane and take her to her hotel. Finally, at six, he had
to admit that the need for his immediate presence was
long over, and he phoned her room to suggest she meet
him down in the hotel restaurant.

"I'm in Room 546, Glen, just come up. We'll order
room service if you want something."

"I, er—"

"For Christ sake, Glen, I'm not going to eat you. I'm
not even going to rape you. Just get here."

The phone went dead. Still, she had sounded more
businesslike than seductive. She also still sounded tense,
almost fierce. He put on his coat and took a taxi to the
hotel.

Glen McCarthy was a pragmatist, and no romantic.
He was good at his job; good, too, at allowing the past to
fade. However, he had to admit that on the rare occasions when he was ambushed by memories, more often
than not they were linked with this strange, damaged
woman and the emotionally draining cases she was involved with. Odd things such as the sound of children in
a park would jolt him with a palimpsest of horror
overlaid with pleasure, a clear image of an array of
young bodies, lovingly laid out and murdered by a madman, superimposed by a strong tactile memory of the
small mole on Anne's left breast, a low bump tantalizing
to the fingertips, two inches northeast of the nipple.

He was hit by such a memory as he stood in the
anonymous hallway of the New York hotel, a vivid picture from the days when he was trying hard to shape her
into some semblance of a law enforcement professional,
driven by the uncertainty of what the hell he thought he
was doing and the fear of how utterly unprepared she
was for the position in which he proposed to put her. He
had shouted at her, in doubt and anxiety, that *Jesus
Christ, you never open a door if you don't know what's on*

the other side. There in the hotel corridor, he saw the tiny dot at the center of the glass eyehole darken as she looked through it. She had not forgotten, he thought in relief, and he was oddly sad that she had not.

The security bolt rattled, the door opened, and the four-and-a-half-year-old memory of a mole, lodged deep in the skin of his fingertips, flitted through his awareness before retreating again into deep storage.

"Hello, Anne."

"Glen." She retreated a step and he followed her into the room.

"Sorry I couldn't meet you. Something came up. How are you?" He watched her loop the security device back over its knob and then limp over to the chairs by the window.

"Not bad. With cortisone injections and a knee brace I can almost do an eleven-minute mile, but I hate the brace and the shots, and in the end I decided to make the limp a part of my new persona. I even carry a cane. You want a drink?" The room had a tiny locked refrigerator filled with tiny expensive bottles, but a normal-sized bottle of a California zinfandel stood uncorked on top of the desk and Glen told her he would have some of that. She stripped a glass of its sanitary wrapping, poured it half full, and raised her own glass in a toast.

"You look well," she said. "You've lost some weight."

"I've been working out. How was your flight?"

"Lousy." She put down her glass and reached over to the desk. "I have something I want you to look at."

To his astonishment and dismay, when her hand came back it was holding out a manila envelope, the same kind of envelope she herself had received from him three times now. He took it reluctantly, studying her face for clues, but she got up and went to stand looking out of the window at the traffic and buildings. Her hair was beginning to go gray, he noticed, but it curled gently down between her shoulder blades, still looking thick and very touchable.

Abruptly, he bent to tear open the envelope. With one glance at the top clipping his heart tried simultaneously to sink and speed up.

Martin Cranmer. One of a number of midwest messiahs, there was a growing file on him in Glen's own office cabinets, including this very clipping. In the photograph, Cranmer was surrounded by the children of the school that he had just donated to the nearby town, there in the Kansas wheat fields. The school was built with his money and the labor of his followers, staffed by fully qualified volunteer teachers from the huge, heavily fenced farm where they all lived, a community outreach project that saved the local children an hour-long bus ride to the next nearest school, a noble gesture that got his picture in the weekly paper and reduced the anxiety level of the suspicious local farmers by a great deal.

McCarthy, when the action came to his attention, had not been so reassured. Neither, apparently, was Anne Waverly.

Her file missed some of the material his contained, mostly letters and missives sent out over the growing international computer network. It did, however, contain half a dozen items his lacked, two of which, had they come to his attention earlier (despite being illegally obtained and therefore legally inadmissible) would have upgraded the level of concern over Martin Cranmer's enterprise a number of notches.

Three of the pages were photocopies of letters to the editor of the county's local newspaper, complaints about suspicious activities on the Cranmer farm. They had not been published, an oddity that took on distinctly sinister overtones when coupled with photocopies of six months of a man's bank statements clipped to an unsigned letter that read:

Dear Professor Waverly,

I know I said I couldn't help you, but I got to thinking, and I don't like the idea of what may be going on. I won't go into detail, and I won't testify or anything, but still, you may be able to use these somehow.

"Who's William Denwilling?" Glen asked, reading the name from the checking account statements.

"The owner and editor of the local paper."

Denwilling had received a postal order for five hundred dollars in the middle of each of the months for which there were photocopies. Glen read on.

The second alarming factor Glen missed at first, because the name on the photocopied obituary, a forty-six-year-old farmer killed in an automobile accident, meant nothing to him. However, the next page Anne had included was an assessor's map with the boundaries of two adjacent properties highlighted: Martin Cranmer's name was in one, the dead farmer's in the other. With that, a small bell rang, and Glen leafed back through the file to find that the man had been one of the three residents who had written irate yet unpublished letters to William Denwilling's newspaper, complaining about problems with their weird neighbors.

The rest of the file contained no revelations. However, the familiar material, from the harangues across the Web to the stockpiling of foodstuffs, took on a darker meaning with the knowledge of editorial bribery and the death of an outspoken critic.

He reached the end of the file, folded the earlier pages back, and sat for a moment studying the grainy photo of Cranmer, the smiling, bearded farmer/prophet.

"There's very little of this I can use, you know," he said.

"You won't have to if I go in."

Even with the evidence of her carefully compiled file in his hand, the blunt offer startled him. He had never expected to use her in anything but an advisory capacity again, and then only as a last resort.

"I don't think that's a good idea, Anne," he said carefully.

"Is there anyone else?"

"We have a couple of—"

She interrupted. "Anyone as good?"

He was silent. She turned back from the window then to look at him, and she was smiling.

"If I don't do it one more time, I'm going to live the rest of my life with the taste of failure in my mouth. My clumsiness in Utah killed seven people."

"Anne, your skill and your willingness to sacrifice yourself saved all the rest of them."

"From a situation I put them in."

"For Christ sake. Anne, not even you can stop an avalanche. Not even you could second-guess a man like Jeremiah Cotton."

"In my head, I know that, Glen. In my gut, I need to try one more time."

"And if it happens that this one goes bad?"

"Well, I guess I'll just shoot myself," she said, still smiling.

"Anne . . ."

"I'm joking, Glen. Surely you must know that if I were going to commit suicide, I'd have done it a long time ago. And anyway, this one won't go bad. We're early enough with Cranmer, we can certainly defuse him and may even get enough evidence to put him away for a while. Very different from the last time. And a nice, tidy investigation might take your boss's mind off Waco."

"I didn't have anything to do with Waco," he said quickly.

"I didn't think you had." It was a simple statement, but Glen heard Anne's faith in his abilities behind it. He looked down at the envelope.

"Okay," he said. "I'll push a little harder."

He had pushed, and Anne had gone in, and in fact, they had been early enough: Cranmer was in prison now for a variety of offenses. However, the night before Anne had gone to Cranmer had not been an easy one. It had taken Glen two hours of concentrated effort to gain Anne's full and undistracted attention, and he had felt distinctly triumphant when she had fallen asleep afterward. When she came back from Kansas, however, she looked immensely tired and had lost an alarming amount of weight. Besides, she was beginning to make him feel . . . uneasy. He went through the motions of preparing a new identity for her, but privately he vowed that he would not again pull her into one of his investigations.

Over the course of his nearly forty years, Glen had been forced to break any number of vows, some of them serious, but never had he gone back on his private word with greater reluctance than with the case that had taken him into Anne Waverly's lecture hall two weeks before that morning, and into her bed last night. In fact, it was something of a surprise that his reluctance had not manifested itself physically. Perhaps if Anne had not been so . . . uncontrolled, he might have had time to consider what he was doing and created difficulty for himself, but she had been. God, had she been.

He only hoped he hadn't hurt her. Whatever had taken possession of her last night had wanted to be hurt, and although Glen knew full well that wife-beaters and sadists the world around always used that rationalization, in this case he thought it might be true. He even had to wonder if somehow he had known it was going to be that way. A month ago, when he was wrestling with the need to call Anne back into service, he had dreamed: He and Anne were lying together on the rug in front of the downstairs fire, just at that urgent stage between caresses and actual intercourse, when the smooth pink scars scattered across her body, remnants of glass shards and shotgun pellets, had awakened under his touch and begun to move, twitching independently of each other until they opened and became numerous tiny mouths, gaping against the palm of his hand and speaking to him in tiny, insistent voices. He instantly shot awake, revolted by the sick eroticism of the image but so turned on, he had stirred Lisa awake and crawled into her for relief.

No, Anne had set the tone last night, as she always did in these encounters; he had only responded in kind. And it seemed to do the trick—she was always different after sex, softer and more womanly, and he knew that sex with him had become a part of the process by which she transformed herself into the character he had created for her. Sure, he had felt like he was knifing her last night when he stabbed into her, but she had responded, and that final gasp of pain had even set off her orgasm. And his.

It was light outside now, and by experience he knew that Anne would soon stir, making a small questioning chirp of a noise in the back of her throat as she half woke to his presence and pressed her back against him. When his rough face had nuzzled its way through her thick hair to the nape of her neck and his fingers located the intriguing mole on her left breast, she would begin to push back with a greater urgency, until after a minute she would twist around and fling her arms around his neck, and they would drown in each other until it was time to start the day.

All in all, Glen thought, smiling into the pillow and

stiff now against the sheets, a hell of a way to begin an FBI investigation.

He turned then to reach for her, and sat up abruptly, his smile fading along with his arousal. The other side of the bed was empty.

CHAPTER 6

Anne Waverly, PhD
Duncan Point University, Oregon

Dear sir,

As the millenium draws to a close, we must be prepared for a sudden rise in the popularity of apocalyptic teaching and millenarial movements. The search for meaning seizes many disparate and apparently irrational handholds, and signs are seen in comets and calendars and anomalous weather patterns.

It is absolutely essential, therefore, that we develop a mechanism for communicating with these so-called cultists, a means of understanding their world-views, comprehending their symbolic language, and establishing a common tongue. In a situation involving a difficult, possibly hostile community, the primary act needs to be the establishment of a groundwork for communication between the governmental agencies involved and the religious community, and particularly the leader or leaders. The vocabulary and structure of apocalypticism may at first hearing seem irrational, even mad; however, if one regards it less as a symptom of delusional psychopathology and more as a complex language to be learned, a long step may be made on the road to communication, and an equally large step made back from the inevitability of confrontation. Previous experience has shown that if we can get the religious dynamics of the community under investigation down pat, when the time comes for intervention, armed or not, at least the two sides are able to speak a common language.

I write, both as a theoretician in the field and as an occasional active participant in investigations, that the FBI Cult Response Team be upgraded, in manpower and in resources. It would be a serious mistake to be taken unawares by a situation we can all see approaching.

Yours truly,

Anne M. Waverly, PhD

Excerpt from a memorandum sent by Dr. Anne Waverly to the FBI Cult Response Team, undated

The sudden panic that seized Glen and swept him to the top of the stairway went still with the awareness that someone was moving around down below and that the stairwell was warm from the woodstove. He stood, straining to hear, and abruptly relaxed into a relief that left him feeling queasy: Anne was in the kitchen, making breakfast.

He stepped back into the bedroom to retrieve the dressing gown she kept in the closet (a man's, size extra-extra large; he had never asked who had left it there, or who besides himself used it, although he knew that the man—or men—would have a lot of dark hair, a lot of upper-body muscle, and a real attitude). He started to pull it on, then changed his mind and went to take a shower first: If they did have a morning session, Anne might find a clean partner more appealing.

He showered and washed his hair with her coconut-smelling shampoo, and as the smell of it hit his nostrils, a cold thought shoved itself into his simple contentment. He looked sharply down at his feet, but the drain was clean of hair. He rinsed off and got out of the shower, took a towel from the rack (dry, he noted) and scrubbed at his head and face, shoulders and chest, and then wrapped it around his waist, tucking in the ends even as he was bending to peer into the wastebasket. It held two tissues and a loop of hair pulled out of a hairbrush—not what he was looking for. The tile around the sink was clean, but hanging off the edge he found one hair, perhaps eight inches long. He dropped to his knees, and on the floor he found it: a swatch of perhaps a dozen brown and gray hairs, cut flat on one end. In the drawer were the scissors she had used, with another long hair caught in the hinges. He stood up, curled the hair around his finger, and absently dropped the tuft into the pocket of his borrowed robe. What had he expected? "No changes," she had told him, and though he didn't altogether understand it, he knew it always happened.

Her toothbrush was not in its usual place in the cupboard, but he found the spares in her drawer and added a cellophane wrapper to the contents of the wastebasket so he could greet her with clean breath. He hung up the towel and put on the dressing gown, stuck another condom in the pocket, and pattered downstairs in his bare feet, happily registering the warmth of the woodstove and the smell of coffee emanating from the kitchen.

So vivid was Glen's anticipation that he took two steps into the room before his eyes informed him that the person sitting at the table with a steaming cup of coffee was not Anne. The man looked up, and Glen recognized Eliot Featherstone.

"There's coffee," he told Glen, and went back to the disemboweled toaster in front of him.

Anne's toothbrush was missing, thought Glen starkly. He flung himself out the door and into the yard, where he was confronted by the sight of the barn door standing open with no vehicle inside it. Her old Land Rover was parked in its usual place with Eliot's pickup truck beside it; the Volkswagen bus she called Rocinante was gone.

Aware suddenly of his lack of shoes, Glen picked his tender-footed way back to the porch, past Stan, who was lying on the edge of the steps with his head between his front paws and his eyes on the empty barn.

"When did she leave?" he asked Eliot in the kitchen. The younger man stared at him blankly for a minute, processing the question and his answer.

"Four?" he said finally. "Thereabouts." He went back to his screws and wires.

Well, thought Glen, of course she's gone, that's what

she was going to do. Am I going to get all disappointed that she didn't wave good-bye?

He looked bleakly out the window, catching sight of the hatchet in the splitting block, and became aware that his skin was prickling with a tainted sense of uneasiness and reluctance. It felt, in fact, remarkably like the sensation of uncleanness, of needing a shower, a really hot one. He had just taken one, but he was after all in the habit of shaving in the shower, so maybe he would just go back upstairs and drain Anne's water heater. He reached for a mug to pour himself some coffee, needing strength before he submitted his face to the crappy little pink plastic razors he hoped she still kept in the bathroom, and then he paused on his way out of the room to open the cabinet under the kitchen sink.

There in the compost bucket, mixed up with coffee grounds and eggshells, lay the thick, wavy mass of Anne Waverly's hair.

Anne herself was nearly two hundred miles to the south, walking stiffly back across the parking lot that surrounded a big Denny's restaurant just off the freeway. She had used their toilet and bought a cup of coffee to go that she did not intend to drink. Instead, she crawled into the back of the bus, tugged the curtains shut, wrapped herself up in the quilt, and slept.

For once, no one came tapping at the windows ordering her to move on, and she woke hours later, sore all over from Glen's violent attentions and feeling the black burden of a massive emotional hangover, but at least rested, and ravenous. She swallowed a couple of aspirin with the cold coffee and went back into the restaurant, where this time she ordered a full meal. She drank some of the strong, hot coffee that had hit her cup almost before the seat of her jeans had come to rest on the bright orange vinyl, and then she got up to use their rest room again before her food arrived. When she saw the woman in the mirror, she wished she had stayed in her seat: Her hair looked as if it had gotten in the way of a lawn mower, her lips were swollen, her eyes bloodshot, and her jaws and cheekbones had patches of what looked like angry red sunburn that hurt to the touch—Glen had evidently needed a shave. She splashed a great deal of cold water on her face without looking again in the mirror, and ran her wet fingers through her strangely cropped hair. She'd certainly lost the knack of doing her own haircut.

She took her time over the meal, and as she paid the bill, she asked the waitress for the nearest no-appointment haircut place. When the woman gave her the information with only the briefest glance at Anne's head, she earned herself the heftiest tip she'd ever had from a lone woman.

It was a day for freedom—what remained of the day, anyway. A haircut and shampoo left her with a brief cap of hair hugging her scalp, after which a visit to the Recreational Equipment store she stumbled across entertained her for more than an hour and provided her with a long black metal flashlight, a brilliant yellow fleece pullover manufactured out of recycled soda bottles, two pairs of heavy socks, and a delightful gadget with knife blade, pliers, two kinds of screwdriver heads, and a can opener. She topped off the holiday mood with a night in a motel, where she took first a deep bath and then a hot shower, watched some delightfully inane and utterly incomprehensible television, and slept for eight hours in a bed designed to fit a ménage à quatre.

The next day it was raining, and she resumed her flight south toward the desert.

Rocinante chugged her way steadily past the well-fed rivers and rich soil of Oregon, and gamely threw herself at the mountain passes. Laden trucks tended to pass her going uphill, but she made it, and Anne dropped with a sigh of satisfaction down into the disturbingly unnatural green of California's central valley, where rice paddies grew at the base of desert hills.

California was even more endless than she remembered, with barely half of it behind her when she finally pulled into a rest stop and allowed Rocinante's poor overworked engine to fall silent for the night. She made up the bus's converting bed and lay on it while the trucks and a few cars pounded by on the freeway fifty feet away, setting the crystal mobile over her head to jingling. At two in the morning she gave up and walked over to use the rest area toilets (avoiding looking at the mirror under the harsh fluorescent lights) and then she walked up and down the dark and deserted picnic area for a while before perching on the edge of a splintered wooden table to watch a feral cat teaching her kittens how to raid a waste bin.

Anne did not know what to think about what she had done the previous night. The sudden elemental up-welling of rage and sheer animal fury frightened her and filled her with self-disgust, that she could be so consumed with the desire to inflict damage on another person, and then by the need to be hurt herself. Her shoulders ached, her wrists and arms were dark with the bruises from Glen's violent hands, but they were nothing next to the inner turmoil.

She did not understand her relationship with Glen McCarthy, had never fully understood it. She had long realized that sex with Glen, a man she both liked and loathed, was her way of cutting herself off from her normal self. Sex was invariably a complicated human endeavor—even when monogamous and marital it was the delight of anthropologists and psychologists, and in this case it seemed to have become necessary to complete the transformation of the cerebral and responsible Anne Waverly into the flightier, rootless personalities of Ana Wakefield or Anita Walls or whatever name Glen had picked out for her. Beyond that, however, she was wary to go: too much analysis, too close an understanding, might well make it impossible to participate in the powerful symbolic energy of the act, leaving her unable to cut her ties and walk away from Anne Waverly.

Now, though, the thing with Glen seemed to have moved from the merely complex to the truly bizarre. It was fortunate, she reflected, that she had already decided to be done with Glen. The next time she might easily find herself going after him with a kitchen knife in her hand.

It was cold, and easing her stiff knee, she got down from the picnic table to return to the folds of Rocinante's bed, and perhaps to sleep.

Still, she thought as she pulled the quilt over her head, she had to admit: It had certainly had its moments. . . .

Late the next afternoon she finally left the interstate and hit the desert, and began to breathe again.

She had forgotten how beautiful it was, how bare and clean and disdainful of human beings. Living a life that was divided between a cabin in the tall trees and concrete buildings in the city, Anne was never greatly conscious of the sky, and the sun and moon were things glimpsed and treasured and quickly forgotten.

Not so in the desert: When the sun was up it was *there,* unarguably present for all the hours of light, and the division set between the light and the dark was strongly felt. There were no buildings and trees here to filter the daylight and prolong the periods of growing dawn and fading dusk, no city lights to take the edge off the night; just the hot white day and the cold black night, and the brief sly times when one handed over to the other.

All these things Anne had managed to forget, and she was caught out by the rapid fall of night before she could find a good side road down which to park. Instead, she found herself peering forward in Rocinante's dim headlights; she eventually gave up and pulled into a wide shoulder used by trucks.

The road was a minor one, and the cars only occasional, heard at a distance and swishing past to fade equally slowly in the other direction. Anne heated up a can of refried beans and wrapped them with some lettuce and tomatoes in a couple of tortillas, and carried her dinner outside with a bottle of beer to sit on one of the old telephone poles that had been laid down to mark the limits of the pullout.

The night was so still, she could hear the bubbles rising in the bottle from the ground between her feet. She left the second tortilla on the plate because the crunch of teeth on lettuce offended her ears, and because she wanted to listen, and to see, and to breathe.

She wrapped her arms around herself and raised her face to the stars, tentatively taking stock. Her scalp and the bare nape of her neck felt cold and light without the thick covering of hair. Her many aches were already fading, and she was beginning to accept what she was embarked on, starting to feel better about the whole thing, abandoning her classes and the puppies and haring off after Glen's community. No, better than acceptance: She was feeling good. Clean and strong, in fact. Reborn.

With that knowledge, in this place, she could finally admit to herself the deep, hidden reason that her nerves had been stretched to the point of snapping ever since she had seen the contents of Glen's envelope: the desert itself.

Since the days of the Hebrew fathers, and no doubt for unrecorded millennia before then, the desert had called out as a place of refuge for the disenfranchised, the oppressed, and the just plain mad. God spoke out in the desert—or perhaps humankind could simply hear the divine voice more clearly in a place clean of the distractions of busy life.

Anne Waverly had once loved the desert places. They had reached out to her as they had to countless others, men and women who had removed their followers from the temptations and distractions of life in the green places and settled them to grow in the hot, rocky soil of Egypt or Israel or Rajasthan. She had loved the southwestern desert and reveled in its purity and silence, in the harsh simplicity of its choices, and would no doubt never have sought out a cabin in the deep woods had life been good to her.

Instead, the desert was where Aaron and Abby had died, and where Anne herself had walked so close to her own death. The desert was inextricably linked in her mind with the color of fresh blood and the nauseating smell of putrid meat.

She knew this. How could she not be aware of the cold feeling in her gut whenever she had to drive through eastern Oregon, or when she was forced to go to Texas or Arizona for research or to give a lecture and fly over all that vast dead land? She loathed the very idea of the desert, and given a choice would never have set foot again outside the rainy Northwest.

When she had laid eyes on Glen's aerial photograph of the Change compound in Arizona's high desert, her stomach had clamped up. It had remained taut, day and night, for the entire time since then, and had begun to loosen only when the dry air had actually hit her face.

Funny, she thought as she had a thousand times in recent years, how the disastrous case in Utah eight years ago, four weeks of tension and despair that had ended with her getting shot, had faded in her memory. Not only was the shooting itself wiped from her memory, with the hours before only vague and sketchy, but all the rest had illogically and inexorably bonded itself to the original disaster in her life, Texas, becoming a seamless whole. In Anne's mind, Abby's death blended in with her own shooting, as if hundreds of miles and the ten intervening years of Anne's survival counted as nothing in the eyes of catastrophe. The two pains had merged, the Utah community under investigation tended to blur into the Texas Farm that she and Aaron had joined, and the desert had become one place, an environment inextricably linked with terror and pain.

She had set out fully expecting to spend the coming weeks shouldering the burden of what the desert represented to her, but now that she was actually here on a log with the grit under her boots and the memory-laden smell of the scrub in her nose, the burden was gone.

The relief was a bestowal of grace she could not have hoped for, so unexpected was it. She felt like weeping with release, or laughing with the sheer joy of living. She did neither; she merely sat with all her skin alive to the night, feeling the cold air waking her up and renewing her.

A dog barked far away, and a rooster crowed with irritating frequency from somewhere closer. A point of light moved across the heavens, becoming an airplane bound for Los Angeles or Asia. A car grew and whistled past without slowing, and faded, and when the headlights were gone, Anne raised her face to the heavens and saw the moon being born.

A delicate sliver of bright new moon hung above her in the cloudless expanse of black sky, sharp-edged and brilliant among the hard points of a million stars. A new moon was a good omen, Anne decided—at least, Ana

Wakefield was sure to think so. Half-humorously, she lifted her bottle of beer to salute the vision, but before she could put the mouth of the bottle to her lips, to her astonishment the moon dimmed, flickered, and disappeared. From one end up to the other Anne watched the darkness crawl over it and take possession, leaving only a faint light shadow, like the impression that a brief glare makes on the retina. It was difficult not to feel uneasy, impossible not to feel relief when the crescent shape crept back into view. Then it wavered again, and was gone.

She watched for a quarter of an hour, openmouthed and oblivious to the cold and the cramp in her neck as the delicate crescent first was there, then gone. Eventually, whatever it was coming between the moon and its sun—high mountains on the other side of the world? distant masses of clouds? or just the curvature of the earth itself?—cleared away, and the moon resumed its place in the heavens, eternal and innocent as if it had never given reason to doubt its solidity.

For a believer in omens this would have been a mighty portent, the infant moon struggling to find the light that gave it definition. Among primitive peoples it would be the basis for myths about moon-eating demons and cause for lengthy political and theological debates, used by opposing sides to prove both divine support and disapproval of some controversial action.

How would Ana interpret the vision? Anne wondered. A woman who had worked her way through the *I Ching* (both coins and yarrow sticks), the tarot major and minor, and the consultation of crystals on a string would not take the birth pangs of the moon lightly. Perhaps I should drive over and buy that damned rooster, Anne mused, kill it, and spill its entrails in an attempt to divine the future.

Oh yes; it was easy enough to recognize an omen. The difficult thing was how to read it.

3.
CALCINATIO

calcine *(vb)* To heat to a high
temperature but without fusing
in order to drive off volatile
matter or to effect changes.

Calcination is the purgation of our Stone.

CHAPTER 7

From the journal of Anne Waverly (aka Ana Wakefield)

The following morning Anne crossed the border into Arizona, and returned to winter.

Working her way south through California, she had seen a concentration of spring akin to the time-lapse film of an opening flower. In the Pacific Northwest the first bulbs had been pushing their determined heads into the cold; by northern California the almond blossoms were out; in the central part of the state the glorious full blush of spring flaunted itself from every apple orchard, every wisteria-draped fence, every front garden, and by the time Anne entered the desert it might have been a Portland summer.

Not, however, in Arizona. The only sign of burgeoning life Anne could see from the window of the roadside coffee shop where she sat with her hands wrapped around a hot cup of coffee was the spray of flame-colored flowers on the tips of the ocotillo cactus, and even those had tufts of snow weighting them down.

For the past half hour she had amused herself with watching snow flurries approach from the west. They began as a dark shadow on the distant rise of the highway, a clearly drawn line that advanced steadily toward her. The thin sunshine would be blotted out and a whirl of thick flakes would pat against the glass for a minute or two before the flurry swept on by, leaving the road clear but for another dark line moving down the far-off rise.

Driving conditions were disconcerting but not dangerous, as long as Anne took shelter among those other refugees from the northern winters, the trailers from Idaho and the recreational vehicles with Manitoba plates. They all lined up obediently in the slow lane, nose to tail at three miles above the speed limit while the interstate big rigs thundered past on the outside, sucking at Rocinante and the other frivolous beings with the vacuum of their passing. What had driven Anne to seek the shelter and coffee of the dubious-looking restaurant was not hazard, but comfort: Rocinante's heater, a vestigial entity at the best of times, seemed to have retreated entirely into the shell behind the back bumper.

The coffee was stale, but the buckwheat pancakes Anne had ordered with so little confidence turned out to be fresh and fulfilled the requirements of their kind to combine a hearty mealiness with the miraculous ability to absorb more maple syrup than any other substance known to science. The café had even disdained the modern notion of miserly glass jiggers of syrup in favor of the traditional metal flip-top jug, so that the final bites Anne lifted with her fork were as thoroughly saturated as the first had been.

It was tempting to stay within reach of this unexpected oasis and use the anticipation of what the cook would do with other diner staples—chicken-fried steak, say, and apple pie à la mode—as a means of getting through the heater repairs (standing with her head in Rocinante's innards and her backside hanging out in the snow). However, it was not to be; much better to make use of the repairs later, when they could become something more than mere repairs.

With a sigh, Anne dropped a tip on the table, carried her tab to the register, and pushed back out into the winter.

Even with long underwear, her new yellow recycled-soda-bottle pullover, a padded jacket, wool hat, and gloves, the cold was pervasive, and Anne stopped every hour to thaw her fingers over a cup of wayside coffee.

The original plan, Glen's plan, had been for her to pass through the town of Prescott and meet her local contact there. However, vague memory told her that Prescott was at a considerably greater altitude than the road she was on now, and a parking-lot conversation with some tourists getting out of a snow-laden camper had confirmed that yes, Prescott was picturesquely deep in snow. However, the couple assured her that the roads were clear and safe all the way to Phoenix, and urged her not to miss the experience. It was an appointment she had in mind, not an experience, but she thanked them anyway.

She did, after all, have chains for the tires, as well as warm blankets and plenty of food if she got stuck, and although she would have welcomed a real excuse to by-pass the local agent who was charged with keeping an eye on her, she thought a few inches of snow a coward's way out.

So she drove to Prescott and found it as pretty as advertised, although the snow in the streets was treacherous, its fresh white purity concealing frozen slush and a substratum of slick ice from an earlier melt. She negotiated a parking place and picked her cautious way into the designated place of meeting, and found a table.

Her contact arrived before her coffee did. He was even younger than she had thought when she spotted him through the steamed-up window of his car in the street outside, and she watched without enthusiasm as he came in the door and ran an elaborately casual eye over the crowded restaurant before doing a theatrical double take at the sight of her. He pasted a look of astonishment onto his fresh young face as he wound through the tables in her direction. An actor, he wasn't.

He greeted her by her new name, saying his own as if reminding her of it while he pumped her hand up and down and expressed his pleasure and surprise at seeing her in Prescott. He looked about nineteen, red-haired, jug-eared, earnest, and eager to get things right, and she hadn't the heart to tell him that probably half the people in the room knew that he was the local FBI man.

Instead, she played her part. She invited him to sit down and maintained her side of the meaningless conversation until he was satisfied that the neighboring tables had no interest in them, at which point he lowered his voice to get down to business. It did not take long to reassure him that yes, she had his phone number memorized; yes, she would call for help if she needed it; yes, she knew how to keep in touch with Glen; and no, she did not need anything. She took a few minutes to explain to him just what she wanted: no interference, no drop-ins, no clever surveillance. His disappointment was profound, but with the authority of Glen McCarthy behind her, she was satisfied that he would not try to put together his own operation behind her back. She relaxed and thanked him nicely, and told him again that she would definitely call if she needed anything at all. Then she left him to pay the tab.

Anne shambled out of the restaurant feeling like a curmudgeon—no, like a bear: a vastly experienced, irritable, wily old bear disturbed too early from a winter's sleep. She climbed behind the wheel, and paused to tug Rocinante's stained mirror around. Same old lines on her face, same new brutal haircut on her head; she made a face into the mirror, baring her teeth and growling at her misted reflection. Where on earth did the government find so many fresh-faced youngsters? she asked herself sourly, reaching down to turn the key, waiting for Rocinante's engine to rattle into life. And why do they all have to be so damned cute?

Christ, Anne, she thought. Don't be disgusting. What the hell is wrong with you?

It was at that point that she realized that something was awry. Sardonic self-criticism and easy mild profanity should not be her response; those were straight from the voice of Anne Waverly, and Anne had no business here. Ana Wakefield was proving very tardy in taking her place behind Rocinante's wheel.

Anne sat in the bus, not aware that the engine was running, staring unseeing at the cracked plastic of the steering wheel and searching internally for the person she had once been: interested, gentle, patient, contemplative Annie, now Ana, a Seeker who believed rather than analyzed, who was open to ideas, not cynical about motivations, concerned with the individual and the immediate, not with patterns and theories.

Ana had to take over; it was as simple as that. There was no way Anne Waverly could act the part in Change without endangering herself and others, because it would be an act, and obvious, and dangerous as hell.

Gradually, imperceptibly, her fingers and toes grew colder and her breathing rate slowed, and the analytical scholar she had forged, through defense as much as inclination, took a small step back, and then another. Ana Wakefield was born in that bus in the snow, as curiosity began to awaken.

First off, she had to forget the details. She had never heard of Steven Change, never seen an aerial photograph of the Arizona compound or a photocopy of its building application, never reviewed the community's Web site or studied its tax returns. These were all things she should not know; that would only trip her up and get in the way of her innocence.

Instead of facts, she had to concentrate on how she felt about Change, to open herself up and make her mind receptive to its nuances. She already had the impression of Change as a growing, energetic, interesting group of people with a strong leader filled with original ideas. Yes, she knew that Glen had reservations, and yes, an ex-member had complained at great length about the secrecy and limitations he had encountered, but that did not explain the almost excessive openness the community displayed when it came to the school or to visitors to its frequent retreat sessions, nor did it account for the presence of a number of educated, intelligent people—a professor of economics, a doctor, several schoolteachers, and a rabbi—who had dropped out of their former lives to join the community. Granted, even the most critical of minds could become gullible, open to the point of emptiness when confronted by the mumbo jumbo of another discipline. And she could not forget that boy's odd and disturbing nightmare drawing of the man in the giant pear-shaped drop surrounded by monsters. Still, Change promised to be sufficiently complex to be interesting.

Who knew? Ana might even learn something there.

Ana became aware that she was sitting in Rocinante staring out at the plowed drifts of snow, and had been for some time. She shook herself mentally and reached for wheel and gearshift, then hastily drew back her bare hands and patted her pockets until she found her gloves. Once they were on, she put Rocinante into first gear, drove out of the parking lot, and turned toward Jerome.

It began to snow along the narrow, mountainous road, but the fat flakes seemed to be blowing about rather than sticking, so she pressed on. The flurries dove toward her hypnotically, a moving tunnel she was driving into. Oncoming cars startled her with their nonchalant speed, but she was also encouraged by their presence—if they contained irritated drivers forced to return by a road closure ahead, one of them anyway would surely give her some sign as to the hopelessness of her progress.

Trees and sheer cliffs and the infinitely reassuring white lines of the road made up Ana's world, and she started singing to herself as a means of keeping alert and talking aloud to Rocinante about the camber and slope of the surface, the unseen depths off to their right, the speed of the oncoming madmen, and the weather.

Coming around one sharp and completely blind turn, she was plunged into icy horror when her entire windshield was suddenly filled with a Winnebago out of Minnesota, its driver trying to avoid the overhanging cliffs by driving along the centerline. She slapped her hand onto the horn and her foot gingerly on the brakes, bracing for the impact. The driver of the tin box seemed to think her panic unjustified; he clamped his hand onto his own horn in reply, drowning out Rocinante's thin wail, and pulled his vehicle just enough to the right that they passed each other with nothing more than a tap on the back of Rocinante's side mirror and a certain momentary insecurity of the right-hand tires.

Ana furiously rolled down the window and shook her fist at the behemoth, but he was already around a corner, gone from sight, and the only recipients of her indignation were the equally frustrated drivers of the mud-stained pickups and four-wheel-drive vehicles caught behind the man from Minnesota. Ana rolled up the window, shivering from the combination of cold and adrenaline, and deliberately forced her mind back to the road ahead.

With her eyes on the pavement, fighting to separate what she needed to see from the constant distraction of the swirling snowflakes, she noticed nothing else of interest the rest of the way down from the mountains aside from a handful of small waterfalls and one valiantly blooming shrub, its pink blossoms looking a bit stunned against the gray stone and white snow.

The small town of Jerome, perched on a steep hill above the mines that had given birth to it, was a welcome interruption as well as being a sign that the worst of the drive was over—and indeed, by the time she was actually in town, the snow had turned to a dull rain. Her target was Sedona, just a few miles away, but she decided to stop here and piece her nerves back together.

She parked alongside the road, careful to turn the wheels into the curb, pulled her knit hat down across her ears, and got out.

The air was magnificent, clean and cold and damp and fragrant. She could smell smoke from well-seasoned firewood, and wet dog from the recesses of the porch behind her, and a faint waft of pipe tobacco. A symphony of odors, but standing out, clear as two instruments in a duet, came the fragrances of fresh coffee and hot chili peppers. She turned, smiling, and went into the café.

An hour later, when she came back out onto the street, she was warm inside and out, her nose still running from the spice in the chili. She tugged on her wool hat, got in behind the wheel, and launched Rocinante's nose downhill, out of the mountains toward the Mecca of the New Age, the town of Sedona.

CHAPTER 8

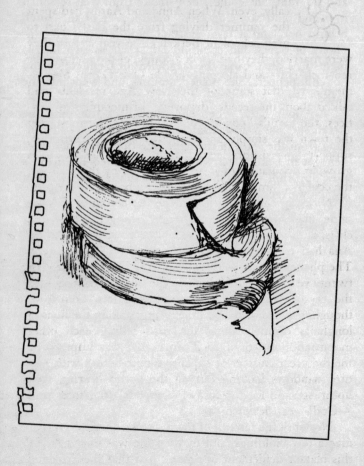

From the journal of Anne Waverly (aka Ana Wakefield)

Sedona had changed, dramatically. Drastically, even. When Anne and Aaron had spent the summer driving from the East Coast to grad school in Berkeley the year before they were married, they had spent a couple of days hiking the red-rock cliffs and sleeping beside Oak Creek. She remembered that some of the New Age residents had talked about the recent "discovery" of metaphysical vortices, the earth's "power points," but for the most part the town was simply another quiet artists' community, supported by visitors from Flagstaff and Phoenix and a growing population of retirees attracted by the clear air, the cooler summers, and the stunning beauty of the area.

Now the only thing that made her certain it was the same place was the unchanging arrangement of red cliffs, dark with the rain, that looked down on the town. Ana had reckoned that differences would be apparent. The phenomenal growth of New Age ideas over the last twenty years had put Sedona on the map of must-sees for the crystal, aura, and alien-abduction sets. Somehow, though, she had visualized the changes along the lines of longhairs camped along the road selling each other moonstones and tie-dyed T-shirts; she was unprepared for the great clusters of expensive new homes with picture windows looking out on the vortex-bearing rock upthrusts, and for the sprawl of motels, drugstores, and —God!—car dealerships.

Not until the far end of town did Ana begin to recognize a few buildings, and by then she was so put off by this blatant defilement of Anne's past that she drove on through and out of town, heading up the precipitous Oak Creek road that proved blessedly free of the intrusions of civilization. After a few miles, she pulled over into a wide spot, cut the engine, and got out to look around her.

Yes, she thought; this is where we slept, back there above that boulder. We'd been driving for hours and hours in the heat, and we got in at night, and couldn't see a damn thing except by the headlights of Rocinante's predecessor. In the morning Aaron got up and made us coffee on the pump-up campstove, and brought me a cup, and we made love in the zip-together sleeping bags. Afterward, there was a blue jay sitting on that branch there, that very branch (although the tree was smaller then), and it flew away when we began to laugh. Aaron always said that morning was when Abby was conceived, and I never argued with him, even though I knew it was ten days later, on our first night in the apartment in Berkeley.

Cars went by on the road, pickups and delivery trucks from Flagstaff and RVs from Montana, but Ana heard only the wooded silence of that distant day and the familiar low, loving groan of the man who was going to be her husband; it was cold, but she felt only the cool air of an early summer's morning on her face and the faint imprint of a pair of rather poorly made elkskin boots beneath her feet, high elkskin moccasin boots worn by a young woman with long hair, a woman who had not only a full scholarship, but a man who adored her and a life opening up before her.

Ah, Annie, she said to the young woman giggling in the sleeping bag with her man's rough black beard buried in her neck; Annie, it's God's true blessing that we cannot see our future, because we'd never be able to bear it, if we had any warning.

The blare of an air horn brought her back to herself, and she looked up to find the red cliffs dim behind low, wet clouds.

She stood for a moment longer to look down at the spot where the tent had been. Good-bye, Annie, she said. Good-bye, Aaron. Enjoy each other. Cherish your daughter. Be grateful for the life you have left.

Despite the cold drizzle, Sedona was bustling with the incongruous life of commerce. On this side of the town, however, it seemed more familiar, a place of galleries and coffeehouses instead of supermarkets and garages, the vehicles at the curbs leaning more toward mud-spattered four-wheel-drives and less to shiny travel trailers. Ana slowed to allow a family in bright, worn anoraks to scuttle across the road in front of her, then pulled into a parking place between a muddy Willy's Jeep with a bumper sticker that declared FRANKLY MY DEAR I DON'T GIVE A DAM and a newish Mercedes with a window sticker showing three almond-eyed aliens. Rocinante's *om* mandala fit right in.

For the better part of two hours, she wandered up and down the street, in and out of shops, smiling at the locals and talking to the shopkeepers. She bought a delicate blue crystal on a deerskin thong, a pair of thick wool socks made in Ecuador, three slim books on Sedona, and a newspaper, which she took into a small café that seemed to cater mostly to scruffy vegetarians rather than the polished tourist classes. She ordered a latte and a slice of apple pie from the waitress, a girl with thick black braids, two gold studs in her nose, and a long-sleeved T-shirt with a Tibetan lotus blossom on it, and then she opened the paper to immerse herself in the printed word and the overheard conversations of the locals.

The coffee was very good, the whole wheat crust on the pie less successful, and the news and conversation had more to do with small-town politics and economics than with the otherworldly considerations Sedona was known for. True, the couple at the next table was earnestly discussing the miraculous reappearance of a medicine wheel a week after the local parks department had kicked the earlier one apart, scattering the rock design in all directions, but the six people gathered around the table in back of her were involved in a vigorous debate concerning the area south of town around the Chapel of the Holy Cross, and although the New Age books in the bag next to Ana's elbow had told her that the Chapel had been built (all unknowing) on the site of a powerful vortex, the four bearded men and two flannel-shirted women were more interested in the sewage problems involving the houses being constructed in that area and the need for a traffic light where the access road met the highway.

It was very comfortable, this snug little coffeehouse with its woodstove, dark walls, and the amateur paintings of red-rock buttes done in a realistic style alternating with visionary depictions of those same rocks psychedelically glowing with the energy of a vortex. The air inside smelled of wet clothing and baked goods and was filled with low music, the clatter of pans in the kitchen, and the hum of voices discussing matters of no earthly interest to her. She felt at home here, just one more aging refugee from the sixties, with no lectures, no papers to read or to write, no Glen watching over her shoulder. All she lacked was a dog to lie across her feet, and she suspected that if she poked her head into the kitchen and asked, she'd even be provided with one of those.

Ana smiled into the dregs of foam in her glass, tipped it back to allow the coffee-stained island of foam to slide slowly down into her mouth, and put it down with a small sigh. She was of an age to know that a person had to take her pleasures when and how they came, and not to grasp after them as they faded. Sitting here had been very pleasant, but it did not, as her grandfather used to say, pay the bills.

The tip Ana left, nearly matching the size of the amount she owed for her latte and pie, was her offering of thanks to the resident deity responsible for this moment of calm. Restored, she buttoned her jacket, pulled her hat down over her brief hair, and went back out into the street.

The rain had let up, though low clouds still hid the taller of the surrounding hills. Rocinante was not far away, but Ana was not about to get back on her mount and ride away, attractive as the thought might be, for five doors down from the café lay the Changing Earth Crafts Gallery, the shop that had been her circuitous goal during the entire afternoon.

She started in the direction of the shop that Change ran, glancing in the windows of the intervening shops with no intention of entering any of them until all her attention was seized by a small display of silver jewelry arranged across a length of dark brown velveteen. Most of the pieces were conventional enough—arching dolphins and delicate fairies—but one piece caught her and would not let her go.

It was a crescent moon, but instead of being the usual small wisp of silver, this one was larger around than Ana's thumbnail and had a thickness and texture to it that invited the fingers. And if the new moon shape wasn't enough, calling out from her vision in the desert, above the moon the cord passed through a single red bead that could be the double of the one Ana had in the medicine pouch hanging from Rocinante's mirror, the remnant of Abby's favorite necklace.

Ana smiled at herself, started reluctantly to move on. Then she stopped. An omen was an omen, after all, and who was she to fight it?

The moon necklace cost little more than the weight

of the raw silver, and it dropped around her neck as if she had worn it for years. She refused a box, rubbed the satisfying shape between thumb and forefinger, and zipped her jacket up over it against the cold.

A bell tinkled overhead when she entered the Change gallery, and the pretty young woman at the desk raised her head to give her the standard greeting, grateful and hopeful, of a shopkeeper on a slow day. Ana started to respond in the browser's usual way, a quick phrase and a duck of the head, when her eyes caught on the other person in the shop; the words in her mouth turned to dust, and shock froze her spine.

Next to the woman sat Abby, hunched up on a stool, weaving a yarn rope from a wooden spool with four small nails in it, one side of her mouth pursed up in concentration, her hair its usual wild mass of intractable black curls. Abby looked up from her work to the young woman at her side, and then glanced at Ana, and the rigid shock melted into a shudder of mixed relief and despair, because of course it was not Abby. Abby was dead. This was another child, a pleasant enough child, no doubt, who resembled Anne's daughter strongly in her hair and her eyes and the quirk of her lips, a child who was looking wary now at a powerful current of something she did not understand.

Ana tore her eyes from Abby's double and glanced at the woman, who she assumed was the child's mother and whose face was now looking positively apprehensive.

First meetings are dangerous moments. Ana pulled off her hat with one hand, ran the other over the brief bristle that covered her skull, and gave a shaky laugh.

"How weird," she said to the woman. "For a second there I could have sworn the child was someone I knew a long time ago. She's the spitting image of my sister's kid at that age. How old is she? Five? Six?"

"Almost six," the shopkeeper said, still cautious.

Ana shook her head and took a few steps forward, careful to stay closer to the mother than to the child. "My goodness," she said to the little girl. "That's quite a rope you've made."

It was, too. It looped around and around on the child's jean-covered lap and trailed off onto the floor, yards and yards of tubular weaving, uneven and full of gaps but gloriously bright, almost fluorescent in intense shades of alternating orange, fuchsia, lime green, and yellow. It was obviously a work of great dedication. "May I ask what you're going to do with all that?"

The child looked down at the spool in her hands, and after a moment of silence, the woman spoke up. "She's thinking of making a rug with it, to put on the floor next to her bed."

Ana studied the immense pile of soft yarn rope, and raised her eyebrow in puzzlement at the mother, who let go of the last traces of apprehension at being in an empty shop with a stranger who had reacted oddly to the sight of her daughter. She said, "Like a braided rug, you know? Show the lady how it's done, Dulcie."

Obediently, the child laid down her spool and crochet hook and slid down from the stool to dig around in the bright mass until she came up with the end, two feet of an almost neon orange dimmed only slightly by collected grime. This she laid on the counter, holding it in place with two fingers, and began deliberately to coil the rope around the center.

"Ah," said Ana. "I see. In fact, I have one like that on the floor of my bus. Only this one is brighter than most of the ones I've seen."

"A lot brighter," agreed the woman.

"It's going to be magnificent," Ana told the little girl.

This pronouncement brought the child's head up, so that for the first time she was looking straight at Ana. After a moment, she smiled, a shy and brilliant smile that acknowledged Ana as a true and kindred spirit, and Ana felt as if she'd been kicked in the stomach, because it was Abby, sharing a moment of complicity against Aaron and the world. In another moment she would be crying for the first time in years.

Abruptly, Ana moved away, reaching blindly for the first thing she came across, which turned out to be a crudely thrown pottery mug with a quail drawn into the side. The bird was nicely done, simple, brief lines bobbing with the essence of quailness, even if the glaze had slipped into it, and the shape of the cup was inviting in the hand. She held it for a moment, finding it oddly soothing, then took it over to the counter.

"I broke my favorite mug last week," she told the woman. "Funny how certain shapes seem just right, isn't it? And the bird is great."

"Isn't it? In fact—is this one of Jason's, Dulcie?" she asked the child. Dulcie looked up from her work, nodded, and dropped her head again. "I thought so. Jason is Dulcie's brother," she told Ana. "Not much of a potter, I'm afraid, but he can draw beautifully."

Ana asked hesitantly, "Is Jason your son?"

The shopkeeper gaped at her for a moment, and then laughed loudly, a noise more uncomfortable than amused, and shook her head in rejection of the idea. "Oh, no, no. And Dulcie's not my daughter. She's just a good friend who's helping out in the store for a day or two. Aren't you, honey?" she said to the girl, and reached out to give her an awkward hug, which Dulcie allowed but did not respond to.

Ana seized the small opening and introduced herself. "I'm Ana Wakefield," she told the woman. "I just got into town, and I'll probably be staying for a while. You have a great shop."

"Carla McIntyre," said the woman in return, and picked up the mug to check on the price. "And the shop's not mine, it's a communal effort." It sounded like someone else's phrase, but she chose not to continue with the quote. Instead, she wrote up a sales slip and gave it to Ana, saying, "That's ten-fifty."

It was more than the mug was worth, but Ana meekly handed her the money and waited for her to wrap it and put it into a bag. She thanked Carla, said good-bye to her and to the child, and went back out onto the street, the bell tinkling behind her.

Thirty-five minutes later, right on time, the shop closed. On the doorstep Carla, bent over the lock, felt Dulcie tug at her sleeve. She pushed away the brief irritation she felt at the child's interference with the always difficult task of locking up, which involved inserting the key and then easing it out the tiniest fraction of an inch before jiggling it and hoping it would turn.

"What is it, honey?" she asked absently. She really was going to have to insist that someone fix the lock. One of these days it wasn't going to work at all.

Her only answer was another tug. Hopeless to try locking the door with the child hanging on her arm. She summoned the patience of the truly wise and reminded herself that a child would lead them.

Probably not this child, but one never knew.

She straightened up and looked to see what had caught Dulcie's interest, and found herself staring down the road at a human backside emerging from the remains of an exploded engine.

That was an instant's impression, but on closer examination Carla decided that the assorted parts and tools lined up along the edge of the sidewalk were too orderly for an explosion, and besides, she hadn't heard anything. Someone was just working on his car.

"Yes, I see, Dulcie," she said, and turned again to the lock. "The man has just chosen a strange place to fix his engine."

Ah, success, and the satisfying click of the bolt sliding across. Carla was so pleased at this minor victory, it was a moment before she registered the fact that the child Dulcie had spoken.

"*What* did you say, honey?" Carla's voice slid upward in astonishment and excitement: Dulcie could talk, and occasionally had in the weeks she had lived at Change, but she had been silent all that day.

Now, however, she even repeated herself.

"I said, 'It's the lady.' "

Carla had been instructed not to fuss if Dulcie decided to verbalize. However, it wasn't easy to be natural, thinking how pleased Steven would be when he heard.

"Lady?" she said. "What lady?"

Dulcie apparently thought that Carla could figure that one out by herself, because she did not answer, merely put the hand that was not busy carrying the canvas bag with the future rug in it into her pocket, and studied the blue-jeaned buttocks of the person emerging from the Volkswagen bus.

Ana dropped back to her knee again, holding a length of frayed tubing in the greasy fingertips of a hand clothed in fingerless wool gloves. She reached behind her for the toolbox, rummaged through it a bit, and then seemed to notice her audience.

"Hi," she said cheerfully. Her frozen hands found a roll of duct tape in the box. "Hello, Dulcie. Going home now?" She began to pick at the end of the tape with a thumbnail, with limited success. Both hands and tape were too cold.

"What are you doing?" Dulcie asked her. Amazing, thought Carla. Three times in a matter of minutes.

"Well," said Ana, "my old friend here sometimes has things go wrong with her. Today it's her heater, which is not very convenient, considering how cold it is. So I thought I should try to patch it together before I turn into an icicle. Can you get that end loose for me?" She held out the roll of silvery tape to Dulcie, who put her bag down between her feet, pulled off her mittens, and worked at the end of the thick tape until she had a half-inch or so of corner free.

"That's great," said Ana. "I can get it from there."

Dulcie gave her back the roll, and frowned as she saw Ana take the loose corner between her right front teeth and tug free a length of tape with a loud, ripping sound.

"You shouldn't do that," the little girl said to Ana in disapproval. "Your teeth will fall out."

"Will they?" asked Ana. "You mean like this?" She worked her tongue across the roof of her mouth and then reached up with her black fingers to pop loose the small plastic plate that held her other front teeth, the two false ones on the left. She then grinned at the child with her jaws clenched, poking the tip of her tongue through the hole left by the missing bridge.

Dulcie stared openmouthed at the gap in Ana's teeth, and at the thin device of pink plastic and wire with the two neat white teeth attached that lay in the palm of the greasy woolen glove, and then burst into a paroxysm of giggles. Tears came to her eyes at the absurdity of the lady with no teeth, and she bent over and laughed so hard, she probably would have wet herself if Carla hadn't made her use the toilet just before they left the shop.

There is nothing more contagious than a child's giggles, and Ana's mouth twitched, then she started to laugh, and soon she was reduced to a weak-kneed collapse onto the wet street and rather needing a toilet herself. Even Carla, who had little sense of humor at the best of times and who was moreover distracted by the unexpected descent of the problematic, enigmatic Dulcie into an ordinary, silly five-year-old, even Carla began to grin at the two of them.

It took a long time for the storm to pass, because every time Ana looked at Dulcie, one or the other of them would snort and set off the laughter, and when Ana put her bridge back in, Dulcie couldn't bear it, and demanded—in words—to be taken back to the shop to use the toilet again.

While they were inside, Ana brushed herself off and tore away (with her fingers) the now-crumpled and stuck-together length of tape, bringing on a fresh piece, which she wrapped tightly around the worn tubing and cut off with her pocketknife. She bent to replace it, deep in Rocinante's guts, and heard the tinkle of the shop bell behind her.

As the child's footsteps came to a halt behind her, Ana whirled around with her finger out and started to growl, "Don't you *dare* laugh," when the words strangled in her throat at the sight of Dulcie stumbling backward in her panic to get away, her face twisted into a mask of sudden terror. Ana immediately took a step back and raised both her hands, palms out in a declaration of peace.

"Whoa, it's okay, Dulcie. I was just pretending. I'm not angry, not a bit, I was just acting fierce so you wouldn't laugh at my wet bottom." She turned and bent to point her forty-eight-year-old rear end at the child, a rear end with a perfect circle of dark denim where she had sat down on the wet street. She looked over her shoulder at the child. "It looks pretty dumb to have a wet butt."

The admission of adult frailty combined with the mildly rude word brought the beginnings of a smile to the child's face. Ana straightened up to look at her.

"I'm sorry, Dulcie. I didn't mean to surprise you like that."

Carla, who had lagged behind to fight with the lock and had missed the exchange, joined them with a puzzled look, knowing something had happened to change the mood so radically, but uncertain about asking. Instead, she gestured to the bus.

"Did you get it fixed, then?"

"Not really. It'll last for a bit and then die when I need it most. She's an old car, and parts are hard to get."

"Is that your only heater? I mean, don't you have a stove or something?"

"That's not very safe. I have some good warm blankets; I just crawl in and go to bed early."

Although Ana was prepared to go much farther than that in laying hints, she did not have to say any more. Carla had been thinking hard about Dulcie's strange openness, and although she wanted to believe that she had been responsible for freeing the child, wanted Steven to look at her with respect and a word of praise, she had to admit that it wasn't her but this woman who had somehow, unknowingly, pried Dulcie out of her shell. Five times Dulcie had spoken—and laughed! There was nothing to do but bring this odd woman with the ugly haircut home and try to hang on to her until Steven returned. He would want that.

"Why don't you come back with us?" Carla said. "We live in a community about forty-five minutes away. There's plenty of room. And lots of fireplaces," she added.

Dulcie did not say anything; she didn't need to, the way she stood gripping the lumpy bag, waiting for this lady to say yes.

Strangely enough, Ana was the one to hesitate. She had been prepared to spend days working her way into the community. Instead, she was slipping in after bare hours, but still she hesitated—for a brief moment, true, but a concentrated one.

She could only wish the child didn't look so much like Abby.

CHAPTER 9

leads to the macho confrontational approach to resolving a standoff--
what I think of as the "create-a-crisis" or "Look you little bastards, you
can't mess with me" point of view. There is no denying the appeal of
having a clear goal and definite action, following in the footsteps of the
Israelis at Entebbe and performing a deft and forceful coup, rescuing the
hostages and crushing the hostage takers.

However, frustrating as it may be to men hedged around by
boredom, testosterone, and the pressures of media and their own
higher ranks to DO SOMETHING, the coup de guerre does not work when
there is no one to rescue, and one must always bear in mind that in a
strong religious community, whether one calls it a cult or a sect or just
a group of believers, there are no hostages; I repeat, there are no
hostages wanting rescue. Typically the men, women and children of
the community love and believe in what they are doing, and will die--
willingly, freely die--before submitting to the perceived enemy, the
hands of Babylon, the government representatives. This is as true now
as it was in first century Palestine when the Jewish rebels at Masada
committed themselves to their own blades rather than surrender their
children to the Romans, or when the Russian Old Believers, who were

From *Cults Among Us* by Anne Waverly, Ph.D.,
Oxford University Press, 1996

As soon as Ana opened Rocinante's door, she knew that Carla had not misled her about the fireplaces. The air was sweet with piñon smoke, that incense of the high country, and the night moved across her face, smooth and cold and clear. It was a sort of night to make even a middle-aged woman with a bad knee want to do something mad, throw off her clothes and raise her arms to the stars, perhaps, or lift her face and howl at the young moon.

Reluctantly, she came back to earth and looked around to see what had happened to Carla. The woman was standing at the passenger door of her pickup truck, laden down with parcels and a bulging grocery bag, exhorting Dulcie to get down and come on. Ana closed Rocinante's door, thought about locking it and decided not to, and buttoned up her jacket while she walked over to see if she could help.

The child had been sleeping, she saw, and was still more than half asleep, fisting her eyes against the thin brightness of the pickup's cabin light and whining the inarticulate protest of the very young.

"Can I carry something?" Ana asked. To her dismay, Carla stepped back from the truck and nodded at Dulcie.

"Why don't you just carry her in?" she said with thinly concealed annoyance. "Otherwise we're all going to freeze to death out here." Carla turned and walked away.

Ana swallowed and stood where she was. Dulcie's arms came up in the natural, trusting gesture of a child waiting to be lifted up, her normally guarded expression rendered soft and vulnerable by sleep; it was all Ana

could do to keep herself from bolting for the safety of
Rocinante.

"Is something wrong?" Carla called.

Ana shuddered and felt the sweat break out under
her hat and along her back, but she bent down and put
her hands under the child's arms. "Come on, Dulcie,"
she said thickly. "I'll give you a ride."

This was not by any means the first time she had held
a child since her daughter had died. All the other contacts, though, had been casual, daytime hugs, pats, or
rough-and-tumble play, and none of the children had
resembled Abby. Not for eighteen years had a trusting
young child reached up to slide her arms around Ana's
neck, hitched herself up to perch on a maternal hip, and
then dropped an utterly relaxed head against Ana's
shoulder. The fierce and immediate response of her own
body to the sensation of holding Dulcie took Ana by
storm, and she could only stand stiffly, fighting for control.

Dulcie was too drowsy to be aware of Ana's reaction,
but behind them Carla, impatient at the delay, had
turned back to see what the problem was. Ana heard the
crunch of her feet and stepped back quickly, kicked shut
the door of the pickup, and hurried to join her, infinitely
grateful for the poor lighting along the path.

The nearly unbearable luxury of the warm, limp
body clinging to her made it impossible to concentrate on
anything more complicated than placing her feet without
stumbling, but she was peripherally aware of buildings
around them, of spiny desert plants and low shrubs behind the light-colored rocks that lined the borders of the
path, of a few lights behind windows. Then Carla was
struggling to open a door, and they were inside.

Rough plaster walls, uneven red paver tiles underfoot, and exposed timbers over their heads placed them
solidly in the Southwest idiom of architecture, even

without the bright rug on one wall and a collection of Indian pottery arranged on a shaky-looking table, little more than lashed-together branches topped by unsanded planks. The scale of the hall and the rooms they passed was large, as if designed for the gathered community, but at the moment they were echoing and empty.

As if reading Ana's thoughts, Carla spoke over her shoulder as she led Ana down the hallway toward the back of the building and the sounds of clattering dishes.

"There's normally a lot more people around, especially right after dinner. But just at the moment we have a busload of kids and adults down in Tucson for a basketball game and to visit Biosphere, and some of us are off at the sister house in England. Steven's there, but he'll be back in a couple of days. I hope you'll stay— we've got plenty of room, and I know you'd love to meet him."

"Who's Steven?" Ana asked ingenuously.

"His name is Steven Change, but we just call him Steven. He's our spiritual counselor. He founded the community."

"Oh. Like your guru?"

"I don't know about that," Carla said disapprovingly. "He's just a very wise man. He sees things, and helps others see them. I hope you'll stay to meet him."

"I hope so, too."

One last door took them into the sudden brightness of the communal kitchen, a room Ana had seen dozens of times in her past: huge, battered stainless steel pans (never aluminum, no matter how cheap it was—the health risks were unacceptable) heaped precariously on open shelves from which hung ladles and spatulas and industrial-sized spoons; stacks of ill-assorted mixing bowls nested on other shelves, dented stainless steel resting inside peeling plastic inside hand-thrown pottery objects so heavy most people could not wrestle them from the shelf. The cupboards would be filled with cheap, chipped partial sets of department-store stoneware plates, graying, scratched Melmac cereal bowls, and all the handmade coffee mugs too lopsided or ugly to sell at the crafts store in Sedona. The drawers would hold vast numbers of flat spoons, twisted forks, ill-suited knives, and all the odds and ends that collect in a kitchen, the balls of twine and meat thermometers, the toothpicks and egg separators and paraphernalia bought or brought by one cook or another, abandoned under the pressures of quantity food production or when the cook tired and transferred over to work in the vegetable garden or weaving shed. One of the drawers would be jammed solid with plastic bags from the grocery store.

It was familiar, as comforting and dreary as a home-coming, and Ana found she was smiling even before Carla started introducing her to the three women clean-ing up the evening meal.

The names made less of an impact on her than did the warmth on her face (rubbery with the cold of the long drive in Rocinante's still-unheated interior), the smells of cooking on her stomach, and the weight of Dulcie on her arms. She nodded in acknowledgment to Suellen (a small woman with a pale blond bun on the back of her head), Laurel (tall, bony, glasses, and thick brown plait), and Amelia (round, glasses, a bad burn scar on the upper part of her forearm, and older than the others, perhaps a year or two older than Ana), and while Carla was easing her various bundles down to the counter and into the hands of the three women, Ana looked around for a chair, found a bench against the wall, and went over to it. She shifted Dulcie's legs to one side and sat down cautiously, but the bench seemed more sturdy than decorative, and she relaxed. Dulcie burrowed into Ana's jacket and gave a little grunt of contentment, a sound that reached straight out of Ana's past and gave her heart a hard twist.

"That sure smells good," she said loudly. "One of the drawbacks of living in a bus is that you find yourself eating the same one-pot meals all the time. And you never have really fresh bread."

The meaningless little speech not only succeeded in attracting the attention of the other women, but also woke Dulcie, who sat up, blinking crossly at the light. Amelia put down the red cabbage she had taken from a bag and came over to where Ana sat, bending to smile into Dulcie's face. She smelled of mint and perspiration and she had a small mole with a pair of dark hairs growing out of it on the side of her jaw. As she bent forward, Ana caught sight of a heavy silver chain under the edge of her blouse.

"Dulcie my sweet, did you have a big day helping Carla in the shop?" Amelia, a born grandmother, had an accent from somewhere in the south of England. "How about a bite to eat before you slip into bed? No? Well, just a glass of milk and a biscuit, then, how about that?"

Dulcie slipped out of Ana's lap without a backward glance to follow Amelia over to the big refrigerator, leaving Ana both relieved and longing to reach for her and pull her back. Instead, she stood up briskly and stripped off her gloves and jacket, dropping them on the end of the bench. She pulled off her hat, added it to the pile. When she turned back, running her fingers through the impossibly short hair on her head, she noticed that Amelia and Suellen were looking at her oddly, and then both of them quickly moved away to resume what they had been doing.

Both women seemed to have been taken aback by Ana's appearance, and she ran her fingers through her hair once more, to calm its apparent disorder. Funny, she reflected, I didn't think it was *that* bad.

Carla showed her where to scrub Rocinante's grease from her fingers, then gave her a bowl of thick vegetable soup and several slices of heavy bread. There was water to drink, tasting strongly of minerals, and the offer of dessert in the form of fruit crumble made with canned peaches or the healthy-looking cookies Dulcie had taken away with her, both of which Ana declined. When they had eaten, when the last of the pans were washed and the surfaces wiped clean, Carla began to dress again for the outside.

"I'll show you your room. Breakfast is next door to the kitchen from six to eight in the morning. I work the shop again tomorrow, but I'll be around until nine. I eat breakfast about seven-thirty, or Amelia and Laurel will be in the kitchen. Got your gloves? It's sure cold tonight —I'll be glad when winter's over. The spring up here is really beautiful."

They went out the same way they had entered, down the gravel pathways that seemed even more dimly lit than before. Ana stumbled once, but Carla did not notice, chattering inconsequentially as she led her charge past the vaguely seen buildings and back to Rocinante, where Ana retrieved her toothbrush, some clothes, and the big metal flashlight.

"Do I need to lock it?" she asked Carla.

"Well, you can," said the woman disapprovingly.

Ana left the keys in her jeans pocket. "I just didn't know if you had problems with intruders, kids in the neighborhood, that kind of thing."

"There isn't a neighborhood," Carla said, "and our own kids wouldn't steal anything, not once they come here."

Ana wondered at the confidence of this statement. The kids fostered out to the care of the Change community had often been through the rounds of juvenile hall and a series of temporary homes, and many of them had

police records; she couldn't believe there wasn't a certain
amount of misbehavior when they came here. Change it
might be, but a leopard's spots didn't fade overnight.

Still, she didn't imagine there was too much to worry
about. The road out was gated and the only valuables
inside Rocinante were hidden beyond the reach of the
average delinquent. She did debate with herself whether
she needed to pursue Carla's provocative statement "not
once they come here," but she decided that she was too
tired, and that Carla was insensitive enough not to notice
her guest's lack of curiosity.

Besides which, they had reached their destination,
and Carla was holding open a door, turning on a light,
and leading her into a building considerably less imagi-
native and carefully built than the communal hall had
been. The walls were simple painted Sheetrock, the dec-
orations desultory and mass-produced. Her bedroom, the
third and last one to the right, was cold and sparsely
furnished. It could have used Dulcie's brilliant rug on
the floor, Ana thought. She was pleased, though, that
when Carla went over to a motel-style heater under the
window and turned a dial, warm air billowed out. Carla
drew the curtains against the night, checked that the two
narrow beds had sheets and that there were extra blankets in the closet, pointed out the towel hanging openly
on the wall, and showed Ana the shared bathroom across
the hallway.

"There's no one else here tonight, though," she said.
"It's kind of early for casual visitors, and with Steven
away, there aren't any retreats scheduled. Anyway, I
hope you're comfortable, and I'll see you in the morning.
Oh yes, let's see. We don't have a lot of rules, except basic
things like no loud music and no drugs, but we appreciate it if you don't wander into the buildings, since most
of them have people living in them, and I should warn
you that the outside lights go out at midnight, so take a

flashlight if you're going to be out after that. And there is a community rule that we don't wear any jewelry except wedding rings, and no extreme dress, and only small amounts of makeup, which doesn't look like it's going to be a problem for you. Okay? Good night, then."

Ana listened to Carla's retreat, easily followed through the flimsy walls, and fingered the hammered surface of her new necklace thoughtfully. In a moment she was alone, left in sole possession of the two-story building reserved, she thought, for unimportant guests and people outside the Change community—quite literally outside, in truth, perhaps half a mile down the road from the central compound.

The fan blew out its warm air; there was no other sound in the guest house. After a while she put her jacket back on and went to explore, but she found nothing unexpected, nothing of interest, just sixteen bedrooms, most of them with two beds, one desk, two chairs, a shared bedside table, and a rug or two on the floor. There were also six communal bathrooms, one tiny kitchen with stove and empty refrigerator, and two storage closets for bedding and cleaning materials. Only two other rooms were made up, ready for occupancy; the others had bare mattresses with folded blankets and pillows neatly stacked at their feet.

She found a heater in the bathroom nearest her room and turned it on to thaw out the chilly space, then went back to her room and sat for half an hour or so with her light out and the curtains drawn back, vague thoughts chasing themselves around her brain while her hands massaged her knee and her eyes watched the young moon. When she judged the bathroom warm enough, she took her towel and the sweatshirt and sweatpants she used as nightwear and crossed over the cold, empty hall to take the first shower she'd had since leaving Oregon.

She used a lot of lovely hot water.

• • •

She was wakened in the morning by the brisk crunch, crunch, crunch of a single person walking past her window on a gravel path. Although she lay waiting for something else, there came no other noise, and no one entered her building.

A look at the clock told her that breakfast would soon be starting in the main hall; she wondered if the members of Change drank coffee, and decided she should resign herself to something herbal or, at best, black tea. The things we do for our country, she thought, and then abruptly recalled the last time she had heard that phrase. She felt her face go red and then laughed quietly to herself, and threw back her blankets to face the new day.

CHAPTER 10

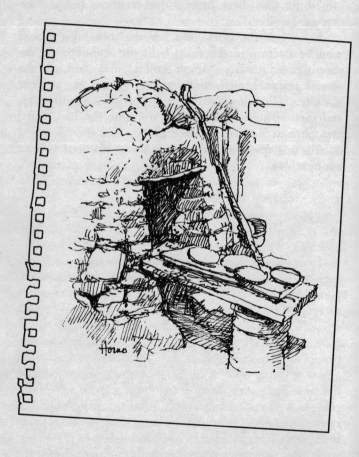

From the journal of Anne Waverly (aka Ana Wakefield)

The desert was still and clear, a morning so filled with promise that one could almost believe the internal combustion engine would never be invented. Ana knew she should wander up to the communal dining hall and begin the process, but the surrounding hills called to her, and she turned her back on breakfast. After all, she did need to get the lay of the land, didn't she? She dropped her compact bird-watching binoculars into her pocket and set out for the nearest hill.

The hill was farther than it looked, and there was no easy path leading to its top. Ana scrambled and panted and prayed that her knee and her bones would stand up to the demands she was making on them.

Finally she stopped, and if it was not exactly the top, it was close. She eased herself down onto a flat boulder, and looked out upon the Change compound.

It was bigger than Glen's aerial photograph had indicated. The seven round buildings of the central compound had looked like African huts in the picture, which threw off the rest of the perspective, but in fact each circular building was much larger than the guest quarters where she had been lodged. She wouldn't be surprised if sixty or eighty people could live in each one, given a propensity for cheek-by-jowl, monastic-style housing. Four of the outside buildings seemed to be complete as well as the even larger building at the hub. The remaining two were still under construction, one of them little more than a circle of foundation blocks.

It was also more beautiful. Seen from overhead, the layout had been flat, two-dimensional. From her angle, the buildings and gardens came alive and took on a relationship to the outlying fields and the hollow of red stone in which they were laid. It still looked somewhat other-worldly, did the compound, like something inspired by space aliens, but it was at the same time clearly of this earth.

She sat on her godlike perch and watched people come and go along the red gravel paths, into the hub building and out again to one or another of the outlying sheds and barns. A group of children accompanied by a couple of taller escorts burst out of a building and swirled along one of the pathways, bright and lively dots of motion, before disappearing into the doors of the building that held the communal dining hall, their adults following sedately behind.

She lowered the small binoculars and surveyed the whole. She was satisfied with how her introduction to Change was proceeding, the familiar patterns of Anne Waverly remaining in suspension, keeping her fears and her doubts locked away to herself while her alter ego and former self Ana Wakefield walked, wide-eyed and eager, into her new and exciting experience. It was not, as she had feared, proving difficult to usher Anne behind her door. Anne was no more real than Ana Wakefield was, and now that she was in place, she remembered how restful it had been each of the earlier times to immerse herself in a passive role, knowing there was nothing she could do except absorb it all like a sponge. And when she was saturated, Glen would reach in, pull her out, and wring her dry, and she would put on Anne Waverly again and go back to the university and the trees and her dogs.

The only thing wrong with the comfortable playact-ing she was wrapping herself in was that child with the frizzy black hair. She always had an uncomfortable few moments when she first met the children of her newest community. The children were always the hardest part, a strong emotional tug reaching out from her past to threaten her equilibrium. She had occasionally wondered if this was why she had ended up teaching at a university, a community that contained very few small children —her way of touching young lives while avoiding the dangerous maternal responses set off by the very young. The surprise of Dulcie, her distressing resemblance to Abby, would no doubt fade with familiarity, but the thought of the child was a bothersome little itch in the back of her mind, an irritation that kept Ana's new skin from a complete and comfortable fit.

Speaking of children, where was Dulcie now? she wondered idly, and then, What time is it, anyway? She did have a supply of food in Rocinante, but a solitary meal was hardly the best way to begin her relationship with Change. Taking a last glance at the view, she set about climbing down to the valley, and gained the bottom unscathed by dint of never raising her gaze from her feet.

Hurrying up the road, she exchanged waves and smiles with the occupants of several exiting cars. Once past the parking area, she greeted Change members with words instead of a wave: Good morning. Beautiful morning, isn't it? How are you? and, nearing the main building, Is there any breakfast left?

When she got to the main hall and pulled open the heavy door, she had to step back briskly and give way to a dozen or more waist-high members of the Change community, all of them chattering away at the tops of their voices and pulling on brightly colored jackets and sweaters. They took the opening door as permission, or opportunity, and washed past her as a unit, breaking into a run and sweeping out of sight around the building toward the playground noises coming from a distance. One of the lagging adults, a woman in her early twenties busily trying to fasten a buckle on a soft baby pack worn on her chest, gave Ana a quick and apologetic smile as she, too, ducked through the conveniently open door.

"The swings are calling," she said in brief explanation, and followed the children in the direction of the playground.

There was breakfast left, though only of the cold cereal, canned-fruit-or-bananas, and sour yogurt variety. There was no coffee, though she could have had a cup of black tea if the big urns hadn't been cleared away. She satisfied herself with a small glass of goat's milk and orange juice made from an inexpensive concentrate.

Ana gathered her bowl in one hand and the two glasses in the other, and surveyed the room for a minute before choosing her seat. There were only nine people sitting down, in three groups. She decided against the young couple, who appeared too wrapped up in each other to welcome an intruder, and the four men who had obviously already put in two or three sweaty hours of dirty physical labor. Instead, she gravitated around to the three women nursing their cups of tea. One of them was Laurel from the night before, who recognized Ana and moved over a fraction to welcome her to the bench.

Introductions were made—Teresa Montoya, pretty and silent, and Dominique Picard, who had an accent and an appearance as French as her name. Ana greeted them, sat down, and made a comment about the beautiful morning; with that simple prime, the well of conversation began easily to flow, even when Laurel excused herself to begin her kitchen duties.

Teresa and Dominique, it seemed, were teachers. All of the older students currently being off to basketball and Biosphere, the two women were free to bring their record books up to date and have a leisurely consultation over an extended breakfast. They were interested to hear that Ana was herself a teacher, and asked her about her experience.

"Well," she said, "I used to teach the little guys—I started with kindergarten, then third grade for several years. Then I wanted a change so I upgraded my certificate and taught high school in a private alternative school —history, English lit, and even beginning Spanish for a year." The two women did not go so far as to exchange significant glances, but Ana could feel that they were definitely paying attention. "Tell me about your school here. How many kids are there?"

"We have about a hundred kids in the community, eighty-seven of them in the school," Dominique told her.

"Really? That's quite a good-sized school. How many people in the community in all?"

"Two hundred seventy, two hundred eighty, something like that. A high percentage of children, you are thinking, no? Do you know anything about us, Ana?"

"Not a thing, really. Carla took pity on me last night in Sedona when she saw me working on my bus's heater, but we didn't have a chance to talk. I did gather that this is a religious community."

"Please, whatever you do, do not think of us as a cult. We are a community of people brought together by a common interest in spirituality and responsible living— personal transformation leading to a change in society as a whole. Steven is first among us here, but he is no cult leader." Ana smiled to show her sympathy, and Dominique, mollified, went on.

"We have a high percentage of children here because one of the ways we take responsibility for our existence on this earth is to nurture young people who have been abandoned by their families. We take in so-called problem children—children who have been rejected by a series of foster homes, who are being released from juvenile detention centers, children too old or too ill-behaved for the adoption agencies—and we give them structure in their lives, the firm hand and good example of mature adults, healthy food for their bodies, fresh air and open space for their spirits, education for their minds, and, when they are ready for it, the skills to personally transform their souls."

"And basketball games," said Ana.

Dominique looked puzzled for a moment, then grinned. "Basketball, yes—and we have a killer baseball team as well. Kids need focused relaxation, and a little friendly competition teaches them how to use aggression, not be used by it—a lot of the boys who come to us have real problems with aggression, learned from their fathers, continued by their peers. Besides which, an all-American team sport is a way we can demonstrate to the community and the state that we're not a bunch of weirdos about to start shooting at the FBI and BATF."

The colloquial familiarity with governmental agencies was disconcerting, particularly as Dominique had hit on the very purpose of Ana's presence here, but it was also amusing to hear the phrase "bunch of weirdos" rendered in a French accent. Ana laughed. "I met a child named Dulcie yesterday, who I assume is being fostered here."

"Dulcie is a sweetheart. But why do you not think she was born here?"

Without pausing to consider, Ana said, "Because she acts like an abused child." Oh God, she then thought, what if Dulcie is actually one of their own? But both Teresa and Dominique were already nodding.

"She has only been with us about six weeks. She speaks only to her brother, who is also here, but she has begun to respond to outsiders by gestures, nodding, or pointing, and occasionally she uses a few words. That is progress."

"Dulcie?" said Ana. "Do you have more than one Dulcie here? The girl I met last night was talking just fine."

"*Dulcie* was?" It was the first time Teresa had contributed; both women were leaning across the table as if to seize Ana by the collar.

"Yeah. When she and Carla saw me working on the engine, she asked me what I was doing. And what was the other thing? Oh yes, when I pulled a length of duct tape from the roll using my front teeth, she was a good little mother and told me I shouldn't use my teeth like that, they'd come loose and fall out. And then she got the giggles when I actually pulled my teeth out. I have a dental plate," she explained.

Teresa and Dominique looked at each other thoughtfully.

"Well," said Dominique. "Interesting. Would you like to see the schoolrooms?"

"Sure," said Ana. "Let me just take the dishes back." She piled up her things and took the empty cups of the two women, turned to carry them over to the kitchen, and then nearly dropped her burden in astonishment.

"Good . . . heavens," she said. It was the first time she had faced the high half-wall that dropped down to divide the high-ceilinged dining hall from the kitchen. Last night she had merely glanced in as she went past, and this morning she had come in at the far door, taken her food from the buffet, and walked over to the tables to sit with her back to the kitchen. Now, however, she stared at the high wall and at the ten-foot-high mural that stretched the full sixty-foot width of the room.

The theme of the painting was proclaimed in foot-high gold letters smack in the middle: TRANSFORMATION. At the left side of the mural a highly realistic portrayal of the untouched desert that Ana had contemplated from her high perch that morning gradually gave way to the gentle civilization of fields and crops from which tumbled baskets of fruit, tomatoes, eggplants, and grain that spilled into the central image, the kitchen. Five figures

stood with their backs to the painter and their arms
raised, giving praise to a fiercely glowing *horno,* the
womb-shaped bread oven found behind native dwellings
throughout the Southwest, its top slightly elongated by
the artist's perception into something closer to a pear in
shape. To the right stretched an abundance of cooked
dishes, breads, casseroles, and pots of soup that nourished
a long row of identical people, again shown from behind,
and then a row of people marching renewed to the fields
while in the background children played on a slide and a
set of swings. The people were followed by a jagged,
half-raised circular stone building, and finally, seated in a
lotus position, a meditating man surrounded by a shimmering golden aura.

Ana laughed in pleasure at the sight of it, and felt
that really, she might as well climb into Rocinante and
ride away: Any group with sufficient sense of humor and
sheer exuberant joy to paint that mural above the entrance to their communal kitchen was not about to twist
itself in self-loathing or paranoia.

She walked with Teresa and Dominique to the
schoolrooms in the central building. On the way she
looked curiously at her surroundings. The buildings
were impressive and original, massive circular objects
slapped together of rock and cement that somehow managed to look crudely primitive and wildly modernistic at
the same time.

The garden, however, was the real delight. Xeriscape
landscaping at its most austere, the carefully scattered
cactuses, boulders, and desert plants had the look of
modern sculpture in the courtyard of an art museum,
softened only by the rises and falls of the ground and the
sprinkled clumps of delicate grasses. There was even,
Ana was charmed to see, a boojum tree at least twelve
feet high, its glorious blue-gray trunk straight and tall in
its cloud of tangly, tiny-leafed branches.

" 'For the Snark *was* a boojum, you see!' " she exclaimed. Teresa looked at her as if she were mad, and Dominique blinked. "A poem," she explained. "By Lewis Carroll."

"Ah," said Dominique.

Ana decided not to attempt further explanation, and as they continued on she turned her attention to the buildings themselves. All of these in the central compound were made in the same fashion, comprising great, rough-hewn hunks of rock held together by reddish concrete. The rocks were not laid so much as tumbled, with the spaces filled by the concrete varying wildly and including a lot of gaps. It was a pleasing technique, looking both massive and delicate, but Ana had to wonder if it wouldn't fall in on itself in an earthquake.

"I don't think I've ever seen buildings like this," she commented.

"Then you haven't been to Taliesen West."

"Frank Lloyd Wright's place? That's in this area, isn't it? No, I haven't been there."

"It's down near Scottsdale. Beautiful. Inspired. Needs a lot of muscle, though. We build the forms, lay in miles of reinforcing bar, heave in the rocks—we have a forklift for the bigger ones—and shovel in yards and yards of very stiff concrete. After a couple of days we take the forms down and do the next section."

"That explains the muscle on the men in the dining hall," Ana commented.

"Steven calls it 'sweat meditation,' " Teresa volunteered seriously.

Ana decided that this was one Change member who had not contributed to the humor in the TRANSFORMATION mural, but she said merely, "I'm looking forward to meeting Steven," and followed the two teachers into the central building.

· · ·

Ana spent the morning with Dominique, exploring the classrooms, shelving books in the nascent library, helping fill out a stack of evaluation forms, all the endless process of running a legally recognized school under the state's watchful eye. They took lunch in the hall, where Ana met more strong, happy young men and women than she had seen gathered together in one place for a very long time. Then, in the afternoon, Ana met the children of the Change community.

Many public schools, Ana knew, had gardens for the students, "life labs" where the elementary classrooms' bean-seed-in-a-milk-carton could be carried through to its fullness, giving the children actual edible beans to harvest. Concepts of biology and ecology were given solid form, and the students learned cause-and-effect by seeing their own plants wither or thrive.

The students here were put in the gardens for pedagogic reasons, but also as a basic lesson in responsibility. Change was as nearly self-supporting as a desert community could be, and the earlier the children learned to become active contributors to the whole, the better, for themselves and for the community.

Today was dedicated to the beginning of the year's cycle. Ana was assigned to a group of six five- and six-year-olds, and the subject was the planting of beans. Instead of small waxy milk cartons salvaged from the lunchroom and bags of sterilized potting soil from the local hardware store, they used rough pots formed out of recycled newspaper and scoops of rich, fragrant soil from a compost heap mixed with the sandy earth of the desert, but other than these surface differences, the effect was the same as any other classroom bean-planting. Clumsy fingers, chubby still with baby fat, spilled more soil than the pots received and either thrust the beans so far into the soil the seeds would be hard put to reach the light or else left them so close to the surface they would be unable to stand upright. Each child then drowned his seeds with water. Muddy, wet, and thrilled, they placed each already disintegrating pot onto flats, and then she herded them out of the potting shed toward the beds where the beans would be planted when the survivors had their first three leaves.

These children knew what was going on, that was clear, even if few of them could handle the gardening implements with any dexterity. They squatted down along the side of the weedy bed and plunged their trowels enthusiastically into the soil as they tried to emulate Ana, who was loosening the soil with a garden fork before she pulled the weeds and tossed them into a nearby bucket. Most of the children overestimated the motion required, and clots of dirt and weed flew all over.

Ana kept them at it for twenty minutes, abandoning the bed with the ravaged edges only when the next group stood waiting to take over the trowels. They then went to scrub hands, brush ineffectually at knees, and gather eggs at the henhouse.

She began to relax in their company. She had only experienced one bad moment, a brief blink of an eye when she seemed to be standing not in Arizona, but long ago in Texas, and it was Abby digging at her side with similar enthusiasm, unearthing an enormous worm and holding it up in triumph. But the memory was gone in an instant and she was again Ana Wakefield in Arizona, and the worst part of meeting the children, the early moments of extreme vulnerability, were past, she was sure of it. Now she could get on with the business of saving them.

Once the kids were delivered, tired and dirty, back to the schoolrooms, Dominique took Ana back in hand. They wandered through the farm sheds and admired the goats, looked at the ongoing projects in the crafts barn, the pots, mugs, and weavings due for sale in the Sedona gallery, saw the bare orchard and the plowed fields and the wide, mulched-over vegetable beds, mature brothers of the beds the students played at, which in the summer would surely resemble the left-hand side of the TRANSFOR-MATION mural.

At about three o'clock, Dominique excused herself, saying that she had her meditation period now. Ana went back down the road to the dull guest quarters, but stopped there only long enough to fetch her camera and her journal, and took them up to the red-rock perch above the compound.

It was only to be expected that a woman like Ana Wakefield would keep a journal, the daily thoughts and meditation of a lifelong inhabitant of the New Age, her inner thoughts, reflections, and a record of her dreams. In it she recorded descriptions, personal details, specula-tions, and interesting asides. She could even make de-tailed if amateurish sketches of her surroundings, and anyone going through her things would see only an inno-cent diary of events. In truth, it was Ana's means of reporting to Glen.

It was small enough to take with her at all times, and she tended to stick it in a pocket and leave it there even when she had no intention of writing or sketching. That way she would have it with her on trips to town, where she could divert into a library or copy shop and in min-utes have the pages photocopied and either into a stamped envelope or faxed to Glen and discarded, before anyone noticed she was gone. She felt like a teenager sometimes, but she kept a diary.

The climb up the hill was not much easier the second time, but she had at least discovered some of the hazards among the boulders, and this time she located a natural seat, shaped for comfort. She took a few photos with her trusty old 35mm, then opened the journal.

Over the years she and Glen had developed a series of code phrases, words that could be used naturally in the journal or a postcard to "Uncle Abner," or even in a conversation, but which had specific meanings to indicate, for example, that things were going either so slowly or so smoothly that she thought Glen might as well go do something else for a while, or that she needed someone to hang around the prearranged meeting place until she could get free, or that she was feeling nervous and wanted to get out soon.

The word used to show this first state of affairs was, appropriately, "placid," and she used it now, twice, in describing the compound with a third of its population missing and then on the following page in speaking about the goats in the field. She did not know if Glen would appreciate the nuances of the mural (though he sometimes seemed to have a sense of humor), so she spent some time on that, reflecting on its hidden meanings without giving too much away herself. She closed the entry immediately after the second "placid," for emphasis, read what she had written (checking to be sure that she had not by accident made use of other, contradicting code words), and climbed back down the hill to see if she could lend a hand in the kitchen.

After dinner, when the dishes were clean and the small children in bed, Ana was invited to join the community in its group meditation. She accepted with the appropriate eagerness, hung up her damp dish towel to dry, and waited while her new friends Laurel and Amelia checked on the breakfast provisions and shut down the lights. They took coats from an entire room dedicated to rolling metal clothes racks hung with hundreds of bent metal hangers, and bundled up fully before stepping out into the frigid night air. The three women walked quickly from the dining hall to the hub building, their breath steaming clouds around their heads, and joined several others just entering the foyer.

This time, however, instead of going left into the school offices or right into the circular corridor that connected all the classrooms, Ana followed the others straight ahead, through a set of double doors that looked so like the walls around them as to be invisible, given away only by the slight discoloration of the wood where a hundred hands every day pushed them open. Inside the doors was another, smaller foyer, this one with a solid wall on the inward side and swinging doors to the right and left, forming a baffle to keep those outside from seeing in. Amelia went through the right-hand door, Laurel through the left. After a moment's hesitation, and aware that Laurel was standing and waiting for her, Ana followed Amelia.

Her first thought on setting foot into the circular meditation hall was how amazing it was that such a room could be concealed in plain sight, surrounded as it was by one of the busiest, most public places in the entire compound, the school.

There were two stories to this building, the school below and the residences of Steven Change and his oldest companions above, but the domed roof made this central part taller yet. The top of the circular skylight was nearly forty feet above the floor. The actual diameter was not great, but full use had been made of the volume by the simple, dramatic device of a pair of circular ramplike steps winding up the walls, forming an external double helix of platforms, each roughly four feet square, many of which were occupied already by seated figures settling into poses of meditation. Some of the platforms were empty, at irregular intervals but mostly in the middle section, which made Ana wonder if perhaps the seats weren't specifically assigned, and their owners absent.

That was later, though. At first all she noticed was the sense of constricted space below, underscored by the near-black carpeting on the floor and the sheer, high walls rising on all sides that gave way to warm reds and gathered light above until at the very top, where outside spotlights shone down through the glass, there was an explosion of warmth and movement and golden light.

Just under the glass was suspended a shimmering golden cloud, a sparkling, breathing entity made up of dozens of fine gold rods held horizontal to the floor and turning freely in the rising air. Ana had seen something like it once in a San Francisco cathedral. That sculpture, though, had served to evoke the cool splendor and ethereal magnificence of the Holy Spirit. This one made a person yearn to be closer, to rise up from the dark commonality and strive for light and entrance to the dazzling gold cloud.

Ana was not the only one to feel the pull. She was bumped twice in the jostle near the door as others paused to throw their gaze upward. For some there was awe, for others an almost ritual throwing back of the head that reminded Ana of the pause at the font when a Roman Catholic entered a church. She watched two of the ritualists, both of whom came in the right-hand door, and saw them climb the rampways to take up seats raised above the rest. Among them, she saw, were Amelia, Suellen, and Teresa. Teresa's platform was high up enough that it would have given an acrophobe problems. Ana settled into a place on the floor with her back against the wall, tucking her knees in with care, and gave herself over to a close examination of this holy of holies at the very center of Change.

The golden mobile and the double helix of meditation steps were not the oddest thing about this room, although they were the most immediately impressive. In their shadow, an observer could easily overlook the peculiar structure that took up the center of the hall, forming a sort of axis device around which the circular room might be visualized as turning.

The axis rose out of the floor in what Ana had no doubt was the precise center of the hall, a dull black pipe about fifteen inches in diameter that ran straight up and through the middle of a circular fireplace with an over-hanging hood until it divided into a Y about two-thirds of the way up the hall's height. The two arms disappeared into the domed roof just below the edges of the skylight. In the arms of the Y a circular platform had been set, connected to the walls by six narrow walkways.

The more Ana looked at this weird structure, the stranger it seemed. It was as if some mad engineer had decided to cross a huge chemical apparatus with the rat-guard of a ship's ropes and turn the result into a tree house. That it was deeply symbolic for the builders she had no doubt—nobody would go to that amount of work for mere decoration—but what that symbolism might be, and if it had any actual function aside from holding the fireplace to heat the room, she could not tell.

What she did know, what she hadn't been sure of until she had walked into this room, was that behind all its apparent openness, Change was full of hidden secrets.

The room began to quiet, until Ana could hear the low crackle of the fire burning behind its circle of screen. After a minute, high over her head, a man stood up. His was the highest occupied platform on his run of the helix, although three higher than his were unoccupied. (Steven and his right-hand man, Mallory, Ana wondered, off in England? And what of the third one?) This man now picking his way cautiously along the nearest walkway to the central platform was someone Ana had met during the day, in the workshop where he was working on a set of chairs. David Carteret, his name was, a big man with scars on his face that looked as if he'd gone through a window. He seemed to be in charge of leading the meditation from his high perch directly above the fireplace. Ana wrenched her mind from speculation and her gaze from the extraordinarily beautiful cloud of gold, and prepared to give herself over to meditation.

David began with a greeting sent from Steven and a couple of brief announcements from the English sister house. He then moved quickly, and with the relief of a person taking refuge from public speaking, into a chant Steven had set for them. "I am Change," said David; "Change am I."

Ana dutifully joined the others, listening to how the voices rose and rang through the dome overhead, hearing the hundred voices slowly become one. It had been a while since she had joined in a group meditation, and it took her some time to immerse her voice in the others', to lose herself in the words. Gradually, imperceptibly, she let go, and as the chant evolved from two statements into the slow two-beat rhythm of "I am Change am I am Change," she moved along with it.

Silent meditation followed, although by this time the protests of Ana's knee were loud and interfered with the purity of her contemplation. The ninety minutes seemed endless, and when finally people began to get to their feet, she followed them out gratefully, stumbling down the road on a leg that felt as if hot gravel had been inserted into the joint. All she could think about was a shot of cortisone from Rocinante's locked cabinet, a jolt of whiskey from her illicit stores, and many hours stretched straight in bed.

An ancient school bus rumbled past her as she approached the guest quarters: the older children and their teachers returning from Tucson. She wished them a silent good night and took her creaking middle-aged body to bed.

CHAPTER 11

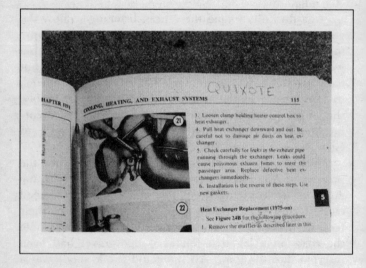

From FBI documents relating to the Change case

Ana walked into the dining hall the next morning and found the community restored to itself, voices raised in a wall of sound, dishes clattering, excited teenagers calling to each other across the room. The energy embodied in the TRANSFORMATION mural no longer seemed unlikely.

The hub building, too, was transformed. What had yesterday been a half-empty nursery school was now a purposeful seat of learning. Halfway through the morning Ana was dragged out of the office to help Teresa with her fifteen eleventh and twelfth graders, who were finding it difficult to settle back into the classroom after two days of freedom.

"I just need another adult today," Teresa told her as they hurried around the circular hallway. "You don't need to do anything—they'll settle down if you just go and stand next to them while I'm trying to teach."

Not a terribly flattering judgment of Ana's abilities, perhaps, but it was true that the repressive presence of an adult—any adult—goes far to smooth down youthful high spirits. Ana dutifully stood, and drifted, and saw the classroom gradually cool off from the near-boil. By lunchtime, concentration had been achieved.

The kids exploded out the door, and Teresa dropped down into her chair with her head thrown back. Ana noticed idly that despite Carla's version of the community regulations that specified no jewelry, this woman, too (whom Ana would have classified as an ardent follower of rules), was wearing a necklace, in her case a delicate gold chain. Teresa sat forward and the chain disappeared under her collar. Perhaps the rule meant only no necklaces on top of clothing?

"It is always so difficult for them to focus when they have been away," Teresa said. "I've come to dread field trips."

"Sitting in a bus for all those hours," Ana said. "Maybe they need some 'sweat meditation' when they get in."

Teresa looked surprised, then thoughtful. "You could be right. Perhaps I'll mention it to Steven."

"Do you have any idea when he'll be back?"

"It was supposed to be tomorrow, but we heard this morning it will be three or four days. Well, let us go and have some lunch."

Three or four days. Ana was seized by an abrupt spasm of boredom at the thought of it, because it would then be three or four more days while the great man settled in and found the time to exchange a few words with the newcomer, plus two or three more before the community got back into its normal functioning.

She told Teresa she had things to do, and excused herself from lunch, going instead to her room to change into her oldest clothes. She spotted the silver moon that she had bought in Sedona and obediently removed the night before, and after a moment she picked it up and dropped it over her head, tucking it under her shirt. She felt obscurely comforted by the small weight, and by the minor rebellion against the rules.

Rocinante's cupboards provided some stale bread and a piece of cheese for lunch, and soon Ana was elbow-deep in the bus's engine, red-faced and muttering, with the ancient, much-taped-together repair manual propped open at the heater section. Forty minutes into it she heard footsteps approach and stop behind her; she looked around and saw Dulcie's serious and disconcertingly familiar face.

"Hello, Dulcie. I wondered where you'd gotten to. I think you must be my good luck, because I just this

minute found what's wrong with Rocinante's heater.
You see this little switch? Well, you can't tell it's a
switch, but the book says it is, and says it's supposed to
flip on to let the heat in, and it isn't. You probably
shouldn't touch it," she said, drawing it back slightly
from the child's inquiring finger. "It's really filthy. So am
I, in fact. How've you been? How's the rug coming
along?"

"Can you fix it?"

"What, the rug? Oh, you mean the switch. I don't
think I can fix it, but now that I know what the problem
is, I can buy another one and replace it. I hope."

"Why do you call your car Rosy Nante?"

"Rocinante? That's her name. Have you ever heard
about Don Quixote, the Knight of La Mancha?" She
rolled the name on her tongue with magnificence and
raised her eyebrows at the child.

Dulcie shook her head.

"Don Quixote was a great man, although he was a
little bit crazy." Ana reached for the small screwdriver
and settled herself into the story while she put the engine
back together.

" 'Don' means 'sir,' or 'lord,' so it's like calling him
Sir Quixote. Anyway, Don Quixote lived a long time
ago, in a country called Spain, where he spent all his
spare time reading exciting adventures about knights
who rode out and rescued maidens and punished bad
guys. Could you hand me that roll of skinny black tape?
And I promise not to bite it with my teeth." Ana pulled
her head out far enough to exchange grins with the
child, accepted the tape, and returned to her task.
"Where was I? Oh yes. Don Quixote loved to read stories about knights and their squires—that's the person
who helps the knight, bringing him food and polishing
his armor. Are you reading yet, Dulcie?"

The child nodded. Ana paused to scrabble through

the toolbox for a stub of pencil she kept there, and printed the name QUIXOTE in clear letters along the upper margin of the manual on repairs, saying the letters aloud as she wrote them. She dropped the pencil stub into the fold; many weeks later Glen McCarthy would find the tattered manual, open it at the pencil, and wonder over the inscription.

"That's what it looks like, with a Q and an X, which aren't letters you get to use very often. Anyway, one day Don Quixote got it into his head that he, too, would be a great knight. He was by this time more than a little bit batty from all his reading, so he really believed that he could do this. He made himself a helmet out of an old bucket and climbed onto an ancient old nag of a horse he called Rocinante, imagining it to be a magnificent steed trained as a warhorse. He talked one of his neighbors, a man named Sancho Panza, into becoming his squire by saying that he would make Sancho the governor of an island when they returned, and Sancho believed him.

"Now would you hand me the crescent wrench? It's that flat metal thing with the shape like a moon on the end. No, I think I need the bigger one. Thanks.

"Don Quixote and Sancho Panza rode forth, Don Quixote on his bag-of-bones Rocinante, Sancho on a donkey, and the first thing they did was come out onto a flat plain, where they saw two or three dozen windmills. Do you know what a windmill is?" Dulcie looked uncertain. "There's one here, though it's a very modern one. You know that thing on the high tower up on the hill past the barns, with little arms that turn really fast when the wind blows? That's a windmill for making electricity; these windmills Don Quixote saw were shorter but wide as a shed, and instead of little metal blades that fly around fast, they had four huge arms stretching almost to the ground, made out of wood and cloth like the sail of a boat, and they went around and around slow and strong, turning a stone that the people used to grind their wheat into flour."

Most of this would be beyond the child's comprehension, but that didn't matter. Ana stuck her head back into the engine and went on with both repairs and story.

"The windmills that poor old confused Don Quixote saw looked to him like an army of giants, each of them with four enormous arms turning around and around. Of course, Don Quixote immediately decided that he would attack them all, wiping this scourge of giants from the face of the earth. Can I have that smaller crescent wrench now, Dulcie?" She waited a minute, caught in a tricky bit and unable to look around. "Do you see it? The one on the top?" she prompted, and was preparing to back out, when the wrench nudged her outstretched hand. She wrapped her fingers around it and continued.

"Don Quixote pulled down the visor on his bucket helmet, stretched out his lance, and jabbed his spurs into poor Rocinante's sides. Off they pounded, straight at the nearest windmill, while Sancho Panza sat on his donkey and covered his eyes so he didn't have to watch.

" 'Cowards and vile caitiffs,' shouted Don Quixote." Ana stuck her arm out behind her to gesture swordlike with the crescent wrench, then reapplied it to the task. " 'One knight will conquer you all!' And he flew across the field at them and charged into the nearest giant. The wind was turning the sail, and it caught Don Quixote's lance, broke it to pieces, and flipped both Don Quixote and his horse over and over, rolling across the ground.

"Sancho was so frightened. He came running up and helped Don Quixote to his feet. 'Master,' he cried, 'what are you doing? These are not giants, they're windmills. You can't destroy them!' And Don Quixote, groaning from his injuries, looked again and saw that they were indeed windmills, and he shook his head. 'My great enemy, the magician Freston, has robbed me of my victory by turning these giants into windmills before our very eyes. But never fear, dear Sancho; my sword will prevail.'

"And off they went to the inn, to bind their wounds and eat their supper."

Ana had timed her conclusion carefully, to coincide with the end of the temporary repair. She emerged from the engine, dropped her tools into the box, closed Roci-nante's engine cover, and turned to look in triumph at her audience.

Except that her audience had grown, and was no longer just a quiet five-year-old girl. Standing behind Dulcie was a dark, well-muscled, devastatingly good-looking young man with his hands in his jacket pockets and suspicion in his eyes.

"This is Jason," Dulcie said proudly.

Ana felt simultaneously fourteen and eighty-four, clumsy, awkward, stupid, and ugly, and could only hope that none of it showed on her face. She picked up the screwdriver and tape and dropped them into the box, got to her feet, brushed off her trousers, removed her fingerless gloves and looked at the state of her hands before deciding that she ought not to inflict her grease on the young man. He looked nothing like Dulcie, except perhaps the eyes. His hair was as black as her tangled mop, but his lay slick against his head, gathered into a short ponytail at his neck, and his skin was a couple of shades lighter.

"Hello, Jason, I'm Ana. I heard that Dulcie had a brother. Did you have a good time down in Tucson?"

"It was okay," he said, a typical teenager's reaction, and although it was not accompanied by a shrug, some-thing about the gesture made Ana wonder if he wasn't younger than the eighteen or nineteen he appeared.

"You're an artist, I think Carla told me." In an in-stant, she could see it was the wrong thing to say: His face, already closed in, went completely blank. She hastened to create a diversion by clearing up the tools and chattering. "I was in the shop in Sedona and bought a coffee mug, and Carla told me that Dulcie's brother had sketched the bird on it. My favorite cup got broken when I had to slam on my brakes the week before—I got coffee all over the car and broke the handle off the cup, but I missed the deer."

She pushed the tools down and snapped the top shut, flipped the manual closed, and put tools, book, gloves, and ground cloth into their place beneath Rocinante's seldom-used passenger seat.

"I think I'd better go clean my fingernails before I offer to help with dinner. Good to meet you, Jason. See you later, Dulcie."

"Good-bye, Ana. Bye, Rocinante," said Dulcie. Her hand snuck out and surreptitiously stroked the bus's faded paint, and then she and her protective, self-contained, aloof, unconsciously handsome and unbelievably sexy older brother walked away up the road to the main compound.

Ana let out a deep breath as she watched them go. He walked like a young athlete, or a street tough, with straight spine and a slight swagger to his hips. However, his head was ever so slightly bent to listen to the now-chattering Dulcie, and when the child's hand came up to his, he allowed it to stay there.

Again, Ana wondered how old he was.

That night after dinner a basketball game was held in the dining hall. While the pans were being scrubbed and the smallest children put to bed, the tables and benches were pulled back to the walls and two men with a roll of masking tape measured off the sidelines and laid out two keys around the baskets that other men were bolting to the walls. It was a practiced exercise, finished before the cleanup was, and when Ana came out of the kitchen, she stepped into a basketball court complete with a facsimile of bleachers and two teams of wildly mixed players warming up by doing passes and layup shots. One of the players was Jason.

Ana worked her way around the room to where Dulcie sat.

"Hey there, Sancho," she said. "Why aren't you out on the court?"

"Hi, Ana. They said I could stay up to watch my brother. Do you want to sit down?"

The woman at Dulcie's side stared at Dulcie, stared harder at Ana, and turned to whisper to the woman next to her. Ana joined them and sat down.

"How is Rocinante, Ana?"

"My trusty steed? Ready to tilt at a hundred windmills, Dulcie. Hey, I forgot to tell you something. You know how I said that Don Quixote thought of himself as the perfect knight. Well, a knight has to have a lady to defend and to dedicate his victories to. And do you know what the name of Don Quixote's lady was? Dulcinea. Dulcie."

The child thought about it, and after a minute she ducked her head and said to Ana in a voice almost too low to hear, "My name isn't really Dulcie."

Ana answered in a near whisper out of the corner of her mouth, "That's okay. Don Quixote wasn't really a knight, either."

Dulcie wriggled her body in a settling-in gesture and ended up leaning into Ana a bit more than she had been. After a minute, Ana placed her arm gingerly around the child's shoulders and turned her attention to the players on the floor.

The game was a contest between the students wearing T-shirts in various shades of yellow and the men of the community in green. At first glance this division seemed unfair, since the men were taller and heavily muscled, and presumably the pick of adult players came from a larger pool than that of the teenagers.

The kids were good, though, and fast. Of the five on the starting team, two were as tall as the biggest adult, four were unusually muscular for teenagers, and all of them looked like they wanted to win.

The two teams assumed their positions in the center of the court, the referee tossed the ball up, and the lanky blond boy rose up and tapped it into the waiting hands of the shortest member of his team, who immediately shot it over to Dulcie's brother. Jason pivoted and began moving down the court in an odd hunched-over stance that looked clumsy but moved him along faster than anyone else on the court. A guard in green swooped up in front of him and without a break Jason switched hands, ducked under the man's outstretched arms, and accelerated for the basket. Up he went in a sweet, easy layup shot seven seconds into the game, and the cafeteria erupted. Everyone in the hall was on his feet shouting, Ana no exception. Even the foiled guard grinned and slapped Jason's shoulder as they jogged back up the court.

Jason heard none of it. A glance at the man was his only acknowledgment of anyone outside his own skin, although he was quite obviously aware at any given moment just where his teammates and his opponents were on the court.

So it went for the whole game. Other players laughed, grimaced, raised a fist in a victory punch; Jason did his job, scored his points, and turned his focus onto what came next.

It was a high-school length game, four eight-minute quarters, and from the first play, Ana could not take her eyes off Jason.

He was a superb player, shambling along in that deceptive way like an elongated chimpanzee and then suddenly shifting gears to streak through the crush near the basket, fast and slippery and untouchable, rising up free of the guards to nudge the ball in with his fingertips. Time and again he did this, and the men in green seemed unable to come up with a strategy to counteract him.

He was no team player. He hunted up and down the back of the court like a lone wolf until he either saw an opportunity to snatch the ball from a green player or until one of his teammates could get free to pass to him, then he was off. Only once did he voluntarily relinquish possession of the ball, when he was trapped in the corner and time was running out before the half was called. The pass he made, a single bounce beneath the flailing arms of the tallest man, was successful, but the boy he passed it to, the lanky blond kid who had jumped at the game's opening, took three steps and had it snatched in mid-dribble. The only emotion Ana saw him show the whole game was right then: A twist of irritation passed over Jason's face, more at himself, Ana thought, than at his teammate, and then he was back to his normal unruffled, ruthlessly focused self.

After halftime a pattern began to develop out on the court, or perhaps Ana was only now beginning to see it. The blond kid, whose name was Tony, had apparently had enough of Jason's successes and decided to start keeping the ball to himself. Four times in the third quarter he ignored obvious opportunities to pass to Jason for an easy score. Twice his strategy succeeded. The third time an opposing player snatched the ball from midair and barreled down the court to score. The fourth time, with Jason, two other players, and most of the audience screaming "Pass it!" Tony chose for a long shot, with the same result. Most of the audience was watching the middle-aged English teacher take off down the court for his two points, but Ana glanced over at Jason and saw the narrowed eyes of a pure, cold rage, so instantly wiped away that she had to wonder if she had actually seen it.

It was fascinating, Ana reflected, how much a person could discover by watching boys play a game of basketball.

She leaned over to ask the woman on the other side of Dulcie the question that had been puzzling her all afternoon. "Do you by any chance know how old the boy Jason is?"

"Fourteen," she said promptly.

"*Fourteen?* No."

The woman shrugged and went back to her conversation with her neighbor. Dulcie took her eyes off the game long enough to tell Ana, "He had his birthday just before we came here."

Good Lord.

Jason now had the ball and he was moving back and forth outside the key, watching and waiting for the opening he needed. He had taken the ball from Tony (whom Ana could easily imagine behind the wheels of a series of stolen cars, grinning in the pleasure of the joyride) and was waiting for the stocky kid to delay one of the guards and open the key. (That boy, on the other hand, had a mean streak, and used his elbows when the ref wasn't watching. He would be the perpetrator of harsher crimes, and on his way to being a career criminal.) Jason would be too serious to joyride, too cautious to commit the obvious crimes.

Perhaps, she speculated, it would be that brief, white-hot rage that was Jason's downfall, a sudden and disastrous loss of control resulting in a vicious and no doubt very efficient act of violence, instantly over, constantly guarded against. Would he regret it? Perhaps, perhaps not, but certainly he feared it. Clearly, too, Carla and the other women were a little bit intimidated by him, Carla

with her loud and uncomfortable laugh when Ana had
suggested that Jason might be her son, the dryness in
Dominique's voice when she spoke of him. The only
person Ana had met who did not seem slightly uncomfortable around the boy was Dulcie, and Dulcie, Ana felt
sure, need never fear her brother's anger.

Yes, a person could tell a lot about the players by
watching a game.

Fourteen years old; the phrase kept running through
Ana's head as she left the impromptu gymnasium and
walked through the cold night to her room. Fourteen
years old, with the angular face of a man five or six years
older and the ropy muscles of a laborer under his sweat-
soaked yellow T-shirt, walking across the court with the
wary self-confidence of a felon and the unconscious grace
of a dancer. He moved through the community in a state
of splendid isolation, shifting easily to avoid contact with
others, always keeping a distance.

Except for Dulcie. Dulcie could touch him; for
Dulcie he would bend his straight spine and dip his head
to hear her childish rambles. For Dulcie he would walk
through a hundred and more admirers, politely acknowl-
edging their appreciative remarks after the game was
won, until he was standing in front of Dulcie, looking
down into her dancing, worshipful eyes with something
very near a smile on his face.

God almighty, Ana mused. What the hell has that
boy been through, to turn him into what he is now?

CHAPTER 12

You are all law enforcement professionals. You have
all been trained in what to do in a hostage situation.
You talk, right? Sure, you're also finding out the shape
of the building where the people are being held, who the
hostages and their takers are, what weapons are involved,
all that. However, you also have to know what the beef
involves--if it's terrorism, well, that's something very
different from a kidnapping for ransom gone bad, and still
farther from a dispute over custody of the kids or a guy
who lost his job, his wife, and his car all in the same
week. And the only way of finding this out, while you're
also trying to let the situation come off the boil, is to
let the people talk.

But what if you're not speaking the same language?
We've all heard the stories about cops who have pulled
over an erratic driver who didn't speak English and
couldn't understand the order to "Get out of the car, sir"
and reached into the glove compartment and got shot. A
terrible accident, maybe; the cop had no choice but to
suspect the driver was going for a gun. Of course, the
truth of the matter is, it probably never happened, it
just makes a great story. [laughter]

But you see what I'm saying? Sure, there are times
when the only response is the immediate one; but the great
majority of times the situation can be resolved
peacefully, if only you have enough time, and if only you
can find the key to the situation.

A group of religious believers speaks a different
language from the majority of citizens. It sounds like
English, but you will be making a real mistake if you
assume that it is. To take a fairly obvious example, when
David Koresh talked about "the lamb", he didn't mean what
he ate for dinner; he meant "Jesus Christ, Lamb of God,
who taketh away the sins of the world." What I want to do
today is give you some suggestions for dealing with a so-
called "cult" situation, in the early hours before the

Excerpt from the transcription of a lecture by Dr. Anne Waverly
to the Northern California Sheriffs' Association, January 16, 1992

It had become clear that nothing could be done, no decisions made concerning Ana's presence until Steven returned. She could be given no permanent position, not even a room in the central compound, until he had approved her sincerity. She wanted to work in the school, had come prepared for it, and knew there was a need for the skills Ana Wakefield brought, but she had to settle for drudgery in the kitchen and around the barn and buildings.

Two days after the basketball game, on Ana's fourth day at Change, she drove into Sedona to order the switch for Rocinante's heater and to fill a shopping list of incidentals that Amelia gave her. "Just a few odd things" nearly filled the bus, and Ana could only be grateful she hadn't been asked to do a week's shopping.

She also mailed a packet of photocopied pages from her journal, sent a roll of film off to a mail order film developer that was actually a branch of the FBI, arranged at the post office to have general delivery mail forwarded to Change, and finally wrote a note to the mail service in Boise to give them her new address.

She had found it disconcertingly difficult to write in her journal about Jason, knowing the attention Glen and others would devote to it. She was very aware of how her unexpurgated reaction to the boy would sound: like some strange, distasteful, even bizarre infatuation of a middle-aged woman for a handsome young boy. Leaving him out entirely would have made for a suspicious gap, but writing about him naturally, about an interesting young male person the age of a grandson, was remarkably difficult.

In truth, though, Jason was interesting, even intriguing; the fact that she was a woman on the brink of menopause did not negate who he was. Still, she downplayed the intensity of her reaction to him, took care to include descriptions of the other boys as well, and trusted that neither Glen and his people nor any potential snoop sent by the Change community to look through her things would notice the difference.

She took dinner in Sedona, in a quiet restaurant with white linen on the tables, where she had red meat and red wine, and two cups of dark coffee with her dessert. Then she drove back down the long, narrow, unlighted road to the Change compound.

At the first hint of morning, Ana rose and set off for her red-rock viewing post.

It had rained the day before, and the morning felt soft against her face. Her footprints had been wiped clean from the sand, but she had been this way several times now and she knew the places where she needed to walk around rather than go straight and be forced to turn back, and she remembered the narrow break between the shrubs that seemed to go down but then turned and took a shortcut to the top.

The last part was a bit of a scramble, around the back of the flat boulder and pulling herself up to the top: It was there that she met Steven. She came up, puffing and grunting with the effort, to find a man sitting on the other side of the rock—seated in *her* place—in full lotus position, watching her appear bit by bit over the edge of the stone slab. She did not notice him at first, since her eyes were watching for handholds and sleepy reptiles, but she plunked herself down in triumph, kneaded her bad knee two or three times to encourage it, and then suddenly became aware of a presence behind her and whirled around, narrowly avoiding precipitating herself backward off the cliff she had just come up.

"Good heavens," she said breathlessly. "You startled me."

"I apologize," he said in a voice as calm as his posture. "You're just in time for the sun."

It had been light for some time, but the high rocks to the east of the compound kept the sun at bay for twenty minutes or so after the shadows stretched long across the adjoining desert. Ana had discovered this her first morning, and had come to anticipate this second, private sunrise into the compound below. Slightly disappointed, but reassured that this man was not a threat, she took a seat at the other edge of the rock from the stranger and waited for the show.

The first thing to light up was the three-bladed windpowered electrical generator on the ridge of hills west of the compound. The light traveled steadily down the metal struts of the tower until it hit the base and spread, flowing along the low hills and bringing to life the brilliant red rock and dark vegetation, and for a couple of minutes a bright spot of light reflecting a piece of discarded glass.

Now the compound itself was touched. The first part of Change to be illuminated was the peak of the glass dome that capped the hub building. Sunlight spilled gradually down it, round and full and red as the hills, and then the other buildings were lit, and the paths, and the darkness crept away, loosing its hold on the parking area, the square guest quarters, and finally retreating to the very foot of the hill below them. The sun was up. Ana let out a small sigh of satisfaction. The man seemed inclined to agree.

" 'Truly the light is sweet,' " he said in a voice that rolled the syllables, " 'and a pleasant thing it is for the eyes to behold the sun.' "

Beginnings are crucial, first impressions far-reaching, and Ana was alive to the knowledge that her success or failure in the Change community began at this moment. A quotation from Ecclesiastes, that crusty Old Testament compiler of epigrams and wisdoms, was not what Ana would have expected, and she ransacked her memory for a worthy reply. She decided on Psalms, to be safe.

" 'Light dawns for the righteous, and joy for the upright in heart.' "

"The righteous?" the man said in what she hoped was mock disapproval, and called on Luke, " 'There were certain which trusted in themselves that they were righteous, and despised others.' "

" 'When one rules justly over men,' " she told him, " 'he dawns on them like the morning light, like the sun shining forth upon a cloudless morning.'

"You're Steven, aren't you?" she added.

It was the man's turn to sigh, and although his was a noise of faint regret, as if at a burden resumed, there was a smile at the corners of his eyes. His voice changed as he dropped the game of quotations, becoming lighter and more clearly American.

"I am. And you, I believe, are Ana Wakefield."

"How did you get up here?" she asked curiously. "I didn't see any footprints."

"I levitated."

Ana could not tell if he expected her to believe this flat statement or if he was making some subtle joke. She smiled uncomfortably, but he seemed occupied with the process of unwrapping his limbs, stretching hard with his hands on his ankles and his face pulled down to touch his knees, and then rising. He stood for a moment, surveying his domain and allowing Ana to run her eyes over his tall, muscular body, and then turned his head to look at her.

"Shall we go down and see if they've kept any breakfast for us? You could probably use some after your excesses of last night."

"What do you mean?" Ana demanded.

"Meat, alcohol, and strong coffee have a tendency to leave a person needing more the next day. Part of the cycle, of course," he said with a smile, and turned to go.

The steep climb down left plenty of opportunity for Ana to assemble her thoughts. He was waiting for her at the bottom, and politely let her come up beside him before he set off for the road.

"I hadn't realized that there was a Change member working in that restaurant," she said.

"Which restaurant is that?"

"The French place on the road to Cottonwood."

"La Rouge? As far as I know, none of us work there."

"So how do you know what I had for dinner?"

He bent his head around and presented her with a grin of pure boyish mischief. "People like you always have a last meal of meat and booze before they confront the decision of whether or not to join us. A last fix of toxins before the threat of the purity regime."

"People like me," Ana repeated.

"Seeker Ana? Isn't that how you think of your role here?"

Ana fought to conceal the deep shock she felt. Did he know who she was? Or was his analysis general? God, she'd never thought her mask could be ripped off so early in an investigation, but the double meaning of Steven's words was frighteningly close to the truth. It triggered panic alarms and the too-vivid recollection of the last time her duplicity had been suspected.

"My role," she managed to choke out.

"You're, what, closing in on fifty? And here you are, still wandering around in your Volkswagen bus, still experimenting with this and that. Don't you get tired of it?"

The massive relief Ana felt when she realized his seeming knowledge of her was mere speculation made her want to sit down suddenly. It also served as a sharp warning against complacency: He could not have been back in the compound for more than a few hours, yet he knew all about her, one insignificant woman who happened to wander in off the street. The man's intelligence-gathering service was as efficient as it was inconspicuous; she must never let down her guard.

"I haven't found what's right for me yet."

He heard the quaver in her voice, if not the cause for it, and his smile deepened.

"So you thought you would try Change, to see if we are 'right for you.'"

"Actually, I came here more or less by accident. If there are any accidents," she added dutifully. "I was in Sedona and I met Carla at the crafts gallery. She invited me to stay here for a couple of days while I fixed the heater in my bus. I've been trying to help out in the kitchen and filing papers in the office, so as not to be a burden."

"But you will be on your way when you have warmth again." It was not a question.

"Well, I thought I would. I don't really have any definite plans."

He ignored the implied request for an invitation to stay. "The real reason Carla asked you here was because of Dulcie. She doesn't talk much for anyone but her brother. And now you."

"I gathered that, afterward; Teresa said something about how disturbed Dulcie had been when she and her brother first came here. I don't know why the child decided to talk to me."

"She may simply have been ready, and you were

there," Steven said. Ana would have liked to claim credit for an ability to restore the voluntarily mute to speech, but she had to admit that he was probably right.

"She seems an intelligent child."

"It is her brother who interests me," he said bluntly, a sweeping statement that managed to discount not only Dulcie, but Ana and even Carla at one stroke. She stifled a protest, realized what she was doing, and stifled, too, her sudden amusement at the exchange. Steven did not notice, just kept walking and talking. "Have you met Jason?"

"Briefly."

"I think that is the most that can be said for any of us, that we've met Jason briefly. He came to us on a court referral last month, some minor brush with the law but with no parental presence or relatives to assume custody. The boy has been handed a bucket of shit by life, and he's managed to turn it to pure steel. It will be interesting to see what he can make now that he has been given the proper tools."

They were nearing the compound now, and very shortly their private conversation would end. Ana turned over her options. She needed to do something that would make an impression on Steven, set her apart from all the other Ana Wakefields who drifted in to sit at his feet. This was a natural human urge, to demonstrate one's superiority to the masses, but it was also essential for Ana's more covert progress. She caught at the phrase he had used concerning Jason and cobbled it together with an assortment of hints and images that Change had set floating through her subconscious, and came out with a lucky hit.

"Funny how some kids are burned up by life, while others in the same situation are just hardened."

Somehow they had come to a halt and were standing face-to-face. And a very beautiful face it was, too, Ana realized, strong, square, and brown, with deep brown eyes, sun-streaked hair curling down onto the collar of his jacket, and a closely trimmed beard with faint flecks of white in the mustache. A lot of religious men, be they cult leaders or ordained ministers, cultivated the Jesus look, but this one was Jesus the carpenter, not Jesus the wimp, a six-foot-three-inch workingman, with an emphasis on man.

The sheer masculine power of Steven's personality set off all kinds of alarms in the back of Ana's mind, even as Seeker Ana was melting into a pliable mess willing to sign away any part of her soul the man might desire.

Hold on, Ana, she told herself sharply. *Watch your ass, you dumb female.*

Something changed in the back of Steven's eyes. There was a slight but definite shift from aloofness to interest in his manner toward her, perhaps even a hint of respect.

"That is very true," he said, and then, "you've taught kids, I think?"

"I've been a teacher on and off during my life. And a student."

"I think you ought to stay with us for a while, Seeker Ana," he said with the air of making a pronouncement. "You might learn something here. You might even have something to teach us."

She had to be satisfied with that, because David Carteret, the woodworker and shop teacher, was coming out of the hub building, had spotted them, and was approaching with purpose in his stride.

But before David reached them, Steven paused to drop one more little bombshell.

"I hope your knee isn't too sore from the climb."

To give the impression of omniscience, a person had only to pick up some small clue (a slight limp or a wariness toward the community) and present it casually as a known fact with long-understood implications. Palm readers and sideshow telepaths did it all the time, but Ana had never known a spiritual leader better at it than Steven.

"First levitation, now mind reading," she replied. "Are you going to tell me how I hurt the knee, too?"

"You would probably call it an accident," he answered thoughtfully.

He was really very good; naturally she would call it an accident, if for nothing other than to deflect interest, though whether it was an automobile or skiing mishap, the act of an assailant, or an accident of birth, only she— and by implication, Steven—would know.

Yes, Ana would have to be very careful around this man, but at least he represented a worthy adversary.

David came up to them then, with a problem for Steven, but before he turned to go, Steven paused to look deeply into her eyes. "I hope you stay with us, Ana. If you do, you will be expected to strip yourself of the ornament you are wearing around your neck."

When Ana got back to the compound, she removed the moon from her neck and added it to the contents of the buckskin medicine pouch hanging from Rocinante's rearview mirror. That afternoon Ana moved into a room in the central compound; the next morning she was given a job.

4.
SUBLIMATIO

sublime *(vb)* **To cause to pass directly from the solid to the vapor state and condense back to solid form.**

If thou can make thy Bodys first Spiritual,
And then thy Spirits as I have taught corporal.

CHAPTER 13

From the journal of Anne Waverly (aka Ana Wakefield)

From the beginning, when Anne Waverly had first opened Glen McCarthy's manila envelope, she had been struck by just how much of an anomaly the school at Change was; now, seeing it in action, it puzzled her even more. In Ana's considerable experience, religious communities tended to regard the education of their children as the touchiest area in their belief system. The single biggest perceived threat to the community's future and purity was usually the interference of governmental agencies of various stripes in how it chose to raise and educate the next generation of believers.

The same touchiness, of course, applied to the opposition as well: Governmental agencies and the general populace will shrug their collective shoulders at the oddities practiced by adults, even when they have to raise their collective eyebrows. A belief in aliens, strange meditative practices, even a bit of discreet drug use are not enough to bring an official hand down on the community's shoulder, but start interfering with the innocent, especially with young children, and hell will break loose. Literally. Most of the truly disastrous confrontations with "cults" have been sparked by the perceived (if often groundless) maltreatment of children.

However, Change was different. Here, not only their own children, but some thirty outsiders in addition attracted the attention of the school boards and Child Protective Services, the welfare, social security, income tax, and housing agencies, the courts and probation officers, and a dozen other suspicious bureaucratic entities eager to lay hands on this cult in the desert, to say nothing of the parents and relatives of the children who had been taken from their tender care.

All of those busybodies were welcomed. Not just borne as a necessary evil, but actively welcomed, greeted with smiles and treated as co-workers in the task of raising children. Books were laid open, problems freely admitted and discussed, suggestions welcomed.

The school, Ana knew, did represent a sizable income for the community. Once the state had been convinced that here was a group willing and able to assume the burden of some of the system's incorrigibles, it had tentatively given Change a grant. When results began to appear, when a handful of hardened young troublemakers were tugged free of the cycle that normally led to the prison door, the money came more freely. And after a particularly noteworthy triumph involving a gangbanger who had lived at Change for two years and then been accepted at U.C. San Diego, the name of Change was heard on the lips of state senators and money was increasingly found, even from the private sector: The hardwood floor in the dining hall had been given by a chain of sporting goods stores based in Phoenix, a computer company donated machines and software, a new roof was provided by a local contractor looking for a tax writeoff.

All of which explained why the Change members should appear to welcome inspectors and pen pushers, but not why they should actually do so. Ana found it puzzling.

It was, oddly, the reticent Teresa who gave Ana what she later found to be an important clue to understanding Change doctrine.

Except in the classroom, Teresa was almost pathologically silent. In front of her kids she was quiet, although she had a considerable talent for dropping a brief phrase that set the students into action or brought them into line, depending on the need at any given time.

Teresa was the widow of a drunken and abusive husband who killed himself and three others when his truck drifted over the centerline straight into a family that was on its way home from a niece's *quinceañera* celebration. Two months after the accident, Teresa, who when her husband was alive had ventured out only to shop and make the rare visit home to her mother and now was almost completely withdrawn into her house, happened to see a program on the local cable television channel about Steven Change and his community.

She wrote him a long, agonized letter. Three days later Steven was on her doorstep, coaxing her out, bringing her back to life.

Ana learned all this from Dominique, who liked to talk while she was involved in meaningless tasks such as filing or folding brochures for mailing. Ana decided it might be a good idea to listen carefully to whatever utterance Teresa might care to make. As with Dulcie, words issued sparingly were intended to count.

Teresa's clue came after Ana had been involved in a particularly harrying telephone roundabout, an attempt to find someone who could tell her where the father of one of the Change foster kids could be found, after the boy had said in a revealingly offhand manner that he wouldn't mind if his dad happened to visit for the boy's birthday the following week.

With forty minutes of argument, cutoffs, and being kept on hold behind her, Ana slammed the receiver down and grabbed at her barely grabbable hair.

"God!" she exclaimed. "Don't they *want* these kids to get their lives together? I don't know how you guys do it, day after day of keeping your patience with the bureaucrats." Teresa was typing fourteen reports for the sheriff's department; Dominique was writing letters to parole officers across the state.

"Steven says, 'The most blessed thing you can swallow is your own spittle,'" Dominique commented sympathetically, although he did not seem to have mentioned that he was quoting the Prophet, Ana noted.

Teresa added, "Heat and pressure are necessary to the transformation process."

"Does Steven say that, too?" Ana asked. Teresa nodded. "Then it must be true," Ana said grimly, and reached again for the telephone.

During the day she caught three glimpses of the child who could have been her daughter. The first was through the open door of the kindergarten room, where Dulcie sat on a tiny wooden chair, her hands folded in her lap and her hair in two thick, short, lopsided braids, while the teacher read her class a story. Two hours later, she again saw Dulcie, sitting on a boulder in the open desert garden between the compound buildings, waiting patiently. When the main door of the school building opened, the child jumped to her feet in anticipation, and when Jason appeared she ran to him—and then dropped in at his side and reached out a hand for his, almost shyly. He rumpled her hair and tweaked one stubby braid, and casually tugged her over so that they walked along with her shoulder bumping against his hip, heading to the dining hall for an after-school snack. And then later still Ana spotted them a last time, on their way toward bed. Dulcie was up in her brother's arms, limp and looking not far from sleep. Jason's proud head was bent, ever so slightly, to fit over hers. It was a gesture Ana could feel in her own neck, the warmth of two bodies reaching out to each other, and she was smiling as she entered the meditation hall.

Inside the hall a number of the formerly empty platforms were now occupied by the Change members returned from England. Ana saw with interest that Steven sat, not on the highest platform, but the second highest. Below him was a man whose muscular body and scowling brows contrasted oddly with a weak mouth that his aggressive mustache could not quite hide. This must be Thomas Mallory, longtime friend of Steven Change, second in command, and occasional dealer in illegal firearms. He looked the sort of small man whose touchiness over his size drove him to pump iron and collect guns; a man who thought of himself as dangerous, and might actually be if he was pushed too far. She studied him for a minute, but found her eyes drawn to the empty space at Steven's right. If the highest place was not Steven's, whose was it? Or was its emptiness permanent and symbolic—a place set at the table for God?

Steven rose smoothly and strode across the narrow walkway to the high platform beneath the golden cloud. He folded himself into a lotus position, took a few deep and slowly exhaled breaths, and opened the evening's session of meditation with a brief but carefully worded sermon on the necessity of discomfort on the road to Transformation. He then gave them the mantra, "Great heat, great change."

They chanted for a while and then came silent meditation, and Ana's mind wandered back from Steven's words to the earlier statement by Teresa, and beyond that to the things he had told her walking back from the red rocks. He had spoken of being put through the tempering fires during the search for enlightenment—what he called Transformation—but she had taken it for a metaphorical reference to inner struggles. If his community interpreted this as a command that they should welcome the pressures and irritations of meddling outsiders because they helped to build character, it explained a great deal. Surely the hair shirts of the early Christian monks, their fondness for mortification of the flesh and embracing of bodily torments and martyrdoms might find modern psychological equivalents in automated telephone systems and the barbs and torments of red tape?

It was actually quite funny, once she thought about it.

Teresa had not thought it amusing, though. Ana began to wonder what other forms of heat and pressure might be applied in the search for Transformation. This was not, all in all, a comforting thought. Nor very amusing.

What else had Steven said, according to Teresa? It was something about the arduous building project. "Sweat meditation," she had called it.

Come to think of it, that had an uncomfortable sound to it as well.

The days passed, five of them, during which Ana saw Dulcie half a dozen times and Jason up close twice and three times at a distance, in the school or walking across the compound, and once she saw him setting out on a morning run. Steven she saw any number of times, but of the three, the only one she exchanged words with was Dulcie.

She lived in the community and she worked alongside the others, but Ana could feel that she was not a fully accepted member. She remained an assistant in the classrooms, people gave slight hesitations before some answers, as if considering her status, and polite demurrals when she offered to help with some project or other.

This clear sense of boundaries indicated a degree of suspicion that Ana could not afford to let stand, but she knew that not until Steven gave the word would she begin to be integrated into the Change community.

She knew why he was withholding his blessing, too. He had accused her at their early-morning interview of a lack of commitment, of flightiness and an unwillingness to dig in, and she had not denied it. He would be waiting for her to ask him for the next stage in her Transformation.

Very well, she would ask. But not tonight. Tomorrow she would give her pledge to commit herself to Change —or, rather, give the nonexistent Ana's meaningless pledge. Tonight, though, was hers—not to drive into Sedona and gorge on meat and wine, not even if Steven hadn't already spoiled that pleasure. No, tonight she would take a solitary walk, playing hooky from the group meditation and wandering by herself through the near-empty compound.

The moon lay on the horizon, past full now but still large and heavy with gathered light. The night was cold and cloudless, the white stones lining the edges of the path luminous in the light. Ana left her flashlight in her pocket and wandered the compound by moonlight and the lights from the windows.

In and out the paths zigzagged, into the hub and back to the edges, each of the outside buildings connecting with each other and with the center. It would make a neat geometrical pattern from the air, she thought, a cat's cradle of pathways strung among the seven buildings. Why hadn't Glen's aerial photo shown it? Were the paths of crushed gravel too like the desert soil in color or the white stones too far apart to form a solid line? Or had she just missed it? And if so, what else had she missed?

They were chanting in the meditation hall, not the "I am Change am I" rhythm or the ¼ beat of "Great hope, great Change," but something slower and choppier, four beats and a pause, four beats and a pause. She listened, and heard the word: *Trans-for-ma-tion.*

Into change in a big way, was Steven.

Ana continued on out to the bare site where the sixth and final building would go, back to the still-chanting hub, and up to the oldest of the surrounding structures, the dining hall.

Ana let herself in, thinking to look again at the lovely Indian pots she had seen the very first night and looked at with pleasure every time she had passed by. One in particular was stunning, a glossy black-on-black bowl worth more than Rocinante and all she contained.

She heard a sound, deep in the building. Not a kitchen noise, but a high, sharp squeak. She followed the hallway back to the dining hall, and soon the echoing thuds of a bouncing ball joined the squeaks: Someone was playing basketball.

Jason.

CHAPTER 14

From the journal of Anne Waverly (aka Ana Wakefield)

The boy was practicing crossovers, dribbling the ball up the court for a few steps and then shifting his body and taking the ball in the other hand for the next few steps, dodging imaginary opponents. As he neared the end, he lowered his body and sped up, springing up beside the basket for a layup shot. He veered outside the unmarked end line of the court to catch up the ball and started back up the other end again, alternating hands as he dribbled.

He was very beautiful, a young human male as he was meant to be, rejoicing in perfect strength before his body discovered that there were things it could not do. For some reason the phrase "I sing the body electric" ran through her mind, and she refused to feel like a voyeur.

He traveled the court three or four times while Ana stood leaning in the doorway with her hands in her pockets. She knew that he was aware of her presence—she had seen the faint falter and sideways glance when he first turned to go back up the court—but he ignored her, concentrating on the rhythm and on the use of his left hand.

She could certainly sympathize. Privacy was a rare enough commodity in a communal enterprise, and it would be a gift of kindness if she were to back away and leave him to the echo of the ball and the squeal of his shoes on the polished floor. Instead, she hardened her heart and began to pluck off her outer garments until they lay in a pile on the bench and she stood in her jeans, long-sleeved T-shirt, and bare feet. She pushed her sleeves up to her elbows and went out onto the floor.

"It's very pretty," she said to him without preliminary, "but it's too slow. You get some kid out there with quick hands, you're going to lose the ball every time you go past him."

Jason had stopped, and stood now with the ball balanced against his hip, his chest rising and falling beneath his sleeveless T-shirt, just watching her, expressionless.

"Here, I'll show you what I mean," she said. Settling down as far as her knee would permit, she stretched out her arms in the guard's position and wiggled her fingers to indicate that he should come at her. He simply stood there. "Yeah, yeah," she said. "I know old women like me don't play basketball, but there's nobody here to see you, and who knows? You might learn something. At the very least you'll embarrass me so that I go away and leave you in peace."

She waited, so long that she was beginning to think that she had underestimated the depth of his need for dignity and credited him with more curiosity than he actually possessed. He waited until her knee was protesting and her doubt was building, and then he dropped the ball to the floor and came at her, driving fast straight down the court until the very last instant, when he shifted and went to the side.

But he did not take the ball with him. Instead, it was traveling back down the court in the hands of this woman with the almost-shaved head, who furthermore came to a halt well outside where the key would be and shot the ball toward the basket. It dropped neatly in. She trotted forward to retrieve the ball and turned back toward him, laughing.

"Now, there was a lucky shot," she said. "I haven't done that in years." She tucked the ball under her left arm and put out her right hand. "Call me Ana. The shortest member of the women's varsity team in high school, tied for second highest score for the season. Couldn't guard, never made a rebound, and slow on my feet, but I had a talent for long shots and I had quick hands. Once upon a time, years before you were born," she added with a grin.

Reluctantly and briefly, Jason let his fingers brush hers. She passed him the ball and moved down the court, taking up a position in front of her basket.

The rhythm of the ball smacking up against the boards started up again, slowly, while he considered things, and then more rapidly when he began to move toward her. He was no longer trying to intimidate her, Ana was glad to see, and he no longer discounted her entirely as a human being. Not that he took her seriously yet, but he was determined to prove to himself that what she had done was a fluke.

It was not. The only difference this time was when Ana tried for a basket, the ball bounced off the backboard and flew into the stacked benches. She talked as she retrieved it.

"You're good, Jason; you don't need me to tell you that. But I don't think you've had much chance to play against very many top-rank players, and I doubt you've had any really good coaches. I was always a second-rate player, but I learned a lot from the good people around me, and I was lucky to have a coach who was a retired professional with a love for girls' basketball. We had four or five of our players go on to university scholarships— this at a time when there was no money at all for girls' sports, when girls did cheerleading or synchronized swimming or gymnastics, period. You want to know how not to get your ball stolen by a pair of quick hands? Come here."

She took him through it in slow motion, so he could see precisely how he was leaving himself open, then she showed him how to pace himself, how to move the ball to the free hand just a shade earlier, so it would already be on the downward trajectory when his opponent was reaching out, and how to extend his elbow and shoulder

as he swept the ball aside, blocking the other's outstretched fingers and giving the ball a boost of speed at a
vital moment.

He was a fast learner, and after a dozen or so tries,
Ana was only occasionally able to snatch the ball away
from him. Four times in a row he dodged around her,
and she could only brush her fingers across the rough
surface, although once she would have had it, had her
knee given her enough speed. It did not, and she did not,
and she stood grinning and applauding as Jason scooted
past her, stopped outside the key, and shot—missing the
basket.

She wiped her forehead with the back of her arm and
watched the boy move. She was drenched with sweat,
her muscles were quivering, and her knee felt as if she
were walking on a red-hot steel rod, but she was more
than satisfied. Contact had been made. Not conversation,
perhaps—Jason's only words to her had been monosyl-
labic answers to direct questions—but a beginning. To
what, she did not know, nor did she wish to ask. She
could only tell that the physical exertion with a boy she
had no real excuse for approaching had been deeply satisfying, an antidote to the cerebral jousting she had done
with Steven.

Ana gathered up her clothing and limped away. The
thuds of the ball and the squeals of shoes on floor started
up again as soon as she was out of the dining hall.

The following morning, she went to see Steven.

Ana rose early and walked out into the desert, a ritual
that had already become a necessary part of her day, half
an hour when the world was hers alone, when she did
not need to watch herself, think of every word, consider
each gesture. She walked and breathed and took joy in
the early-morning life of the high desert, the skunks and

wild pigs, the tiny pygmy owl returning to its home in a saguaro, and once a family of coatis flickering along the floor of a wash, tails high and long noses snuffling. Snakes were too lethargic to be a concern, scorpions were still asleep, and for some reason, few Change members ventured out of the compound.

This morning, however, one person was at large aside from those residents heading for a car or the milking sheds, a person dressed in shorts and a sweatshirt, running easily along the side of the road. She knew 'without pausing to think' just who it was, knew even though she could not make out anything other than his dark hair in the dim light. Jason was on another morning run, trying to get rid of some of that energy that burned in him.

He ran fast, his head bent, and she watched him for a moment. Who would be the more embarrassed, she wondered wryly, if he were to find out that he had a forty-eight-year-old admirer? She shook her head and turned her back on him; she needed to concentrate on the coming interview with the community's founders.

Steven Change, she had decided, was a natural and unconscious manipulator rather than a deliberate one, more a distorting mirror than a calculating plotter. He was very quick to pick up hints and intimations, turn them around, and give them back in their reworked form to their owner, but Ana was not convinced that he considered what he was doing. As far as she could see, Steven believed in himself, was convinced that this showman's knack was the pure manifestation of his religious authority.

This made him more dangerous—a messiah convinced of his own divinity was always the least likely to listen to reason—but it also made him easier to get around for a person able to match his abilities, precisely because he would be unaware that for others the gift of prophetic speech could be a conscious and deliberate means of manipulation: a trick.

He was not by nature a cynical or suspicious man, but he was highly intelligent, which meant that Ana had to be extremely careful. As always in these situations, her biggest problem was concealing her knowledge. She might have left her personality behind, but she could not lose her brain, and Anne Waverly was, after all, a historian with a specialty in alternative religious movements, qualified to offer instant analyses of the roots and precedents of pretty much anything resembling a religion. Early Church heresies, doctrinal controversies, the influence of Islam, the contributions of Judaism, and the effects of the Reformation were all at her fingertips, and beyond Christianity, the modern influences of the East, from Theosophy and Madame Blavatsky to neo-Hinduism, Reverend Moon, and the Heaven's Gate comet-seekers.

Ana Wakefield, though, did not know all this. Ana Wakefield's concept of religious inquiry was experiential and personal, not academic, and if she knew anything at all about Theosophy, it was because someone had once given her a book on Krishnamurti.

Ana Wakefield knew a little bit about a lot of religious traditions, but the only one she knew intimately was the Christianity of her fictional Midwest childhood, a revelational, New Testament Christianity supplemented by her own early rebellious excursions into the foreign territory of the Old Testament. In dealing with Steven Change, Ana could not know too much or come on too strong. She must somehow suggest to him an immense and untapped potential beneath her innocence. She must present herself as an undiscovered, unspoiled treasure ready and willing to respond to his teaching. Ana Wakefield: every teacher's dream student, a seed ripe and wanting only soil and water to burst into lush growth.

She walked for an hour, trying to think herself into the person she needed to be and finding it inexplicably difficult. She had done it before. Four times, in fact, had she presented herself behind a new mask. In North Dakota, twelve years before, she had been a lone woman needing to be taken in hand by the protective men of the survivalist community Glen was interested in. Three years later she went to Miami to inquire happily about Satanism, trying hard to make her amusement at their antics look like the pleasure of enlightenment. Then on the heels of that case . . . Utah. In Utah she had never really been able to construct a plausible persona, because the social dynamics of that community had already begun to turn inward, and whatever she did, she could only be an outsider, forever a source of distrust. It had proved disastrous, fatal for five adults, two children, and nearly her.

In Kansas, though, with Martin Cranmer, she had slipped easily into the household, a potentially useful female damaged and made prickly by the ills of a corrupt society, wanting only the right man—Cranmer—and the right message to make her a good woman once more.

This time it ought to be easy. Here she was, a New Age seeker faced with an exciting community and hints of an intriguing religious experience. She fit here far better than any of the other four places she had entered. The face she was about to present to Steven Change was close enough to her own to be comfortable, nearly natural.

Yet she was distracted. A bare ten days before she had come into the compound not really caring if she succeeded or not—half wanting, if the truth be told, to fail and prove Glen wrong. Then she had met Dulcie, and her brother, and for some reason as she walked attempting to picture the face she needed to be, she saw theirs instead. It was disconcerting at first, then annoying. Finally she just threw up her hands and decided the problem must be that she really was too close to being Ana Wakefield, that it was futile to work at constructing something that already existed.

She went to find Steven in his office just inside the entrance to the building that held the kitchen and dining hall. Thomas Mallory was there, too. Ana had consigned Steven's second in command to the category of Professional Shadow, one of those attracted to leadership but incapable of it. It showed a great deal of sense on Steven's part not to have given Mallory a permanent Change center of his own; as his temporary leadership in Los Angeles had demonstrated, any place given to him would have fallen apart in a matter of months.

Instead, Mallory accompanied Steven whenever the Change leader left the compound, acting as secretary, calling himself bodyguard (for which role he dressed all in black, wore dark wrap-around sunglasses, and taught a class in karate in the evenings—wearing a black belt). Mallory delighted in stirring up discontent among the other potential shadows, his inferiors in the hierarchy. Ana had spoken to him twice, and thought that he would not recognize her in a lineup. He only glanced at her this time, too, before saying, "He's on the phone. It's an important call, and he may be a while."

She sat down. "I can wait."

It annoyed him, as she had known it would, although there was not much he could do about it. He hunched his muscular little body over his paperwork, lips pursed tight. She sat and waited.

She could hear the sound of Steven's voice, though not the words. He seemed to listen a great deal, and contribute only brief phrases, for a long time. Fifteen, twenty minutes crawled by, and though she was careful to show no impatience, she could feel Mallory's growing satisfaction in this small vengeance.

Eventually, Steven seemed to have outlasted the speaker on the other end of the line. His answers grew longer, his tones sharper, until one stretch of perhaps three minutes, when he spoke continuously. He stopped, listened, said a few words, went silent again, and finally launched into the truncated rhythm of farewells. Silence fell. After a minute the inner door opened and Steven came out, already speaking to his right-hand man.

"Jonas is getting all worked up about—" He saw Ana and caught himself. "Good morning, Ana."

"I wanted to have a word with you. I can come back later if this isn't a good time." But, damnation, how she wished he had finished that sentence first.

"This is fine," he said. "Thomas, remind me to give Jonas a ring before dinner, see what's happened during the day. Come on in. A cup of tea to warm you up after your morning walk?"

"Thank you, that would be nice." She took a chair in front of the open fire, placed the armful of heavy outerwear on the floor at her side, and planted her sandy hiking boots on the floor in front of her while Steven went over to a small sink-and-electric-kettle kitchen arrangement in the corner. He asked her two or three general questions while waiting for the water to boil, and she gave him general answers while studying the room.

This was a public room, intended for consultations not only with Change members but with outsiders as well. The bookshelves were impressive, their contents generic and little used, with many titles on psychology, educational theory, and the rehabilitation of juvenile offenders. The art was a combination of Western landscapes and small sculptures from the East, with a nice bronze *nataraj* taking pride of place above the fireplace. She wondered briefly whether the statue depicting Shiva dancing amid the flames of the earth's destruction meant anything to him other than a decorative piece of tourist art.

"Milk?"

"Please," she said, and reached out for the mug. When she took a sip, she nearly choked: The tea was Earl Grey.

Fortunately, Steven had turned to lower himself into the chair across from her, for he could not have missed her look of shock as Antony Makepeace flitted through her mind and was gone again.

"I'm glad you came to talk with me, Ana. I always like to get to know new members. Teresa tells me you've been helping out in the school. What do you think of it?"

"It is impressive. The kids are impressive."

"Yes. Ironic, considering how grateful society is to get rid of them. We couldn't have a stronger bunch of kids if we had the entire school system to pick from, rather than a handful of castoffs."

"You're allowed some choice, then?"

"Well, in a sense. There are more kids than we could possibly absorb, so we only take those who we feel would most benefit by the structure of Change. I don't encourage them to send us hard-core drug users, for example. There're too many peripheral problems with druggies that we're not equipped to deal with. Have you ever taught special-need kids?"

"Not exclusively, but I worked for a while in a tough urban school where half the kids were nodding in their seats and the others were bouncing off the wall. I didn't last long, but I sure learned a lot."

"Why didn't you last long?"

"I was young. I took it all too personally, couldn't distance myself enough. The kids were far tougher than I was. I burned out."

"The kids had no choice but to stay; I imagine that

was the primary difference between you and them. They burned out by retreating into drugs and violence. Like the ones presented to us, ninety percent of whom are brain dead by the age of fifteen."

"And you take the remaining ten percent?"

"I grab them for the valuable resource they are, kids who have been, as you yourself put it the other day, through the fires of hell—abuse, neglect, violence—and come out toughened. Purified, if you will."

"Transformed."

"Precisely."

"But not easy kids to handle."

"Give them a goal and a reason to reach for it and they handle themselves."

Ana thought it was not quite as simple as that, but then, Steven did not work inside the classrooms, and might not realize how much the teachers did.

"It all comes down to Transformation," she commented, casting around in growing desperation for a lead that would take her to the heart of this conversation.

"Transformation is the only goal that matters," he replied.

"But do the kids understand that?"

"All of nature understands it. All of nature—rocks, trees, animals, human beings—yearns toward becoming greater, even if only to become the seed of a new generation. It is our duty, as beings somewhat further along in the work, to aid and direct the yearnings of those in our care. Teaching is a sacred occupation, Ana. A great responsibility."

She took a deep breath. "Is that why I've been kept from it? Until I prove myself worthy?"

He studied her over the rim of his cup. "What do you mean?"

She crossed her fingers and launched her shot across his bow, praying fervently that it wasn't a dud, or wouldn't blow up in her face. "I don't feel a part of the energy here, somehow. Like there's a secret handshake or something and I don't have it. Of course, I'd expect that from the people who wear the necklaces, but even the people who have been here only a few weeks are—" She broke off, seeing his expression.

Steven had gone very still. "Who told you about the necklaces?"

"Nobody. Why, what is there to tell? I saw people wearing them and assumed they were a sign of rank."

"Rank," he repeated.

"Or accomplishment or time here. Apparently I was wrong." She allowed a thread of curiosity to creep into her voice.

Steven moved quickly to squelch it.

"No, you weren't wrong. It's just that in Change we try to keep any signs of . . . rank to ourselves. The pendants we wear are meant as a private reminder and acknowledgment of accomplishments, not a badge to be flaunted."

"Nobody's flaunted anything, not that I've noticed. In fact, I've never even seen what's on the end of the chain, just the chains themselves."

He looked relieved, then moved to lead her away from the topic. "I'm sorry you feel we are being aloof, Ana. I will speak to some of the members about it. And I also think it's very probable that Teresa is about to turn her class over to you on a permanent basis."

"Really? But what about her?"

"Teresa will go back to the administrative job she was doing before she had to fill in, which is more to her taste. She'll thank you for showing up."

"Oh. Well, thank you. I'll enjoy teaching again."

"And learning?"

"Oh yes. I wouldn't be here if it weren't for the possibility of learning."

"You who have spent all her adult life in the pursuit of learning?"

Ana did not think she was imagining the faint mocking tone in Steven's voice, nor the tiny quirk in one corner of his mouth. He would allow her to teach children because the school needed her, but unless she did something right now, he would forever see her as yet another middle-aged butterfly flitting from one spiritual flower to the next. She had to be taken seriously, yet without stepping outside her persona. She stared into the depths of the empty mug on her knee as if it would give her the words she so desperately needed to convince him.

"All my life," she began, "I have been, as you called me the other morning, a seeker. I've lived in half a dozen communities, followed the yoga sutras and done *zazen*, learned a little Chinese and a little more Sanskrit, and sat at the feet of any number of men and women who I thought could teach me something. I have never stayed with one discipline because none of them seemed to me complete: I found them either all ritual or all philosophy, negating the body or discounting the mind, either bogged down in their own tradition or else rootless and shallow, and none of them succeeded in integrating everyday life with the search for enlightenment, or Oneness, or revelation.

"Here, I get the feeling that you are trying to do just that. There's the day-to-day, gritty reality of raising kids and growing food, but not at the expense of nurturing the flame of spirit. Change is a flourishing plant with strong roots deep in the earth. I would like to be a part of that."

Ana did not look up from her mug. She had thrown out a number of hooks here, from her linguistic background to the use of loaded words like "ritual" and "integrating" to just plain flattery, and she held her breath to see what he would respond to.

"In what way do you see us—how did you put it? 'Nurturing the flame of spirit'?" he asked.

A wave of relief swept through her—she was right, fire *was* central to the belief system of Change. Perhaps on his trip to India Steven had picked up the Zoroastrian dualism of light and dark, good and—but there was no time for that now. She had to keep the tenuous upper hand, and impress Steven with the potentialities of his new convert. Keep it general; keep it provocative. Ana raised her eyes to look, not at Steven, but at the fireplace.

"The Hindu god of fire is Agni, depicted as a quick and brilliant figure with golden hair. He is young and old, eternal and ephemeral, friendly as a domestic fire and ferocious as the flames of sacrifice. The human spirit is the same—you can see it in those kids. Easily quenched but waiting to be rekindled, flaming out of control but wanting to be brought in to the hearth."

She could spout this noble bullshit for hours; it was one reason why Anne Waverly was such a popular teacher. That she had not actually answered his question was beside the point, to Steven most of all. His face had gone rapt.

"Have you ever walked through flames, Ana?"

"Do you mean actual flames, as in Nebuchadnezzar casting the three young men into the fiery furnace?"

"Shadrach, Meshach, and Abednego. 'The hair of their heads was not singed, their mantles were not harmed, and no smell of fire had come upon them.'"

"Well, no."

"I have, Ana. I went in bare feet across a stretch of burning coals, and I was not harmed. On the contrary, I came out a new man."

Firewalking, Ana thought—found in cultures as diverse as Polynesia and Greece, and closer to home as well among the New Age.

"I saw it once in the desert outside San Diego," she told him with enthusiasm. "It was unbelievable."

"Believe, Ana."

"Oh, I do believe. Maybe not enough to commit the soles of my feet to it." She laughed in deprecation of her cowardice; he looked at her with pity.

"Perhaps you will," Steven said portentously. "Perhaps you will."

" 'The fire will test what sort of work each one has done,' " she returned, venturing into the New Testament to follow his line from Daniel.

" 'When you walk through fire you will not be burned, and the flame shall not consume you.' "

Isaiah, she noted. Then before he could launch off on the burning bush, Elijah's chariot, or the fiery Day of the Lord, she asked, injecting her voice with earnest solemnity, "That's what you're saying happened with the kids here, isn't it? That they have been through hell already, and some of them were merely hardened."

" 'Behold, I have refined you, but not like silver; I have tried you in the furnace of affliction,' " he quoted, adding, "like your young friend Jason has been tried."

Ana kicked herself mentally for assuming that anything she might do would be overlooked by Steven's eyes and ears. She hoped to God that she wasn't blushing.

"He's a fine young man."

"I agree," said Steven in his all-knowing voice. "I have great hopes for that boy."

CHAPTER 15

Men and women seeking a time of reflection and spiritual renewal have always sought out the empty places. From time immemorial, God has spoken in the desert or in the mountains, away from the hustle of everyday life. Contemplative religious communities have established themselves outside of the towns, in places where the living is harsh, because the simplicity pares things down to the essentials.

There is a tendency to think of all such communities as slightly odd, if not dangerously antisocial, to see their choice of environment as a flight from rather than a seeking out. And it is certainly true, many of the souls who choose to live out in the desert are damaged, even unbalanced.

However, we must guard against our assumptions. A close analysis of the Branch Davidian community in Waco in the period before the FBI and BATF entered the scene reveals it not as a tightly self-isolated group of fanatic believers, but as an independent community with regular interactions with the neighboring individuals and communities. Branch Davidians came and went, held jobs in the area, formed friendships with outsiders. With the raid and the long standoff that followed, a community with roots and branches in the outside world was abruptly truncated, stripped down to an edgy leader and his isolated followers.

The Branch Davidians might eventually have withdrawn from the world on their own decision, but as it was, before that time came they found themselves walled up away from it. They were kept from communication with anyone but the FBI, they were not allowed to come and go, they were forced into an irrevocable choice between staying and leaving, forever abandoning their home and family inside what was now a compound.

Self-chosen isolation may be a positive thing; being cut off from all contact with the outer world is not, and must in a "cult" situation be avoided at all costs,

From the notes of Professor Anne Waverly

In the days that followed, the sun grew marginally warmer, the nights fractionally shorter, and the community considerably more welcoming; slowly, Ana grew to have a deeper understanding of Change and how it functioned.

It did not take her long to verify that Change was indeed built around secret teachings, that initiates worked their way into the higher levels, moving by steps upward into greater knowledge and proximity to Steven. This was represented not only by the necklaces that certain initiates wore and the position each had in the multileveled meditation hall, but it extended to living quarters as well—the room Ana had been given was in a building populated almost entirely by newcomers. The only person in the building who had lived at Change for more than a few months was a young man with a vile temper, who had been demoted by Steven after getting angry at another member and hitting him. The young man stormed around furiously for a couple of weeks before he finally left, to the unvoiced relief of all.

Steven himself lived in the central building over the meditation hall, in the northern quadrant of the upper floor. The other upstairs rooms were all filled with the oldest, closest Change members. Most were men. The building to the northeast of the center was the communal dining hall with the kitchen and several offices, including Steven's, and upstairs the quarters for the youngest children. Walking around the circle counterclockwise, the next building housed older members on the ground floor and older kids above, then came a building filled with earnest but inexperienced members, and finally the recently completed building where Ana was housed.

It was a bit worrying: Ana had no intention of staying out her promised year, but in a hierarchical organization where secret doctrine is given out in slow degrees, it would not be easy to speed her trip to the inner circle. All she could do was keep her ears and eyes wide open, and hope for a chance to bypass the preliminaries.

It helped, being a teacher, particularly as she convinced the others that she was best placed with the older students where her background of history could be used and her less-complete but still broad familiarity with English literature might assist in preparing the students for the state's standardized tests. Even in an alternative community, test scores mattered.

Within a couple of weeks, Ana was well on her way to becoming an accepted member of the Change community. She taught her kids, she participated in group meditations, and she listened intently to Steven's nightly talks.

One morning when Ana went in for breakfast, small, blond Suellen was not at her usual place behind the serving tables. When she did not appear again for lunch, Ana asked casually if anyone had seen her, and received only tight lips in answer. At the very end of dinner the young woman walked in, making an entrance into the dining hall, her hair wet from the shower, her body moving as if it ached all over, a small blister on the inside of her left wrist and the light of a radiant vision in her face. Ana watched thoughtfully as Suellen made her way proudly through the room, nodding regally at the respectful greetings her passage earned. Steven came in a short time later, and over the next ten minutes, Ana noticed three high-ranking Change members approach him, exchange a few words, and then glance at the radiant Suellen with knowing smiles—expressions that were affectionate, experienced, and not the least bit lewd. Whatever test the woman had faced during the day, she had obviously passed it, and Ana would have sworn that it did not involve sleeping with the leader.

Ana added Suellen's religious glow and the smiles of the others to her growing store of Change evidence. She studied the novels in the library and the paintings on the walls, she asked questions of the older members (most of whom were younger in years than she) and listened for the hidden references and intonations behind their words. She looked at the architecture and the arrangement of the buildings, at the TRANSFORMATION mural over the kitchen and the shape of the meditation hall, at the intriguing, glittering gold sculpture that was suspended over the hall and the way Steven and the higher initiates gazed at it, and she began to have some interesting ideas.

From the first she had seized on Steven's continual references to heat and fire and the presence of the round suspended fireplace at the center of the meditation hall. Fire was not, she decided, merely one metaphor among many; as a symbol, it lay at the heart of the Change process.

That suspicion had led her to consider the phenomenon of fire worship, which was why she had talked about Agni at the crucial meeting in Steven's office, and not Shiva or Jesus or any of the other figures she found present in Steven's theological vocabulary. Steven and his three friends had spent time near Bombay, where they might have met Parsi thought and begun to develop a kind of neo-Zoroastrianism, fire-reverence with the Parsi tendency toward secrecy and an appreciation for the metaphysics of change.

However, wouldn't she then see more tangible signs of Steven's preoccupation with fire, like a continuous flame in front of each building or a ritual involving the meditation hall's fireplace? Still, she remained convinced that fire entered the religious equation in some way.

And then one evening during Steven's talk he used a

word that sent a shudder through the ranks of the higher initiates, and it all fell into place.

The chant that night was "Great heat, great hope," which started out with four beats and ended up being little more than "heat" and "hope" with a brief pause between the words. That night Steven spoke not before the chant, but after. As usual, his subject was change, and specifically some problems the community had run into with a building inspector.

"I want you to regard the rules of the world," he said, "not as the work of an enemy out to thwart you, but as the vessel for our transformation, and from our personal and communal Transformation to the transformation of the world. If the world brings pressure to bear, if it turns up the heat of tribulation, do not hate it, do not seek to escape it; welcome it as the means whereby change is effected. We are tried in the furnace of affliction, refined by the flames of daily torment. We do not turn from it— no, we enter into it freely, as the alembic of our own Transformation, the power nexus of our change."

He continued in this vein, but Ana was too busy with her own thoughts to listen. The word "alembic," the ancient chemical apparatus used to heat and distill, had jolted the people nearest to Steven, all the men and women on the platforms; she had felt their sudden intake of breath and the straightening of their spines, could still see it in their faces and their posture. She could feel it in her own. Because with that single noun it all came together in her mind, and she knew with certainty what Change's hidden doctrine was all about.

Alchemy.

Good heavens, she thought in amazement—alchemy. Is there nothing new under the sun?

It was, she had to admit, the ultimate in transformational processes, extending beyond the spiritual to transmute base physical matter into pure incorruptible gold, never to be tarnished, more valuable than any other metal. Her knowledge, unfortunately, was sparse: From a hodgepodge of roots and the earliest stages of chemistry, in China and through India and Arabia and finally to Europe, great minds had worked to develop a sort of physical philosophy, a method of intellectual and spiritual inquiry reflected in solid results. Base material such as lead was put through an elaborate series of processes (all of them involving, as Steven had said, heat) that led to its perfection into gold, while the alchemist, struggling over the years to perfect the process, was simultaneously being refined, purified, and ultimately transmuted into a being of untarnishable wisdom and immortality. And didn't a branch of alchemy seek to make not just gold, but the Philosopher's Stone—a tincture of immense power capable of changing any base substance it might touch into gold?

There was no doubt that charlatans abounded in this burgeoning science, but the mere possibility that a person might have a recipe for gold put that person into danger; for centuries, alchemists were kidnapped, tortured, and murdered for their formulas. As a result, the secret doctrine became even more so. Rich symbolism and heavily allegorical writing served to obscure the process to all but those who were already in the know. Poetic imagery rather than clear description was used for speaking of the stages the metals went through within the alembics: the Peacock for the rising up of colors from the substance being heated, the Dragon for the fighting of the elements. Zodiacal symbols were used to refer to chemical substances, drawings of men with suns for their heads and women with moons for theirs represented gold and silver, and a king and queen in connubial embrace showed the joining of opposites that was necessary to the success of the Work.

Beyond that, Ana's knowledge began to dissipate,

becoming thin and frayed around the edges. Deadly explosions in alchemical laboratories—fulminate of mercury?—Roger Bacon—Alexandria and the Arab Jābir, all bubbled up and burst in her mind, along with the conviction that Jung had written at some length about the symbolism of alchemy, and the clear memory of an illustration by Arthur Rackham that showed a dark and cluttered workshop peopled by a squat gnome of an alchemist, holding up a small glass vessel in which the gleam of gold provided the only light in the shadows; the alchemist was gazing at his miraculous creation in astonishment and dawning awe.

Ana felt a bit like the gnome in his workshop herself, all her discomfort and distraction swept to the side as she held up her shiny discovery, studying it from different angles. It was truly a beautiful thing, this pure knowledge of the distilled essence of Change, but as with any treasure, possession was not enough. How could she use it? And even more urgent, how could she add to it? Knowledge here was both the key to authority and a resource doled out in tiny dribbles. She had no intention of waiting years to earn her right to a silver chain around her neck. One obvious shortcut was Glen, but as a member of Change, she could no longer just climb into Rocinante and drive into town without attracting too many questions, and the U.S. mail and the telephone system were far too vulnerable to Change eyes and ears.

Still, she had to reach Glen somehow, both to show him her treasure and to request a heavy dose of additional information about the alchemical process. Retrieving his gathered information, then finding a means of studying it in private, was a problem she would face when she came to it. Now, however, how could she free herself up to reach Glen?

•   •   •   •   •

The next day a slim opportunity came up. In a moment Ana had seized it, wrenched it wider, and ruthlessly pushed her way through it.

One of the many advantages of working with a relatively small group of students is the ease of combining parts of the curriculum. Math lessons can spill over into English, a practicum such as filling out an income tax form or balancing a checkbook can be worked into government classes, and economics can be made to include family planning. (Just how much does it cost to raise that failure to use a condom up to college age?)

A few days earlier, Ana had been making her way along the circular hallway, the classrooms opening off to her right and to her left, the blank wall broken only by displayed notices, papers, and assorted pieces of student artwork, and she had idly thought what a waste of a long, unbroken stretch of wall it was.

She had mulled it over during the morning and at lunch she had turned to Teresa.

"You know that inside wall of the hallway? Has anyone thought about having the kids do a mural on it?"

"A mural?"

"Yeah. Each class could have a segment, maybe the one across from their doorway, and it could be along a theme like the one in the dining hall, only longer. I was thinking that it would be kind of fun to have the kids trace the historical development of Arizona, from dinosaurs to Anasazi cliff dwellings and settlers to now. It would be a great history lesson for them, and even useful for kids in the future. Of course, there are lots of themes they could work up, but it would be interesting to have the entire wall an integrated unit."

"It would be an enormous task," Teresa said dubiously, but Ana had made sure before she began that there were others within earshot, and she pressed on, aware that they were listening.

"It would take a lot of organization, but once it was done it could be left in place for years. Or painted over, if teachers wanted to do their section over again. We could ask about getting the paint donated. The biggest problem I can see would be covering the floor so the carpet doesn't get trashed, but I think we could manage that."

Dominique had been one of those listening in, and she spoke up.

"I think it is an excellent idea. We probably wouldn't finish it before June, but we could stretch it out—or even let the kids work on it over summer vacation if they wanted to. Which they would."

It was discussed some more and tentatively approved, depending on the cost. The school buzzed, preliminary sketches were made, themes were hammered out.

In the meantime, the business of school went on, and Ana prepared the other half of her plan.

For convenience and interest, Ana had combined her two high-school-level history groups into one. At this time they had been working on the idea of colonialism, with the eleventh graders covering the historical and social aspects and the seniors concentrating on economics and governmental choices. When the topic of the mural came up, she brought the discussion around to their own backyard, as she tried to do with regularity, and asked them what effect colonialism had had on the local inhabitants, the Navajo and Arapaho, the Hopi and Zuni peoples.

She was not actually surprised when few of them could think of any particular effect offhand, nor that fewer of them, even those of minority blood, thought of the white intrusion as colonialism. She professed astonishment, however, and again during lunch she told the story to her colleagues, exaggerating slightly both the ignorance of the students and the consternation of their teacher.

"You know," she said to Dominique as if the thought were suddenly occurring to her, "we really ought to take these kids down to the ethnology museum in Phoenix, not only for this but as research for the mural. It's possible to do field trips, isn't it? Just for the day?"

Ana knew it was possible; after all, the students had all been on a field trip when she first arrived. Dominique objected that they had just gotten back from a trip, and Ana retorted that soon it would be too late in the year, that they needed to get the future muralists started in the right direction, and furthermore, she pointed out, they would soon all be so concerned with the end-of-the-year testing that the opportunity would be lost. She kept on, stubbornly finding more reasons that it was a good idea, convincing two or three of the other teachers to join in, until suddenly all opposition collapsed and the trip was set, in ten days' time.

She had forced open the door to an opportunity to make contact with Glen; the delay made her impatient, anxious to get to the heart of this community, get the information Glen needed, and get out again. On the other hand, she did not have a lot of time to fret over the delay, since in addition to planning the mural and her other duties of teaching and taking turns in the manual labor of the community (chicken shed, kitchen, and clean-up crews—gardening and building duties were still on winter status), she had also to prepare herself and her students for the field trip, which involved numerous telephone calls to the museum docents and the school district.

Dozens of times during those days she would look at the telephone sitting on the desk in front of her and think how simple it would be just to phone Glen. She could punch in the familiar numbers and in thirty seconds tell him what she needed and when she would be accessible, but in the end she did not, because she was fairly certain that she would be found out, and that the repercussions would be heavy.

She was fully aware that she was being watched. It was only to be expected. All of the newcomers were under careful scrutiny. She suspected that she was more closely watched than the others simply because she was involved in teaching the children, and the Change authorities needed to be certain that she could be trusted not to introduce subversive outside ideas. Her classes were monitored, the papers the students wrote for her gone over by Dominique or one of the others, her reading list vetted, her computer time observed. She took care to stick to the syllabus, and allowed only those diversions and creative ideas that fit with the community beliefs. She kept a tight lid on her personal thoughts, was careful not to voice too much criticism of the outside authorities, and left religion in the realm of sociology. She did not think her rooms had hidden microphones, but she took no chances. She wrote in her diary, she meditated with the others and by herself, she walked out into the desert each morning to watch the sun rise, and she took no chances.

Her main goal was the gathering of information and worming her way into Steven's confidence, and in both of these the school became her focal point. At first it seemed an ordinary enough teaching institution, despite its setting, with very little Change doctrine working its way into the curriculum. Gradually, this picture deepened.

Ana had been given Teresa's class—or, as she discovered, the class Teresa had been forced to assume when Change had lost two teachers, one to apostasy, the other to Boston. It seemed to Ana that her colleague stepped back into her former role as the school's administrator with a trace more relief than a seeker after psychological hair shirts ought to display.

Teresa's removal from the classroom after five months inevitably created a great deal of reorganization and makeup work, and many after-school meetings with the other teachers. It seemed to Ana that the number of these requiring the presence of one particular instructor, Dov Levinski, was quite high, although as he was responsible for the math and science side of the curriculum, it made sense. Still, Ana was intrigued. When Steven began to come down for those meetings as well, although she recalled that Steven, too, had been trained in the hard sciences, she thought she might take a closer look.

So it was that one afternoon two days before the planned museum trip, she walked into Teresa's office with an administrative problem she had been saving up and found the three of them sitting at the round conference table. Teresa looked irritated at the disturbance and Dov surprised, but Steven merely wore his customary look of mild interest and wise inner amusement.

"Oh, I'm sorry," Ana said, coming farther into the room. "I needed to give you something, but I didn't realize you were busy. I'll just stick this on your desk."

Teresa nodded coldly and closed the file she had on the table in front of her, which may have hidden the specific information inside but at the same time revealed the cover to be PROPERTY OF THE ARIZONA STATE DEPARTMENT OF CORRECTIONS. Seven such files lay on the table, four of them stacked in a pile to one side, the others distributed among the occupants of the conference table.

"Anything I can do to help?" she asked brightly on her way past the table.

"No thank you, Ana," Teresa said repressively. Dov had closed his folder, too, and was patently waiting for her to leave the room, but Steven sat back in his chair and pushed his own file a couple of inches in her direction.

"Yes," he said. Teresa's mouth dropped open and Dov looked equally startled. "Let's see what Ana makes of this decision."

Ana stood and looked the situation over with care. She wanted to see what the files were, but she did not wish to alienate the two teachers, and although Dov was merely surprised at Steven's words, Teresa's dark cheeks had flushed. However, she couldn't very well withdraw the offer once it had been accepted, so she walked over and sat down in the chair next to Steven's, pulling the folder over in front of her.

It consisted of the brief biography and not-so-brief criminal record of a fifteen-year-old boy named Edgardo Rufina, who three years earlier had gone to live with an alcoholic aunt in Kingman with two charges of prostitution in her past. He had been in and out of trouble ever since. In school he was getting one B, one D, and the rest Cs, and had spent at least a week in custody every term. His violent acts were escalating, with his last offense the serious one of assaulting a police officer.

She read to the end and looked up. Steven reached across the table to retrieve the two folders from in front of Teresa and Dov and pushed them over to her. As she opened the first, Teresa stood.

"Does anyone else want something to drink?" she asked in a taut voice. Dov did, Steven did not, and Ana thanked her and said no. Teresa took her time in the lounge, and returned with two glasses of iced tea as Ana was nearing the end of the third and last file. They waited until Ana closed that one, which like the second had concerned a young boy with few offenses but those serious and escalating, who had a family but one that was broken and itself marked by legal wrongdoings. Gabe Martinez, the boy of the second folder, had dropped out of school in Tucson; the third boy, Mark

Gill, was in the process of flunking out in the border town of Nogales.

"Which of the three?" Steven asked.

Ana had been a teacher long enough to know a test when she heard one.

"Well, it sort of depends on what you want," she replied immediately, although keeping her voice casual, even diffident. "If your goal is to get a bad kid off the streets for a while, then by all means take Gabe or Mark and do society a favor. On the other hand, if you're looking for a bright boy who's acting out an impossible home situation and might respond to a positive environment, whose troublemaking has been spontaneous and emotional rather than premeditated and self-serving, then I'd say grab Edgardo. He's even bright enough to keep up in school despite his brushes with the law."

"He's not bright enough to avoid being caught," Dov pointed out.

"Some kids find the structured setting of being in custody a nice change compared to their home life," Ana suggested mildly, and stood up. By the smug expression on Steven's face she seemed to have passed his test, and nothing would now be gained by outstaying what small welcome she'd been given. On the contrary, enigmatic statements and tantalizing glimpses of Ana Wakefield's abilities were precisely the effect she was striving for. A game, yes, but one she had to win.

CHAPTER 16

August whatever, 1995 (That's still the year, isn't it??)

Dearest Tonio, just a short one to let you and Marla know I'm out and okay, as okay as I ever am at this stage. I'm off to the boys in Virginia for a couple of weeks for debriefing (which always makes me think of male strippers, most inappropriately) so let Eliot know he needs to stay on for a bit longer. I don't know if I'll then be directly home or if I'll go somewhere for a few days to let my nerves jangle--Glen says they have a safe house somewhere in Wisconsin that's not being used, but I'm torn between peace and quiet (God, communes can be noisy) and putting my head down and getting back to work to take my mind off everything. I'll let you know. It'ss probably a good thing I don't have any decisions to make for a while, since the choice between tea and coffee reduces me to tears. Poor Glen.

Anyway, I will be back in time to open up shop, so don't let anyone cancel my classes like they did last time. I'll send you confirmation of the reading list for the bookstore, when I can concentrate on it, and if you'd get in touch with those three people whose names I left with you, and tell then I'll definitely want them each for a guest lecture or two.

Tell Marla hello. Give her my love, tell her I look forward to many long sessions.

The children are the worst, walking away from them and not knowing if I should be doing anything else for them. I hear their voices in my sleep, over the sound of the water when I take a shower, when the kettle is coming to a boil. Absolute silence is tolerable, or noises loud enough to drown out anything in the back of my ears, but in between is difficult. Funny--you'd think I'd be grateful for the absence of children's racket, the arguments and continuous uproar, but I suppose one gets used to things. God, I hope they will be all right.

Enough. I'll let you know when I'm home.

--Anne

**Letter via e-mail from Anne Waverly to Antony Makepeace,
August 25, 1995**

The drive to the Heard Museum in downtown Phoenix took a little over three hours, so the bus carrying twenty-nine students and the twelve adults necessary to keep them in line left at seven in the morning. This would be the first time some of the students had been off the compound in months, and excitement was high. The adults, scattered throughout the bus, were kept busy asking them to sit down, changing seat partners who in some way or another rubbed on each other, and deflecting teenage misbehaviors.

Ana was sitting toward the rear of the bus, looking four rows forward at the back of Jason Delgado, who, along with about half of the other eighth graders, had been included in this high school outing. He was rigid, staring out the window and radiating animosity, and the source of his discomfort was not difficult to determine: It was seated right beside him.

In the aisle seat was an overweight blond boy with bad skin and a worse attitude. Bryan was two years older than Jason, looked younger, and resented the fact—and Jason—mightily. Ana already knew him as a troublemaker, although the school avoided that judgmental term, and she could see that he was deliberately provoking Jason with regular incursions of elbow and shoulder into the younger boy's space and the odd muttered phrase, inaudible in the next row over the noise of the bus but causing Jason to stiffen further.

After an hour and a half, the bus stopped to allow the cramped passengers to stretch and use the toilets. Ana walked her way over to the two teachers sitting in Jason's section, one of whom was Dov Levinski, and suggested that either he or Bryan be moved.

"We can't, sorry," said Dov.

"Why not? Just trade seats with somebody—Bryan gets along okay with Marcos; put him there."

"Bryan and Jason have to sit together," he said. "Steven's orders."

"Steven? But that's—"Ana caught herself before she committed the offense of criticizing Steven, and changed it to "He must not be aware of the problems between the two boys."

"He knows," Dov said curtly, and moved away to suggest that two girls might not want to squirt each other from the drinking fountain.

Strange, Ana thought. Why would Steven force two boys who hate each other to sit together? And particularly when one of them was a boy in whom he had expressed an interest?

They got through the rest of the trip without a scuffle and were met at the museum by three strong and determined-looking docents, who divided them up into groups with the big, scar-faced woodworker and shop teacher David Carteret in charge of the first group, Dov Levinski the second, and Teresa Montoya the third. As they went inside, Ana glanced at the map in her hands, looking for the location of the public telephones, and found one under some stairs near a rest room on the other side of the courtyard. It was very exposed, but she needed only two minutes to make the call. There didn't seem to be much choice but to leave her group when everyone was safely in the depths of the museum and take an emergency bathroom break, hiding her diary and a brief note for Glen somewhere—in the towel dispenser perhaps, or the toilet seat cover case—and make the call.

No time to find a photocopy machine; Glen would have to arrange the journal's return somehow.

Accordingly, halfway along the tour and deep in a lecture on Navajo building techniques, she sidled up to Dov and told him, "You guys'll have to watch the kids by yourselves for a couple of minutes. I have to go use the rest room."

Dov looked annoyed. "Can't you wait for twenty minutes?"

"I don't need to pee," she whispered cheerfully. "It's this menopause business; a person has really hard flows at the weirdest times."

He turned scarlet and pulled away from her as if it might be contagious, and Ana strode off toward the ladies' room.

To her irritation, there were two women already in the rest room and another followed her in the door. Even worse, there was no seat cover dispenser in the stall she entered, and the toilet paper holder was too small for her diary. The women left, Ana flushed (her period was quite regular, and not due for a week), and went out to see if she could jimmy the towel holder, and there stood the woman who had followed her in, waiting for her.

"Agent Steinberg, FBI," the woman said, and flashed a badge in front of Ana's startled eyes before making it vanish into a pocket. "Glen McCarthy told me to follow you around the museum, to see if you had anything for him."

For a moment, Ana could only stand and gape at this evidence of the FBI man's all-seeing and omnipotent presence, but then her brain kicked in. Of course—with all the activity involving the school board to set up this trip, the news had leaked to Glen's ears somehow. She yanked her diary out of her bag and thrust it at Agent Steinberg.

"Photocopy all the pages after the marker and give

them to Glen. Tell him I need information on alchemy. Got that? In two days—not tomorrow morning but the next day—I'll walk down the road at dawn. I need this diary back, along with any material he can get together; have him put them underneath the big rock with the white chip out of it exactly half a mile outside the gates, on the east side of the road. Now go."

"Alchemy," the woman said. The diary was already hidden.

"Go." Ana turned to wash her hands, and Agent Steinberg was gone before she could reach for the towels.

The half-closed door was pulled open and Teresa walked in.

"You okay?" she asked.

"Just fine," Ana answered, and left to find the others.

The trouble erupted over lunch.

Jason and Bryan were in the group behind Ana's, the last to finish. When the assorted students and teachers spilled into the small courtyard behind the bookstore where the others were already settled with sandwiches and drinks in hand, Teresa and the other woman chaperone were looking extremely apprehensive, and two men, whom Ana knew only as Dean and Peter, were trying to position themselves between the two boys, with limited success. Bryan's sneers and feint pokes were kerosene to Jason's smoldering anger. Watching them, she could see the meaning of the slang term "mad-dogging." The two boys glared at each other, daring the other to be the first to move, encouraged by the low remarks and glances of the other students.

Steven be damned, Ana cursed to herself; those two have to be separated.

She grabbed Teresa by the arm and hissed in her ear, "Do you want a fistfight right here in the museum?

Wouldn't that make Change look really good? I know Steven said to keep those two together, but Steven isn't here. Split them up, and we can settle it with him later."

Teresa looked over at the two boys and decided to agree with Ana. She went over to speak urgently into the ear of David Carteret, who then moved his six-feet-six-inch bulk over to the table where the sandwiches had been set out.

"C'mon, man," he said to Bryan. "Time to cool down."

Ana went to stand next to Jason, who was positively vibrating with repressed fury. She spoke his name, picked up a wrapped sandwich, and thrust it into his hand, trying to distract him, make him focus on her and return him to himself. He glanced at her distractedly, but then from behind her came Bryan's voice saying something she barely heard but which sent Jason's control through the roof. He dropped the sandwich, whirled, and reached out for Bryan, roaring his fury straight into Ana's face. She was caught up in a swift whirl of movement. Her shoulder slammed against some hard object, men were shouting, a woman shrieked—she shrieked—pain shot up from her knee, and then a shocking impact spun her face around and she was buried beneath two furious and very strong young men. She cried out again when a shoe ground down hard across her fingers, and then just as suddenly as it had begun it was over, leaving her crouching on hands and knees, waiting for her body to report its injuries. Her head spun, her hand throbbed, her mouth hurt, and she watched the drops of bright red blood across her bruised knuckles splash regularly down onto the courtyard tiles.

Hands tentatively touched her back, heads were bent to hers, shocked voices came from nearby, and at a distance a man, full of rage and disgust, harangued.

Jason, she thought suddenly. Where—?

She raised her head, grimacing at the taste of blood in her mouth, and tried to see him through the legs.

"Ice," a voice said. "Get a wet cloth," said another, and "Who's got the first aid kit?"

A dripping towel appeared; Ana took it with her right hand and put it gingerly to her mouth, which seemed to be alarmingly full of sharp pieces of tooth. No —not teeth.

She sat down on the pavement and pulled out the remains of her two front teeth, which caused a quick frisson of horror to run through the crowd of onlookers until they saw the broken plate of the bridge and the wire bits that were attached, and the tight laughter of relieved stress replaced the horror. Several of the girls began to giggle uncontrollably, and Ana was reminded of Dulcie. Great icebreakers, missing front teeth, she thought. Well worth all the trouble of getting shot up and crashing your face into a steering wheel.

Ice was brought and wrapped in the gory towel. After a minute, Ana decided the ground was too hard and her injuries too light to continue sitting where she was, so she allowed a couple of the men to help her to her feet. Her knee functioned, her left hand was scraped and already swelling but all the fingers seemed whole, and the bleeding from the cut lip was slowing down. She no doubt looked a sight, but what did that matter?

"I'm fine," she said indistinctly to the people fluttering around her. "I'm fine. It was an accident, and the only thing damaged is my bridge, and that can be replaced." She lisped and enunciation was difficult, but calm communication was reducing the anxiety level. Time to move on. "Would somebody go and buy me a T-shirt in the shop so I don't go around looking like an escapee from the emergency room? I'll pay you back. And did somebody tell the museum people they don't need to call in the riot squad?"

A babble of voices started up, and she squelched them. "No, I do not need to see a doctor. There's no point in even seeing a dentist until the swelling goes down. Finish your lunch, I'm going to go wash my face."

She pushed through the would-be Samaritans until she could see Jason. Both he and Bryan were unscathed other than a small, already dried cut on Jason's knuckle where it had connected with her mouth. His face was taut and pale, and not, she thought, because of the infuriated woodworking teacher looming over him. The sight of her blood-smeared face emerging from the crowd brought a look of mingled relief and horror to his features, and he took in a great gulp of air. He looked ill.

"I'm okay, Jason," she said as clearly as she could. "It looks worse than it is. And it wasn't entirely your fault."

She came out of the rest room still looking as if she'd fallen in front of a truck, but cleaned up, wearing a shiny new T-shirt with Anasazi pot designs printed on it and beginning to see the humor in the situation.

And the benefits: This would mean at least two trips into Sedona to see a dentist, great opportunities to contact Glen. Silver linings, she told herself, and would have chuckled if it hadn't hurt so much.

The first group had already been taken away by their highly reluctant docent. The second group, her own, was assembling near the door, but she saw that neither Bryan nor Jason had joined them. Without hesitation she marched up to Jason, took his arm, and moved him over to her group. There was one tentative objection, inevitably from Dov.

"Look, Ana, we were specifically told—"

"I'll talk to Steven when we get back," she interrupted him, wishing it didn't have to come out Thteven. "I want you with me, Jason." Jathon.

The authority of her shed blood shut them up, and the tour resumed. Ana felt distinctly unwell, and would have opted out but for the strong need to maintain her poise before, and because of, Jason. She absorbed not a word of the lecture and demonstration by a Hopi carver on fetishes, and when the bus doors opened before her, she staggered for the opening as if for a lifeboat. The only thing she had accomplished was keeping Jason safe, and with her. It was enough.

Jason had not appreciated her protection. He was firmly back in his shell, refusing to meet her eyes, sitting at the window, hunched away from her. She might have been an arresting officer. Ana slumped back in her aisle seat, her mouth, hand, and knee radiating sharp pain and the rest of her just sore, hoping that a degree of energy and wits would seep back before Jason had shut himself away for good.

It was afternoon, and the traffic out of the sprawl that was Phoenix seemed endless. Ana had been to the city half a dozen times before, but she always forgot how big it was and how long it took to cross it. The occupants of the bus had fallen silent by the time the driver finally shook the suburbs off, exhausted by the trudging and the thinking and the emotional surge over lunch. A few people talked, several fell asleep on each other's shoulders, but most simply sat, rocking with the motion of the bus. She still felt ill and old, but if she was to reach the boy, it had to be now.

"What was it Bryan said to you?" she asked Jason quietly. He sat up straighter and seemed intent on melting holes in the window with his gaze. "It was something about Dulcie, wasn't it? Something about her being retarded."

The side of the young jaw was clamped down hard, working against her words. Ana had dredged Bryan's shouted sentences out of the back of her mind, and she thought that what he had actually said was a criticism of Jason, and indirectly of Dulcie: "He's a retard like his sister."

Ana did not for a moment believe that Jason had resented the derision against him, but a threat, or even a mere insult, aimed at his sister would easily have the power to pry the lid off his self-control.

"Well, do you think she is retarded?" she asked.

Had she been any other person on the bus, he might well have hit her. She knew what his reaction would be, though, and she braced herself against his surge of emotion, instantly repressed. The moment his face was closed again, she leaned toward him and said urgently, "Think, Jason, think. Would I call Dulcie retarded? Me?"

She watched his hackles go down and she drew a relieved breath. "You know I wouldn't, because she's no more retarded than you or I. Of course, Bryan's vocabulary is about as extensive as his moral sense, so he may have meant not that Dulcie is mentally deficient, but that she is unbalanced. Ill. What Bryan would think of as crazy. In which case, Jason, do you think Dulcie is crazy?"

Fury mixed with fear instantly welled up in his eyes, fear for Dulcie and fear that Ana might so readily see it, fear that her saying it must make it true and fury that he could not change his own fear. She smiled at him.

"Jason, your sister is fine. Whatever it is you two have been through, Dulcie is working it out. You being there, you being strong and stable and loving, makes it more certain. She's not sick, not nuts, not disturbed. She is a true individual, and I for one cherish her for that.

"Personally," she added, "I think she's a hoot. Did you hear about Dulcie and my bridge, the day I met her?" Jason shook his head, so Ana settled down and told him the whole story, drawn out and decorated with extraneous details.

And he laughed. Jason Delgado, tough guy and basketball star, first snorted and then gave forth a brief
guffaw of laughter. It startled half the bus and was instantly stifled, but it was there between them, and it
remained in his eyes, that picture of his silent little sister
almost peeing herself giggling at the lady who took out
her own front teeth.

That short, unguarded laugh was to sustain Ana
through some hard days ahead. That laugh bound her to
Change far more closely than she had intended or anticipated. She knew she would sell her soul for that laugh, if
it came to that.

In the deep, still dark of the desert night the bus came
into the compound. The weary travelers climbed stiffly
down (Ana more stiffly than most). The adults staggered
off to the dining hall behind the revitalized teenagers,
and respectively sat in silence or in excitement over the
meal that had been kept warm for them.

Ana managed a few mouthfuls of soup and a glass of
goat's milk, and looked up to find Teresa standing next
to her.

"I'll take your classes tomorrow," she said. Ana protested feebly, then allowed herself to be talked into
spending a day doing paperwork. She thanked Teresa,
helped herself to a tureen of ice cubes, and went to her
room, where she arranged one ice-filled washcloth on
her mouth, another one on her left hand, and lay with
her right arm thrown over her eyes, aching and thinking.

What was she doing? What the hell was she doing?
She had no business becoming involved in the lives and
affections of two orphaned or abandoned kids. Let's
make another joke about menopause, Ana, with the hormones running wild and the old brain melting in a hot
flash. She acted as if she were falling in love with a boy

of fourteen, a tough, swaggering child who shaved once a week whether he needed to or not. Hell, who was there to kid here? She *was* falling in love with him. Oh, it was not a physical thing, she was not out to seduce him, not even tempted to fantasize about him, but God, this felt like a high school crush, looking for The One across a crowded room, studying him from a distance, casually meeting and flirting and making him—yes—making him laugh.

That laugh.

She really should get out of here before someone got hurt. Glen would insist, if he figured out what was happening.

But she knew she wouldn't go.

CHAPTER 17

Let's say one day you discovered that your next door neighbors were in the habit of slitting open live chickens and watching them run around the back yard. What would your reaction be? If this family was of your everyday middle-class Anglo-Saxon background, if the people doing it were young boys, and if everyone there seemed to be drinking beer and having a fun old time, you'd be more than justified in locking the doors, shutting up the cat, and ringing every emergency number you could find from the police to the SPCA, because the chances of that being pathological behavior would be very high.

But what if you found out that the offending family was freshly arrived from, say, Haiti, and if the people doing the slaughtering were grown adults with not a breath of hilarity in the air? What if you knew that the sacrifice and reading of auguries was a deeply ingrained part of the family's society and religious heritage? You might still check on the whereabouts of the family pet, you would no doubt still be disgusted, and you would still have a problem on your hands, but the phone calls you made would probably have less panic in them and more concern for long-term socialization efforts.

Cultural relativity is the acknowledgement that what your Caribbean neighbors were doing was in their eyes a valid religious expression. After all, a hundred years ago it was absolutely acceptable that my great-great grandmother married at the age of thirteen, and for a large part of the Muslim world today, circumcision is a thing for eight to twelve year-old boys.

Are these seekers of auguries wrong? Was my female ancestor old enough to become a wife and, ten months later, a mother? Are these boys mature enough to make the decision to submit to the knife? Or are my grandmother's marriage and the circumcision of fourteen year-old boys both examples of child abuse, and the inhumane slaughtering of chickens strictly a legal matter?

Excerpt from the transcription of a lecture by Dr. Anne Waverly to the Northern California Sheriffs' Association, January 16, 1992

Ana slept fitfully and woke early, imagining she had heard a scratching at her door. She lay for a minute, waiting for the sound to be repeated, and then dismissed it. She had not yet regained the immunity from external noises one needs in communal living, and she tended to hear every closed door, every toilet flush and cough.

She eased her legs over the side of the bed and groaned herself upright. Her face ached but her hand was on fire, and she reached over and turned on the bedside lamp to examine the damage.

It looked surprisingly normal, though it was scraped from the bits of gravel embedded in the shoe that had come down on it and the fingers were as fat and immobile as sausages. Tomorrow the whole hand would be black, but today it was only darkly suffused with blood. She forced herself to bend each fingertip and wiggle each sausage; they all worked, but maybe she would go see the nurse about it after all.

Now for the mirror. She gained her feet, and the scratching noise came again from the door.

She tottered over and pulled it open: Dulcie sat shivering on the floor outside, her arms wrapped around the canvas bag full of bright yarn rope.

"Dulcie?" Ana exclaimed. "What on earth—? Come in, child, let's warm you up." She bent down, but with only one usable hand she could not lift the girl. "Dulcie," she said in a clear voice, "you'll have to help me. I hurt my hand yesterday and I can't pick you up. Come on, sweetheart, stand up and come inside, where we can get you warm. That's a girl. Good, good. Now let me get a blanket—you'll have to let go of my hand for a second,

Dulcie. Okay, let's just sit over here and warm each other up."

Ana whipped the blankets from her bed and sat down in the room's soft chair, pulling Dulcie onto her lap and wrapping the still-warm blankets around them both. The child's shivering seemed more like shock than mere cold, but in either case warmth seemed the best treatment. Dulcie put her thumb in her mouth and nestled down between Ana's breasts; in two minutes she was asleep.

Memory was a terrible and intensely physical thing. Unlike guilt, it lost none of its power over time, and if it hit less often than it had in the early years, it still hit hard and unexpectedly: The sight of a furry infant skull would trigger the warm, round sensation of cradling Abby's head in her cupped palm, all of her daughter's humanity and future in her hand; a blend of fragrances on a street would jerk her back to a particular mad evening with Aaron in New York before they came west; a certain kind of tree-lined street in the fall would evoke the heady beginnings of graduate school.

Now it was her breasts that betrayed her, heavy and warm, tingling with the gush of nonexistent milk down to her nipples for Abby's greedy mouth. Dulcie slept on, unaware of the turmoil within the woman she knew as Ana, aware only of the rare and dimly remembered bliss of being held in comforting arms, aware that Ana must be trustworthy, since Jason had told Dulcie to go to her if she needed anything while he was away "helping Steven." She was aware only that she felt safe.

Dulcie's thumb dropped from her slack mouth and half woke her, so that she turned against Ana's chest, nuzzling like an infant until sleep pulled her down again.

It was agony, it was sheer delight; eighteen years after the fact, Ana had been given back her daughter. Dulcie was not Abby and Dulcie would never be Ana's daughter, but Ana's arms craved the child and the bone-deep love of a mother tugged at her, and she knew she had only two choices: She could put Dulcie on the floor and walk away from her, or she could permit the indulgence of her body's yearnings. It was no choice. She wrapped herself around the sleeping child and rocked her in the ageless rhythm of mothering, and when Dulcie woke fully an hour later, Ana more than half expected to find the front of her T-shirt drenched with leaking milk.

Her shirt was dry, but Dulcie was frowning at her face.

"I had a little accident yesterday, Dulcie. It really doesn't hurt very much, but those teeth of mine that come out got broken right in two, so I'll have to have them fixed. Looks funny, doesn't it? Thounds funny, too. Remind me not to smile, okay?"

Dulcie's only response was to turn and look at Ana's hands. Ana held the left one up. "This one does hurt. I don't think anything's broken, but it'll be sore and ugly for a few days.

"Now tell me, Dulcie: Where's your brother?"

She was unprepared for the extremity of Dulcie's response. The child wailed and flung herself against Ana, curling up to make herself small, burying her face in Ana's T-shirt.

Ana's immediate urge was to burst out of the door and find out what had happened to Jason, but she forced herself to sit and calm Dulcie with drivel first.

"Okay, we'll talk about that later. Dulcie sweetie, let me tell you about the time we had in Phoenix yesterday. There was a display in the museum that showed all these beautiful clothes the Indian women used to wear, all covered with beads and stuff, and the house they used to live in made of logs and mud, with a fire built right in the middle of it. You ever see one of those? Maybe you can go on a trip with the school next time. It's a long drive but it's fun. You know, I'm feeling a bit hungry. I think I'll get dressed and go have some breakfast. Do you mind coming with me down to the dining hall? I think I'll have a bowl of oatmeal with lots of brown sugar on top, that'll be nice and soft to chew on." She waited until Dulcie had given her a small nod, and then worked herself out from under the child. She went to the closet and chose clothing with loose cuffs, pulled on her boots and pushed her untied laces into their tops, and eased on her jacket.

Dulcie was more of a problem: She was dressed, but she had no shoes on. Ana had her climb onto the arm of the chair and propped her awkwardly on her right hip. Fortunately, it was not far to the dining hall.

Once inside the building, Ana could loose her precarious hold and let the child slide to the floor. They walked hand in hand toward the breakfast noises. The instant they came in the door, Teresa leapt to her feet and scurried over to intercept them.

"Dulcie! Where on earth have you been? We've been looking all over, we were so worried about you. Come along and let's get properly dressed."

She reached for Dulcie's hand, and the child twisted around behind Ana to avoid her. Despite Ana's protests, Teresa pulled the child's hand away, and Dulcie naturally reached up for Ana's other hand and grabbed it hard.

The pain was literally blinding. Ana sank to her knees with a breathless squeal, and with infinite tenderness tried to peel the little fingers from hers, all the while chanting, "No, no no no no no, Dulcie, oh please, no no no." The grip suddenly dropped away as the horrified child realized what she had done. She stepped back, looking ready to bolt, but Ana scooped her around the shoulders with her right hand and pulled her back, mur-

muring all the maternal phrases of condolence while the
agony in her left hand subsided and her right hand
stroked the back of Dulcie's hair. The child threw her
arms around Ana's neck and began to weep. The pain
retreated and became bearable; when Teresa saw the
change, she started to fuss again. Ana took a deep calm-
ing breath, and let it out.

"Dulcie, it's over," she said firmly. "It's uncomfortable here on the floor, I feel stupid with everyone staring
at us, and I want my breakfast. What say we eat?"

Teresa started to say, "Yes, Dulcie, let's let Ana—"
when Ana gave her a glare that instantly silenced her.

"Dulcie is going to eat breakfast with me. We'll talk
to you later."

Teresa opened her mouth, closed it, turned on her
heel, and left. Ana persuaded her limpet to let her free
enough to rise, and the two of them continued their
interrupted journey to the breakfast line.

With Dulcie holding firmly on to her jacket, Ana
carried their tray over to an unoccupied table. Dulcie
seemed uninterested in food, so in the end Ana spooned
oatmeal into the child's passive mouth. It was like feeding a baby, down to the close-lipped shake of the head to
let Ana know she'd had enough. Ana finished the bowl,
drank her herb tea and the remainder of Dulcie's juice,
and piled their dishes on the tray. No doubt about it; the
brain functioned better with food.

She took Dulcie's hand and bent down until she was
looking into the young face. "Dulcie, would you please
tell me now where Jason is?"

Dulcie was feeling the stabilizing effects of breakfast
as well; her lip quivered and her eyes filled, but she did
not wail and fling herself at Ana. Neither did she answer
her.

"Dulcie, I want to help you find Jason. Did he tell
you where he was going?" Dulcie gave her a tiny nod,

dislodging the tears from one eye so that they spilled down her face. "Can you tell me? Please?"

"He went to help Steven," she said in a tiny voice. "Two men took him."

At first Ana refused to hear the meaning of Dulcie's words. Even when the horror of what it might imply was roaring through her, she tried hard to remain objective, sensible. Eventually, rationality won out. Had there ever been any indications, in the weeks she had lived here, that Steven was a sexual predator? Any record indicating that he might be a pederast, straight or gay? Any sign of ongoing sexuality among even the abused outsiders in the school? No, no, and no. It was possible, yes, but it was also possible that something else was going on—some kind of initiation, perhaps, or a punishment for yesterday's fight, or a hundred other things. She needed to find out, but she also needed to keep her head. As she'd said to Jason: Think!

Her first responsibility was to Dulcie, temporarily bereft of her brother and clinging mightily to the only other support she could find. There was no possibility of abandoning her.

"First step," she said to Dulcie. "We get your shoes and your coat, brush your hair and your teeth.

"Second step," she said, in answer to the unvoiced objection of the small person, "we find out where your brother is. Okay?"

Dulcie nodded, content that Ana was not proving herself yet another untrustworthy adult. This time Ana carried Dulcie piggyback to the room in the next building where she and Jason slept. Teresa went with them, but she did not try to interfere, she just tied Dulcie's shoes and put her hair into braids after Ana had demonstrated her inability to do either of those things. She even tied Ana's flopping boots for her, to Ana's embarrassment and gratitude.

When Dulcie was dressed and scrubbed, Ana asked her to sit down and work on her rug for a few minutes while she talked with Teresa. She reassured Dulcie that she was not going to leave her, just step out in the hall and talk privately for a minute, and led Teresa out, shutting the door.

"I need to talk to Steven," she said.

"You can't."

"Is he here? In the compound?"

"Yes, but he's busy."

"Teresa, be sensible. I don't know what that child's background is, but it's obvious that it was pretty hellish. Jason is all she has. She's accepted me, heaven knows why, as a substitute, but I have to know what Steven is doing with Jason in order to help Dulcie. She's too fragile to be kept in the dark."

"I know, but there's nothing anyone else can do. Jason will be back when he's . . . when he's ready."

"You know where he is."

Teresa would not meet her eyes.

"Is it a punishment for yesterday? It wasn't his fault."

"A consequence is not a punishment."

"That sounds like Steven."

She didn't answer, but Ana could see it was true.

"Where is Steven now?"

"Meditating. You can't—"

"I sure as hell can," Ana said, and pushed her aside to yank the door open. "Come on, Dulcie. Let's go ask some questions."

She did find Steven, and she did ask questions, but he did not answer them. He did not even respond, but merely sat in the full lotus position, unseeing and unhearing on his high seat in the very center of the meditation hall, the golden sparkles from the mobile directly over his head moving slowly across the wall.

Thomas Mallory, inevitably, was there. She entered

the meditation hall and saw Steven, and addressed him
in a loud voice. Steven did not react. Telling Dulcie to
stay where she was, Ana started for the rising platforms
on the side of the room, intending to clamber over to the
platform and seize Steven by the shoulders, shaking him
from his trance, but Mallory stopped her, his scowling
eyebrows nearly meeting over his nose. She knew better
than to resist physically, not when Dulcie was looking
on. She also suspected that Steven's assistant would have
picked her up bodily and put her outside the meditation
hall had it not been for Dulcie's presence.

"Steven!" she shouted. The hall had excellent acous-
tics, but Steven did not move. She retreated from the
platforms and angrily hammered her fist against the
great black pipe that rose out of the floor to support
the fireplace and Steven's platform. It was metal, and
oddly warm, but it gave out only an unsatisfactory dull
thud instead of the clanging echoes she had hoped for,
and then Thomas Mallory came up behind her and
grabbed her shoulders, whirling her about effortlessly
and propelling her toward the exit. She retreated, but at
the door she turned to plead with the man.

"Look, Dulcie is worried about her brother. She just
wants to know where he is and when he'll be back.
Surely you can tell us that."

Mallory studied her, and then the child, and his petulant mouth softened a fraction.

"Her brother is in meditation with Steven," he said.
"He'll be back in a day or two."

That was all he would give them. Strangely enough,
it seemed to reassure Dulcie, whose level of anxiety went
down a great deal, although she refused to venture from
Ana's side. All that day, wherever she went, Dulcie was
her shadow, a silent and determined presence working
eternally on the cumbersome bulk of her yarn rope.

Ana's own concern for Jason, her unresolved anger

against Steven, and Dulcie's presence, silence, and absolute trust all began to prey on Ana, and the bright, aggressive cheeriness of Dulcie's rope began to rub on her nerves.

Three times in the course of an hour Ana got up and left the desk where she was doing paperwork; three times Dulcie put her spool into the bulging canvas bag and followed her: into the supply room, into the computer room, and to the bathroom, where she stood outside the door, waiting for Ana to come out.

Patience was a good thing, Ana decided, but at times did not go far enough. Dulcie was beginning to look like a miniature Madame Defarge, knitting as the heads rolled.

"Dulcie, don't you think it's time you started to make your rug out of that? I'm sure you have enough there for a nice big rug."

The child nodded, and went back to looping the bile-green yarn over the nails on the spool, one stitch at a time, around and around.

"You could set it out here on the floor and get it started," Ana suggested. "I'll be here for another hour or so."

Dulcie dropped her hands into her lap. "I don't know how," she said, sounding sad to the point of despair.

Ana turned and looked at her. "You've never done this before, have you?" she asked slowly.

Dulcie shook her head.

"Did Carla get you started?" Dulcie nodded. "But she hasn't shown you how to make the actual rug?"

Dulcie looked up at Ana, her eyes not far from tears with her anguish. "I don't know how to stop," she cried.

The pathos in the child's manner made Ana's lips quiver for a moment. "You poor thing," she said. "Did you think you were going to knit away on this thing forever? That one day we'd go to look for you and all we'd find would be a pair of feet sticking out from under a gigantic pile of brightly colored rope?"

Dulcie's own lips quivered, but not from amusement. "It's very bright," she agreed sadly.

"You mean— Didn't you choose those colors?"

Dulcie's head went back and forth, slowly and emphatically. The two of them sat looking at the dirty canvas bag with the pink loops and the orange coils and the green tail emerging to dip along the floor and disappear into the wooden spool in Dulcie's fist, and Ana began to laugh at the tragedy and the absurdity of the whole situation. She gathered Dulcie into her arms and the two of them howled and howled.

When that was over, she found some tissues and she and Dulcie sat up and dried their eyes, and she helped the child blow her nose. Then, with great ceremony, she took a large pair of scissors from the drawer of the desk and laid them in the center of the desktop.

"Bring me the spool," she ordered Dulcie.

"If you cut it, the whole thing will fall apart," Dulcie said quickly. "Carla told me."

"Not if you tie the end off first," Ana replied grimly, hoping it was true. Perhaps she should tie two knots, just to be sure.

Dulcie hopped down from Ana's lap and fetched the spool, the instrument that had produced all those yards and yards of rope. Ana did not know if it had functioned as a meditation device or as a form of penance, but be it rosary or hair shirt, she was declaring it finished.

She snipped the yarn that led from skein to spool, tucked the end in, and set the unused yarn to one side. Working slowly because of the awkwardness of her left hand, she looped the rope below the spool into a knot, and had Dulcie pull on the rope to help her tighten the knot. They then repeated it to make a second knot beside the first, and she picked up the scissors and offered them to Dulcie. They were too big for the child's hand, but Dulcie took them with two hands and chewed with them at the rope until it parted, and Ana was touched by a brief vision of Aaron with a pair of obstetrical scissors in his hands, his face showing mingled revulsion at the effort of cutting through the tough flesh of Abby's umbilical cord and dawning wonder at the separate new person lying in red, angry splendor on his wife's breasts.

Dulcie's face showed mostly relief, and wonder at her daring, and trepidation lest the sundered end should suddenly burst into life like some live thing or cartoon entity, spitting furiously and peeling back countless loops of yarn until her weeks of effort were reduced to a room-sized heap of kinked-up wool.

It did nothing, just sat there with the two snug lumps at its end. Dulcie noticed the spool and picked it up. She worked the stub of yarn rope from its nails and thoughtfully pulled at the loose end. Around and around the yarn unraveled, each loop pulling free. When she held only a length of kinked chartreuse yarn in her hand, Dulcie dropped it into the wastebasket, put the spool and hook out of sight in her pocket, and bundled the now-severed rope into the bag.

"You know," Ana suggested, "when you're finished with the rug, if you decide you don't like it, you could always give it to Carla."

CHAPTER 18

The word "cult" has become meaningless as a description of human behavior, so laden is it now with negative emotional baggage. Any small and vaguely eccentric group of religious seekers-after-truth is apt to find itself slapped with the label and instantly converted in the minds of outsiders into a potential People's Temple or Branch Davidian. This is a heavy burden to carry, and serves primarily to increase the level of paranoia in even the most level-headed group.

Of course, short words with hefty emotional impact are the stock in trade of the media. When a newspaper reporter describes a group as a "cult," it has nothing to do with the actual technical definition of that word. The media are not interested in matter-of-fact; that sells no papers. It speaks in polemic, describing not what is, but what has been in the past and, more to the point, how we as readers have to feel about it: outraged, righteous, and moved to demand action.

Cults--or as they should usually be termed, sects--can be vicious, stupid, paranoid, murderous, suicidal, incomprehensible, and hysterical; as indeed may any group of human beings involved in a quest and immersed in passion. They can also be gentle, contemplative sources of creativity and peace, but we do not hear much about those. We must keep firmly in mind, however, that most of the picture we see of cultic activity has been drawn for us by ex-members, and if in some cases their withdrawal from the community may be seen as a return to sanity, in other cases the ex-member's dissatisfaction may have its roots in political, personal, or even financial reasons. To expect a calm and balanced image of their former life would be to hope for rational words from a jilted lover about the ex. Grains of salt must be applied with a generous hand--an exercise the news media has never shown much interest in. [laughter]

Excerpt from the transcription of a lecture by Dr. Anne Waverly to the FBI Cult Response Team, April 27, 1994

During the afternoon, Ana found a dentist in Sedona who would see to her teeth, and made an appointment with him for the following day. Teresa agreed to take her classes again. Teresa also agreed that unless Jason had reappeared, it looked as if Ana would have to take Dulcie along, since the child showed no sign of relinquishing her hold on Ana. They ate dinner together, and then Ana borrowed an armful of bedding from the stores closet and made up a bed for the child in the corner of her room. She showed Dulcie where the bathroom was, supervised a bath and the brushing of teeth, and settled the child into her makeshift bed.

"I have some reading to do," she told her. "I'll turn out the lights in a little while."

"Ana?"

"Yes, Dulcie?"

"Jason always lets me read for ten minutes when I go to bed. We used to watch TV," she confided, "but then one of my mom's boyfriends broke it and so Jason said I could read instead."

"Oh. Well, books are better anyway. Except that I don't know if I have anything you'd like."

Dulcie promptly sprang up and trotted over to the bag of things they had fetched from her room, and came back to the heap of tumbled sheets and blankets with two well-thumbed paperback picture books. Ana laboriously remade the bed with her one hand, tucked Dulcie in again, and returned to the papers her students had written. For ten minutes all was quiet but for the turning of pages; then Ana told Dulcie it was time to put her books away and go to sleep.

"I have to go to the bathroom, Ana."

"You go ahead, then. Just try not to mess up your bed when you get up."

Five minutes later: "What are you reading, Ana?"

"I'm reading papers I had my students write about what they expected to see on their trip to Phoenix. Next week they'll hand in papers on what they did see."

"Did any of your students say they were going to see you hurt in a fight?" Dulcie knew all about what had happened to Ana; everyone on the premises knew.

"No, none of them so far has mentioned that."

"What does Jason's paper say?"

"Jason isn't my student, Dulcie. I don't know what he wrote for his teacher."

"Jason hit you, didn't he?" said a small voice.

Ana let the paper she was reading drop onto the table. "Jason's hand hit my mouth, somebody else's elbow hit my back, and I think Dov Levinski the math teacher stepped on my hand. No one was aiming for me, Dulcie. There were a lot of people moving quickly, and I just happened to be in the way."

"So you're not mad at Jason?"

"Of course not. I'm sorry that he lost his temper, and I'm sure he's sorry he did, too. But I'm not at all angry at him. I like your brother."

"I love Jason."

"And Jason loves you. Now go to sleep."

"Ana?"

"Yes, Dulcie."

"Is Jason okay?"

"Jason will be fine, Dulcie. There are just some things he needs to do, and then he'll be back."

A few minutes later: "Would you say my good-night prayer with me, Ana?"

"Why don't you say it and I'll listen?"

"Now I lay me down to sleep," Dulcie began to

chant. Ana winced. She had always considered it a sadistic idea to make a child's final words for the day "If I should die before I wake"; after Abby's death the thought had become truly appalling. She steeled herself, but when the second half of the poem came, it was, instead, "Thy love guide me through the night, and wake me with the morning light." A much better version.

"Amen," Ana said.

"Ana, is the Lord like Don Quixote?"

"What?"

"The Lord. You said that Don Quixote's name meant 'lord.' "

"Well, no. 'Lord' is the way we speak to noblemen, to knights and kings and very important people, and when we talk to God, we use the same word, because it's one of the most important words we have. God is much bigger than any king; it's just that language doesn't go far enough to describe how we feel about things as big as God. You could say that God is bigger than language."

"Is Steven God?"

"No! For heaven's sake. Did somebody say he was?"

"I don't think so. But Amelia said that Steven sees everything and knows everything."

"Steven is a human being, so he can't be God. You could say—" Ana paused to choose her words. "You could say that Steven tries to act for God, that he knows something of what God wants and helps others know it, too. Steven may be a man of God, but he can't be God. No person can be God."

"Wasn't Jesus God?"

Ana had to smile. "That, my dear, is a question that better minds than yours or mine have dedicated their lives to thinking about. Now: Sleep."

Five minutes later, in a tiny voice: "Ana?"

"What, Dulcie?"

"If you're not here when I wake up in the morning, you'll be back as soon as you've finished your walk?"

"That's what I told you. I promise I'll be back."

"Like Jason. He goes running in the morning sometimes."

"Yes, I know. I've seen him."

"Ana?"

"What?"

"I love you, Ana."

Dulcie was asleep before Ana could formulate an honest response to that last statement. She sat with her papers, listening to the child's even breathing, the occasional hitches and pauses in the rhythm, an indistinct mutter and chewing noise when Dulcie entered a dream.

I love you, Mommy. All the various meanings that simple phrase had once held. It could mean, Thank you, Mommy, for the great birthday party, or it could be a spontaneous and inarticulate recognition of the joy of human companionship. It had even, once or twice, been a preemptive strike, an attempt at disarming Ana's probable anger when she found out that something had been broken, spilled, or otherwise spoiled. "I love you, Mommy."

Oh, God; what was she doing here?

Ana had no difficulty waking early the next morning; she had not actually been asleep. Shortly after she had turned out the light and gotten into bed, Dulcie woke crying. Ana took her into bed with her, warmed her back into sleep, and then, when the child was limp and deep, she had moved herself over to the bed on the floor. It was amazing how hard six blankets on the boards could be, and how vivid pain became in the dark. Her hand pounded, her lip hurt, Dulcie snored and muttered, and dawn gradually crept near.

It was still dark when she went outside, but the stars were beginning to fade. The Change members with early-morning jobs were on their way to barn or kitchen, or to the cars that would take them to employment in Sedona or Flagstaff. Ana exchanged a couple of greetings but she did not stop to talk, just made her way along the road out of the compound.

She passed the boxy guest quarters, where four or five visitors now slept, and walked by the rocks where she had first met Steven and watched the sun come up over the compound. She stayed on the road, which was growing more visible by the minute, and went through the gate until she reached the heap of spilled rock a half-mile from the Change entrance, the heap that included one boulder that had sheared off in the fall to reveal a white face. In cross-section the white would appear as a vein, but now it was a bright flag visible even from the small planes that from time to time overflew the area.

Ana went over to sit atop the rocks. She gathered her knees to her chin and waited while the land took form around her. A car drove out of the compound, its headlights on, and Ana raised a hand. The lights dipped in response, and when it was past, when she was as certain as she could be that no one was watching, she reached underneath the white-marked stone for the papers she had told Agent Steinberg in Phoenix she needed.

Her fingers encountered only stone, sand, and one small slip of paper. She pulled it out, opened it, and saw written on it: *I will be in Sedona today.*

It was Glen's writing, though looking at it carefully she decided it was a faxed reproduction rather than the real thing. So, he was flying in to talk with her.

What could be so urgent that he would get on a plane, then drive up from Phoenix or Flagstaff to see her in person? And even more disconcerting, once she thought about it, were the implications of how he knew she would be in Sedona. It was one thing to have a friendly ear in the local school district offices who could pass on the news of an impending field trip to the museum; it was quite another to have a legally sanctioned wiretap on the community's phones, which was the only way she could think of that he would know of her dentist appointment. Glen was not the sort to arrange for rogue surveillance, not if he had any other options. Had something happened to boost the Bureau's level of anxiety about the Change movement? And if so, why wasn't she aware of it here?

She crumpled the paper and finished her morning walk, tossing the small, tight wad among some thorny cactuses along the way. When she got back to her room and opened the door, Dulcie immediately sat upright on the bed, so wide-eyed and alert that Ana knew she had been fast asleep until the instant her hand hit the doorknob.

"Come along, Dulcinea, you slugabed," she said cheerfully. "There's a bowl of cereal with your name on it in the dining hall."

There was no sign of Jason at breakfast. When she was preparing to leave for her appointments with the dentist and with Glen, the teenager had still failed to emerge from hiding and Dulcie was looking even more miserable. Ana sat down on the bed so she could look the child directly in the face. Feeling like a traitor, or a wicked stepmother, she took Dulcie's hand in hers.

"Sweetie, I think you'd be happier if you stayed here and waited for Jason. You can help Amelia in the kitchen—she'd love to have you—and you'd be right here if Jason gets finished with his work. If you come with me, you'll have a long, cold ride in and out of town, and a long, boring wait in the dentist's office. He'll probably make you sit in the waiting room, too, while I'm in with him."

Dulcie wavered, torn between the possibility of Jason's restoration and the sure security represented by Ana. In the end, the deciding factor was something else entirely.

She asked Ana, "Will we go in Rosy Nante?"

When Ana admitted they would, that was all Dulcie needed to hear. Ana drove to Sedona with Dulcie in the seat beside her.

As Ana had predicted, the dentist suggested firmly that Dulcie occupy herself with the children's books in the waiting room while he and Ana went back to mull over the choice between repairing the bridge and starting from scratch. In the end they did both, making temporary repairs on the shattered plastic and taking impressions of it and her mouth.

"No apples," he ordered. "Don't bite anything. And don't get in the way of any more fighting boys."

Ana thanked him distractedly, her attention caught by the voice she could hear coming from the waiting room. Sure enough, as she approached the nurse's station she could tell that it was Glen in monologue. No—he was reading something aloud, a story about a pony.

She made an appointment for Monday, four days away, which seemed quick work on the part of the lab that would be making the bridge. She said something appreciative to the receptionist.

"Yes," said the woman. "You're lucky—the new delivery man for the lab happened to be through today, and he said he'd wait for your impressions. That saves you two or three days. In fact, that's him out there, reading a story to the little girl."

It was indeed Glen, dressed in the uniform of a medical delivery-man, bent over that ubiquitous magazine of pediatricians and children's dentists, *Highlights for Children,* its pastel monochrome cover at once dull and soothing. Dulcie was sitting a polite distance from this friendly stranger, back straight but her neck craned to see the illustrations. Glen turned the page, read to the end of the story, and closed the magazine. He handed it to Dulcie.

"Thank you, young lady, I enjoyed that. I don't think I've read one of those magazines since I was your age. May even have been the same one. Is this your friend Ana?" he asked, and without waiting for an answer he stood up and introduced himself in a voice that twanged of the South. "Glen York. And you're Ana—?"

"Wakefield," she supplied.

"Ana Wakefield. Your young friend here is a most talented listener. Doesn't talk much, but boy, can she listen."

"Glen is going to take your teeth to be fixed," said Dulcie.

"That I am, if the nurse here is ready. That them? Anything to sign? Right, that'll do me, then. You don't mind if the young lady hangs on to the magazine, do you? And I don't suppose you could recommend a good coffee shop around here? I don't think I actually had lunch today. In fact, maybe this young lady and her friend Ana would like a cup of coffee or something. How do you take your coffee, Dulcie? Strong and black, am I right?"

Ana was amused to see that, considering he was a man without children, he had struck a note likely to loosen up the most reticent child. Dulcie very nearly smiled at his quip.

"She'd probably rather have an ice cream," Ana suggested. "Do you like ice cream, Dulcie?"

The girl nodded hugely. Ice cream was not high on the list of supplies in the Change walk-in freezers. As they walked to the café, Glen slipped Ana's diary back into her bag.

They sat at a booth with a booster cushion to raise Dulcie's chin above the table. Glen ordered a ham sandwich and black coffee, Ana a bowl of vegetable soup, and Dulcie had a grilled cheese sandwich followed by a hot fudge sundae complete with cherry. As they waited for the food, Dulcie read the borrowed magazine under the edge of the table. Glen opened his mouth, and then shut it firmly at Ana's vigorous shake of the head and her pointed glance at the seemingly oblivious child. He was seething with impatience, both to tell and to hear, but he could see that it would not do to speak openly in front of a wide-eared and obviously bright child. It might have to wait until Ana came to town again to retrieve her new bridge.

She began telling him, an amiable stranger, interesting things about the Change community, including that Dulcie was with her today because the child's big brother was away for a couple of days. He could tell from the faces of both of his table companions that there was more to it than that, but he did not give vent to his questions. Ana looked relieved. Dulcie went back to her pictures.

Glen studied Ana over his coffee cup. She looked as banged-about as he had expected, having had Rayne Steinberg's report of all that had happened at the Heard Museum. Her hand was ugly and obviously giving her pain, but he had seen her in worse shape. She would recover.

Only at the very end of the meal did he manage to have an unobserved minute with Ana, when Dulcie was in using the toilet.

"Are you bugging the phones?" Ana asked him as soon as Dulcie was safely on the other side of the door.

"We just started. The branch in Japan is acting strangely and there's an uproar brewing in England over their kids, with Social Services sticking their noses in and Change resenting it. I thought the combination justified a greater degree of concern, and I found a judge here who agreed with me, that the presence of children made it urgent enough to justify a tap." One bleak consolation after the Waco affair, Glen reflected, was the way the name made judges want to reach for their pens. "What's this about alchemy?"

"It's too complicated to go into now. Did you get me the books?"

"I planted them in the used-book store, just down the street. Pick them up when you leave. Look, are you all right?"

"I'm fine. A little sore, that's all."

"I meant . . . you're sure?" Truth to tell, Glen thought, she did look fine beneath the bruises, healthy and strong and considerably more alive than she usually did when she was immersed in one of these operations. Change obviously agreed with her. Which was, somehow, worrying. Still, there was no time to dig into it now, because the door to the ladies' room was opening. "And there's the young lady now. Dulcie, it was a real treat to meet you, and I hope I come across you again someday. Good-bye, and good-bye, friend Ana."

He waved and strode out whistling, Agent Glen Mc-Carthy in his full Uncle Abner mode, the talkative, ever-genial Southerner. Ana suppressed a smile and looked down at Dulcie. "I've got another idea that might be an even bigger treat for you than ice cream," she said.

It turned out Dulcie liked bookstores just as much as she liked ice cream, and while Ana searched out the books on alchemy that Glen had arranged there for her, Dulcie studied the riches of the children's corner, where she chose the three books Ana had said she could have, and then a fourth one, asking tentatively, "For Jason?"

Ana laughed and said she could have four, and she

put them with her own three choices (Glen had left six or seven, but these were closest to what she wanted) and paid for them with her virginal credit card. It was accepted without hesitation. As she was picking up the bag, a thought occurred to her.

"Do you by any chance have a copy of *The Hunting of the Snark* by Lewis Carroll?"

"Let me see," said the cheery young woman. She went to the shelves and returned with a copy of *Alice*. "This is all we have at the moment."

"Can you order me one?"

"Picture book or text?" she asked, already calling up the title on her computer.

"Picture would be nice, if there is one." Ana glanced at Dulcie, who was immersed in a book and not paying any attention to the conversation. "And hardback, if there's a choice."

"I can have it day after tomorrow."

"Great," said Ana, and told her she'd be in on Monday.

Back in Rocinante's passenger seat, Dulcie buried her nose in her picture books, spelling out words for Ana to translate, until the light failed and she had to put them away. She fell asleep, and did not even stir when Ana stopped the bus to retrieve a thick blanket from the back to wrap around her. Ana drove on with the window open, battering herself with fresh air to keep the weariness at bay. The child was still asleep when they bumped into the compound parking lot, but she woke and gathered up her books to carry them to Ana's room.

They were halfway to the central buildings when Dulcie gave a loud cry, let her precious books fall to the ground, and flew into Jason's embrace. The boy wrapped his arms around his sister and buried his face in her hair, clinging to the child as if she were the last living thing on earth.

CHAPTER 19

From the journal of Anne Waverly (aka Ana Wakefield)

Ana slept very well that night. At dawn she continued her habit and, putting one of the books she had bought the day before into her pocket, she climbed the red rocks and watched the sun come up over the compound.

Steven did not turn up.

She went down to breakfast and read the book while she carefully chewed her cut-rate cornflakes, banana, and yogurt. No one commented on it, although she was certain that at least two of the higher initiates saw it. Both of them glanced at her quickly and then moved away.

She conducted her classes, talked about the essays the students were writing about the museum, reviewed for a test she was giving the next week, and handed back the essays they had already done. During lunch and while she was in class she left the book on her desk, its title facing up for all to see, but Steven did not come to see her, and no one seemed to take notice of the topic.

Saturday morning came and went atop the red rocks, and Steven did not approach her, and the day passed as Saturdays did around Change, with hard physical work that included the schoolchildren and a night of relaxation, with basketball and communal music in the dining hall.

Sunday morning came, and Steven was there at the red rocks when she arrived, watching the light creep over the compound and, she knew, waiting for her. She smiled a very quiet smile, put the book down next to her knee, crossed her legs, and surrendered herself to the moment.

The sun rose and grew in warmth, and half an hour later, Steven was the first to stir. "Your hand is healing," he said, his eyes still closed, his face raised to the sun. It was not a question, but a statement from an all-knowing observer of human frailty.

"It's much better, thank you."

"You have some interesting reading material, Ana Wakefield." His eyes were still shut.

"This?" She stretched out her legs and picked up the battered volume, which looked as if Glen had rescued it from a Dumpster before selling it to the woman in Vortex Books for fifty cents. The inside was in better condition and, to her relief, had barely been written in by the previous owner: Volume 12 of the collected works of Carl Jung, a group of related essays entitled *Psychology and Alchemy*.

"Have you read any of Jung's writings?" she asked him innocently, very sure that he had.

He stirred, and she felt him looking at her. "Some of them."

"Well, I was thinking about the things you were talking about the other day before meditation, about the need for pressure in striving for personal transformation. Somewhere Jung says something along the lines of enlightenment being found at the point of greatest stress. That got me thinking about Jungian psychology in general and the goal of transformation, and I remembered that he wrote a couple of things about the symbolism of alchemy as a paradigm for change. When I was in Sedona the day before yesterday I found this book of essays in the used-book store. I'll have to see if I can hunt down the other ones." She stopped leafing through the book and made herself meet his eyes, making absolutely certain that she gave him only the face of Ana Wakefield, earnest Seeker Ana with no challenge or knowledge or academic superiority in it. She was in luck, because the sun was rising behind her, and whatever it was he saw in her face, it was not Professor Anne Waverly.

"I have them. You may borrow them if you like," he said. "You might find Volume Fourteen of interest."

"That's the one with the Latin title, isn't it? *Mysterium Coniunctionis*? Am I right, then, in thinking that Change—the Change movement—incorporates some of the ideas and symbolic processes of the alchemical tradition?"

He said something under his breath.

"I'm sorry?" she said. He rose fluidly to his feet, although he had been twisted up on the hard, cold rock in full lotus position for at least an hour.

"It's time we were going," he said. She stood up, more slowly than he had, and when she looked around she saw his head disappearing down the hill. He descended the rough terrain with the ease of a cross-country runner, leaving her to pick her way among the rocks and bushes and wonder if she had heard him correctly, and if so, what he could have meant by "not just symbolic."

Rather to her surprise, he was waiting for her at the bottom of the hill, the very picture of a man in deep thought as he stood with head bent and hands clasped behind his back. She came to a halt, not before him as a suppliant would but next to him so he had to turn his shoulders as well as his head to shoot her his piercing glance.

"Ana," he pronounced, "a little knowledge is a dangerous thing."

She couldn't resist. " 'Learning,' " she said, and for the first time she saw Steven Change disconcerted. He blinked.

"I'm sorry?" he demanded, impatient at her apparent non sequitur.

" 'A little learning is a dangerous thing; Drink deep,

or taste not the Pierian spring: There shallow draughts intoxicate the brain, And drinking largely sobers us again.' That is," she added, "supposing you were referring to Alexander Pope. It's a common misquotation, and granted it's a subtle distinction, but as an English teacher, I feel obligated to be pedantic."

God, she thought, in a minute I'll be waving my cane and calling him a young whippersnapper. "I admit, though, that I've often wondered what a Pierian spring is." Actually, she knew quite well what the words referred to: An area in Macedonia where the Muses were worshiped, it was used as a classical romanticization of learning. Steven did not seem to know this, however, and merely allowed his ruffled feathers to be smoothed by her disarming admission.

"In either case, having an insufficient command of a path of learning can be hazardous," he said firmly, and began to walk again. She fell in at his side.

"A person has to begin somewhere," she protested.

"Very true. And in some cases, personal exploration that allows for random discoveries and spontaneous growth is for the best." He paused, choosing his words carefully—or perhaps considering how much to tell her. "However, with the ideas that lie at the heart of Change, such unguided stumblings are more likely to result in disaster than in enlightenment. There are immense forces at work here; a misstep can be very dangerous, for you personally and for those around you."

Ana looked at the unrevealing side of his face, wondering uneasily if that had been a threat. She reached across with her right hand and laid it on his arm, stopping him and causing him to face her. No, there was no explicit threat in his eyes that she could see, just great seriousness. There was nothing to do but grab the ball and run, and see where it took her.

"Are you telling me that you are doing alchemy

here?" she asked bluntly, an unfeigned edge of incredulity in her voice. "Is that what you're saying? That I mustn't mess around in things I don't understand because I could, in effect, blow up the laboratory?"

He stood for a long time studying her. Finally he said, "Yes, I am."

"But—you're not talking about real alchemy," she said. "Not furnaces and alembics and actual gold."

"The Philosopher's Stone," he said reverently. He put his hand up to his collar and reached inside for the sturdy gold chain he wore and pulled at it. Up came the chain, and on the end of it a gleaming drop of pure soft gold about the size of a small marble, an uneven shape smoothed by years of wear under his clothing.

She reached out a finger to touch it and drew back. "You mean—"

"I created this, under the guidance of my own teacher. Three of us here have transformed lead into gold, and twelve have transmuted silver."

Ana sat down abruptly on a convenient boulder. She did not have to feign astonishment; the man clearly believed. If she was any judge of charlatans at all, this man, this trained scientist, truly believed that he and who knows how many others had actually changed the atomic structure of one metal into another. Nothing metaphorical about it; "not just symbolic," indeed. A phrase from the other book she had been reading came vividly to mind: "The Middle Ages did not have a monopoly on credulity." She did not think Steven would care much for that quote.

Suddenly, all the oddities she had noticed about the upper echelon of Change fell into place: the calloused hands and hard muscles on men and women who rarely worked out-of-doors; Suellen's day-long absence, to reappear exhausted, famished, and glowing with an inner light; the small burn on her arm, very like Amelia's large and oddly placed scar, more easily explained by nearness to an open flame than to a cookstove. Alchemy was hard labor around hot flame—and glass: The tiny scars on David Carteret's face could easily have come from an exploding glass vessel.

She drew in a breath and blew it out between puffed cheeks. "Wow."

"Alchemy has been a secret doctrine for millennia, precisely because of the value of this." Steven dropped into a squat in front of her and held out the pendant, letting it swing back and forth in the gesture of a stage hypnotist before he caught it up and tucked it back under his collar. "Alchemists who created gold were doing so as a by-product and an objectification of the internal transformation they were undergoing, but the gold was nonetheless there. That's why they welcomed and encouraged the skepticism, even ridicule, of the outside world—it kept them safer.

"But even without the external threat from greedy men, Ana, alchemy has always been a dangerous occupation. Explosions in laboratories were common when chemicals were heated carelessly. Impatience, Ana. Impatience is the killer of the would-be alchemist. You have it in you to do a great Work, Ana; I can feel it. But you must submit to guidance. You have to work slowly, or it will all blow up in your face."

There was the threat again, but still she did not feel any malice behind it. Instead, Steven gave her a smile of great sweetness and wisdom, and then rose and walked away. She watched him go, watched him shrink into the distance and finally leave the road and disappear behind a building. Then she herself rose, turned, and walked out into the desert.

•   •   •   •

She was gone for seven hours, long enough for people to notice her absence and approach Steven about it. She walked out into the scrub, down into the dry wash and out again before she turned up to the hills that lay a few miles off, and there she sat and thought and came to some uneasy decisions.

Ana rarely outstepped the bounds of her role during the course of her investigations. Her success in her investigations depended on blending in, on being who she appeared to be and acting strictly as that person was expected to act, at all times, until she even thought as that person would. Her means of gathering information was more along the lines of passive receptivity than picking locks in the dead of night. Not only did illicit snooping scare her shitless, it was too dangerous to her investigation. From the very beginning, Glen positively forbade it (even as he taught her the rudimentary skills) not only because it was a threat both to her personally and to the continuation of the case, but because anything she discovered was apt to be contaminated or otherwise rendered useless as evidence: The FBI took its rules of evidence very seriously indeed.

However, this case didn't seem to be going like any of the others, and Ana did not know what to make of that. Anne Waverly kept intruding into her thought processes at the most inconvenient times, and this seemed to be one of them: Anne badly wanted to know what was behind Change.

During the course of that long day in the dry hills, Ana gradually shed her reluctance. She needed to know what Steven had up his sleeve; she somehow had to shortcut the lengthy initiation process involved in any esoteric teaching; she itched to see what he was hiding; but mostly she wanted to convince herself that Steven did actually believe that he had made gold, and was not using the pendant he wore as a subtle joke along the lines of the claim he had made to levitate up the red-rock viewing platform.

Also, she admitted to the flock of small gray birds that had settled around her, Steven's superiority grated on her. Ana liked to win as much as the next person, and during these investigations it pleased her, tickled some deep part of her nature, to know that she held the upper hand—even if her opponent never found out about it and the only person to appreciate her was Glen. Steven was a prig and it would be a pleasure to undermine him; that alone would be justification enough.

Most important, though, was the niggling suspicion that there was something funny about Change. She caught the thought and it made her laugh aloud, startling a small desert iguana that had settled down near her boot. Come on, Ana: What could possibly be funny about a community whose belief system was based on the manipulation of atomic structure to transmute material? Sure, medieval alchemists had believed in the possibility of creating gold from lead, but they had no means of testing, no analytical apparatus capable of distinguishing true gold from sulfurous mercury. To find seventeenth-century ideas coexisting with silicon chips, electron microscopes, and the robotic exploration of Mars said a great deal about man's deep need to believe that he had some control over his environment. Witchcraft, magic, and alchemy. No funnier than a belief in a personal God, was it?

Still, there was something she didn't understand yet about Change, some group dynamic she didn't have her finger on. Something told her that it was represented by Steven's necklace. Something also told her that she would not find out by simply waiting to be told.

She got to her feet and slapped the dust from her rear end. She wanted to know what was literally underlying the Change community, and tonight she would see if she could find out. Nothing dramatic, no blackened face and silken rappelling rope, just some judicious nosing about where she was not supposed to be. Ana Wakefield, after all, seemed to be the kind of pushy female who might well do that. If she was caught—well, she would tell them that she was nosy. Steven would believe that.

But she would try very hard not to be caught.

When she got back to the compound, she went straight to her room, where she drank about half a gallon of water and stood under the shower for twenty minutes, feeling like one of those desert plants that unfurl from a state of desiccated hibernation with the rains. It was stupid to go out in the desert without water. A few weeks later in the year the consequences might have been serious, but the day had been cool and overcast and she emerged from the shower only slightly sunburned and a little trembly.

She put on clean clothes and went over to the dining hall, making straight for the serving line, where she filled a plate, put two large glasses of fruit juice onto her tray, and got to work on it. She did not look up from her dinner until half of the food was inside her, when she paused for a breath and a long drink of juice. She glanced distractedly around the room over the rim of the glass, still more interested in nourishment than in her surroundings, but she put the empty glass down slowly, and when she resumed her fork, she did so with the air of a person who is not really tasting her food.

At first she thought that her conversation with Steven had made the rounds and her precipitous introduction to the community's secrets had set her apart. When she caught two of the members who wore silver chains around their necks staring at her, only to have them shift their eyes and pointedly resume their conversations, she felt certain of it.

However, the other twenty or so other early diners neither wore necklaces nor seemed to find her worthy of attention, yet they, too, seemed subdued, even troubled. She appeared to be the only person in the room with an appetite.

She finished her food and cleared her dishes, but instead of leaving them in the trays she took them on through the swinging doors and into the kitchen. Suellen and another woman were there, already up to their elbows in soapsuds, and Amelia (who shot her the same speculative look that she had received from the two initiates outside) was spooning the last of the food into the stainless steel warming trays. Ana put her plate among the stack on Suellen's right, and then reached for a single rubber glove to help out, pulling it onto her good hand with her teeth.

"Man," she said, "it's so quiet out there, I thought I was too late for supper. Did something happen?"

"You didn't hear?" Suellen asked.

"I was gone most of the day."

"Some of the children in England have been taken away." Her voice was both genuinely troubled and secretly cherishing being the bearer of bad news, which Ana had counted on.

"Taken away?" Ana exclaimed. "Do you mean they've been kidnapped?"

"By the government."

"What?"

"What Suellen means," said Amelia's disapproving English accent from behind them, "is that Social Services has got involved in a custody dispute between one of the members and her ex-husband and has temporarily removed the two children while the accusations of the fa-

ther are being investigated. It has happened before."
And, her voice clearly said, it would happen again.

"Still," said Ana, "it sounds unpleasant for the
mother."

"Unpleasant, yes, but hardly the end of the world,"
Amelia said repressively.

They had to wait until Amelia left the kitchen, but
when she did, Suellen was happy to fill Ana in. The chief
trouble, it appeared, came about because although the
mother was British, the father who was trying to pry his
children free from the hold of the "cult" was an American. The dual citizenship of the boy and girl confused
matters no end and, being a disgruntled ex-member of
Change himself, the father was more than willing to
drag in every authority he could, from Social Services
and the American embassy to the tabloids. Not, Ana
agreed, a pretty picture, but she had to agree with
Amelia that it would probably quiet down in a few days,
particularly if the British authorities had the sense to play
it low key.

She worked one-handed alongside the other two
women, carrying in plates and wiping surfaces until they
had finished the heaps of pans, and then she fixed herself
a cup of tea (one of the perks of working in the kitchen)
and went to use the toilet before the evening meditation.

Steven began his talk by mentioning the situation in
England. He sounded untroubled, though, and his attitude proved contagious. The chant was a poetic image if
an awkward phrase: "Boiling water, peaceful clouds."
When meditation was over, Ana slipped away and went
to her room, and there to bed.

Setting the tiny alarm on her wristwatch for 2:00 A.M.

CHAPTER 20

We Were All Once Cultists

Anne M. Waverly

Duncan Point University

All religions were once new, and all established religious were once a brash hodgepodge of ideas and images snatched and cobbled together in an attempt to put revelation into words. The prophet Mohammed built his house on the foundations of The Book, using bricks made of his own native soil; Jesus the Messiah was a believing Jew with a new vision of man's relationship with God; Judaism itself bears clear imprint of the people who worshipped in the land before they came, the psalms and images of Canaanite gods, even to the very shape of its Temple.

Archaeologists glory in (and despair over) the immutability of stone and the thrifty habits of one generation of builders to make use of the decrepit structures of previous generations in building anew: Gravestones are turned into paving stones, inscribed triumphs reversed to become part of a blank wall, and Roman markers tumble out of a medieval wall under demolition. Theological historians take equal joy in the discoveries of one tradition taken up and used by another: a theophanic hymn to Yahweh that preserves the cadence of a song dedicated to the storm-god Baal; a set of characteristics-- beard, tent, age, wisdom--that speak of the authority of the God of the Israelites which are also seen in the physical description of the Canaanite El; the Gilgamesh story and certain mythic elements in the Old Testament stories

From "We Were All Once Cultists" by Anne M. Waverly, in *Modern Religious Expression,* ed. Antony Makepeace, University of California Press, 1989

The outside lights were shut down at midnight, except those along the road between the gate and the parking lot and one hanging from the front of the barn, the purpose of which Ana had not been able to figure out. The halls of the buildings remained lighted, but anyone who needed to negotiate the paths after that time was expected to use one of the wild assortment of flashlights that were kept near the outer doors.

Ana took her own, pencil-sized flashlight with her as she let herself out of the sleeping building.

She ducked into the shadows away from the door to allow her eyes to adjust to the darkness. The night was clear and cold—not as cold as when she had first come to Change a month ago, but still with the crisp, dry temperature drop of the desert. A waning moon lay near the surrounding hills, casting enough light to give shape to the buildings now that her eyes were adapting, and enabling her side vision to pick out the white stones that edged the walkways. The sky was black from one horizon to the other with no city lights to dilute the hard brightness of the stars. In the distance, coyotes were chattering their eerie call at the moon, and one of the bats that lived among the eaves of the barn darted overhead.

Other than that, there was no sound, no movement.

Ana was wearing the thick Ecuadorian socks she had bought that first day in Sedona, which had the combined virtues of complete silence on the gravel and the innocent evocation of someone who couldn't be bothered to put on her boots just for a brief nocturnal stroll. She also wore the dark blue sweatpants and sweatshirt she habitually slept in, and her hair was uncombed from the pillow.

The small flashlight in the pocket of her sweats was a natural thing for anyone to take on a restless-night excursion, and she carried nothing else except one crumpled tissue.

She stepped away from the dormitory and onto the path, winced as her heel came down on a sharp rock, then walked quickly across to the hub building. The austere planting of cactuses and shrubs looked alarmingly like men standing by the path. The boojum tree loomed large and pale, although she was expecting it, and it took some effort not to turn and check on the still figures as she went past them.

Inside the building, she scurried across the dimly lit foyer, feeling as exposed as a rabbit in headlights, and went through both sets of swinging doors into the meditation hall. There she paused, catching her breath. The room was pitch-black, with only the faintest light coming from right up at the top, where the moonlight on the translucent dome showed as a vague glow. She stood listening for a couple of minutes, and nearly leapt out of her skin when a small rustle and crackle came out of the dark not twenty feet away. Dry-mouthed and with pounding heart, she strained to hear, and when it came again she nearly laughed aloud in relief: It was the last coals in the suspended fireplace, collapsing in on themselves. She snapped on the flashlight, playing it around and above to confirm that she was alone, and then went forward to investigate.

The night she had come here looking for Jason she had approached the great central stem of the structure that supported the fireplace and Steven's platform. She had pounded on it with her fist in anger, hoping for a loud echo to jolt Steven from his trance, but the dull thud it gave indicated a heavy degree of insulation inside the pipe. What she had only dimly noted at the time, but which had returned to niggle at her, was that despite the insulation, the pipe had felt warm.

The fireplace above it could conceivably have sent its heat down along the base. It was, in fact, the most logical explanation. However, Ana had seen the original plans for this structure, submitted to the county planning department, and she was quite certain that there had been a partial basement included in the drawings. Heat could travel down from an overhead fire, yes, but heat more naturally traveled upward. Was there just a central heating boiler down beneath the meditation hall? Or was there something else?

An alchemical laboratory, perhaps?

Ana left the meditation hall and went back through the main foyer and into the school offices. She had been around the school long enough to know the handful of places where a door to the basement might be hidden. It was not in any of them: not in the back of the storage closet in Teresa's office, not in the men's rest room, not in the cluttered depths of the janitorial closet. She rather doubted that the entrance would involve ripping up the carpeting or rotating an entire wall with a secret switch, but she found herself pushing at the spines of the books on Teresa's shelves, just in case the switch was hidden there. She made herself stop that pointless exercise: It was nearly three o'clock, and Change, with its combination of rural demands and long-distance workers, began to stir by five. She had no time to waste, and it did not seem that the entrance was here.

That left either the meditation hall or upstairs, and she had no wish to venture up among the sleeping authorities. She went back out to the school entranceway and from there into the great circular hall, and stood playing the beam of her light over the walls, thinking hard. After a minute, she started to climb the platforms up the side of the hall. At first she looked closely at the walls, but then she stopped that and just climbed straight for the top, to the single seat that was higher than Steven's, the platform she had never seen occupied. And there it was, a narrow rectangle built into the wall and concealed by the dim lighting, the wall hangings, and the reluctance of the Change members to venture beyond their proper places.

It was locked, but before climbing down to retrieve the key ring Teresa kept in her desk, Ana looked around for the equivalent of the key-under-the-doormat, and she found one, under Steven's thick meditation pillow on the next step down. She used it to unlock the door, then put the key back where she had found it and pushed the door open.

If it was dark in the meditation hall, the doorway was a black pit. She gingerly stepped inside, pulled the door shut, and switched on her flashlight. The steps were slightly tapered, narrower at the inner side to fit into the circular wall, but otherwise even and perfectly sound. They continued on, featureless, past the place where she estimated the floor of the hall lay, a gentle spiral leading into the depths. There were lights, but she stuck to the flashlight—no telling what else the light switch would turn on.

The stairway ended at another narrow wooden door, this one unlocked. She nudged it open, and stepped into a medieval laboratory into which a computer had been dropped.

The room seemed to be the same shape and size as the meditation hall overhead, but it seemed smaller because the ceiling was so low: If Steven were to give an uncharacteristic leap of enthusiasm down here, he would brain himself on the rough beams. The room was strewn with worktables and cluttered with equipment that ranged from shiny new glass beakers to crude redbrick furnaces with huge bellows leaning against their sides, but at the moment what took Ana's attention was the object at the precise center of the circle and hence directly below the black pipe that rose out of the hall floor.

It was a shiny, pear-shaped, potbellied . . . *thing* nearly the height of the room and perhaps six feet across its thickest part, made of some shiny metal like stainless steel or polished aluminum. Its smooth sides were punctuated by six large oval designs that did not quite meet, looking vaguely like seams. She examined the thing closely and decided that whereas five of the circles were indeed laid-on welding, the sixth one was meant to give way: There was a small, sturdy latch on the right-hand side.

She pulled the Kleenex out of her pocket and, using it to keep her fingerprints from the shiny surface, wiggled the latch until it gave. The door drifted inward. She leaned inside and saw the same ovals repeated there. A large circular pad took up the middle of the object's nearly flat bottom, but as far as Ana could see, there was no source of light.

She bent over to thread herself through the door, and straightened up inside. "Ommm," she tried softly, and the noise hummed and echoed around her. She smiled. This was, she guessed, a variation on the sensory deprivation tanks so popular with the human potential movement, although she had never before seen one that didn't use warm salty water to induce the hypnotic feedback of the mind denied external stimuli. She had spent any number of hours in such tanks, finding them slightly claustrophobic but immensely restful.

She climbed back out, refastened the latch, and made a circle of the room.

Evenly spaced around the silver tank were the six small redbrick kilns or fireplaces. Their flues joined together in a six-pointed star just at the pear-shaped thing's top—the source, no doubt, of the heat she had felt com-

ing from the pipe the night Jason was missing. Next out
from the furnaces were three long, battered work-
benches, each with two workstations and situated so a
person could move easily between bench and furnace.
The benches were strewn with the ancient tools of a
metallurgist or chemist: alembics, yes, as well as retorts
and scales with weights ranging from the minute to the
massive, mortars and pestles of various sizes and composition, scoops and pipettes, funnels and mallets, long-
handled pincers and galvanized buckets, heavy gloves
with high gauntlet tops, and an assortment of jewelers'
loupes, hammers, and tweezers. Actually, she realized,
she had seen something very like it before, somewhere in
Europe—Heidelberg, was it? Or Köln?—where an alchemical laboratory had been re-created for the benefit of
the tourists.

One section of wall had a bookshelf, sagging under
the weight of numerous thick volumes. Some of them
were merely bound photocopies of books attributed to
"Hermes Trismegistus," "Miriam the Jewess," and other
well-known alchemical authorities. Other volumes were
ancient leather-bound tomes that looked original. Ana
winced to think what someone had paid for them, only
to have them stored in a dusty environment where the
only climate control was in six coal-burning fireplaces.

And then there was the computer. Ana's hands itched
for it, but it was not a kind she knew well and she
doubted that on a strange machine she would be able to
hide her footsteps, were anyone to wonder if unauthorized persons had been perusing its electronic innards.
Reluctantly, for the time being, she left it alone.

Beyond the bookshelves were supply cabinets with
jars and canisters, all labeled. Ana had not done any
chemistry since high school, but she could identify that
the vials of mercury and the jars of sulfur were what
they said, and the blue packages of ordinary table salt,

looking peculiarly homely and out of place, still bore their factory seals. She didn't know what antimony, salt-peter, or half a dozen other labeled substances ought to look like, but she could think of no real reason to doubt that they were what they said. A large bowl contained an incongruous heap of dried half-eggshells; a topless shoebox sagged out under the burden of twenty or so large lead fishing weights; and six small stoppered test tubes held granules of what appeared to be silver.

She searched the back of each shelf with her light, careful to move nothing. Everything was dusty, the dis-used substances at the back more so, until she got to her knees to check the contents of the very bottom shelf, and noticed a small box, nearly hidden behind some stone-ware mortars, that seemed remarkably dust free. Taking note of its precise location, she reached in and eased it out. It was a grocer's package of ordinary blocks of par-affin wax.

She ran a thumb thoughtfully over the cool, slightly greasy surface of the wax block, struck by the combina-tion of pushed-to-the-back abandonment and its cleanli-ness. After a minute, she began to smile.

A useful substance, wax. Children made strange, amoeba-shaped candles on the beach with it and handymen rubbed it onto sticking drawers. Ana's mother used to pour a thick layer of melted wax onto the top of her jams and jellies, and Ana could recall the childhood magic of pushing down on the round wax plug and having the other side rise up to reveal the sweet preserves underneath. Wax was useful, too, in molding itself around a shape, in providing weight and bulk to a hollow core—or, conversely, in obscuring whatever it surrounded.

She bent down and carefully put the box back into its original place. One of the commoner tricks of the al-chemical charlatan, according to one of Glen's books, was to soften a lump of dirty gray wax and wrap it around a piece of gold. When the resulting "lead" was heated in its glass alembic, the wax burned away as black smoke, miraculously revealing a puddle of pure gold.

The word "sincere" literally translates "without wax," Ana mused, brushing the dust from the knees of her sweats. Unadulterated. Pure. The presence of *cere* in this laboratory was very interesting.

Although she would have sworn that Steven truly believed that he himself had actually created gold.

She glanced at her watch: nearly four A.M., and time to leave. She walked a last time around the man-sized alembic in the center of the room, and suddenly knew where she'd seen the shape before: as an aura, surrounding a meditating figure at the end of the TRANSFORMATION mural in the dining hall.

She closed the laboratory door behind her and hurried up the steps. At the top she paused to catch her breath, and then cautiously pulled the door open. The hall was still dark; her straining ears could make out no noise. She stepped out onto the platform, closed the door, and stood rigid for a long time before she was satisfied that the hall was empty but for her. She switched on her flashlight, retrieved the key, and used it to lock the door, then replaced it just as she had found it, tugging the corners of the pillow to straighten the cover. She retreated down the platforms to the shadowy floor and out of the first set of doors into the hall's small foyer, and was just reaching out to push open the doors to the school entranceway, when she heard voices. She snatched back her hand and turned to leap back into the hall before she caught herself: To be caught in a panicky retreat would be the worst possible thing. She lived here at Change, and if she felt like meditating at four in the morning, so what?

Still, she couldn't quite bring herself to walk brazenly

out to the voices, and in the end it was just as well that she did not, because the two men—it was Steven, his low voice shockingly loud as he came into the entranceway—did not enter the hall. Instead, his voice faded in the direction of the school offices, saying, "I'll go make the call; you see if you can find some milk in the kitchen."

There was a swishing noise as the office door shut; it was followed by the distinctive click of the main entrance. Ana pulled her own door open a fraction of an inch, fully expecting the two men to be standing there ready to pounce, and looked out onto emptiness. She counted out thirty seconds, which was about seventy heartbeats, and pulled the door open all the way. She walked briskly through the hallway and slipped out into the cold night air.

CHAPTER 21

From the journal of Anne Waverly (aka Ana Wakefield)

A few hours later Ana staggered out of bed and drove again to Sedona to pick up her new bridge. Two different people threatened to come with her, but she managed to put them off by simply offering to do their tasks for them. The solitude within Rocinante's thin walls combined with sleeplessness and the exhilarating feeling of Having Gotten Away With It was a heady mix; she spent most of the trip down singing old rock-and-roll songs and grinning widely at the passing cactus.

The intoxication lasted through the dental visit. The new bridge settled into the front of her mouth as neatly as the old one had, restoring a sense of security to her face. She smiled at the dentist, the nurse, and at everyone she passed on her way back to Rocinante, where she found not Glen, but a tourist brochure for the Chapel of the Holy Cross tucked under the windshield wiper. None of the neighboring cars bore them. She folded it into her pocket and went on to the post office, where she collected two imaginary bills forwarded by her Boise mail service and the heavy parcel she had agreed to fetch. She left the parcel in the bus and walked a few doors down to a stationer's shop to buy the supplies she had been asked to get, and incidentally to copy the recent diary entries on the shop's photocopier. They did not, of course, contain the details of the previous night's excursions, but they gave in great detail her conversations with Steven.

After all that busywork, the day's bubble began to go a bit flat. She was aware of being very low on sleep, and her hand ached, particularly as the day was turning cold. Still, she was alive and free, and was about to have a

conversation with Glen that might help her make sense
of the situation. Euphoria faded, inevitably, but she remained what in her long-skirted youth had been called
"mellow."

She drove out of town on the Phoenix road, past the
pseudo-Mexican shopping center that contributed mightily to the Sedona tax base and through an area of carefully scattered homes and looming rock buttes to the
turnoff to the chapel, and found it as she remembered, a
blunt, angular block of glass and concrete that some
woman had commissioned to be jabbed down among the
lifting, organic shapes of the rock, back in the days before planning commissions.

There were half a dozen cars parked in the marked
area and tourists wandering up and down the steep hill.
Ana joined them (feeling tired now, and distinctly under-
dressed without a camera) and pulled open the heavy door
of the chapel. Inside, she found Glen disguised as a tourist,
complete with video recorder and even a wife in the shape
of Agent Steinberg, whom Ana had last seen leaving the
museum rest room in Phoenix.

Ana sat down in the pew behind them and waited for
two elderly women making the rounds to struggle their
way out the door.

"Hello, Glen," she said over the back of the pew.
"You look like a real snowbird, down from Nebraska for
the winter."

He shifted sideways and gave her a lopsided grin that
went with the image. He didn't have a cowlick but he
looked as if he did, and Ana was briefly visited by the
memory of Antony Makepeace's disparaging remarks
concerning Glen's undercover abilities. "Howdy,
ma'am," he said. "You know Agent Steinberg. My right-
hand woman."

"We met. Do you have a first name?" she asked the
woman.

"Rayne."

"Originally Rainbow?" Ana ventured.

Agent Steinberg actually blushed, an endearingly human reaction that caused Ana to wonder how far the woman would get in the Bureau. She was about the same age that Abby would have been, and for a moment Ana played with the amusing idea that one of the many hippie babies she had known named Rainbow might have become this young woman. "Never mind," she told her. "None of us is responsible for our parents. Anything new from your end, Glen? You heard from Gillian, or that Dooley woman in Toronto?"

"Gillian has nothing new to offer—she's got a loaded desk at the moment and has put the Change case on the back of it. And the Toronto situation is . . . frustrating. The woman's community where she's supposed to be is bristling with lawyers and there's no way we can get a warrant to talk to her if she's not interested. Rayne went up last week to have a try, and they just told her that they have too many women hiding out from their abusive husbands to want the FBI poking their snouts in. I quote."

"Is that why Samantha Dooley is there? Is she in hiding? And if so, from whom?"

"Who knows? There's nothing on the books connected with her name, here, in Canada, or in the U.K. She just doesn't want to talk to us, and so far we haven't been able to find someone in the community who will. We'll keep trying, of course."

"Good luck. I, on the other hand, have had an interesting time." She took the photocopies out of her coat pocket and handed them over the back of the pew. "Why don't you two take a look at what I've written first? Save me going over it twice."

Glen turned his back to her and unfolded the sheets. Ana leaned back and closed her eyes. She should have had something to eat back in Sedona, she thought; it might have helped boost her blood sugar. She would stop off and get a large coffee before driving back, and buy something to eat then. Maybe that café next to the bookstore. Which reminded her, she had to pick up the Lewis Carroll book for Dulcie.

Pages rustled in front of her as Glen passed each one over to his assistant. The chapel was cold and a far cry from the old wooden building where she sometimes went with Antony Makepeace and his wife, Marla, for the Quaker services that passed for worship. Ana's own rather more complicated relationship with God was personal, both spiritual and intellectual, with little room for the formal and liturgical. However, this place was too cerebral even for her.

Glen finished reading. She heard him shift on the seat, imagined his elbow coming over the back of the pew, felt him looking at her, but she did not move. She had gone as lethargic as a snake in winter, and wondered idly if she looked as decrepit as she felt.

"Alchemy," Glen mused.

"'S a funny old world, ain't it?" she replied, and opened her eyes to find him looking at her worriedly.

"Are you really feeling okay?"

"Ah, Glen, it's a young woman's game. Time to give it over to young Rainbow, here."

Curious, she thought, how it was only during these odd moments in the course of an investigation that she actually liked Glen McCarthy. They smiled into each other's eyes in brief but perfect understanding, and then she pulled herself upright and leaned forward, speaking quietly.

"I'd swear that Steven truly believes he created gold, but I know he also uses trickery to make his initiates think they're doing the same thing, only with silver."

"Why do you say that?"

"I saw the strings and mirrors. Or in this case, the wax."

"Would you say he thinks he's encouraging lesser minds?" Glen wondered. "Or just stringing along the marks?"

"Maybe a little of each. But he himself believes it is possible, that he and others have actually made silver and gold. That's how I read him, anyway."

He looked down at his knee and nodded. Rayne tapped the photocopied pages straight and folded them, but did not look around. Ana felt the tug of dread pulling at the edges of her mind, and sighed. "Okay, Glen, what's going on? Why have you brought your assistant all the way out here instead of using the man I met in Prescott, and why are you bugging the phones? Is it this thing with the two children in England?"

"I don't know what the hell's going on in England. As you know, communication with foreign police departments isn't always what one might wish, and in England something like this falls into the spaces between departments even more than it does here. So far it's just the local Somerset police involved, and I don't have any personal contacts on that force." He shook his head. "No, the problem's in Japan. A kid in the Yokohama Change center died about three weeks ago. You probably don't want to know his name?"

"Not unless I have to."

"I don't think so. Anyway, we just found out about it on Monday and had the autopsy report faxed over and translated. They're treating it as a mugging—he was a mass of bruises, found dumped by the roadside."

Ana heard the emphasis on "they." "You don't agree that he was mugged."

"All the boy's bruises had diffuse edges—no sharp-edged marks such as you'd expect to find after someone was struck with, say, a bat or a board or kicked by a shoe. Most of the bruises were along the sides and back of his upper torso and head, with a concentration on his shoulders. He may have been naked when the injuries occurred, because there were no marks on the skin from fabric or seams or buttons. His legs were not bruised other than his hips and knees, but his feet were badly damaged—he had three broken bones in his left foot. No defense marks on his arms, but all the fingernails on both hands were broken and bloody. Actual cause of death was a cerebral hemorrhage caused by the blows to the head."

Ana did not hear the final sentence. The image of those destroyed fingernails, the clear picture she had of the Japanese boy clawing at something, kicking and throwing himself violently and repeatedly at some smooth, hard surface, rose up inside her and blotted all else out. All the blood in her body seemed to turn around and flow backward. She felt like vomiting, her head buzzed as if she were about to faint, and she stood up and stumbled rapidly away, unseeing, just to be moving.

She felt Glen's hand on her back, felt his solid presence by her side, and wanted either to turn to his arms for comfort or beat at him for putting her there. He was saying something in a low, urgent voice and she was looking through the window at the hills beyond the cross, and she shuddered.

"God. I've got to get out of here, Glen. I need air."

It was better outside, seated on a bench overlooking the world, with the clear desert breeze sweeping away the nausea and light-headedness and with Glen and Rayne standing between her and the curious tourists. Glen saw her begin to shiver and he took off his heavy jacket and wrapped it around her.

"I saw a death like that once," he said quietly. "A kidnap victim closed into a shipping crate. Differences, of course. What did Change lock that boy into?"

"I don't— He's— Oh Christ." Ana sat perfectly still for a long moment with her eyes clamped shut, and then sat up straight, took a deep, steadying breath, and, addressing herself to the red-rock cliffs, summoned the analytical words of Anne Waverly.

"As I told you, the doctrine of Change is based on alchemical beliefs concerning transmutation of substances into higher forms. Whether or not Change as a whole believes in the actual production of gold is still open to question, but in its metaphysical form—the transformation of human beings—it permeates the Change creed.

"The alchemist believes that a person can transform base matter using heat and pressure, as a means of speeding up the normal processes of nature. The matter being worked on is closed inside . . ." Ana gulped and started again. "Inside a hermetically sealed vessel. An alembic. It is heated on a furnace and, if the alchemist does it right, it passes through a defined series of stages to become gold or, alternatively, a tincture or 'Philosopher's Stone' which, added to a substance such as mercury or lead, changes it into gold.

"This paradigm of heat-generating transformation is used by Change to effect the transformation of the human spirit as well. Their mantras—meditational chants —often concern the benefits of heat and pressure. Psychological pressures are positively welcomed, on individuals and on the community as a whole. Members are taught to welcome intrusive outsiders, hard physical labor, unpleasant tasks. When I was hurt at the museum the other day, it was a direct result of Steven's instructions that two antagonistic boys be forced to spend the entire day in close proximity. When one of the boys, Jason Delgado, snapped and struck out—the other boy was insulting his sister. Dulcie. When Jason—" Ana stopped, her jaws clenched. In a minute she continued.

"When Jason lost control, Steven took him away for two days."

"That was when you came to town with Dulcie. What do you mean, 'took him away'?"

"I mean that early on the morning following the museum trip, Jason was removed from the room he shares with Dulcie. The men who led him off are two of Steven's closest associates. And Dulcie was told that Jason was 'helping Steven with his work.'"

"But he's back now? Unharmed?"

"He was returned during the day while Dulcie and I were here. I've barely seen him since then, but he looked . . ." How far could she expect Glen to understand? "Jason looked changed. Exhausted. Depleted. Fulfilled. I'd say he had some fairly profound experience.

"Glen, you remember those drawings that Gillian sent me? There was one of a child's nightmare, a man trapped—" She paused to swallow. "A man in what I took to be a giant pear or a raindrop, with two monsters outside. Glen, I think Change uses an alembic big enough for a man as part of their process of transformation. Steven called it 'the power nexus of our Change.' I think they shut people in there, an alchemical version of a sensory deprivation tank, as a means of applying pressure. I think the child's drawing is a textbook illustration of the hallucinations a person experiences under enforced, long-term sensory deprivation. Probably not the child's own experience, since the drawing was of a man with a beard, but possibly that of a father or friend who talked about it in the child's hearing, and frightened him. I think . . . I believe that Steven shut Jason into the alembic that's in the basement under the meditation hall, and I think there's a good possibility that the Japanese boy died in one just like it."

"Hell. Have you seen this thing?"

"Last night."

"Where did you say it was?"

"In a locked room underneath the meditation hall. You enter it by a door off the highest meditation platform."

"Damn it, Anne, what were you doing there?"

"I wanted to see if Steven had some kind of alchemical laboratory in the basement. That's what I found, a complete alchemical workshop out of the Middle Ages. Plus a box of paraffin wax. There's also a computer in there with a modem, in case any of your pet hackers want to play with it."

"You didn't open it up?"

"I didn't touch it."

"No sign of anything else in that lab?"

"No dismembered clocks or clippings of wire, no nice, labeled bins of Semtex, or even fuel oil and ammonium nitrate." Those two harmless ingredients when combined had proven spectacularly deadly. "No heaps of pretty little balloons or scatterings of mysterious white powder, no distinctive smells other than the sulfur, and the lab equipment I saw couldn't have been used to process any drug I know. Sorry—no bombs or drugs that I could see."

Glen stood up and looked out over the rocky valley for a minute, thinking. Four days ago Ana had struck him as being far more healthy-looking than he had expected to find her, and he had been unable to get that unnatural cheerfulness out of his mind. It had not been like her, and this sudden venture into derring-do was not like her either. Besides which, the vulnerability and emotional involvement sounded more like Anne than Ana; it was all very worrying.

"I don't like the sound of any of this, Anne," he said abruptly. "I'm pulling you out."

"My name is Ana, and it's gone too far for that, Glen," she said flatly. "The only way you can keep me from going back to Change is if you get out your hand-cuffs." She looked at him, and Rayne was amazed to see on her boss's face a thing that on anyone else's she would have called a blush. She dismissed the unlikely thought immediately.

Ana turned back to the landscape while Glen thought about this unexpected shift in authority. When he spoke again, it was in a voice gone dead with the realities of his profession. "Did you see any evidence that the boy Jason was locked into the thing against his will?"

"No."

"Would he or anyone you can think of be willing to testify?"

"No," said Ana. "No." God, she felt like moaning aloud at the thought of that beautiful, strong boy stuffed into a dark, smooth space with the door shut behind him, and here was Glen thinking about warrants and rules of evidence. She dropped her face into her hands and scrubbed at her skin, which felt thick and insensate. "Jesus, you're a cold son of a bitch. No, there's no justification for a raid. You could argue that Jason is too young legally to have given his permission, but I'm sure you'd find he would refuse to testify. Nothing's changed, except a boy in Japan is dead. I'll go back to watching and listening, and if I need anything, I'll develop problems with the tooth and make another appointment with the dentist." She felt so tired, and old, and sick. "Go away, Glen. Christ, go away before I throw up on your foot."

She tugged his coat away from her and held it out without raising her head. It was taken from her, and a hand rested briefly on her shoulder—Glen's hand or Rayne's, she could not tell—and then she was alone at the side of this sharp-edged concrete-and-glass building set down among the round red hills of Sedona. She leaned up against the side of the building, and in the darkness behind her eyelids she saw the dining hall mural, which held it all: The progress from the prime matter of the desert on the left to fully actualized human on the right, and in the middle, looking like an elongated version of a Native American bread oven, the power nexus, the instrument of the proclaimed transformation, an alembic. What she had taken for a symbolic journey was physical and literal, an actual vessel in which sensitive human beings were subjected to the pressure of their own undiluted minds.

Still, now she finally knew the shape of this community, the essence of belief that lay at its core. Knowing, she could watch over the two children; at least she could do that.

Ana opened her eyes, got to her feet, and trudged down the hill toward Rocinante.

CHAPTER 22

Section 44 Children Act 1989

The court	To be completed by the court
████████████	Date issued 21 May 199█
	Case number ████████████
The full name(s) of the child(ren)	Child(ren)'s number(s)
James Anthony Parker (age 11)	
Steven Parker (age 8)	
Sophia Louise Parker (age 6)	
Elias Arthur Parker (age 4)	

1 Description of the child(ren)

If a child's identity is not known, state details which will identify the child.
You may enclose a recent photograph of the child, which should be dated.

2 The grounds for the application

The grounds are

ANY APPLICANT

A ☑ that there is reasonable cause to believe that [this] [these] child[ren] [is] [are] likely to suffer significant harm if

    ☑ the child[ren] [is] [are] not removed to accommodation provided by or on behalf of this applicant

    or ☐ the child[ren] [does] [do] not remain in the place where [the child] [they] [is] [are] currently being accommodated.

LOCAL AUTHORITY APPLICANTS

B ☐ that enquiries are being made about the welfare of the child[ren] under Section 47(1)(b) of Children Act 1989 **and** those enquiries are being frustrated by access to the child[ren] being unreasonably refused to someone who is authorised to seek access **and** there is reasonable cause to believe that access to the child[ren] is required as a matter of urgency.

AUTHORISED PERSON APPLICANTS

C ☐ that there is reasonable cause to suspect that the child[ren] [is] [are] suffering, or [is] [are] likely to suffer, significant harm **and** enquiries are being made with respect to the welfare of the child[ren] **and** those enquiries are being frustrated by access to the child[ren] being unreasonably refused to someone who is authorised to seek access **and** there is reasonable cause to believe that access to the child[ren] is required as a matter of urgency.

C11(M) (11.94) Printed by Satellite Press Limited

Request for Child Emergency Assessment, signed May 14, 199_

It was difficult to return to Change. It was difficult that night, when she dozed off over the wheel and nearly overturned into a stand of cow-tongue cactus, but it was worse the next morning, when she had to force herself to walk to the dining hall, to eat breakfast, and to speak in her normal manner to Suellen and Dominique across the table from her. To her relief, Steven did not happen to cross her path, because she was not certain that she could conceal the violent agitation of her feelings about him that had been set off by the death in Yokohama—or by the image of Steven in meditation while below him Jason sweated and confronted his inner demons in the prison of the dark alembic.

Was it child abuse? Yes—but. But there was no sign of physical injury on the boy. And manipulation of belief is monstrously hard to prove compared with overt aggression or abuse. And even fourteen-year-olds have freedom of religion in this country. And despite any apprehension he might have felt when the two men came for him, Jason came out of the experience a willing participant.

Yes, but. Even at the moment when the truth of the alembic's purpose first struck her, she had known that a prosecution based on that alone would be futile and short-lived. Certainly if she informed the local Child Protective Services of what was happening with one of their charges, it would set Change on its ear, and might even lead to the end of the fostering program, but was the responsibility for that a price she wanted to pay? She loathed the idea of doing nothing, but she knew without question that if she were to stay on with this investigation, she had to accept that Steven had the right, not to lock Jason into the alembic, but to ask Jason to submit to it.

Still, she needed a day, or perhaps a bit more, to assume this attitude. She could sense Anne Waverly stirring in the back of her mind, wanting to step in, sweep aside Ana Wakefield's natural diffidence, and set things right. That would be disastrous, and she remained grateful as the day wore on that she did not meet Steven. She didn't even want to see Jason or Dulcie until her fury had a chance to subside.

Steven believed, she told herself time and again; therein lay the difference. She reminded herself of that until she nearly believed it, and thought that she might look at Steven again with equanimity.

She got through her teaching day, distracted but functioning, but as soon as school was out she fled for the solitude of the desert. This time she took a bottle of water and a wide-brimmed hat, and she sat among the rocks, listening to the wind blow.

Late in the afternoon, another human being entered the landscape in the form of a desert rat whom Ana had seen two or three times before, once close enough to exchange a brief greeting. He was a prospector of some sort, she supposed, since he carried with him a small rock pick and a canvas sack. Perhaps he was gathering arrowheads or small petroglyphs to sell to tourists and collectors. He looked, however, like any of the other desert creatures she had seen—dull, dusty, leathery, and intent on his own business—and seeing him working his way along the hillside a mile off was like watching any other wild creature going about its business, unaware of being observed.

It was restful, leaning up against some rocks in the shade of an ironwood tree and following the man's mysterious progress, his bendings and straightenings and the occasional long period when he stood, bent over something he had found, before either placing it in his sack or tossing it over his shoulder.

She could feel the tension ease from her body, the clamor in her head go quiet. She may even have slept briefly, or retreated into that inner place where there is no time, because she came out of her reverie to realize that the shadows across the dry wash were immensely long and the prospector was no longer there.

She stretched luxuriously and took a long drink of warm water, and then tentatively, as if touching a finger to a wound, she brought Steven to mind.

She still felt empty, but at some point in the last hours the feeling had changed slightly, turning from confusion and turmoil into a cool, focused determination, from bleakness to calm. The death of the Japanese boy might even have been an accident, she finally admitted, and his being dumped on the road the result of panic. Stupid, but human.

The desert had done its work. She would now be able to look Steven in the eye without flinching.

There was a new man at dinner.

In itself this was not unusual, but this was no visiting newcomer. On the contrary, he ate surrounded by a knot of high-ranking initiates, who hung on his words and gave all the signs of knowing him well. Ana had little doubt that the man wore a silver necklace beneath his shirt, if not a gold one.

"Who is that man?" she asked Dov over the warming tray of baked potatoes.

"That's Marc Bennett. He used to live here for a little while, taught science until Dennis came and then he went back to England. He's a close friend of Jonas—Jonas Seraph, the founder of the English community.

Sort of his right-hand man. An important man in Change, anyway."

"You'll be glad to have him back, then."

"Oh, Marc's not staying. It's just a short visit."

Ana moved to a nearby table and watched Dov return to the group around the newcomer. A short visit might mean recreation or family matters, or peripheral to some kind of business trip. It could also be the work of a courier.

Steven did not lead the meditation that night, which had happened only twice since Ana had been there. Instead, Thomas Mallory took the central position, stumbling and stuttering his way with even more awkwardness than he normally displayed in public speaking. Marc Bennett was seated at the highest level of the row of meditation platforms across the hall from Steven, who sat unmoving the entire time. The whole Change community left the meditation hall unsettled.

She spotted Steven the next morning, too, still looking distracted, even troubled. He was walking with his hands locked behind his back and his head bent. Mallory was following him at a distance, also looking upset. As she watched, a third figure appeared: Jason on his morning run. Steven's head came up and he thrust out a hand to beckon Jason over to him. They exchanged a few words, Steven clapped Jason on the shoulders, Jason resumed his run, and when Steven turned to watch him go, Ana's silent presence must have caught the corner of his eye. He swiveled to face her across half a mile of scrub and rock and stood intent for what seemed a very long time. Then he half raised his left hand in a gesture of greeting, or benediction, and continued his walk. She ignored Mallory's glare and set off in a different direction.

A high initiate, a close friend of one of the original four Change founders, arrives from England; Steven is troubled. Had Glen's phone taps been discovered, or even suspected? Or had Steven just then learned about the Japanese boy's death from this old Change member, sent to bring him news too sensitive to be overheard?

It fit all the circumstances, and Ana knew that she would have to get word to Glen of the possibility. The knowledge, even a strong suspicion, of official scrutiny would have powerful repercussions in the community; it was exactly the sort of paranoia trigger she dreaded. She reminded herself, too, that the general anxiety did not necessarily mean they feared her in particular, that she must take care not to be a victim of her own paranoia. That time in Utah she had given herself away, but those circumstances did not apply here. Change had a long way to go before its instability escalated into violence. This community was not about to turn on her.

She did not sleep well, but over breakfast she discovered that no one looked particularly rested, that all the adult faces revealed a heaviness and degree of preoccupation that she had not witnessed there before. Talking to the other members and listening carefully, though, she did not think they knew of a specific problem, simply that Steven, their center, was out of sorts, and therefore Change as a whole was unbalanced.

Rumors began to circulate. Steven was leaving Arizona. Steven was not leaving, he was ill; no, he had simply received bad news from his family. Steven and Marc Bennett had had a raging argument; Marc had slammed out furiously to return to England; Marc had not slammed out, he was scheduled to go back anyway.

Ana had the fact of the argument between the two men confirmed by Dominique, who overheard the raised voices if not the words, but she could find no truth in any of the other rumors except that Marc Bennett had left. The whole Change compound began to feel as if somewhere on the horizon a storm was stirring, making the inhabitants feel prickly and on edge.

So it was with great relief that after Ana's last class, when she was sitting at her desk doing paperwork and thinking that she ought to go by the kitchen and put in some time there chopping vegetables or at least setting out plates, she heard a light tapping noise at the door and looked up into Jason's face.

He looked as old as Glen, this kid of fourteen. "Jason, how are you?"

"Okay. How's the hand?"

In answer, she held it out and curled the fingers up until they touched the palm, then straightened them out again. The swelling was almost gone, the tenderness bearable unless she smacked it against something. She noticed that, half hidden by the doorjamb, his left arm cradled a basketball, and he was wearing sweats.

"Going to shoot a few baskets?"

"Yeah. It's warm enough now to use the outside court, so we don't have to quit every time people want to eat."

"Maybe I'll come down and watch for a while."

She wasn't sure, but she thought he looked pleased at the prospect. She doubted that was why he was there, but he seemed disinclined to say anything else, so she tried to bridge the gap by asking him, "How are you enjoying the mural? Has your teacher got you painting yet?"

She had thought it a harmless enough question, given the interest and talent that according to Carla he displayed, but she seemed to have hit it wrong again. She looked at his abruptly closed face, his eyes that had gone to study the corners of the room, and she sighed.

"I can't paint," he finally muttered.

"Maybe not, but that sketch of the quail on my coffee cup shows that you can certainly draw."

"I mean I can't. She won't let me."

"Your teacher? Why on earth not?"

"Steven thinks it's a good idea if I lay off drawing and stuff for a while. But it's okay, really. It's just a stupid mural, anyway."

"I beg your pardon," she retorted in mock resentment. "I'll have you know, the mural was my idea. Don't call it stupid." She laughed at his expression and waved away his embarrassed attempt at backtracking. "But look, Jason, let me get this straight: You like drawing?" He nodded. "You're good at it." A shrug, of course. "And you'd like to help on the mural but Steven said no." A convulsion of the shoulders and head that Ana took for a combined nod and shrug. "Did he tell you why?"

"Sacrifice." He looked at her and misread the expression on her face. "That's what he said."

"Not punishment?"

"He didn't say so."

Heat and pressure, and if a child with great potential and few outlets likes to draw, you take that away from him to increase the pressure. What was next: no basketball and a cancellation of all morning runs? And his only advocate another newcomer who was in no position to raise a stink. Dear God, what an impossible situation.

"Well," she said, "it seems like a massive waste to me. I know my classes could sure use some help in sketching things out—I'm actually the best artist in the bunch, heaven help us." Jason seemed relieved by her willingness to let the subject slide. "You going down to the courts now?" she asked. "I'll probably see you there."

"Okay. Look, I just wanted to say," he began abruptly, then stopped. "Um, I mean, the other day, I don't know why I told Dulcie to come to you. It wasn't your responsibility. It's just that, well, she likes you, and

I couldn't think of anyone else in a hurry. So, thanks for taking care of her. I hope she wasn't too much of a pain."

"I was happy to help, Jason. Dulcie's good people. But I hope," she added deliberately, "that it doesn't happen again for a while. She was very upset."

"I know," he said with a grimace. "She's having nightmares again. Look, I've got to go. They're waiting for me."

Nightmares, again? "Right. I'll come down in a bit."

She did not manage to make it to the kitchen to help prepare for dinner that afternoon.

Marc Bennett was gone by dinnertime, and that evening Steven returned to his central position in the meditation hall. Ana could feel the relief washing around her when he rose from his second-highest platform and started confidently across the walkway to the leader's perch. He seemed restored—a degree more intense, perhaps, but back in control of himself and his community. Change breathed a sigh of satisfaction and stepped back into its former path.

Ana did not. Perhaps her equilibrium had been too disturbed, reminding her what she was actually doing there; perhaps it was just the residue of her own inner tension, but she could still sense the storm in the distance.

It came, sooner than she had expected, and in a form she could not have anticipated.

The next morning when she took her walk, Steven was there. She had gone west this time, up to the hills on which the high wind-run generator stood, on the opposite side of the compound from the red-rock platform where she had met him before. He was seated to one side of the path, his face raised to the growing sun. Mallory was nowhere in sight.

She hesitated. When he gave no sign that he had noticed her, she decided to continue on her path. She drew even to him and was starting to pass him by, when he spoke.

"Good morning, Ana of the Sunrise. Strange, to be a child of the West, where the sun sets, and yet be so drawn to the early manifestations of light."

"Well," she said, not quite sure how she wanted to respond. He went on regardless.

"What do you make of your reading on the philosophy of chemistry?"

"The philosophy—? Oh, alchemy." She raised her eyes to the distant hills, and thought briefly how fortunate it was that people saw only what they expected to see. Steven had no idea. She looked down at him again and smiled, then sat down on a relatively flat place a few feet away from him, her legs out straight, leaning back on her hands.

"Most of the things I've been reading raise more questions than they answer. If, as you say, it is possible actually to make gold, then why did the science fade into a mere quest for spiritual growth, and then die out entirely?"

"Disbelief breeds failure," Steven said promptly. " 'Crush a fool in a mortar with a pestle, yet his folly will not depart from him.' Everyone knows that men can't possibly walk on red-hot coals without burning their feet to the bones, but people do. I did. And men can't transform one substance into another, but they do. If, however, the person trying to firewalk is afraid, if he does not believe he can do it, he will indeed lose his feet.

"Alchemy was the beginning of scientific method, and the great irony is that the more the alchemists discovered about the nature of matter, the more improbable the whole thing seemed. Belief became divorced from intellect, and they have continued to move further apart. Until the two are rejoined, the Philosopher's Stone remains an impossibility."

"You seriously think that the scientist's state of mind affects the result of an experiment?"

"It is not an experiment," he said sharply. "It is a process. A Work. Ana, all matter is related. This is a thing the ancients knew and we Westerners rejected in our single-minded quest to take things apart. We are reaping the results now, in a world poisoned by our convenience products, in children distorted by our providing them food and no wisdom. The only hopeful trend of the last thirty years is the faint stirring of realization that everything is interconnected, that the ozone layer over Australia is depleted by air conditioners used on the other side of the world; that the prisons are full because kids in the ghettos don't have basketball courts and trips to the beach; that women die of cancer because their mothers took the wrong kind of drug when they were pregnant.

"Ana, look: The medical world has admitted that a person's attitude has a strong bearing on how he or she fights off a disease. Alchemy says precisely the same thing: that the material in the vessel needs to be healed of impurity by a person whose mind and heart are both turned in the same direction."

Ana had been caught up in far too many sophomoric arguments on religion to fall into the temptation of pointing out his glaring flaw in logic, but it was not necessary, because Steven was off and running, and she had only to sit and feel the warmth of the sun on her face and chest.

"The alchemist was regarded as mad precisely because of this singleness of intent. His family went hungry, his clothes turned to rags, while he stared into the glass alembic and waited for the *nigredo* to give way to the peacock colors of transformation, through the white *albedo* to the glorious red of the final stage. 'I blew my thrift at the coal,' George Ripley wrote, 'my clothes were bawdy, my stomach never whole.' It would all be worth it if he could only reduce the universe, all the millennia of creation, into this alembic in front of him. It is a feeling like no other. It is like being God."

This was the first glimpse of the fanatic she had seen in Steven Change: It brought a sudden chill to the morning. Her words were impulsive and her voice harsher than she intended.

" 'Behold,' " she quoted at him, " 'I will gather you into the midst of Jerusalem as men gather silver and bronze and iron and lead and tin into a furnace, to blow the fire upon it in order to melt it.' "

"Ezekiel's God is an angry God. Remember, also, that 'the city was pure gold, clear as glass.' "

"The God of Revelation can be angry, too. 'I saw what appeared to be a sea of glass mingled with fire.' "

To Ana's surprise, Steven threw back his head and laughed. "I know. I would make a lousy messiah. I'm far too softhearted.

"Which is why," he said before she could react, "my dear Seeker Ana, I am sending you on a journey.

"In the very first conversation we had, you and I, I wondered aloud whether or not you had the commitment you needed to transform yourself. It was a natural enough question—most of the people who come here are so taken up with the pursuit of comfort and instant gratification that they will never go beyond what they are, will never learn that 'No birth without labor' and 'Great heat, great gain' are more than slogans. Most of the people who come here are content to warm their toes at the fire. They will never tear off their shoes and walk on the coals, because they are unwilling to submit themselves to the hotter, harder disciplines that Change requires.

"You are surprised that I am so blunt," he said, as indeed she was. "It is my job here to help people along the path to Change, yes, but it is also my responsibility as an adept to seek out those with greater possibilities than the masses, those with iron already in their spines. Teresa was one of those. The boy Jason Delgado is another, a young man with enormous potential. And you, Ana Wakefield. It is not my habit to speak like this to a person who has not been through the Work, but you have a natural affinity even without the experience. And not just intellectually—I feel in you a person who has been through the fire more than once, and has been strengthened by it. I feel in you the willingness to be worked and tried, to submit to the refining fires and be pounded into shape. To be transformed.

"I hesitated because I thought you were too frivolous for The Process. It is a long, hard journey. It has broken men and women before this." (Was it just her imagination, Ana wondered, or did she hear sorrow in his voice? At the nameless Japanese boy's death, perhaps? Or a different loss?) "I want you to begin your Change. I want you to set off on your journey, and to do so, I will send you on an actual journey, not one that is 'simply allegorical.' I am sending some of our children to our sister community in England. You will go with them, as a teacher, and as a student."

"What?" Oh shit, she cried to herself. Oh shit. I'm nowhere near ready to pull out of here, I can't give Glen what he needs yet, and Jason—and Dulcie, what the hell am I going to do, oh *shit*—

"To England. I like you, Ana. I can't teach someone I like. I may be further along in my journey than you, but I am not yet purified enough to overlook my own affections. It is one of the reasons we have more than one community, in recognition that none of us has attained our pure state. I want to send you to my own teacher. You will find Jonas, our Change leader in England, considerably farther along on the Path than I am. I want to send him you and Jason and one or two others whom I cannot teach properly. He will help you."

"Jason," she repeated, grasping the name like a straw. "What about Dulcie?"

Steven sighed. "Jason is not ready to move away from her. His sense of responsibility is admirable, but it distracts him. He must concentrate on his own Transformation."

"He's only fourteen."

"There is never time to waste."

"Is that why you've taken his art away from him? His 'sacrifice'?"

Steven's face darkened. "He should not have spoken to you about his Work. It is his alone."

"I wanted to draft him to help with the school mural; he had to tell me why he couldn't. Why take that from him?"

"I think you know, Ana."

"Heat and pressure, right? And the last time you put pressure on him, look what happened. My hand is still sore."

"He has to learn to direct his energies."

"Steven, how many alchemists were killed by explosions when they misjudged the pressures inside their vessels? More to the point, how many of their students did they take with them?"

So there was a degree of uncertainty in him, she thought, seeing his face. However, he said merely, "He will learn. Jonas will direct him."

Ana did not much like the sound of that, but Steven had at least opened a door. She could stay with the community as a whole and with her job. And with Dulcie and her brother. Glen would have a stroke, but if she chose, she might just stay long enough to give him a complete picture of Change. Going by what Steven just said, the center was in England, anyway.

(But—in England, where she had no authority, no Glen, no alarm bell or automatic pistol hidden inside Rocinante? No backup at all, in fact. She would be alone, and with two children on her hands. God, Glen wouldn't bother with handcuffs—he would just straight out murder her for even considering it.)

"When do I need to decide?"

"The tickets will be purchased tomorrow morning. The names of the passengers need to be on them."

"And when would we actually go?" she asked, reassuring herself that the end of the school year was still a long way off.

"In three days," he said. "You do have a passport?"

Two days later, she drained Rocinante's refrigerator, disconnected the propane tank, gave her knee enough cortisone to keep it numb for weeks, and spirited away the gun and cortisone needles from the hidden compartment to bury them in the desert. Before she pulled the tarpaulin over the bus, she stood looking at the medicine pouch that she had made from the objects in her past that meant something to her: the hairs from two dogs, the stones from her creek, and Abby's red bead. She reached in to remove it from the rearview mirror, and slipped the smooth leather cord over her head and around her neck, where it lay beneath her shirt like a talisman.

She did not manage to speak to Glen before the plane left, although she did rip out the most recent pages of her diary and put them into an envelope addressed to "Uncle

Abner," dropping it surreptitiously into a mail slot at the airport. On the last page she scribbled a note:

> No time to contact you, surprise trip to England
> with some kids being transferred there. I'll write you
> from the U.K. when I can. Do we have any family
> members in the area I can look up while I'm there?

—A

5.
SEPARATIO

separate *(vb)* To set or keep apart; to make a distinction between; to sever conjugal ties or contractual relations with; to isolate from a mixture.

Separacion doth each part from the other devide,
The subtill fro the gross, fro the thick the thin.

CHAPTER 23

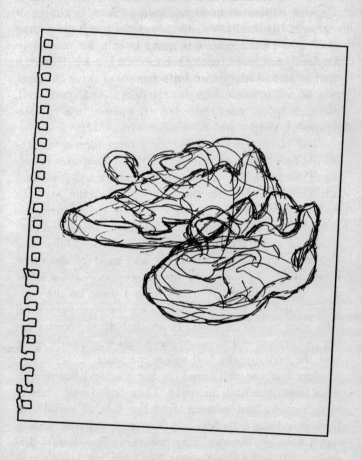

From the journal of Jason Delgado

The seats had been booked too late to enable them all to sit together, so Ana, in charge of Dulcie, Jason, and a boy not much older than Dulcie who was going to join his mother in England, sat apart from Dov Levinski, a kindergarten teacher named Margit, and their group of three children, two of whom were Margit's. It suited Ana quite well, particularly as the little boy Benjamin was sweet-tempered, sleepy, and no trouble whatsoever.

The plane was scheduled for a three-forty-five take-off. At four Ana took out the hardback illustrated *Hunting of the Snark* she had bought in Sedona and presented it to Dulcie. At four-ten the copilot came on the intercom and admitted that they were still on the ground, although the moment the deicer had been unclogged they would be away. By five-fifteen Ana had read Dulcie and Benjamin the *Snark* four times and most of the other books twice. At five-thirty the passengers heard a series of bangs and thuds from below, and those on the starboard windows were gratified to see the repair truck fill with men and drive away. In another three minutes the big jet lurched and began to creep backward, and Dulcie said she really, really had to use the toilet.

Ana had the child back in her seat and buckled in with twenty seconds to spare. They taxied and accelerated, rattling and roaring until the tons of metal and flesh gave their little hop and they were airborne. Dulcie did not notice, she and Benjamin being busy loudly discussing life in England across Ana's lap, but Jason's eyes shifted constantly, particularly upward to where the overhead baggage compartments were vibrating madly.

If one of them drops open, Ana thought, he's going to land five rows back, taking his seat with him.

"Have you flown much, Jason?" she asked to distract him.

"Uh, no."

"Planes always look like they're about to shake themselves to pieces, but as I understand it, they build the flexibility and movement in. If everything was completely rigid and nailed down, it would be too brittle. Even the wings bend a surprising amount. Much safer that way."

"Oh yeah?" he said, looking dubiously up at the rattling bins.

"Actually, I don't have the faintest idea if that's true or not. It's just what I tell myself when I fly because it's better than believing the plane is about to fall apart."

That did distract him, to the point of making him meet her eyes and smile. He leaned back, looking less nervous.

The plane leveled off, drinks and peanuts were handed out, and then there was such a delay before the meal was served that Dulcie and Benjamin both fell asleep. They woke when the food trolley bumped down the aisle, picked at the strange food, eating the cake and some noodles, but Benjamin found the milk strange after a lifetime of goat's milk and Dulcie spilled half of hers. They then wanted to play together with the packet of games and colors the flight attendant had given each of them.

Ana got tired of the elbows digging into her thighs and the constant chatter of excited voices directly under her chin, so she changed places with Benjamin and allowed the two small kids to have the middle of the row, bracketed by her and Jason at the ends. The children colored and played with the headphones, Jason watched the movie, and Ana tried to read the Jung book she had bought in Sedona and tried not to think of Glen.

The movie ended, reading lights were dimmed, toilets were visited, and the two children attempted to get comfortable. A thousand squirms later Ana got out of her seat and arranged pillows and blankets for Benjamin over both seats. Dulcie put her head into Jason's lap, and Ana took her book back a couple of rows, where there were a few empty seats. To her surprise, after a while Jason joined her with his own book, *The Old Man and the Sea.* He smiled shyly and read six or eight pages before closing it with an audible sigh.

"Are you reading that for school?" she asked. She took off her reading glasses and rubbed her tired eyes, leaning her head back on the headrest.

"Yeah. It's really boring. Nothing happens."

"I remember. The old man talks to himself a lot and the scavengers eat his giant fish." There was no response. After a minute she opened one eye to see whether he had gone back to his reading, but he was looking at her with an odd expression on his face.

"What? Isn't that what happens?"

"Don't you like Hemingway?"

"Oh yes, Hemingway was an immensely creative and influential writer, but that's the problem. So many writers have tried to copy his style that the original has begun to seem like a cheap imitation. Unfair, but I find it hard to get past the sense of caricature."

This may have been the first time the boy had heard that there might be differing opinions about the great literary works he had been required to appreciate for the last few years of his life.

"Anyway," she said, closing her eyes again, "I'd have thought the family Dumas more to your taste, or Dashiell Hammett. Someone with more flair and sense of romance than Hemingway. Romance in the sense of adventure"—she added in an aside—"not as in love story."

He said nothing, and she allowed herself to be lulled by the noise and the vibration, drifting into a light doze.

She woke and slept and woke, each time checking on her surroundings, on Jason, and on the forward row where she could see the top of Benjamin's head. Jason had abandoned Hemingway and was looking at Jung, reading at her marker. She slipped away a third time, and woke greatly refreshed. She stretched and looked around for an attendant, but the plane was still dim and quiet. Jason was awake, still working away at the alchemy essay. She glanced at the page, and saw that he was staring at the drawing of a fifteenth-century alembic.

"Jason," she said. He jerked and quickly turned the page.

"Jason, look—"

"I can't talk about it."

"I know it's part of the Work that Steven gave you, but—"

"I can't talk about it," he repeated brusquely, and started to lift himself out of his seat.

She laid her hand on his arm to stop him. "Okay, Jason, I understand. But can I say something? As a friend?"

He gradually subsided, and she took that as a yes. She thought for a minute, trying to find words that might open a door rather than shut him off.

"Steven is a good man," she said, "and he cares for you. There aren't a lot of people like that in the world, and when we meet someone like him, someone who really reaches us, our automatic response is to accept him fully, every part of him. Add to this the fact that no one your age believes that they have a lot of choices in life, and it is natural to think that you either have to accept all parts of Steven's belief system and teaching style, or reject him completely. You don't want to talk about what went on between you and him during those two days, and I respect that. I just want to say that if you have any doubts or even questions, if anything someone wants you to do doesn't seem quite right or fair, you can come to me and I'll try my hardest to keep an open mind. Okay?"

Jason gave his trademark shrug-and-a-nod, and she had to be satisfied with that. She reached down and unlatched her seat belt.

"I'm going to get a cup of coffee," she told him. "Can I bring you anything?"

He looked up at her, his face clearing with the relief of having gotten off so easy. "Can I have a Coke?"

"You can have anything you want except alcohol."

"I haven't had a Coke in three months."

"I haven't had a decent cup of coffee in five weeks. And four days, but who's counting?"

She found the attendants talking quietly in the galley. They exchanged a few words about the "cute kids" she was shepherding (Dulcie and Benjamin) and Ana went back to Jason with a can of Coke, a cup of ice, and two cups of stale instant coffee for herself.

"What else do you miss at Change?" she asked him when they were both settled in again with their drinks. "Your friends?"

"Nah. Most of the people I knew were jerks. I guess at first I missed all the normal stuff—you know, Mc-Donald's and TV and music and everything. Ice cream —me and Dulcie both miss that. I kind of got used to the place, though."

"It's a different life. But, you know, I wouldn't be surprised if they have ice cream at the English house. I remember when I was in London in the dead of winter once, I was amazed at how many people I saw eating ice cream."

"I don't know, I hear it's a weird place. Not the whole country, just where we're going."

"What, the Change community? Weird how?"

"I don't know," he repeated. "There was a kid in my house who just came back from there. He said they never went anywhere and it was like living in a jungle."

Ana had to smile at the thought of a jungle set down in the civilized English countryside. "He's probably exaggerating."

"Maybe. Anyway, he's kind of weird himself."

Ana Wakefield and Jason Delgado sat elbow to elbow with seven miles of air between their feet and the ice-studded surface of the northern Atlantic Ocean, drinking their respective beverages. Jason poured the second half of his Coke into the plastic cup and glanced at the book she had stuck into the seat back ahead of her.

"Do you read a lot of stuff like that?" Jason asked with a gesture at the worn black cover. She was mildly surprised that he would raise an obviously forbidden topic, even obliquely, but she thought the best thing to do was just treat it as an innocent question. She had, after all, told him that it was up to him to talk about his experience in the alembic.

"When I'm living in the bus, I tend to read more demanding things such as that," she said. "There just isn't room to collect masses of books. But when I settle down for a while, I usually go a little nuts at the local libraries and bookstores, catching up on all the novels I've missed."

"God, that must be so great, living in a bus. You can go wherever you want, eat when you want, pull over and sleep when you feel like it."

The wistful tone in his voice did him great credit: Most boys of fourteen, faced with the prospect of twelve years of responsibility for a minor sister, would feel more than mild regret.

"I have to tell you, Jason, how impressive your attitude toward your sister is. Dulcie is a sweetheart, but she's also a major burden. It can't be easy."

Praise on the basketball court was easy to ignore; from a person sitting at your side it was more difficult. Jason fiddled with the contents of the seat pocket in front of his knees for a moment, and then stood up to go check on Dulcie. He came back and continued on to the toilets in the far rear of the plane, where he spent a long time.

When he returned he paused by the seat, then walked forward again to look at the sleeping children. When he was finally in his seat he looked straight ahead at the rumpled white hair of the old man in the next row and began to talk.

"Dulcie and me, we're not orphans, you know. Our parents are still alive. At least, I know my dad is—he's in jail, and last I heard Dulcie's father was around. He lives in Vegas, I think. Our mom is a crackhead—or, she used to be, until about a year ago she started shooting up, and things got a little crazy. She'd bring these really creepy guys home, real narfs, you know? and they'd . . . Well, anyway, I finally got pissed off and told her she couldn't do that, not with Dulcie there, and I . . . I kinda beat one of them up, so she started just not coming home. I had a job, just part-time at a building site, but I had to give it up because I couldn't leave Dulcie home by herself. I mean, I know people do, but she'd get scared, and when I got home she'd just be lying in her bed shaking and she wouldn't eat her dinner. I used to wish Mom would get arrested so the city would step in and take care of things, but I couldn't go asking for food stamps or child care or anything because then I'd have to tell them why Mom wasn't the one doing the asking, and then she really would get arrested.

"I got . . . I don't know. I guess I got kind of fed up after a while, trying to do the school thing with

Dulcie and no money. I thought I deserved a break. Some time for myself, you know? I mean, all the other guys I knew used to spend hours just hanging out, not dragging their little sisters to all the games and wondering where their damn mothers were half the time. I know most of them don't have fathers and a lot of them have moms who work or spend time in jail, but there's always grandmothers or the welfare or something. Dulcie and I just had us."

He turned and gave her a hard look. "I'm not complaining, you know? I'm just telling you. Okay?"

"I understand."

He looked as if he doubted that, but he continued.

"Anyway, I started to go out sometimes at night after Dulcie was asleep. I never went anywhere, not far, because I kept thinking, 'What if she woke up and went looking for me?' or 'What if there was a fire?' I'd just sort of hang out with the guys who lived around us, listening to music and stuff.

"And then one night . . . God, I still can't believe I could be so stupid. We hadn't seen Mom for about a week, and there was almost no food in the house, and school wasn't going too good, and—I don't know, a lot of stuff. So after Dulcie went to bed I went out with some of the guys. And one of them stole a car. And I went for a ride with him, and the stupid bas—he crashed the car.

"We were miles and miles from home, and it was about two in the morning, and all I could think of was Dulcie waking up, and I just kind of lost it and started beating on him. And"—he shook his head—"somebody called the cops. Probably a good thing or I would've killed him, but instead of letting us go they arrested me, 'cause I was the one with blood all over my hands, and they took the kid who'd stolen the car off to the hospital.

"As soon as they closed me in the back of that cop car

I knew I'd really done it. I had to tell about Mom, or else Dulcie would wake up in the morning and find an empty house and go nuts. She did go kind of nuts, I guess, with this strange woman showing up at the door with another cop and no brother in sight, because after a while they brought her to me to settle her down. Some psychologist came along and told them it'd be a bad idea to put her in a foster home by herself, so we got to stay together. We were in and out of half a dozen places, but for some reason nobody wanted a little girl who didn't talk and her brother who liked to beat people up, so we ended up at Change."

"Did you like to beat people up?"

"No! It's just, sometimes you don't have a choice, you know? I used to think that, anyway, but Steven's been helping me see that I really do have a choice, that I hit people because it's easier than not hitting them. Steven told me that sometimes what looks like being strong is really being weak, and what looks like weakness takes greater strength. There's some stuff in the Bible about it."

" 'If anyone strikes you on the right cheek, turn to him the other also.' "

"That's it. And if he wants to sue you for the coat off your back, give him your shirt as well."

A loose translation, she thought, but a happy one.

"He also talked a lot about what you said, about thinking before I get mad."

Ana took a deep breath. "Have you had a blood test, Jason?"

"A blood test? Oh, you mean because I was in that fight?"

"And the other one, with your mother's . . . friend."

"Sure. I had two, six months apart. I'm clean."

"That's a relief. I should tell you that I am, too. Your

hand," she said when he looked at her, puzzled. "You cut your knuckle on my face. If I had HIV, you'd have been exposed. Something else to keep in mind next time you're tempted to pound some drug addict into a pulp."

"Yeah," he said. His face suddenly relaxed into a crooked smile that would have melted stronger women than Ana. "Next time I'll wear gloves."

She laughed. "So, do you like it at Change?"

"It's okay. There's a lot of rules, but I'm learning a lot. And Dulcie's happy."

Dulcie is happy, and Dulcie's brother shoots baskets and runs in the morning, and fantasizes about living the unencumbered life of a gypsy, sleeping when he likes and surviving on Cokes and hamburgers.

"You know," she said after a few minutes, "I went to Japan one time. It's a very crowded little country, the cities anyway. When you get on the subway during rush hour, they literally push the passengers in the door to pack them solid. Traditionally the Japanese lived in houses with walls made out of paper, and right on top of each other.

"People can't survive like that, though, so they developed methods of achieving privacy for themselves when surrounded by people. Small areas, like a language that is filled with double meanings—they can say thank-you in a way that means 'piss off' with nobody to know or be insulted. There are elaborate forms of politeness and dressing—all ways of hiding in a crowd. Even their art reflects this. In the West we've developed big, sweeping art forms, things that catch at you and won't let you walk by. Japanese art tends to be subtle and intense, so a person has to be looking for it to see the beauty of a teapot or a stroke of calligraphy.

"It's a little like that bird you did on the side of the mug I bought," she said as if the thought had suddenly occurred to her. "Controlled lines that say just what you wanted them to and no more, no less. The essence of 'quail' with no superfluous decoration. I like that mug very much."

He nodded, a motion closer to a squirm. After a minute of staring off into space, he said casually, "Steven said I could draw again if I wanted to."

"Did he? That's good to hear. Do you generally do a lot of drawing?"

"Not a lot. Sometimes, when I see something I like. Once I . . . um, I made this book for Dulcie once, for a Christmas present. She wanted this doll, but there wasn't enough money, so I drew her a story about the doll, making it have all these adventures and stuff. She still has it somewhere."

"I'll bet she does." She probably slept with it. "The reason I ask is that Japanese idea of privacy. If you were gifted at poetry, I might suggest that you . . . oh, write a poem about how Bryan made you feel at the museum that day, for instance. Since your form of expression seems to lie in your hands rather than with words, you might think about using them to create a place that is all yours, a place that is Jason Delgado's alone. Small, intense drawings that capture how you really feel about things. You see, I've lived in communities like Change for a lot of my life, and although I do understand the importance of participating in communal life, I know also that if you don't keep a little piece of yourself apart, you go a bit nuts."

"Like you with your walks," he said. "Dulcie said you like to walk in the mornings, by yourself."

Ridiculous, the pleasure in knowing that the two children talked about her between themselves. "I do. I also keep a journal, with thoughts and descriptions and a few really clumsy drawings." Not, admittedly, that the journal she had going at the moment was much more than a sham.

"Can I see it?"

"What, the journal?"

"Not to read. I just wanted to see your pictures. Oh, never mind, it's not important."

"No, I'd be happy for you to look at my drawings, if you promise not to laugh at them." She reached into the nylon backpack at her feet and dug out the journal. He lowered the seat-back tray and put the journal on it, opening it methodically at the beginning, where Anne, still in her home in the mountains, had written:

Sedentary life does not seem conducive to keeping a journal. I finished the last one nearly 4 months ago, & have not felt the urge to open this one until today, when I noticed that a colony of bats has moved in under the eaves of the house.

The journal continued for half a dozen pages of purely imaginary non-events and the rough sketch of a nest with three eggs in it that according to the journal she could see from her bedroom window but which in truth was a long-abandoned nest brought to her by Eliot after a windstorm the previous fall, which she kept on her mantelpiece (empty of eggs).

Jason studied the delicate lines of the nest under the blue light of the overhead spot, while she sat back in the shadows and studied him.

When she first met him over the repairs of Rocinante's heater, he had worn his black hair long and slicked back into a short ponytail. A few weeks ago, the urban-shark look had been replaced by a short buzz cut that looked less extreme and threatening but by its very lack of distraction served to emphasize the sharp edges of his nose and cheekbones. Even if he'd had an ordinary haircut flopping down in his eyes, though, she doubted that he would have looked like anything but what he was: a young man with the eyes of a boy who had given up on hope, and the expressionless face of a killer.

This Jason now sitting next to her was no longer that same young man whose devastating good looks and icy aloofness had sent such unexpected and disconcerting ripples down Ana's spine. He had matured dramatically in the few weeks she had known him, and paradoxically shed much of the hard defensive shell that made him appear so much older than he was. There was a boy in his eyes now—a wary boy, to be sure, ready instantly to snap back into his shell, but still a person who had experienced the first faint glimmerings of hope and who might, given time, come to believe in it. That this change had taken place despite the trauma of the alembic was eloquent testimony to his strength of spirit and the incomprehensible workings of the human mind. It was even possible, she had to acknowledge, that the change had been worked, in part, precisely because of the trauma.

Whatever the cause, and whatever the long-term effects on the boy, Ana was pleased to find that in recent days, a shift had taken place in her own perception of the boy as well. A month ago she would have been hard put to sit with her arm brushing casually against his, their faces eighteen inches apart, talking about Hemingway and drawing; the electricity of his taut personality would have left her as dry-mouthed and sweating as a teenager. On the other hand, it could simply be that familiarity had bred relaxation.

And she was relaxed with him now. She was still intrigued by him, amused and impressed and—yes—secretly in love with him, but her libido or hormones or whatever it was seemed to have rolled over and gone back to sleep, a condition for which she was truly grateful.

"How did you do this?" he asked, pointing to a

drawing she had made of a tumble of rocks in the bright sun, a shape defined by its shadows.

"That's called negative space," she told him. "You use your pencil to draw around the object, treating the thing itself as minimally as you can without making it just a white blob, but working up the background and the shadows. You have to see it with your eyes out of focus, if that makes sense."

He nodded, cocking his head at the drawing before turning the page.

Ana tensed slightly as he approached the section where she had first written about him. One's own name had a way of leaping off the page to catch the eye, and she would rather he not read even the sanitized version of her reaction to him. But there was not a drawing on that particular page, and he turned past it, safely now into school and Steven territory.

When he had reached the end (a small horned lizard she had seen sunning itself the other morning) he handed it back to her.

"You don't have any drawings of people in there."

"No. People's faces are too subtle for me. Lizards are about the closest I come, and even those might not be recognizable to a herpetologist."

"The cat was good."

"Anyone can draw a cat."

"That's true," he admitted. He shifted in his seat, and Ana edged aside to give him a bit more room, under the guise of leaning forward to check on Benjamin. She sat back into the edge of her seat, and then saw that Jason was holding out something to her between the thumb and finger of his right hand. It was a very small sketch book, about three inches by five, the wire coil of its binding bent and flattened, the green cardboard cover cracked and limp with long use. She took the artifact, opened it with the edge of a fingernail, then put it down

on her lap and resumed her reading glasses, feeling
around for the light button.

The drawings were necessarily tiny, the details often
smudged by the treatment the book had withstood and
by the graphite on one page rubbing off onto the facing
one. Densely worked, the subjects varied from a figure
out of some video game (horns, huge grimace, and exag-
gerated muscles) to a sleeping Dulcie who looked little
more than a baby.

After a few pages she looked up. "Are you sure you
want me to see these?"

"Yeah. I do."

She went through the book from cover to cover, seeing images of the Change compound worked into pages
already containing drawings of an earlier time: A coiled
rattlesnake had been fitted into a blank corner next to
the ear of a seated teddy bear, a spotted goat Ana recognized from an unsuccessful time in the milking barn
appeared to be walking toward a futuristic airship belch-
ing flames from its engines.

She closed it and gave it back to Jason, who shifted
again and made the small book disappear into an inner
pocket of his jacket.

"I apologize," she said.

"What for?"

"Teachers get into the bad habit of teaching all the
time. You don't need to be told about making a personal
space with your drawing. Sorry."

"That's okay." He squirmed again with embarrassment.

"And you draw mostly from memory."

"Yeah. You can tell?"

"In drawings this size it's easier to hide the fuzzy
detail, but mostly it's that the outside objects like the goat
and those dogs are more abstract than the things from
your room or Dulcie. You're remembering how you saw

them, not recording how they look. They're very beautiful. Some of them are very fine drawings. You should have some training."

He did not answer, and she bent forward to look into his face, which was blank.

"What did I say wrong?"

"Nothing."

"Please, Jason. Tell me."

"It's just something I do. It's a kid thing. Guys don't make pictures."

She actually laughed aloud. "God, Jason, you have some learning to do about artists. Some of the randiest, most macho guys in the world make pictures. And earn an incredible amount of money doing it."

He looked at her sideways. "Really?"

"Really. Keep drawing, Jason. Even if you don't do anything with it professionally, it'll teach you to see the world."

"You should laugh more often," he said earnestly. "It makes your face relax." He then went scarlet with embarrassment.

"I used to laugh a lot," she said, keeping her voice light. "I'll work on it."

After a minute, he asked her, "Can you show me how to do the 'negative space' stuff?"

Ana opened her own journal to a blank white page and found a pencil. "It's not so much a technique of drawing," she began, "as a different way of seeing and thinking about space."

6.
ALBIFICATIO

albedo *(n.* fr L *albus,*
whiteness)* Reflective power or:
Albion *(n. L)* Great Britain;
England.

It is of soft things induracion of Colour *white,*
And confixacion of Spirits which fleeing are.

CHAPTER 24

The single touchiest place by far in any "cult" situation involves children. An ex-member will come in--or worse, go directly to the newspapers--with a graphic report of child abuse, sexual or otherwise, Satanic rituals involving young children, the perverse habits of the leader and his closest associates, human sacrifice of newborns, you name it. There's no choice but to investigate it, obviously, even though any divorce lawyer can tell you how easy the accusation of abuse is to make, how hard it is to fight, and how often it is completely without basis in truth.

People use children as tools, for petty revenge, for manipulating someone, to build themselves up in their own eyes and in the view of society as a hero, and basically because dragging in kids makes for the biggest splash. The judges trying a custody case, and the public judging a community in the papers, can't afford to ignore claims of abuse of minors.

You as investigators are not immune from the emotional pull of the need to protect our children. However, in investigating these claims, no matter now plausible they sound, how sincere the accuser, the chief thing I would ask you to remember is the cop's first and hardest lesson: distance. You must not feel outrage, not even with the most appalling accusations; you must not leap to action, even when immediate intervention seems to be absolutely essential. You have to bear in mind at all times that in the vast majority of these cases, these children are seen by their community as they are in any community: they are the future. If you reach out to touch their kids, they will strike back, and the kids and everyone else will get in the way.

Excerpt from the transcription of a lecture by Dr. Anne Waverly
to the FBI Cult Response Team, April 27, 1994

They bent over her drawing pad for about half an hour before the flight attendants began to drag the carts up the aisles again. The smell of sausages and artificial maple flavoring floated through the cabin, and people began to stir. Benjamin woke, and then Dulcie, and Ana's brief idyll was over.

They were hours yet from London, their two kids bored and fractious with the need for exercise. Books and games and drawings and stories dragged on, until finally came the faint change of their angle of flight, heralding their descent into Heathrow only two hours late.

The great plane tipped, giving them a view of a vast expanse of red brick, black slate, gray tarmac, and a dollop of river, and then they straightened out and came in for a landing. They taxied, and they taxied some more; they came to a halt and they waited, half the passengers standing back to belly in the aisles for long minutes while the gangway was run out and first class was offloaded. Finally the jerk of motion as the aisles began to clear, and soon they were saying thank-you to the flight attendants and back on solid ground.

A lot of solid ground, carpeted and glassed-in and stuffy with the fumes of jet engines. After a hundred yards of skipping in joy, Dulcie began to lag; at two hundred yards Jason was carrying her, and Ana hefting Benjamin. She remembered Heathrow as endless, and it was.

The long, looping rows awaiting the immigration desks were next, and then the luggage hall, and both small children were limp now, stunned with exhaustion and strangeness. Ana and Jason were in a similar condition, although Dov and the others had slept and claimed to be refreshed beneath their ill temper.

Luggage piled on the trolley carts, steered through customs' gauntlet, where they all made it through undetained, around a bend and into an enormous echoing hall filled with electronic announcements and colorful motion, and there were two strangers greeting Dov, shaking hands, introducing themselves as Richard and Vicky, and taking over the baggage carts. A parking lot, windy and vast, a large van, child seats for Dulcie, Benjamin, and the other small children. Ana buckled in, checked to make sure she hadn't lost Jason, and gave herself over to the massive tiredness that crept into her very bones.

She slept across a large chunk of southern England.

Ana woke when the van descended from the freeway—motorway, it was called here. As cookies were called biscuits and tea was not just a beverage you drank but a meal you ate at six o'clock, and the steering wheel was on the right and roads had roundabouts instead of stop signs, a country where ordinary people did not have cheap guns in their bedside tables and the ordinary policeman was armed only with a stick, a radio, and an intimate knowledge of the patch he patrolled. There would be an equivalent to Glen here, who (if Glen was very persistent) might come to know of her presence, but Glen was a very long way off, and Ana was on her own.

But only for as long as it took her to read the signs here. (As Ana rubbed the back of her neck and shifted on the hard seat, she realized that she had clarified the decision in her mind, on the plane or while she slept.) She would finish her job, even on this strange ground, so that her report to Glen on the Change movement would be as complete as she could possibly make it. Two or three weeks ought to do it; after that she would seize Jason and Dulcie by the hands and remove them from the clutches of Change, even if it meant blowing her cover for good and throwing the Change community to the media, whose appetite for paranoid scenarios involving children was voracious. She would try very hard to take her two charges away quietly, but if she was forced to cling to the figurative gates of the American embassy under the glare of the television lights, so be it.

Then home in time for summer, with potentials and possibilities she wouldn't let herself think about.

Meanwhile, the countryside out her window was proving very compelling, lush and vibrant with the fast growth of late spring. She had been to this country in the summer twice and once for a memorable week in December, but now she saw why the poets gushed and the painters invented new shades of green: May was incredibly beautiful, field and hedgerow and country lane bursting with the full, exuberant rush of life held in during the long, cold winter. Lambs actually did gambol, she saw in amusement as they drove past a field of bouncing white quadrupeds. A long-legged foal inquiring among the nettles at the base of a fence skittered away at their passing, his ridiculous stump of a tail flapping wildly. A neatly tended orchard of thickly flowering trees filled the low curve of a creekside hollow, giving the impression of a white cloud come to earth. They passed a small, perfect stone cottage set back from the road behind a low picket fence, its garden a riot of wildly mixed color. There were even two black kittens playing on the brick walkway leading to the rose-bowered front door, for heaven's sake. Ana raised her face to the soft air blowing in the window and felt like laughing aloud at the sheer glory of the place.

Ana would have missed the first sign of wrongness

completely had she not been seated directly behind the driver. A police car was parked in a lay-by at the side of the lane. Ana might have dismissed it—a local patrol choosing a pleasant spot to have their tea break—but for Richard's vigorous two-fingered gesture at the official vehicle that punctuated his slowing, putting on the turn signal, and turning off through a set of electronically controlled gates and into a worn track so overgrown, it was more tunnel than drive. No one said anything, but Ana was quite certain that in England two fingers jabbed into the air was not a sign of "V is for victory."

They bumped along the track for ten minutes or so, waking up the little kids, but Ana had no ears for Dulcie's cries of protest, because near the beginning of the drive, off in the undergrowth near the gates, she had seen a man dressed in camouflage clothing; in his hands he held something very much like the bulky shape of a shotgun. She opened her mouth, and shut it, but when she looked up she saw Richard's eyes on her in the rear-view mirror. She turned to soothe Dulcie with a story about the lambs and kittens she had seen, furry, warm things to counteract the sudden cold tendrils that had begun to unfurl along the pit of her stomach.

The van emerged from the undergrowth and lurched through a section of slightly better road with fencing on both sides before entering a graveled farmyard where the spring weeds were winning. The buildings showed signs of recent labor, new windows and paint renewed in the last two or three years. All of these seemed to be out-buildings, and indeed the van did not stop there but continued around and past some more fences until it pulled up at the towering backside of what looked like a large country home belonging to a slightly down-at-the-heels family.

Ana thought the building was probably early Victorian, a blunt, purposeful edifice built of a harsh red brick that a century and a half had not dimmed. The kitchen door was standing open and three or four dogs and a large number of cats were scattered about, looking vaguely expectant.

Dulcie made for the cats as soon as she was freed from the van. Jason stood gaping up at the vast and uninspiring redbrick wall that loomed above them, punctuated by four rows of windows and surmounted by a gathered stand of half a dozen chimneys. Ana waited until the driver was by himself at the back of the van, pulling out luggage, and then she approached him.

"Richard, was that man in the woods a policeman?" she asked.

"Better not've been. If he was, there'll be hell to pay. We keep them out—we know our rights, they know our boundaries. Doesn't stop 'em from sitting at the back entrance, writing down plate numbers and playing silly buggers."

"Oh. But I thought . . . He did have a gun, didn't he?"

"Keeps the rabbits down," he said dismissively, and then over Ana's shoulder he shouted, "Where do you want this lot?"

"In the dining room," a woman's voice answered. "We can sort them out from there."

The bags were whisked inside, followed by the people (Dulcie protesting when a cat was plucked from her arms). They passed through the long kitchen, immediately comforting in its familiarity and the post-lunch clutter, although to Ana's eyes the corners could have used a good scrub. She wished they could have stayed there for a while, been handed a stack of dirty plates for what she remembered the English called the washing-up, but they were ushered straight through, past three kitchen workers who stopped to watch their passage. One of them was a tall, straight, blond girl with a peaceful face and oversized rubber gloves on her hands. She openly watched Jason walk past her; he in turn ducked his head to say something to Dulcie; Ana smiled absently to herself.

There was no TRANSFORMATION mural in this dining room, just a lot of mismatched chairs and tables in states ranging from new and cheap to old and rickety. The room had probably begun life as a ballroom, a place for the Victorian father's numerous daughters to display themselves and catch husbands, but the decorative wallpaper, velvet drapes, and gilt-edged mirrors had all long since been removed from the walls and the wooden dance floor was worn and speckled with white emulsion from a clumsy paint job. It echoed; the noise in there during a meal would be riotous.

Richard dumped the last of their things and vanished. In his place a familiar tall, dark-haired, asceticlooking figure walked into the room. Ana had been correct to suspect, when she saw the way the Change members in Arizona acted toward him, that Marc Bennett held a high rank in the organization, because here he was to give them their welcome speech—although very little welcome did it contain. He waited imperiously for their attention before he began his carefully composed talk, delivered in portentous tones.

"Before today, you have known Change as through a glass, darkly. Here, you will see what Arizona will eventually become, years from now. You stand at the very center of the Change movement, and you will find things here very different from what you're used to at Steven's place." ("Steven's place," thought Ana: Was it imagination, or had that phrase sounded dismissive?) "The Change compound you're used to is just getting started, and it has a long way to go before it makes Transformation. We've been here almost three times as long. Steven began his Transformation here before Jonas sent him to

Arizona, and he comes back here to continue his own Work.

"Age, of course, is no guarantee of either wisdom or authority." Bennett flicked a brief glance across Ana, the oldest person in the room by nearly a decade, and she felt herself bristle at the implied judgment. "However, here you will find a degree of concentration, a level of physical and spiritual activity that the Arizona community cannot begin to approach. We have been here for twelve years, and not a day has been wasted time.

"Dov has been with us before, but the rest of you were chosen to come here because in Steven's opinion, each of you is worthy of our greater efforts, capable of faster progress than he could give you in Arizona. We are on the edge of a great Work here, and Steven wanted you to be a part of it.

"I don't think I have to tell you what that means in terms of daily life here. I assume you all know that 'Great heat, great hope' is more than just a saying." His eyes bored into each of them except for the small children, seeing comprehension in all, even Jason. Perhaps especially Jason.

Benjamin had clung to Ana during the disembarkation and as they passed through the house, and he still stood clasping her hand and pressing his body up against her leg. The child seemed frightened of Marc Bennett. Behind Bennett a small cluster of men and women had appeared in the doorway, waiting for him to finish. One of the women moved slightly to see better, and Benjamin spotted her.

"Mommy!" he shouted, interrupting Bennett's dramatic monologue and startling them all. He flew across the wooden floor with his small feet pounding, missing a collision with the speaker by inches before he threw himself into the woman's arms, shouting his greetings and gladness, oblivious to everything else. His mother, however, was not. She tried to shush him, and when he would not contain his joy, she shot Bennett a glance of apology and more than a little apprehension before she ducked out of the door and away.

Bennett, expressionless, waited until the noise of their passing disappeared behind a closing door and picked up as if the interruption had not occurred.

"Here, 'Great heat, great hope' is an everyday reality. The pressures here are greater than you have known in Arizona. You were not ready for them there; now you are. They would have broken you there; now they will make you change."

Ana shifted from one flight-swollen foot to the other, wondering uncomfortably why she had heard none of this in Arizona, and also what it was about men of religion that made them so damnably long-winded. Immediately his hooded eyes flashed back to rest on her. This time the scorn in them was clear.

"I'm not going to lie to you: You will not be comfortable here. You will work hard. You will sweat and strain and come to hate us all, but you will stay because you will be able to see and feel the results of your Work. Some of you will stay," he added, and again his gaze touched Ana. She couldn't think what she had done to offend him, unless if, as she had come to suspect, there was rivalry between the two men, and Steven's approval alone had condemned her in Bennett's eyes. Ah, well— all the better if she could turn his disapproving gaze from Steven's other protégé, the teenager at her side. Even if Bennett was not the community's leader, he could make life difficult for Jason.

"I have nothing to say at the moment about the deeper implications of your life here. It is up to Jonas to set each of you on his or her Work, and tell you what you need to know. Jonas will speak to each of you alone over the next few days. If he thinks you belong here, you will stay; if not, you'll be going back to Arizona.

"In the meantime, let's talk about rules. Our pressures here are very intense, so it shouldn't come as any surprise to find that our regulations have to be tighter. It goes without saying that the same basic ground rules you had in Arizona apply—no drugs or drink, no music or distracting clothes, no personal possessions you're not willing to share, and absolutely no unauthorized jewelry. Beyond that, we have three requirements.

"One: Everybody works. If you're not carrying your weight, you go back.

"Two: No outside contact unless it's absolutely unavoidable, particularly in your first eight weeks here. In Arizona you welcomed outsiders, you came and went, you used the phone and wrote letters home, because you were at an early stage in your Work, where it didn't matter. Here we are higher. Because things are more concentrated, more delicate, outside interference can have terrible consequences. We have wrapped this estate around us to allow us to work undisturbed; none of us can endanger the whole by coming and going without supervision.

"Be aware, too, that the authorities are harassing us —issuing us writs, plaguing us with financial inquiries, and just plain watching us. Some of you saw the panda car parked in the road, but they're a load more high tech when they want to be. Just assume that they're watching overhead at all times, and keep under cover whenever you can. When you're working in the fields, wear one of the hats we keep in the garden shed so they can't see your face. And never go near the boundaries—they have cameras."

Ana found that she was standing with her arms crossed tightly over her chest. She wished Benjamin had not deserted her. She wished she were holding Dulcie.

Most of all she wished she knew what the hell was going on. Why, for one thing, was Marc Bennett standing there pontificating? Where was Jonas Seraph? Both Steven and Glen had led her to believe that Jonas was in charge here, and Bennett's words had indicated that Jonas was present. Was he ill, and capable only of limited, individual interaction with the new members of Change?

Whatever the explanation, she did not like this at all. Forty minutes earlier she had been laughing in quiet pleasure at the gamboling lambs and the kittens, and suddenly here she was, listening to a speech about the terrible threats of the outside world that could have come from the mouth of any of a hundred mentally unstable leaders whose names went on to make the headlines. Cameras and spy planes? The abruptness of the change was shocking, as if she'd been dropped into an icy lake. She began to feel dizzy. Bennett went inexorably on.

"And rule three: You're newbies. Assume that anybody here knows more than you, do what they tell you, and you won't get in trouble. Once Jonas has approved you, you're going to work long hours, you won't get much sleep, and the only time you'll sit down is to eat or to meditate. Or in school," he added in afterthought with a glance at Jason. "And God help you if you fall asleep during meditation, because Jonas sure won't."

By this time Dulcie was up in Jason's arms, hiding from her tiredness and confusion and the strange man's big voice. She cringed at his gust of laughter and turned a wary eye on him, but Jason was listening to Bennett with no small interest, and merely patted her absently.

"So," Bennett said. "There're the three main rules: work, apartness, and obedience. If you don't like it, tell us by lunchtime tomorrow, and we'll send you back to Arizona, nothing lost but a return ticket and a couple of days. Look around, talk to people, stay out of sight, and make up your mind. Steven sent you because he thought you needed the greater heat here to help your Transformation. If he was wrong, it's his fault, not yours." The prospect of Steven's being wrong obviously pleased him. "Any questions?"

Questions? thought Ana. By God, she had questions, but they were hardly the sort Bennett would answer for her. Why hadn't she been warned? Oh yes, she'd been told that there were guns in the Los Angeles branch of Change and that a boy had been killed in Yokohama. But why had Glen neglected to mention the little fact that the English group was an armed camp run by a drill sergeant who saw camera lenses in the birds' nests? Damn you, Glen, she raged, though her face remained stiff and unrevealing.

She held the anger tightly, and fed it with the sight and sound of Marc Bennett and the thought of the flaying she would give Glen when she saw him next, and the anger was a relief and a bulwark against what lay beneath, trying to break through.

For underneath lay dread, the chill, memory-laden fear of the inevitable, composed of images: Abby lying wrapped in Aaron's swollen arms on the hard-baked Texas earth; Calvin Vester in Utah, a friendly man who had cooked her breakfast, seen in Rocinante's side mirror with his gun coming up; Martin Cranmer with the Kansas wheat fields stretching out behind him, brutally knocking one of his followers to the ground, laughing. She could almost smell the burnt-steam stink of the ruptured radiator mixed with the hard, hot smell of her own blood; above all she felt the clear sensation of being trapped in a room filled with flammable gas and the only way out involving a lighted match—staying was unthinkable, leaving impossible. It was Texas, driving away from Abby and Aaron, only Texas with the foreknowledge of what her action would lead to.

Bennett ran out of words, nodded brusquely, and left

the room, but Ana stood paralyzed and unseeing as the meeting broke up and people began to lead the newcomers and their possessions away. She watched Jason and Dulcie leave without a backward glance, and only gradually became aware of the plump, ordinary, sane-looking forty-year-old woman who was standing patiently in front of her.

"Hello?" The woman's humorous, questioning intonation indicated that she had greeted Ana several times already. This time she saw Ana focus on her, and she smiled. "Hi. I'm Sara. Shall I show you where your room is?"

"Sorry," Ana said. Her mouth felt numb, her voice not her own. She tried a return smile, apparently with success. "I was miles away. That would be good of you, thanks."

Sara picked up one of Ana's two bags and started briskly for the stairway, chattering in an enchanting English drawl about how "disorientated" jet lag left a person, and then about the weather. Ana followed slowly, only half hearing.

Don't overreact, she was telling herself; this is neither Utah nor Texas. You've spent weeks in the Arizona community and seen no signs of problems, and then you come here and take the rude gesture of one anti-authoritarian driver and the speech of a self-important member—not even the group leader—put them together, and build a toppling tower.

Calm down, woman. This is not Texas; this is not Utah. They'll ship you back to Arizona whenever you want, and there are certainly no jugs of poison waiting in the cellar; no one is about to run out with an automatic pistol to stop you from driving away. Just think of it as a brief enlistment with the English army.

The surface of her mind began to clear, so that by the top of the second flight of stairs she was paying attention to what her guide was saying about the recent spate of long, dry summers and the mixed feelings the entire country had about warmth in May.

Ana responded with a comment about how amazing the eyes found the rich green foliage that they had come through compared with the sparse, dry landscape, even in the rush of spring that they had driven through on their way to the airport in Phoenix. They talked while Sara marched her up to a small, cold, north-facing room with ill-fitting curtains and a lumpy mattress, showed her the bath, toilet, and linen room, and helped her make up the bed (Sara's half had tight, sharp corners) before leading her back down the stairs.

All the while, though, grinding down in the deeper reaches of her mind and repeating over and over was the thought: I should never have let Dulcie and Jason on that plane. Never.

CHAPTER 25

Jonestown began as an attempt to build a paradise in the wilderness, a garden of Eden carved out of the Guyana jungle, populated by multiracial refugees from the oppressive policies of the American system. A thousand people followed the Reverend Jim Jones into the wilderness; within a year, more than nine hundred of them would swallow poisoned fruit drink and lie dead beneath the tropical sun.

However, one cannot explain away the suicide of Jonestown as merely a product of mass delusion and hysteria with a charismatic madman deliberately manipulating his gullible followers. This was a community of well meaning, deeply committed believers who saw the enemy at their gates, about to break in and break them apart. These were men and women willing to take their own lives, and the lives of their beloved children, rather than submit to the contamination of the outside world. When Jewish rebels gave themselves and their children to the knife in first century Masada, theirs became a cry of resolute freedom through the millenia; the followers of Jim Jones will go down as poor deluded losers.

One obvious difference between Jonestown and Masada lies in the degree of actual threat involved. The Romans would indeed have executed some of the rebels and sent the others into brutal slavery; Congressman Ryan and his team were merely investigating, the first bureaucratic trickle in what would have become a deluge. To the minds of the two communities, though, the threat was identical, primarily because the residents of Jonestown were as isolated and pressured as the community over the Dead Sea was 1900 years before.

Isolation and pressure are the two deadliest enemies of any volatile situation. Heat from outside, added to the heat generated from within, and kept under tight pressure by isolation (be it voluntary or enforced) is a sure recipe for disaster. Isolation by itself is a useful tool, if kept sufficiently low key; pressure too can be valuable, if a clear _and_ _acceptable_ (to the community) outlet is provided. Put the two forces together, though, and you have a pressure cooker waiting to explode.

Excerpt from *Religious Communities and the Law: An Alternative Approach,* by Dr. Anne Waverly (a publication of the Federal Bureau of Investigation)

But then the next morning Ana woke to the joyful noise of a thousand birds singing their hearts out, and the sound, shouting forth the magnificence of life and hope and normality, blended with the golden light pouring in and brightening the spare furnishings and the stained ceiling, and her heart was glad. Yesterday had been a dark dream plagued by a neurotic fantasy, created by pressures and anxieties and fed by jet lag, her personal history, and an accumulation of sleepless nights. Today she would start afresh, and give herself a chance to see this branch of Change with clear eyes.

Her wristwatch had suffered from the journey, though. Either that or she had made a mistake in setting it to local time, because although it told her that it was not yet five o'clock, her eyes and the birds outside insisted that the morning was well and truly broken.

She dressed and went out into the hallway, where she stopped, puzzled by the complete lack of activity. There were no plumbing noises, no voices from downstairs; surely someone would have mentioned it if Change rose with the dawn? However, when she got to the kitchen and found the only indicator of life to be the fragrance coming from the coffeepot, she took it as a sign that only early risers were about. Actually, if she thought it over, it was a twice-good sign: Here, it seemed, she would be allowed to start the day on something more powerful than a tea bag.

She looked around for a kitchen clock, and was chagrined to discover that no, her watch was not wrong. She had just forgotten how far north England was, how incredibly early it grew light there in the summer.

Well, she was not about to go back to bed, not with fresh coffee at hand and the glories of an English morning outside the door. She tried various cupboard doors until she found a mug, poured herself some coffee and added a splash of rich yellow milk from a glass jug in the refrigerator, and opened the back door.

And nearly whirled around and slammed it behind her, until her mind registered that the pack of baying dogs was not actually going for her.

"Quiet!" she ordered, and then, "Shut up!" A simple "No!" seemed to do more than either of the first commands, so she repeated it sternly until the noise died down to a few growls and whiffles and her heart rate returned to normal. When most of the dogs were quiet, she lowered herself onto the top step and extended her hand for their examination. One or two seemed happy enough to adopt her as their own, two or three stayed well back, eyeing her suspiciously and grumbling to themselves, and the other half-dozen, a motley collection that included a slim boxer very like Livy, sniffed her hand, accepted a pat, and then ignored her.

She would have to wait awhile before she tried to walk through their midst, though, so she settled down with the cup of coffee (which miraculously had not entirely sloshed over the steps when she was first confronted by the pack) and a pair of hairy heads immobilizing her feet, and breathed in the day.

Ana's previous trips to England had concentrated on the cities and on tourist sites. The closest she had come to a farmyard were one visit to a farm museum near Oxford and a night in a rural bed-and-breakfast when she and Aaron had been caught by night on a dark road somewhere between Stonehenge and Bath.

There was no doubt that this was a working farm; the very smell in the air told Ana that, even without the sounds of rooster and cow and the memory of three large tractors parked in the yard the afternoon before. The weeds might be thick but the fences were maintained, and although there had appeared to be a leak somewhere in the roof over Ana's bedroom, she would have bet that the barn was sound.

When the cup was empty, Ana figured that she had sat there long enough to become familiar to the dogs. She put her cup down onto the side of the step where no passerby would kick it, and got casually to her feet, standing for a minute while the dogs around the edges gave a few disapproving whuffs. Her two closest admirers waved their tails expectantly; the others waited to see what she had in mind. She addressed her companions.

"Want to go for a walk, guys?" she asked in a cheerful voice. "Yes? Okay, come on."

The disapproving ones started barking, which set off the middle-of-the-road members, but Ana merely slapped her left thigh encouragingly and strode off.

She ended up with five dogs in all, sailing back and forth across the gravel in front of her, but before she reached the end of the yard, she heard a woman's voice behind her, calling for her to stop and wait. She stopped and turned around to wait for the flustered young woman, who was securing a floppy straw hat onto her head with one hand as she ran and holding an identical hat in her other hand.

Hats—oh yes; Bennett had said that hats were to be worn out-of-doors to foil the intrusions of the telephoto lenses, spy planes, and satellites.

The young woman stopped in front of her, panting from the run, and held out the extra hat. "You need to wear this," she said. "You mustn't forget again, or Marc will get angry."

Ana looked at the hat. It was a ridiculous piece of headgear with a low, round crown guaranteed to shift around on the head surrounded by ten inches of soft, grubby, sweat-stained brim. The ribbons necessary to hold it in place were colorless with age and had been tied together in a couple of places. She did not want to have this disgusting object between her and the magnificent blue sky.

Ana, she told herself, in Israel you cover yourself neck to wrist to ankle even in August; in New York you cripple yourself with heels. Here you will wear a hat.

She clapped it on her head and thanked the young woman with as much good grace as she could muster, and without another word turned her back and continued on up the lane.

The wide brim and musty smell of the object on her head dimmed the morning somewhat, and when she reached the point where the road went into the woods, tempted by the thought that in there she might remove it, she paused. The vision of a man wearing camouflage gear was vivid. Perhaps until she knew the ground rules she'd better stick to the open fields, she decided, and turned left onto a muddy track that ran between a fenced field with half a dozen cows in it on one side and on the other a wild thicket of nettles, blackberries, and bushes where the woods began. It was not as nice as the lane, and she had to take care not to put her foot into a cowpat or lose her hat to a branch, but the dogs were pleased and her spirit was content.

It was a nice long circuit with many pleasing ins and outs and dead ends, but it was also a puzzling one. On her left for the entire time lay civilization in the form of cows and sheep, two massive draft horses and a well-populated duck pond, fenced pastures and vegetable garden. Extending out from the house was a twelve-foot-high brick wall lined with espaliered fruit trees, with a gap in the bricks revealing a glimpse of an acre or more of enclosed garden with a gleaming greenhouse, more trees espaliered against the wall, and rows of ruthlessly neat planted beds.

It was a beautiful farm, ageless in structure and vigorously modern in intent; it left Ana with a clear idea of just where all that hard work Bennett had referred to went.

The whole time, however, with the civil arts of the gardener displayed on her left, the right-hand prospect was nothing but a wall of overgrown shrubs, tangled vines, and impenetrable thicket. It was beautiful, too, in its wild way—magnificent, even, such as the huge rhododendron that had grown up and then toppled, rooting and resprouting where it lay until it formed a single plant nearly fifty feet long. Its clusters of red blossoms were fading now, but a few weeks earlier they must have been spectacular in spite of the heavy tangle of bramble that was clambering over the great bush. The rhododendron gave way to a wall of privet that cried out for the attentions of half a dozen strong men with chain saws; farther on, a tree three feet across at its base had fallen onto the lane and had its upper half cleared away while the rest of it was left to rot on the ground, after which a gate, so overgrown as to be unopenable with any tool short of a bulldozer, showed where a narrow lane had once joined with the home farm. So it continued, all the way around: tidy industry and the clean fragrance of grass on the left, a high wall of wild vegetation and the smell of rotting things on the right, hacked back as if a line had been drawn, untouched beyond that boundary. Order versus chaos—the early American colonies must have felt a little like this, settlements carved out of the wilderness. Or an enchanted castle, insulated from time.

From down at the bottom of the farm, the house was softened by the outlying walls and structures, its lower half hidden by trees. The top of it rose up, though, and Ana saw for the first time that it was not just a box, as it had appeared from the back door. The central portion of the main block stepped up, two or three stories higher than the sides, and that section was topped by the tangle of chimneys. It looked a bit like a flattened pear, an overripe Comice dropped from a height onto its bottom, and would, she reflected, have been much improved had someone alleviated the unimaginative symmetry by propping a giant leaf up against the central stem of chimneys. She grinned at the whimsical image, and went on.

Back at the walled garden near the house, Ana turned to survey the gently sloping terrain down to the jungle, and was hit by its unlikely but striking similarity to another would-be paradise, the remnants of which she had once visited, a *hortus conclusus* whose inhabitants had tried to keep the outside world at bay while an ideal society was being constructed within the boundaries. Sealed in, like this place, by the hermetic walls of the jungle, with stringently limited outside contact and a strong sense of oppression, the pressure had built until it could be held no longer. People called it Jonestown—and why the hell, thought Ana, was she dwelling on that tropical, blood-soaked patch of insanity, here on this glorious morning on this piece of God's green earth less than three hours from the edges of London? Macabre thoughts had no business intruding, and paranoia was clearly a two-way street. Yes, it was a good thing that she would never do this for Glen again; academia was an outpost of rationality by comparison.

Still, as she looked back at the abrupt wall of vegetation she found that she was again wishing for the last two days back, so she could walk straight through the Phoenix airport and put Dulcie and Jason in a taxi and drive them straight to Glen or Agent Rayne Steinberg or even the FBI boy with the protruding ears in Prescott. Looking at the forest walls pressing in on her, she could not shake off the fanciful image of bringing Jason and

Dulcie to be hermetically sealed into these green walls, awaiting Transformation. She shivered and pushed the idea away violently. Enough! Time for breakfast and human contact: The mind of the individual, like that of the community, needs contact with others to keep it balanced.

Life was stirring in the house when she returned. She removed her mucky boots at the kitchen door, carrying them inside for fear one of the dogs might take it into his head that they were chew toys, and propped them and the distasteful hat in a corner. She found a washroom and cleaned her hands, then presented herself in the kitchen.

"Good morning," she said to the room at large. "Anything I can do to help?"

There was.

Some years before, Anne Waverly had come to know a visiting pair of eminent anthropologists who were spending half a year at her university. Most of the team's publications were in the husband's name, but he freely admitted that a lot of the research, and indeed all of the research done into the women's side of the society being studied, was conducted by his wife, a frail, white-haired woman whom Anne had come to think of as the Miss Marple of the anthropology set.

The woman's approach was to present herself to their new society—be it in Africa, highland New Guinea, or northern Canada—as precisely what she was: a grandmother. Out would come the knitting and the photographs, the stories and the remedies for arthritis, and with the babies crawling around their feet and the pots bubbling in the background, the women would freely submit to having their brains picked and their communal souls bared. She was a formidable weapon in the anthropological array, and Anne imitated her methods whenever she could. A community's mind and pocket may be in the meditation hall and the office, but its heart and soul are found on the cooking hearth, and although Ana might not have snapshots of the grandchildren or a woolly sweater on her needles, she had found that a person could ask anything if she did it with her arms immersed in greasy soapsuds.

Until the schooling arrangements for the Arizona newcomers were straightened out, which according to Dov would take a couple of days, Ana had no responsibilities, so she washed pans and scrubbed shelves and peeled vegetables. And she talked blithely, and she listened to their complaints and their squabbles, and she wondered at the level of antagonism in the kitchen and at the plethora of convoluted difficulties they were having with health inspectors and school inspectors and Social Services inspectors and banks. She had thought the United States was drowning in bureaucracy, but it would appear that America had nothing on the United Kingdom. By the time the lunch dishes were cleaned up, she had a clear sense of the mental state of this community—which she found filled with sharp little tensions while maintaining a powerful sense of self-confidence in the face of the world's vexations—and had gained a basic idea of how the community functioned.

She was struck, first of all, by the extent to which Marc Bennett had been right: There were profound differences between Steven's compound and this one—differences that went far deeper than the presence or lack of a coffeepot. The English group was actually much smaller, though it was longer established, and because it did not import children for a school, the population was older. Also, although Steven had referred to Jonas as the leader here, the unseen figure seemed to occupy more a position of aloof but ultimate authority than being involved in the day-to-day operations of the place, which were firmly in the hands of Marc Bennett.

Bennett was not universally popular. In fact, two of the women agreed that they had seen a number of members leave over the last year or so, since he had assumed (or been assigned?) a greater degree of control. He was respected, though, and the general consensus seemed to be that whereas Jonas was incredibly wise and authoritative, he was too otherworldly to be burdened with lowly details. No, they were fortunate to have Marc Bennett to direct the daily operations of keeping Change together in a largely hostile universe.

During the course of the morning spent working with the women, it struck Ana how like Change was to a certain kibbutz she had spent some weeks with on the West Bank—surrounded by the enemy, committed to the way of life, unconsciously preserving the traditional gender-linked work roles, scornful of the soft life led by outsiders, and dependent solely on themselves for all the necessities of food, shelter, and defense. Change even had a system of pantries and storage lockers like that of the kibbutz, three great rooms loaded with airtight canisters of grain, plastic drums of dried fruit, and cartons of candles, toilet paper, and canned meats.

Like the kibbutz—or the survivalists in North Dakota she had lived with, her very first job for Glen, when she had learned what it was like to breathe and eat with fear continually touching the back of her mind. This Change community was even populated by the same kind of people as both kibbutzim and survivalists: straight-spined militarists, tightly disciplinarian with their children, and energetic to the point of edginess. The closest she had come to finding a placid individual here was Sara, and even Sara had trotted briskly up the stairs and made her side of the bed with knife-edged corners. It was like being in a hive of type-A personalities, bristling and focused and extremely clear about what they were doing. And to think that in Arizona she had found Dov tight-assed.

She shook herself and reached out for the reason she had come into the storage room: a broom to sweep the crumbs from the floor of the dining hall. It was where she had been told it was, with a dustpan. She took them into the former ballroom and got to work.

It was an awkward job, since the broom was not the nice flat shape she was used to but rather resembled a janitor's push broom, only smaller. The wide head caught at all the chair legs, and though it did not feel right to pull it, pushing it seemed even more awkward. Still, she fumbled and cracked her way through the room, pulling the debris into the dustpan as she went and using the time of uninterrupted, mindless labor to think about lunch.

Perhaps because this Change community was smaller, they all ate at the same time. At least, most of the members gathered together—she had not seen Bennett there, nor Jonas. She had not yet laid eyes on Jonas at all, in fact, although she had been watching for the bearded face from Glen's three-year-old photograph. She did not know if the higher echelons had their own dining area or even a separate kitchen, but she took it that here, rank's privileges held. Or maybe they were just too spiritually uplifted to eat.

At lunch she had seen Jason and Dulcie come into the dining hall, but she had also seen the blond kitchen girl walk in with them, so she went to sit with Sara and tried to get her talking. It proved not to be difficult.

Sara had been with Change nearly four years, but as far as Ana could tell had not made much progress in her personal transformation. Certainly she wore no silver necklace. She seemed mildly aware of her failure but not very troubled by it, and Ana decided that Sara had a good heart but not a great brain—perfect for her purposes, although she would have laid money that Marc Bennett had little time for Sara other than for her obvious willingness to work.

It was confirmed when Ana's tentative remarks about Bennett made Sara almost physically wince. Bennett, it seemed, made no effort to conceal the irritation and impatience Sara caused him to feel, so she tended to stay out of his way. Jonas, however, had once said something terribly kind and supportive to her (which she wouldn't tell to Ana because it had been a part of her personal Work), so although he usually wandered around the place too distracted by his great thoughts and meditations to notice someone like Sara, she still found him a paternal figure. Strange, slightly scary and awe-inspiring, but paternal nonetheless.

Before lunch ended, Ana had arranged to join Sara in the walled garden, where Sara was due to set out seedlings. They then went their ways, Sara to private meditation and Ana to the dirty dishes and then the awkward broom.

She found that she was quite looking forward to meeting Jonas.

In the meantime, she was enjoying the respite from people, working her methodical way down the still, warm room with its high ceiling and jumble of furnishings. The dust motes she raised hung in the shafts of sunlight that streamed through the wide, uncurtained windows, and the collection of bread crumbs and lettuce leaves in her pan grew.

When she looked up, Marc Bennett stood in the doorway watching her.

"I don't know if anyone has informed you," he said without preliminary, "but we do not welcome newcomers to group meditation until Jonas has spoken with them."

Ana opened her mouth to respond, framing the appropriately meek response of a novice to her master that would reduce some of the animosity he demonstrated toward her, but she found that the words would not come; her spine would not bend. Instead, her shoulders went even straighter and her face and voice clearly showed how unimpressed she was, and what came out of her mouth was simply "Yes, that's probably for the best." She went back to her sweeping, to all appearances completely indifferent to his presence.

A moment passed, and he gave a sharp laugh. "Steven thinks you're hot stuff. He says you know things before you've learned them. But then, Steven has always been gullible. That's why he's in Arizona."

"He's a good leader," she said easily, tipping a chair to reach a clot of dried mud next to its leg.

He took her mild emphasis on the pronoun as a criticism, as she had intended. "You assume because he's in charge there, he's higher than I am? Think again, Ana Wakefield. You're not as clever as you think you are. Actually, you're here only because Jonas wanted to see the boy Jason, and you're the easiest way of prising him loose from his sister. You're not an adept; you're a glorified baby-sitter with a sore hand that excuses you from any real work.

"And," he added spitefully, "if I hear of you going out again without a hat, you're on your way home to Arizona."

She paused in her work and turned on him the haughty, professorial raised eyebrow that had intimidated furious thirteen-year-olds and irate FBI agents alike. She just stood and looked at him until he whirled and left her alone in the empty, sun-filled dining hall, sweeping the floor and thinking mordant thoughts.

Stupid. That was a stupid, stupid thing to do, she told herself—a newcomer who had yet even to begin her

Work doesn't stand up to the second in command. Bennett could make a great deal of trouble for her, and the worst part of it was, she did not know why she had not simply put on her humble face and ingratiated herself to him. It would have been easy enough to do. She'd done it a hundred times before, but for some reason, the automatic response had been overridden by a pride that might cost her dearly.

Was it just another inconvenient intrusion from her past, because Bennett reminded her of Martin Cranmer, the Kansas wheat farmer she had chosen to pursue, the man Glen had dubbed the Midwest Messiah? Even physically they were similar, that same tall, thin build and deep-set, burning eyes. Cranmer had been easy to manipulate in some ways, because he did not expect opposition from a woman, but he was difficult in others, for precisely the same reason. He had gathered to himself a high proportion of women in Utah, along with a number of men with low sex drives who seemed happy to turn a blind eye on Cranmer's adoption of their wives. Fortunately, Ana had still been fairly gaunt, and her short-cropped hair and a lack of makeup, combined with a stubborn commitment to loose jeans and baggy men's shirts, had kept her out of his grasp.

Not that Marc Bennett seemed to have made a private harem for himself at Change. Far from it; the most overt display of sexuality she had seen in the past twenty-four hours was the blond girl's flirtatious laughter when Jason made a joke over the vegetable stew (which laughter had caused Dulcie to scowl).

Bennett wasn't actually anything like Cranmer, was he? Tall and pushy, sure, but that was about it. No, the problem was with her, Ana, and her inability to keep the door to memory shut. Something in the past twenty-four hours had jostled her badly—jet lag, perhaps, or something random like the chimneys on the house or the garden or Bennett's speech, maybe even the dog that resembled Livy—and the past was now scrambling back at her, lost incidents washing in with every new sight, repressed images pressing at the back of her retinas. Jonestown, Abby in Texas, the armed kibbutz and the encampment of survivalists—once a memory had its toe in the door, it dragged a dozen more with it. Dangerous, distracting, and distorting to judgment, it was equally difficult to suppress.

It had happened in the past, most strongly in her second case in Miami when the first stressful phase was successfully negotiated and her defenses had relaxed just a bit, and in swept all the anxieties and discomforts that were waiting at the gates like a horde of importunate peasants demanding audience. At home, when she was Anne Waverly and the ghosts crowded close to her skin and whispered just beneath her ability to hear, she had found that the only solutions lay in tranquilizers or alcohol, or long hours of exhausting labor.

The artificial controls were beyond her reach here, but she certainly seemed to be in the right place for hard work.

She reached the end of the room and carried the last dustpan load to the garbage can, then hung up the broom and pan where she had found them, retrieved her boots and the loathsome hat from the mudroom, and went outside to find her informant in the walled garden.

CHAPTER 26

From the journal of Anne Waverly (aka Ana Wakefield)

Sara was in the greenhouse, rearranging flats of seedlings. Ana greeted her and looked over her shoulder at the plants.

"Broccoli?"

"Cabbage," Sara corrected her. "But close—they're hard to tell apart when they have only four leaves."

"Boy, I love these greenhouses. They look like something out of Kew Gardens."

"Aren't they beautiful? It took months to rebuild them, apparently, they were in such terrible shape. Now they look like a place you should hold a garden party. Here's a trowel. You'll find some gloves in the wardrobe over there."

Ana had noticed the object, a tall mahogany clothes closet more suitable for a cool bedroom than this hot, humid atmosphere. She wrenched open the doors with some effort and rummaged through the heap of mismatched gloves until she found two that fit and had a minimum of holes. Then she took up the trowel and a flat, and followed Sara out to the bed that had been set aside for the young cabbage plants.

"What a luxury to have the ground already prepared. And what gorgeous soil."

"We dug it over yesterday and let it rest. And yes, that's what soil looks like after five generations of care. Do you want a kneeling pad? I don't know about you, but I can't squat for two hours like I used to."

Ana didn't think she had ever been able to squat for two minutes, let alone hours, and accepted the offer of a peeling slab of thick, closed-cell foam rubber. She gingerly lowered herself onto her right knee and prepared to follow Sara's lead in planting.

For twenty minutes or more, the only sounds were the gentle, soul-satisfying noises of trowel parting rich earth and then tapping it down again. Marc Bennett faded in her mind, Martin Cranmer might have been a thousand years ago, but eventually, reluctantly, Ana stirred herself to work around to the questions that had brought her out there.

"Have you always been a gardener, Sara? Or just since you came here?"

"Oh, I always had at least a patch of potatoes and lettuces, even when I lived in the city."

"Was that London?"

"York. You know it?"

"I've been to the cathedral."

"York Minster."

"That's right. And that area around it with all the narrow alleyways. It has some funny name."

"The Shambles?"

"That's right, the Shambles. York's a beautiful town. Do you have family there?"

"My ex-husband and daughter are probably still there."

"You're not sure?"

"It's been four years. Two since I heard from them, when there were some papers to sign."

"You haven't seen your daughter in four years?"

"Thereabouts. I think maybe come autumn I'll go outside and look her up."

Ana glanced at her, but couldn't see Sara's face behind the brim of the floppy straw hat.

"You like it here, then?" she asked.

"It's where I need to be," said Sara, which didn't exactly answer the question. "I am growing and fulfilling myself in a way I never could outside. That's worth the ache of not seeing my child."

"I just asked because it seems, I don't know, tense

here somehow. Like there's a lot going on that people are worried about."

"That's always the case. But you're right, it's not an easy time for you newcomers to fit in. We're going through a difficult time with the Social Services—the people who oversee the schooling and welfare of our children. One of the boys who left earlier this year, poor misguided soul, is trying to get back at his wife by making her choose between her life here and her children. It's one thing to enter into it fully like I did with a nearly grown child, and quite another to be torn apart. A very difficult time all around," she repeated. She had briskly planted the last of her seedlings in neat rows, and got up to go to the greenhouse for another flat. Ana worked more slowly, and with less tidy results. The natural look, she told herself.

When Sara came back, Ana maneuvered the talk around to Marc Bennett, giving Sara a shortened version of what had happened between them in the dining hall. Sara shook her head.

"He means well, love, but even he feels the sort of pressure he's under. He hasn't been here even as long as me, you know, and it's a big responsibility he's taken on. Hardly surprising he's a bit tetchy, times. I know that 'great heat makes for great growth,' but Marc's not had all that much time to prepare himself for it. Jonas just saw him standing there and dumped it all on him."

Ana was astonished at Sara's loose tongue, under the influence of common labor and the warm sun, but she was more than willing to take advantage of it.

"Why? Who was doing all the work before Marc?"

"A lovely woman name of Samantha, called herself Sami with an I. She'd been here forever, far as I know, and then she upped and left."

Ah, thought Ana, at last, a trace of the elusive Samantha Dooley, whose main characteristic seemed to be her ability to slip away—from her family and Harvard University to India, from Pune to England, from Change to the women's community in Toronto. "Really? Why did she leave?"

"Ask ten people, you'll hear eleven stories, as my grandmother used to say. I do know that she and Jonas were having a lot of disagreements. About his Work, mostly. We were having a spell of difficulties with the county council around then, a building permit they were holding back or some such nonsense. Sami wanted Jonas to deal with some of the inspectors; he just said he had his Work to do and to let him be. There was a load of other stuff, I'm sure, but as far as I remember, that was the final straw for her. A few weeks later we woke up one morning and she was gone, she and a couple of other women who'd been here for a year or two."

That seemed pretty much a dead end, unless Sara had stood with her ear to the door during Sami's final conversations with Jonas, and a few more casual questions established that no, Sara knew nothing other than what she had already said. Ana had to move away from the topic before Sara began to wonder at all her interest in a woman she had never met. "And when she left, Jonas gave all her responsibilities to Marc. That was when?"

"Oh, last autumn. After the main harvest, before the frosts. October, maybe?"

"Jonas sounds like a real character."

"You haven't met him yet? Oh dear, I probably shouldn't be talking to you about any of this. You're not really one of us until you've talked to Jonas."

"Shouldn't you? Oh. Well, all right, but I'm not exactly new to Change. I've been in Arizona for a while, and Steven himself sent me here."

"That Steven's such a pleasant man. I don't think I'd

mind too much if I was sent to Arizona, if it wasn't so terribly hot there."

Ana wiped the sweat off her forehead with the side of her glove and shoved her hat onto the back of her head. "Actually, it was cooler there when I left than it is here. It's up in the hills, so it doesn't get quite as hot as the lower desert. A very different kind of gardening, though, because of the shortage of water. Sparse, but beautiful. You'd like it, I think."

"Do you? I'll consider it."

"Jonas is Steven's teacher, too, isn't he? That's why Steven comes here so often. He must be terribly . . . wise."

"Wise?" For the first time in their conversation, Sara paused in her quick, methodical actions, a tiny root ball cradled in one hand and the trowel in the other while she considered this description. "I suppose he must be. Most of the time he just seems, I don't know. Unreachable, maybe. Like he's so far above most people, he doesn't really see us. I mean it—Jonas seems to look straight through you, unless you happen to say or do something that catches his attention, or his imagination. When I first came here, it bothered me. I mean, it seemed a bit rude. I talked to Sami about it one day, and she said it wasn't rudeness, when he ignored you or said something that was kind of insulting; it was like a jolt he'd give you, to help you with your Work. Do you know anything about Zen Buddhism?" she asked unexpectedly, returning to her planting.

"A little."

"Well, you know how there were Zen masters who used to slap their students or clout them over the head with their staffs, and then the students would enter a state of *satori*?" Ana nodded, fascinated by this new side of Sara. "It's kind of like that."

"You mean Jonas hits people?"

"No, no, no. Oh, well, I suppose he does, times, but not very often. Only when someone is being particularly blocked by their mind's assumptions."

This sounded like a lesson learned—painfully, perhaps, taught by the flat of Jonas's hand? Ana thoughtfully dropped the last two plants into their holes and tamped the soil down, and as she went for a second flat, she made a mental note not to turn her back on Jonas if he approached her with a walking stick in his hand.

Sara helped her set out the last of the four flats of cabbages, and then they took two watering cans from the shed next to the greenhouse, filled them at the tap next to the house, and hauled them back and forth to water in the new roots. Apparently, English gardens did not have what Sara called hose-pipes, but relied on rain or muscle. At least, this one did.

They hauled water until Ana's shoulders burned, Sara making three trips for Ana's two, but finally she was satisfied, and the two of them stood looking at their handiwork, dozens of small, spindly green plants lying limply on the damp earth.

"They'll pick up by tomorrow," Sara predicted cheerfully. "And they'll keep us in soup all winter."

"Do you ever use vitamin B_{12} to keep them from transplant shock?"

"Never anything but clear water and the earth they're put down in."

"You don't fertilize them?"

Sara turned to her, surprised. "Oh, no. This is an organic garden. The only things we use are *Bacillus thuringiensis* and sometimes a bit of oil spray when the whitefly gets too thick."

It was Ana's turn to be surprised. She would have sworn that Glen's information included a high use of ammonium nitrate fertilizer in the British Change compound. Or was that the Boston group? Damnation.

Sara gathered up the flats and put them to soak for their next use. They then began to clear out the side of the greenhouse that had nurtured the numerous varieties of plants now growing outside, stripping the growing benches of plant stakes, shards of broken pot, empty seed packets, and all the rest of the debris. It was not the time of day Ana would have chosen to work inside a glass house under the blazing sun, but when she mentioned the possibility of doing the job the next day while the sun was still low, Sara looked at her without comprehension and said she had something else planned for the morning. Ana shrugged, and sweated, and finished the job without complaining.

Afterward, the water that gushed from the tap was deliciously cool and sweet. And then they weeded for a while—in the shady areas—until it was time to pull some lettuces and wash the grit from them. As Ana carried the rich armful into the kitchen, she reflected that her afternoon in the garden had borne some thought-provoking fruit.

Perhaps it was only that Ana had spent the afternoon with her hands in the earth and her ears soothed by Sara's easy accents, but the kitchen staff seemed even more irritable than it had that morning, with pans slapped down smartly and very little of the usual boisterous conversation that kitchen work often gives rise to. Later in the dining hall, she found the same state. Unidentifiable currents and tensions ran through the room.

Not that people were openly irritable with each other; it might have been better if they were. Instead, they seemed grimly determined to remain calm. Residents presented one another with taut smiles, edged away when another person sat down too close, and listened politely with faraway gazes.

Even the children seemed either listless or fractious, with two separate incidents of tears before the meal was over.

Toward the end of the meal Marc Bennett presented himself at the door and waited for silence.

"I need you all to be sure you know where the torches are on each floor." Ana was struck by a brief, bizarre image of flaming brands stuck into holders on the wallpapered hallways until her internal dictionary reminded her that "torch" was simply English for flashlight. "The local utilities today informed us that as we may not be working to code, they may cut off our power. It is simply further harassment, and if it does happen, I am sure we will all use it to drive us a step further along on our Work. I am merely telling you so there will not be any panic as there was the last time the power went out."

He nodded and left, and behind him rose up a murmur of dismay and annoyance tempered by a surprising amount of philosophical acceptance. Another thing to remember, Ana thought: Have someone point out the caches of flashlights.

After she had cleared her dishes she looked around for Jason and Dulcie, and found them sitting with three or four other teenagers. Jason was deep in conversation; Dulcie looked bored and truculent. Ana went over and sat down beside her.

"*Hola,* Dulcinea. Did you enjoy your apple crumble? I helped make it."

The child nodded, and Ana wondered if her former silence was returning, but then she elaborated grudgingly, "It would've been better with ice cream on top."

"I know. Oh well. Hey, I have to go help with the

dishes, but afterward I wonder if you'd like me to read you a story?"

Dulcie nodded, animation seeping back into her face.

"Great," Ana said. "How about you come to the kitchen and save me from the dishwashing after you've had your bath and brushed your teeth? Is that okay, Jason?" she said, turning to face him. He looked up at her blankly, having obviously not heard a word she had said before his name.

"What?"

"Can you bring Dulcie down to the kitchen when she's ready for bed and I'll read her a couple of books?"

"Sure. No problem." He went back to his conversation and Ana studied him for a moment. The hardness was leaving his face, dropping years as it went. The tough, sexy street kid she had met was now visible only in the edges of his face and the angle of his head. He had put on a little weight, true, but that was not the only reason that the harsh lines of his face had softened. Unlikely as it might be, here, yanked from his native land and set down among strangers, he had already made friends. Here he was free to be a different person.

Ana looked away before he could catch her staring at him, and smiled a bit sadly at Dulcie.

"See you in a bit, okay, Sancho? Bring me a couple of good books."

Two books translated into four, and after Ana had suggested that Jason come back in twenty minutes or so, they settled down in a comfortable armchair that smelled of dogs in a small room off the kitchen, a space Ana thought might originally have been the butler's domain. Dulcie was warm from her bath and tired from the long day and the time change and the turmoil, and she fell asleep in Ana's arms halfway through a book she had found about a tribe of mice who lived in a church and earned their keep polishing the brass. Ana finished reading the book silently, then settled back in the chair and was nearly asleep herself when Jason returned for his sister.

"Hey," she greeted him.

"She fell asleep, huh? Thought she might. Sorry."

"Why be sorry? Sit down. So, what do you think of the place?"

"It's okay."

Ana grinned at him, and, slowly, he returned it. "I mean, it really is okay. That Bennett guy's a—" He stopped and glanced around guiltily. "You know, he's not real friendly, but some of the kids are pretty cool, and Jonas is great."

"You've met Jonas?"

"Oh, yeah. I spent most of the afternoon with him."

"Doing what?" She hoped she didn't sound as startled as she felt.

"Oh, just talking."

"Talking? About what?"

"Just stuff. My family, how I grew up, the neighborhoods I lived in, things like that."

(Was that a twinge of jealousy she felt, that Jason should confide so freely in a stranger?)

"You know, it's true," the boy went on with a note of discovery in his voice, "it does help sometimes to talk to people about things. Problems and stuff. It makes things clearer, you know?"

"I know," she said, and bent her head to look at Dulcie and hide the twisted smile she could feel on her lips.

(Yes, no doubt about it; it was jealousy.)

"Have you noticed that our names are the same?" Jason asked suddenly. "Jason, Jonas—they're just turned around."

"Did Jonas point that out?"

"Yeah. He has a funny way of looking at things. Original, like. He'll go all quiet for a while and then he'll say something really off the wall. Sometimes I could sort of understand what he meant, but most of the time I really couldn't. I mean, you know how you sort of laugh when someone tells a joke you don't get? Well, I did that a couple of times and I think it kind of pissed him off, because the second time he just stood up and kind of waved his hand like he was brushing me off, and then he walked away.

"I was kind of worried, you know, in case I'd done something wrong, but I asked a couple of people and they said it was no big thing, Jonas was like that. It's like his brain gets full and he has to go think about things for a while."

"I see."

Dulcie stirred then, and Jason took her limp body up in his arms and said good night. Ana responded automatically, but for once she was not thinking about them. She was too preoccupied with Jonas Seraph, the distant figure around whom this tense little community turned.

The dynamics of the community were not at all what she had been led to believe, although she had to admit that was because of her own assumptions and expectations, not due to any overt flaw in Glen's information. She had expected Jonas to be dynamic and involved; instead, he was playing the role of the distracted alchemist buried in his thoughts and in his laboratory, and it appeared that Change had been given much of its shape not by Jonas or even by Steven Change, but by the now-departed Samantha Dooley. Samantha, vanished with her two friends into the women's community in Toronto, where no doubt her intense interest in growing things, in transforming the earth to cabbages and winter soups, was being given free rein. The information on Change had all been there from the beginning, but like an iceberg, the reality changed beneath the surface.

Jonas was beginning to take shape in Ana's mind, this shadowy person defined by the reactions of those around him. Jonas was wise, Jonas was aloof, Jonas occasionally struck those who were being, in his opinion, particularly slow in understanding, although his outbursts of violence were attributed not to any lack of control, but to the teaching methods of a superior being. Jonas did listen to Steven, and he had brought Jason and his sister and babysitter Ana all the way from Arizona just to look at the boy, but Jonas could not be bothered to explain his pronouncements to Jason, and had grown quickly impatient with the shy overtures of a fourteen-year-old boy. Ana speculated for a moment about Jason's reactions if Jonas had tried to backhand him into a state of *satori,* and decided that Jason would almost certainly not have struck back. He was already as much in awe of Jonas as everyone else.

Ana had met any number of people who were as wrapped up in themselves as Jonas seemed to be. Some of them had been profoundly retarded; others were off-the-scale geniuses. Sociopaths were this way, and the severely neurotic, and madmen of various flavors, for that matter—as well as think-tank employees, high-ranking business executives, high-flying academics, half the archbishops she had met, and even, it is true, one or two genuinely holy people. The utter self-absorption of these individuals would have seemed brutal if there had been any awareness in it; as it was, it often seemed only other-worldly. Into which category, she wondered, did Jonas Seraph fit?

The big Victorian house was quiet now, the smaller children abed and group meditation absorbing the adults. Perhaps she might find some hot water in the pipes to soak away the aches.

Ana pried herself up from the soft chair, laid the story about the church mice on the seat, and took herself to bed.

At about the same time that Ana was brushing her teeth and splashing water on her bleary eyes, the diary pages she had mailed at the Phoenix airport landed on Glen's desk. Glen happened to be there, having a tense phone conversation with his fiancée about a dinner party. When he saw the handwriting on the label, he told Lisa that he had to go, hung up on her, and ripped open the envelope.

White-faced, he skimmed the final entry and Ana's guarded note to Uncle Abner. Then, more slowly, he read both again. Gone? Ana Wakefield suddenly up and vanished into England's Change compound, out of his reach, his authority, his sight even. What the hell was she thinking of? What kind of an amateur game was she pulling? His phone rang and he reached out automatically to switch on the answering machine, then sat back in his chair and stared out the window at the uninspiring view for several minutes. When he moved again, he looked his age and more. He reached down to open a desk drawer and take out a fat file, worn and dog-eared with age. He leafed through it until he came across a photograph, which he removed and laid on his desk. From another, much newer file on the corner of his desk he took a second photo, a kindergarten portrait of "Dulcie" Delgado taken not long before she and her brother had come to Change. He laid it next to the older picture, which was a duplicate of the snapshot of Abby that Anne Waverly kept in the bottom drawer of her own desk.

The two girls could have been sisters.

He had seen the resemblance before, of course he

had. Why, then, had he not stopped to consider the implications? Or had he, and then dismissed them? Anything that made Anne Waverly vulnerable was his responsibility, but the question was—the question that would be asked was—should he have seized on that potential weakness in his operative and immediately upgraded the level of surveillance on her? In other words, was his ass covered?

He had nearly lost her before, eight years ago in Utah. If she had died then, or if her presence in the Utah community had not been so obviously crucial in saving as many lives as it had, Glen's job would have been quietly phased out. He might even have found himself removed from fieldwork. That success, tainted though it was, followed by the clean, almost elegant conclusion of the Cranmer investigation, had left Glen with firm ground beneath his feet, which he had laboriously reinforced during the intervening years until it was nearly as solid as rock.

If anything happened to Anne this time, he would again feel the mud squishing up around his toes. His job was safe—even his enemies would have to admit that if one of his operatives took it into her foolish head to go waltzing out of his sphere of influence and beyond his ability to protect her, it was regrettable, but it could not be construed as his fault.

Which did not mean that he should not move heaven and earth to drag the crazy woman back home. His job might be safe, but his position would not be, and if she failed, the voices behind his back would be poisonous. To say nothing of the reproachful voices inside his own head, telling him that he should somehow have known, and put a watch over the airports, even without the disturbing memorandum that had arrived that same afternoon.

Since his conversation with Ana in Sedona, he had

become more and more uncomfortable with the dangling thread that was Samantha Dooley. He had finally sent Rayne up to Toronto again with orders to talk her way inside the women's community where Dooley had taken shelter the previous October. To his great satisfaction, this time Rayne succeeded. His satisfaction was short-lived; Samantha Dooley was not there. She had never been there, and one of the two women who had left Change around the time she disappeared swore to Rayne that the Change founder had not come with them.

No one had seen Samantha Dooley since the middle of October.

Glen pulled forward the Rolodex file that had once been his father's, flipping it open at the H section. There it was: Paul Harrison, National Crime Investigation Service, with two numbers.

He dialed the fifteen digits of the man's private number and sat back, studying the photographs of the two curly-headed girls he held in his free hand while he listened to the double ring of the English phone system.

"Paul? Glen McCarthy here. Sorry to disturb you at home, hope you weren't in bed. Oh, just fine, and you? You heard right—her name's Lisa. Of course she's gorgeous, you know I have great taste. Oh, blond, of course. And how're those two kids of yours? Great. Yeah, I'd like that—Lisa's never been to England. But look, Paul, I've got a kind of situation here I need some help with. Like, yesterday."

CHAPTER 27

Change: I knew you'd like the boy. You don't intend to send him back, then?

Seraph: Of course not. He's wasted there. And the woman. Ana. She's...intriguing.

Change: I thought so. Almost too good to be true.

Seraph: You mean you suspect her?

Change: Suspect her of-- Oh, I see. No, of course not. Since when would the police have that kind of imagination? No, I meant she seemed almost too perfect. A born adept, or someone who has spent her life preparing for the work without knowing it. She's got a lot of depth to her.

Seraph: I look forward to plumbing it. I might wish she wasn't so ugly.

Change: You think she's ugly?

Seraph: Her hair looks like she's undergone radiation treatment.

Change: I guess. But then you've always been a man for the hair. Remember those two women in Madras? [laughter] She has nice eyes, though, Ana does. How--[pause] How is the other thing coming along?

Seraph: The same. Nothing.

Change: Is there anything I can do?

Seraph: You believe you can succeed where I fail?

Change: Of course not, Jonas. I am only an apprentice, compared to you. We both know that. But if there's any service I can perform as an apprentice, you only have to say.

Seraph: I know, Steven. You're a friend. But it's my battle, my work, and I just need to return my mind and soul to a state of balance. Come next month, as you planned. We'll talk then.

Change: Everything else going amoothly? The Social Serices--

Seraph: Not on the phone, Steven. Marc seems to have it all under control.

Change: Marc is an asshole. He's manipulating you.

Seraph: He does Sami's job and lets me concentrate on the work. That's all that matters. You know, Steven, there is one thing you can help me with. There's a book I think you took with

**Excerpt from the transcription of a telephone conversation between
Steven Change and Jonas Fairweather (aka Jonas Seraph)
4:46 P.M., GMT, May 21, 199_**

Even when she was Anne Waverly, Ana did not have many nightmares. The male psychiatrist assigned to her following the Utah debacle eight years before had found that absence worrying, and kept suggesting that she must be having nightmares and be repressing even the memory of having had them. She had found his attitude unbearably irritating, and soon after that had gone back to Marla, but privately she had to agree: Surely a person who had witnessed as many vile and unnerving sights as she had ought to have more broken nights?

She eventually decided that since she had already gone through two or three real, living nightmares, her subconscious had simply thrown up its hands at manufacturing pale imitations. When she did have disturbing dreams, the actual content was usually innocuous, even when the emotional overtones were oppressive enough to send her bolt upright in her bed, all cold sweat and pounding heart.

That night she dreamed, lying in her narrow metal bed in the women's wing of the Victorian industrialist's run-down mansion, and she came awake in a flash of absolute pounding terror.

As usual, there had been nothing to the dream. Abby, aged three and a half or four, sat in the sandbox that Aaron had built for her in the yard of their house in Berkeley, the house on the quiet street that they had lived in for several years until they had moved to the commune in Texas when Abby was five. The child sat shirtless in the warm sunlight, dribbling sand from an old soup ladle into a series of discarded yogurt tubs and Styrofoam egg cartons. A small black cat, one of the neighborhood animals that Anne chased off because it liked to use the sandbox as its cat tray, sat on one corner of the box, watching the concentrating child. Ana, or Anne, was in turn keeping her eye on the cat, not wanting to break into Abby's serious experiment by shooing the animal away, but also not willing to have it pee in the sand. She was weeding the flower bed that ran along the side fence, tossing clumps of grass and oxalis into an old bucket and glancing up from time to time to be sure the cat had not ventured down from its perch, when she became aware of a man standing half hidden by the shrubs in the front of the yard, his hands in his pockets and his eyes on the browned, half-naked child with the sun in her gleaming tumble of coal-black hair.

Ana came gasping awake, cold with terror and choking on the protest caught in her throat, a cry that she had to stand up and move into view and chase the man off but she couldn't because she was waking up now, and she could not reach back into her sleep to save Abby.

She lay still until the silence of the house overcame the pounding of her heart, and then swung her legs over the edge of the lumpy mattress and put her face in her hands, trying to think if she had actually seen that man. There had been just such a threatening stranger while they lived in Berkeley, a situation that involved meetings of the local parents and police. She remembered clearly how reluctant they had all been, good Berkeley radicals all, to call in the police department over a problem they felt they ought to be able to deal with themselves, and how a core group of the mothers had finally forced the issue by pointing out that it was they who were usually alone with the kids during the day, not the fathers, so the decision was theirs to make, and they wanted the police. And regular uniformed presences had done the job, at least locally and temporarily, for the man had moved on, taken his disturbing and disturbed watching self away to haunt another neighborhood.

She had not thought of that episode in years, had not even thought of the Berkeley house for a long time. What would Marla make of the dream? she wondered, beginning to feel angry. She knew damn well that what she was feeling here in England was the same helpless rage she'd felt then, the same feeling of threat and oppression and the need to take some kind of action to protect a child. Why the hell did she need a dream to tell her all that?

She raised her head and looked at the bright shaft of bluish light that came through the gap in the curtains. Her first night in the room she had barely noticed it, one more strangeness among all the others, but the house was surrounded by brilliant floodlights. Presumably intended to keep away intruders. Tomorrow she would borrow a clothespin or a safety pin to close the gap so it wouldn't disturb her again.

The light cut diagonally across the foot of her bed and showed her the thin coverlet, the worn braided rug that reminded her of Dulcie's colorful efforts, left behind in Arizona for safekeeping, and her book, reading glasses, and wristwatch on the bedside table. It was not even three A.M., but Ana's body was trying to tell her that despite the position of the hands on the watch face, it was actually time to be awake and having some kind of meal. She wondered idly if Dulcie, too, was awake and begging Jason to play with her or find her something to eat.

She lay back down for a while, staring at the bare room. She had left the window open when she went to bed, and as she lay there she became aware of a heavy, sweet smell on the night air, the rich odor of the roses that grew in the bed below, underlaid by the dank fragrance of vegetation that arose out of the surrounding jungle. Ana had never much cared for heavy floral fragrances and had been known to remove pots of blooming narcissus from a room to an external windowsill. She found herself thinking about the Arizona landscape, its spiky shapes and small, waxy leaves, with an affection that verged on longing. What she wouldn't give for a boojum tree. There had been a similarly scented rose trained on an archway leading to the herb garden in Utah, she remembered, an annoyance due to the bees it attracted and the thorns that snagged at the unwary passerby—but she was not thinking about the past now; she would think about something else. Dulcie's church mice, perhaps.

It was no use. The whispering ghosts of memories continued to paw at her mind and her inner clock showed no signs of turning over and going back to sleep, so in the end she got up, pulled on jeans, a sweatshirt, and the pair of Chinese cloth shoes she wore as house slippers, and walked down the hall to the bathroom. She took care not to flush the toilet, a massive water closet that must have been the latest in sanitation technology when it was installed at the turn of the century but which roared its presence throughout the house when the chain loosed its eight-gallon tank of water.

She went down the two flights of stairs to the ground floor kitchen, turned on a small light over the stove and clicked the switch on the electric kettle, then began sorting through the nearby cupboards for tea bags and edibles.

The electric kettle had come to a boil and turned itself off before Ana had assembled mug, tea bag, and milk, its speed reminding her that Britain functioned on 220 current rather than the American 110. She poured the water over the tea bag, which instantly turned the water so black the milk did not make much headway even when she had fished out the sodden, scalding bag. Tea, too, was stronger here, it would seem.

She found cheese and a packet of something called digestive biscuits, which looked like round graham crackers and turned out to be a good foil for the cheese. She longed to go outside to eat, away from this house of turmoil, where she could breathe the clean, unscented night air and search for the moon, but she thought of the dogs and reluctantly decided not to risk waking the house with their barking a second time.

Instead, she took her mug and her plate and wandered through the downstairs rooms, her way lit by the shafts of cool light from outside. The dining hall was too big and empty to have much appeal for a solitary diner, so she went on, through a corridor, past a sitting room with a dark television set in the corner and on into the main entrance, a marbled expanse of pillars and stairways, shadowed and mysterious. The rustle of her clothing sent whispers crawling off into the reaches overhead. Not a place to crunch and slurp, she decided, and continued her search for a friendly corner.

The dining room/ballroom on the one side of the house was mirrored on the other side by a room of similar size and shape. This one seemed darker despite the bright patches from the windows, because the walls were paneled with wood. It was also the first room in the manor house that did not echo emptily, for the simple reason that the walls held tapestries and the floor had carpets. The change was soothing, but as Ana walked farther in she saw that the soft floor was practical as well: Probably originally a gallery to display the family portraits that the industrialist would have commissioned, this large room was now the Change meditation hall.

Unlike the Arizona version, this room made no attempt at circularity. The far end of the room had a dais with a cushion for the meditation leader and a fireplace at his back—the only similarity she had seen to the Arizona compound, come to think of it. She climbed on the dais to examine it as best she could in the uneven light, but found it unexceptional, except perhaps for the locked door at the back of the raised area. She wondered if this, too, led down to an alchemical laboratory, but she had no urge to investigate. Not until she knew the community a whole lot better than she did now.

Ana swallowed the last of her tea and patted the remaining crumbs from the plate with a wet fingertip, and when she turned to go her heart lurched at the sight of a dark figure looming in the entrance to the hall. She gave a squeak of surprise, and then said in a voice that betrayed her attempt at control, "Good evening. Or morning."

"You are aptly named, Ana Wakefield," came the man's voice in return. It was a deep, confident, melodious voice, and as the man moved up the hall toward her, she could see that his body matched it. He was a bear of a man, at least six feet four and broad with it, but he moved with absolute silence.

"Jet lag," she explained as he came closer. "It makes me wake up at strange times and get hungry at weird hours. I hope nobody minds that I helped myself to the cupboards and walked through the house."

"Why should anyone mind?" he said, close now. "Are you not one of us?"

Moving in and out of the patches of blue light pouring through the windows, she had seen his dark hair and thick, dark beard, and although she could not see him well enough to compare with Glen's photograph of Jonas Seraph (né Fairweather), she had no doubt of the bear's identity.

"Are you by any chance Jonas?" she asked.

" 'By any chance,' " he repeated thoughtfully. Ana became aware that she was standing in a shaft of light, although he was at the moment quite invisible in the shadows. She had always been partial to big men; she even liked them slightly scary—Aaron had possessed a little-seen but ferocious temper, and she had once had a mild flirtation with a huge, scarred ex-convict until good sense got the better of her odd physiological susceptibility to the pheromones given off by dangerous males. Still, this creature approaching was a bit much even for her. She took an involuntary step back, and suppressed an urge to slip back into the dark as he rose up the two steps to the dais and loomed over her. "Yes," he said. "I am Jonas."

"You and Steven have a way of appearing in unexpected places," she told him. "Is that something he learned from you?"

"It is something that comes with Change. A person's awareness expands."

I'll bet, she thought; I wouldn't be surprised if there are motion detectors hidden in the wainscoting. She nodded in a way to show her interest in the possibilities of Change and waited for him to go on, but he just stood there, a large, dark presence in front of her. She could see nothing of his face, although the band of light that she stood in also fell across his shoulder and upper arm. He was wearing a corduroy shirt, bleached colorless by the outside lights. His shoulders were broad, his arms beefy, and she was beginning to feel very uncomfortable even before he stepped forward and grasped her arms with his strong hands.

She jerked, nearly letting her mug and plate fall to the floor although she herself moved not at all in his hold, and she fought down the urge to struggle. He bent his head to peer into her face, inches away, so close she could smell the coffee on his breath and the faint astringent odor of his bath soap, an incongruous odor at odds with the heavy carnivore smell that the back of her mind had anticipated. She badly wanted to open her mouth and shout at the top of her lungs, rousing the house and forcing him to let go of her, but the impulse stayed down, even as her head reared away from his, partly because she knew that this was a test of some sort, and in part because she did not feel that he was about to attack her further. Mostly, though, she was afraid that her feeble attempts at self-defense would only make him laugh.

In the end, he let her go—gently, so she did not even stumble back.

"Let me show you what I mean," he said, and walked away. Mean by what? she thought, confused. After a minute, her heart still racing and her breathing ragged, she followed him.

She found him in the marble entrance foyer, where he had stopped to burrow inside a pair of doors under the stairway. He pulled out two coats, tossing one in Ana's direction. It reeked of cigarettes and sweat and was far too large for her, but she found a small table to hold her dishes and pulled the coat on. Jonas continued out the front door, where Ana heard a low growl, immediately cut off when her guide—her abductor?—snapped his meaty fingers. When she got to the door she saw three dogs, awakened from their sleep in the shrubbery, coming up to fawn around his legs. One growled when it saw her step onto the porch, and without hesitation Jonas's hand shot out and delivered a massive slap to the side of the dog's head that sent the animal spinning. It yelped once and picked itself up from the ground to come groveling back up to them with its tail between its legs, but Jonas had already set off across the weedy gravel drive beneath the harsh lights. The dog did not seem to have reached a state of *satori,* Ana thought wildly as she hurried after Jonas; still, at least its neck wasn't broken.

They traveled along the drive for perhaps half a mile with Ana in Jonas's footsteps. It was closer to the ridiculously early English dawn than she had realized, because when the floodlights faded behind them she could still make out the shape of the ground, the wall of trees pressing on her left, and the rails of a fence on her right.

When they left the road, the stars were fading in the gray firmament overhead, but as soon as she followed Jonas into the narrow gap between the shrubs, she was blind again. She stopped. He firmly gripped her upper arm and began to draw her deeper into the tangle. She held her free hand up in front of her face and allowed herself to be led.

It was the strangest blind walk this child of the Sixties had ever been on. She was being taken into this jungle by a man she would not have trusted with a pot of beans, much less her life, yet even as she placed her bones and flesh in his hands, she felt nothing of the panic that the situation would have justified, nor even much fear beyond a nervous awareness of what her disappearance might mean for Jason and Dulcie.

The surface underfoot was thick with decomposed leaves and small twigs, but blessedly soft for someone wearing thin-soled slippers and nearly smooth—an old road, perhaps, overgrown for decades but as yet not completely overtaken. Jonas seemed to know the way well, because he walked without hesitation, pressing on for at least twenty minutes before he halted and let go of Ana's arm.

"There's a bench directly in front of you," he told her. "Sit down on it and listen for a while, tell me what you hear."

She patted her way forward to the light shape that turned out to be a very old stone bench, rough with lichen but sound and dry. She sat, and listened. With all her being she listened, and she heard absolutely nothing, not even a breeze stirring the leaves. The silence was weighty, even oppressive; her own breathing was the only sound to brush her ears, and once a tiny twig giving way beneath Jonas's weight. Finally, she could bear it no longer. She raised her head and spoke to his dim shape where it squatted a few feet away.

"I can't hear a thing other than my own breath," she said loudly. "What did you want me to hear?"

He rose, more twigs crackling under his feet. "Very good," he said enigmatically. "Now come."

He plunged off again down the overgrown road, Ana stumbling along helplessly at his heels, and they entered an area that felt more like Lost World or a dinosaur movie than an estate in southern England. Huge fleshy leaves pawed against her face, massive fans that looked like the leaves of rhubarb plants growing downstream from a nuclear power plant. Overhead, lacy fronds clogged the still-dim sky, the prehistoric tendrils of a stand of magnificent tree ferns that any park in New Zealand would have been proud of. In one place in this jungle, even Jonas had to give way, edging around a stand of timber bamboo with stems as thick as Ana's upper arm. She felt as if she'd been fed through a shrinking mechanism, or a time machine.

And then after about ten minutes they stepped suddenly out from the jungly growth into a sloping stretch of open ground, still indistinct but beginning to take form in the dawn. As soon as they were free of the trees, Jonas dropped to the ground, his bearlike shape fitting as easily into a lotus position as if he were sitting onto a chair. Ana sat down a distance from him and pulled her knees to her chest. Wrapping the borrowed coat around her, she tried to ignore her wet, bruised feet.

There was a faint breeze here, and from somewhere the crisp music of water trickling down stone. The sun was coming quickly now, and details became visible— trees, a small building on the other side of the clearing, a stream winding down the hillside in a delicate curve to the gleam of a pond below. With more light came the

colors, the rich green turf and the yellow of a few late
daffodils growing up through it; the pale blossoms, white
or pale yellow, of a scattering of shrubs Ana could not
identify; the creamy white marble of the little building,
its four narrow pillars reminding her of the main house's
entrance foyer and giving it the air of a shrine; the deep,
vivid, and unexpected blue of the roof tiles.

And birds, even before full dawn. Distant and tentative at first, then becoming near as others showed themselves and joined in. A far-off rooster contributed its
crow, and Ana nearly smiled at the sound.

The chorus grew around them, until all the world
rejoiced at the coming of day and the grove rang with
life.

Ana felt well and truly out of her depth here. A Marc
Bennett she could get around, a Steven Change she could
manipulate, but what could she possibly do with a force
of nature like the Bear? She hadn't the faintest idea what
they were doing out there, what it was that he expected
her to see, how she should react to him. She did know
that the method she had used to impress herself on
Steven—Ana the enigmatic Seeker who knew more than
she realized—would be utterly useless here. Jonas had
already, with a few terse sentences, out-enigmaed the
Sphinx, and she had no chance to match that. It would
just puzzle him.

"Sex is a curious thing, is it not?" Jonas mused, startling her.

After a minute, when no explanation followed, Ana
asked a bit uncertainly, "I'm sorry?"

He waved a big hand at the grotto. "Male birds sing
to attract females and to proclaim their territory. In pri-
mates, the male pounds his chest and the female aligns
herself with the most promising male. A woman's great
fear of violation is not only the personal threat, but the
fear of the species that her choice might be taken from

her. Just as a man's great fear, castration, is not only the loss of his own strength, but having his presence in the gene pool taken from him."

Despite her nervousness, it was very, very tempting to respond to this with a complete non sequitur of her own regarding the Dalai Lama's teeth or the migration of the monarch butterfly, but she resisted.

"I don't understand," she said apologetically.

"You were afraid of me. Now you're not."

This was patently not true, but Ana responded carefully. "It was dark and you were a stranger. Now it's not, and you're not."

"And you have stopped to listen to the morning," he said with no recognition of the validity of her statement.

"It was very quiet earlier."

"It still is quiet back there in the deep woods."

"Really? Why?"

"This estate was built in the 1830s," he said. "The family was wiped out in the First World War and the flu epidemic that followed. The gardens deteriorated, the rides grew over, the outbuildings fell into disrepair and then into ruin.

"Change came here twelve years ago. This grotto we're sitting in was one of our first attempts at Transformation. It was so overgrown as to be impenetrable, a solid thicket of laurel and other shrubs grown to vast proportions. Not even bramble could grow. And like the area we were in earlier, there was no life. No birds, no animals, just the insects and funguses of decay.

"Our first action was destruction," he said with no small degree of relish. "Chain saws, bulldozers, and poison for the stumps—when we finished, there was devastation: a few top-heavy trees, a pile of stones where the summerhouse is, and bare, gouged earth. It resembled a First World War battleground, and had about as much life in it.

"And now birds and squirrels live here, the pond that was little more than a mud hole supports half a dozen kinds of fish, the soil that was sour and hard now smells sweet and gives life to a myriad of growing things."

The bearded man, seen clearly now, had a faraway, almost dreamy look on his face. His head was tipped back so that the thick black hair tumbled back on his shoulders; the untrimmed beard covered his face nearly to his cheekbones. Daylight confirmed nighttime's impression, that this was indeed a bear of a man. He was, oddly enough, the sort of man Ana normally found physically attractive, as big and furry as Aaron had been, or Antony Makepeace, or most of the men who ended up in her bed (other than Glen, but then, Glen was another thing altogether).

This bear, however, was no comforting presence, and Ana had no desire whatsoever to sink her fingers into his hair. She felt a fascination, certainly, but it was like the compulsion of reversed magnets, repellent face-to-face but with a strong tug from the back. This bear was more grizzly than teddy, appealing from a safe distance but murderous when crossed. Ana had a strong urge to sit, quiet and small in her corner, although at the moment he seemed almost unaware of her presence.

"The land and its Transformation is a paradigm for our real Work here. From destruction comes forth life. From the ashes of fire beauty is born. Personally, I wanted to set the glade to the torch, to purify it down to the ground and the stones and see what came of it, but my friends and the county council disapproved of the idea. It would have been interesting, however. There are many seeds that come to life only after the touch of fire."

The deep, detached voice sent a cold thread down Ana's spine; she hugged the borrowed coat more tightly around her and closed her eyes.

She was abruptly aware of how terribly afraid she

was, although she could not have said precisely why. Fear, like pain, was an old and familiar companion. She had long ago learned to distance herself, to use the very intensity of the sensation to create a wall between it and her. Pain or fear alike could rage through her body, but her essential self was left quiet in one small corner, aware but not overtaken.

This was different. The normal barriers refused to stay up, the spark of her being was flaring and fluttering madly in the gusts of emotion—the affection she felt for Dulcie and Jason crossed with the battering of memory and the assault of Change—and she could not find the point of balance that kept the fear-ridden Anne Waverly away from the calm essence at the center and allowed Ana Wakefield to get on with her work. There were too many pulls, too many anxieties and memories, and Anne would not go away. The situation was massively dangerous, to herself and to those around her. Ana had to be allowed to slide free; her intuitive and unthinking response to people and events was the key element that made her work for Glen possible. Why was that proving so difficult this time?

She opened her eyes. The morning was still sweet, and Jonas Fairweather was still looking at the side of her face. She turned to him and gave him a smile that felt like a rictus.

"Jonas," she said, "tell me about alchemical transformation."

CHAPTER 28

"Change" Abbey

From the journal of Anne Waverly (aka Ana Wakefield)

"Alchemical transformation," Jonas said thoughtfully, sounding for all the world as if this were a new idea to him. "Ah yes, Steven seemed to think you had hidden talents in the field. Actually, my friend Steven knows I've been having some problems with my Work, and thought you might help. God knows he's tried everything else."

"Can I help?"

"I doubt it," he said flatly.

"So do I," she said. "But you never know."

He looked at her. "No, one never knows. So what are these hidden talents of yours, Ana Wakefield? What do you know about alchemy? What can you tell me about the fading memory of success, and experiments that fail, and a power nexus that has gone dead? Hmm?"

He was waiting. In a moment he would tire of her and walk away, and her opportunity would be lost, but for the life of her she couldn't think of anything clever enough to catch his interest. All she could come up with was his use of the phrase "power nexus," words Steven had used to refer to the alembic of transformation in which he had locked Jason, but that connection was too thin to build much on. In the end she was forced to fall back on the bare and aching truth.

"If I have hidden talents, they are hidden from me, too. And I know almost nothing about alchemy. I do know a great deal about memory, and about failure. And sometimes I think I know everything there is to know about being powerless."

After a minute, he said, "Refreshing, if nothing else. Shall I tell you how I became interested in alchemy?" He actually waited for her to say yes before he went on.

"It began when some friends and I decided to take a sabbatical from life and travel across Europe and the Middle East to India. We had money, we had time, so we went slowly and saw everything there was to see along the way.

"When we got to Bombay, we went to the caves at Elephanta, and there, before the image of Shiva's power, we met a young Parsi woman. A guide, as it turned out, in more ways than one. We talked, we went to her home and met her family, and there I encountered the old man who was to teach me everything.

"The Parsis are called fire worshipers, although that is a typically simplistic description of a complex tradition. I'm not going to bother telling you about them—if you're interested, read a book. The point is, the old Parsi was a questioner. He had reached back through his own tradition to a time when the essential fire—the fire of creation and not of destruction—had been accessible to man.

"To make a long story short, he taught me to transmute matter. I would not have believed it possible—I did not believe it possible—but I saw it, a number of times, and in the end I had to lay down my doubts. He created gold. It was costly and it took weeks of great effort and intense concentration, but it was gold, created out of a lump of lead. And if you give voice to the disbelief that is in your face I shall hit you."

Ana gulped and erased any reaction whatsoever from her mind.

"I stayed with him for a year, I effected transmutation of matter six times under his supervision and three times alone, and I began the even longer and more laborious process of the Fabrication of the Tincture, about which I shall say nothing more.

"The time came to leave Bombay. We went across Iraq and Turkey, through southern Europe to Germany, and there we stopped to see some of the cities of the great period of European alchemy. While we were in a ridiculous, childish, so-called re-creation of an alchemical laboratory, I had a vision.

"I saw the moon clad in white, with great streams of colored sweat pouring down her face as she gave birth to a man with a thick head of golden hair, lying right there on the floor of the museum. When the man was fully birthed she held him out to me to take, and when I reached forward, my vision sank into a great bed of flame and disappeared. What do your hidden talents and powerlessness say of that, Ana Wakefield?"

Before she could formulate any semblance of an answer, Jonas unfurled his legs and stood up, setting off down the hill in the direction of the lake. She scrambled upright and tottered off after him. On the close turf at the edge of the water, they stood looking at a family of ducklings plopping off their nest into the water.

"Steven told me you and he have practiced firewalking," she said.

"It was part of the learning process, that the *artifex* might be aligned with the product in his alembic."

"Do you still do it? Firewalk?"

"Not in some time. It was necessary only at the beginning. Why do you bring it up?"

"Just interested. Something about what you said, the 'bed of flame' in your vision, I guess it was, made me think of it."

He fixed her with a long and peculiar look. She felt pinned down by it, caught by the intensity of his gaze, and when he opened his mouth, she braced herself for revelation. In anticlimax, all he said was, "I want my breakfast now."

They walked on through the restored woodlands, and although he was still difficult to read, she thought

Jonas seemed as pleased as if he had found a new disciple
—which, Ana reflected, he had.

"You should thank alchemists for the distillation of
alcohol. Do you drink?" He did not pause for her answer. "The scientific process, the discovery of ammonium sulfate. Algebraic formulation we owe to Jabir ibn
Hayyan, nitric acid . . ."

The words washed over her, but she made no effort
to remember them, merely listening intently for a clue, a
sign of what he needed from her. Elixirs and dragons;
the characteristics of mercury; the alchemical references
in Ben Jonson; the names Kalid ibn Yazid and Cheng
Wei, Robert of Chester and Albertus Magnus, Roger Bacon and Isaac Newton, Abu Bakr and Charles II; the
magnificent Latinate stages of the alchemical process, the
seven or twelve or more levels of transformation from
the *prima materia* and the *nigredo* of *dissolutio* to the
white of *purificatio* and the red of the Stone itself; the
links between the planets and the metals; the alignment
necessary between the *artifex* and his universe and the
work going on within the alembic.

On and on he went, like a breached dam it poured
out, and although the half-hour walk back to the house
seemed interminable, it also seemed too short, because
listen as she might—and how she listened!—she did not
hear the clue she was waiting for.

Did Jonas want an assistant? An interpreter? Twice
she ventured a remark into his flood. The first time,
when he was describing the role of the alchemist in society, she ventured a comment about shamanism that he
seized with glee and approval. He talked about Siberia
and Native American shamanism, the sacred journey
and the return to the tribe with a holy object. When that
merged into a description of the properties of the Philosopher's Stone, Ana listened attentively before interjecting
a remark about longevity. This time the remark was

ignored, as if she had not spoken. She did notice, though, that eventually he included a lengthy review of the evidence of immortality among alchemists, which took them as far as the house.

Once in the grand marble entrance hall, shucking off the borrowed coat, Ana said tentatively, "You said there were photographs of the gardens . . . ?"

Clear breakfast sounds came from the dining hall, but Jonas swept her into the first room, the one with the small television set, to display a series of before-and-after pictures. The grotto in its earlier stage looked like a jungle—she would not have been surprised to see a sloth or a monkey peeping out of the greenery. A montage showed a narrow path through a wall of branches being peeled back to become an airy ride, with two helmeted riders perched atop a pair of horses. A stretch of muck from which emerged dead trees, a few bog plants, and the handle of a shopping cart achieved its transformation as the pristine lake that she had seen at the foot of the summerhouse, complete in the photograph with two children in a rowboat and a trio of swans.

Jonas tapped a blunt finger on the glass over a tree. "We counted seven birds' nests in that tree the year this picture was taken. Two years before there was not one."

"A remarkable transformation," she said.

Jonas displayed a lot of white teeth surrounded by hair, which she assumed was a grin, although it looked more aggressive than appreciative.

"Breakfast," he said, and left the room.

Ana followed slowly, so that she was still in the corridor when he entered the dining room. There was an immediate drop in the hubbub of conversation and clatter as his presence was acknowledged, but the pause was nothing compared to the brief moment of absolute stillness that fell over the gathering when Ana walked in on his heels. Surprise, speculation, and consternation, all over in a moment when the scores of conversations were resumed in loud and nervous tones to cover up the silence.

Ana cursed under her breath. She should have thought of how it would look, the new woman walking in for breakfast with the guru. But surely they couldn't think— Okay, she wasn't completely hideous, and she was about his age, but surely—

They could, and some of them obviously did.

At first she was annoyed by the community's swift assumption, irritated at the obsessive childishness of the group when it came to their leader. Then she caught a glimpse of herself in one of the stainless steel covers of the warming trays, and she had to laugh at the thought of this crop-haired, graying, peculiarly dressed woman who looked all of her forty-eight years accused of vamping the guru. It was too silly.

It had been a long time since the three A.M. cheese-and-crackers, and she filled a plate and carried it to an unoccupied corner to reflect. Her thoughts fluttered around madly like a cage full of panicky songbirds: Jonas and Jason, Dulcie and the absent Sami, cabbage seedlings and a grotto put to the torch, a dog sent tumbling by a massive hand and a dead boy in Japan with bloody fingernails. She did not know what to do, she could not control the images in her head, and she had never felt so far from home. I've got to get out of here, she thought. The hell with Glen, and except for two people, I don't care what happens to Change. I can't do this. I can't. Not this time.

She heard the panic building in her thoughts, and wrenched them back from the abyss. Grabbing the handle of her fork like a weapon, she stared furiously down at her plate.

Jesus Christ! she raged at herself. You go around ordering a fourteen-year-old kid to use his head—what about you? *Think,* for God's sake! It's supposed to be what you do best, isn't it? You study a religious vocabulary, you figure out how to speak it, and then you use its symbols to manipulate people. What the hell difference does it make if it's an individual instead of a community? Jonas Seraph speaks a language: Learn it. What is his key? Don't think with your guts, woman—that won't help anyone. Stand back and look at the problem sensibly. Use the brain that God gave you and that Glen and Antony Makepeace and a score of others pounded into shape.

First, review the facts: What had she learned that morning between the time when she had woken up with the floodlights shining through her curtain and the moment she had sat down at this scarred table?

Well, she had learned who the mysterious Jonas was. Oh, yes.

She'd learned that he was nuts, just to be technical, and that he liked to . . . She went still. She'd learned that he liked to talk. He needed to talk, and yes, he had indeed told her what he needed of her, not in a word or a phrase but in a spate of them. He did not want her to *do* anything; he just needed someone to listen. Not necessarily someone clever enough to work with, or knowledgeable enough to suggest alternative processes to his own Work, but a bright smile with an adequate mind behind it to talk to. Yes, a disciple. Whether by accident or by the machinations of her subconscious, she had struck precisely the right note, and she had found her role: intelligent passivity. A boy like Jason would not do as a sounding board because he tried too hard and lacked the experience; a man like Marc Bennett had his own agenda; and the woman Sami had lost patience with his genius and left.

And there was no doubt of his genius. He was, as she would have anticipated, extremely knowledgeable about everything to do with metallurgy, from the mining of ore to atomic structure, but he had obviously also spent a lifetime ransacking the world's disciplines for shiny bits of knowledge. Botany, physiology, astronomy, linguistics, history—you name it, he had at least looked inside.

Right. She could fill the position of intelligent audience. It might drive her mad, but she could do it. What else did she know about him?

She'd discovered that he was a man who could drag a woman into the dark woods, lay hands on her, stand inches from her, even talk about sex with her and yet not rape her, not come on to her, not even sound remotely suggestive to her. Not a talent possessed by many men. And she might have thought him to be one of life's intellectual eunuchs but for the communal reaction when she had followed him in: The Change community believed that Jonas was currently without a woman but that such a state of affairs (so to speak) was quite possible, and in this tight-knit group, she was willing to credit common belief with sure knowledge.

Sami, then, had been here, had been his woman in some way or other, and had not been replaced.

Yet.

Ana stopped chewing. No, she would not—could not —seduce Jonas with her body; the very idea was as absurd as it was distasteful. But with her mind—no, go for the man's weak spot: With her *spirit,* she could indeed offer to fill the gap in his life. His spiritual life.

Think, woman.

Alchemy: The key to his mind and method had to lie there. Alchemy was by no means just a phenomenon of medieval Europe and the Age of Reason; the very name was from the Arabic, and alchemical writings and speculations were spread in a wide swath across the Middle East, out from the China that most probably gave it birth. In China as in India, the miraculous transformation of base matter into gold was inextricably linked to the idea of energy centers rising in the body. The erotic disciplines of *Tantra* and *Kundalini* in India, the esoteric sexual branches of the tree that was Taoism in China, all were rooted, back in their beginnings, in alchemy, and all . . . all rested squarely on the dual nature of the human being: a union of opposites, *coniunctio oppositorum;* The Hermaphrodite, a name for the Stone; the symbol of king and queen joined together; the alchemist as *artifex* with his *soror mystica,* his mystic sister, at his side. As another discipline put it: Male and female made He them.

Man and woman together explore the mysteries, yang and yin, sun and moon, gold and silver. If she could remind Jonas of this tradition, far older than that of the solitary European male working in his laboratory, if she could convince him of it, she might at the very least buy herself some time while he thought it over.

At this point, time was gold.

Ana put down her fork and looked around for Jonas.

With half the community watching, Ana went after Jonas, and when she had tracked him down in the small and separate dining room used by the high-ranking initiates, its tables elegant with white linen and crystal glasses, she arranged with him for another interview at five that afternoon. She walked with dignity back through the dining hall and up to her room, planning to have a bath (it being England, "shower baths" were few and far between) and offer her labor to the garden for the day. When she reached her room, though, and shut the door behind her, she was hit by a wave of exhaustion and jet lag combined with the shuddering release of tension, and she dropped down onto the bed fully clothed, for a ten-minute nap.

Three hours later, the sound of voices going past her door woke her. She took her oldest jeans and a T-shirt down the hallway to the bathroom, splashed herself in a tub of tepid water, and dressed. Downstairs she found lunch being set out, so she assembled a sandwich and went outside to present herself to the gardeners.

She was given the inevitable wide-brimmed hat and a short-handled garden fork, and as she took the tool, she realized wryly that her faraway dream of spending her free hours turning soil was about to be fulfilled. She dug until blisters opened along both palms, when she was sent to tote instead: hay to the horses, firewood to the house, and finally stones in a wheelbarrow to a wall being restored.

After four hours of hard labor, she felt as if she had been beaten about the shoulders and back. Her legs trembled, her hand and knee throbbed, her palms were aflame; every muscle in her body protested. Worst of all, she had not given a thought to her coming interview with Jonas. Whoever said that mindless labor gave one a chance to think had never hauled rock in a barrow with a crooked wheel. But the haunting memories had drawn back momentarily into their pit; for that she was willing to suffer greater discomfort than this.

At four-thirty Ana laid down her load and went in to grab a mug of tea and another bath. There was no getting the soil from under her nails, but at least she didn't stink when she presented herself at Jonas's study.

The Change leader's room was at the bottom of a dim, dank set of stairs under the kitchen, in a part of the house that the Victorian family upstairs had probably never set foot in. She stood on the uneven stones that formed the floor and looked longingly at the three firmly closed doors in front of her. All three had new, sturdy-looking locks. Although she would have given much to see behind them, she had no choice but to turn and walk beneath the stairway to the open door of Jonas's study.

"Lair" might have been a more accurate description. It was a big room, twenty-five feet across and nearly twenty high, and from the looks of it had been the original kitchen, back when servants were expected to run upstairs with heavy platters of hot food rather than taint the upper air with the sounds and smells of cooking. The high windows, excavated below ground level, may once have lit the space adequately: Now they were so covered with uneven bead curtains as to be indistinguishable from the walls, aside from a certain glow behind the beads.

Or not beads—objects, thousands of objects hung up against the light on strings and ribbons and fishing line. With themes—one window held nothing but drinking vessels, from commemorative teacups to the small mended pottery amphoras of an archaeological dig, while the next one had figurines from all over the world, all less than two inches in height. The third one seemed to be sticks and rocks until Ana looked more closely and saw that they were bones: chicken bones, bird skulls, the articulated foot of some small mammal, and near the bottom an object that looked disconcertingly like the skull of an infant human being. She hoped it was a monkey.

Jonas was reading a newspaper, apparently a current one, which seemed to her somehow extraordinary, particularly as he wore steel-framed half-glasses to do so. He had looked up as she came in, and his eyebrows rose as if he had no idea who she was or what she wanted. She tore her gaze from the strange window coverings and offered him a tentative smile.

"Ana Wakefield. You told me to come at five?"

His face did not change as he said, "I hope you are

wearing more adequate footwear than you did this morning."

She nodded, and he pulled off his glasses and tossed them and the paper on top of the huge wooden desk that was piled high with papers, journals, used coffee cups, and more books than Ana could have gotten through in a month.

"Wait here," he told her. "I need to urinate."

It was indeed a lair, or a den, or one of the illustrations of medieval alchemical laboratories come to life, lacking only the actual tools of the trade. She would not have been surprised to see Rackham's awestruck alchemical gnome lurking in one corner. Tables were heaped high with books and papers, plates of half-eaten food and cups bristling with pens and pencils. The ballpoint pens seemed anachronistic, to say nothing of the elaborate computer array with scanner, phone line, and an industrial-strength-sized external hard drive: Quills and an abacus would have been more appropriate. High, dark bookshelves held literally thousands of books, many several inches thick and hand-bound in ancient leather, but others considerably more recent, and she had a true shock when she saw a familiar spine tucked between two books from the end of the nineteenth century: Jonas had a copy of Anne Waverly's *Cults Among Us* on his shelf, and she was very glad that she had refused to have an author photo placed on the inner flap. It was disconcerting, as if she had caught sight of Glen peeping through the windows: Comforting, but she could only hope no one else noticed.

Jonas came back and found her standing in the same spot as when he had left. He ran his gaze over the room as if to make sure he had not forgotten anything, then grunted, and walked out. She took the grunt as an invitation, or a command, but as she turned to follow, she glanced over at the headlines of the paper he had been reading, and caught the words AMERICAN CULT. She swore under her breath; all she needed was another notch of pressure on Change. If the media climbed onto the current load of problems, it would not make her time there any easier.

"Why do they so love the word 'cult'?" Jonas was saying irritably. "They use it as a term of opprobrium, certainly of derision. Did you know that 'cult' is from the Latin *cultus,* from the verb *incolere,* meaning to inhabit or care for a place? And that it is related to the Greek *kyklos,* wheel, which in turn is linked to the Sanskrit *chakra*? You do know what a *chakra* is?" he demanded, stopping on the stairs to peer down at her.

This time he seemed to want his question answered, so she obediently said, "It means wheel, too, doesn't it? Or the energy centers of the body that are depicted as wheels."

He grunted and continued. "Cultivate, culture, they're all the same, though I would say in this country we're more a cultigen than a cultivar. You don't have the faintest idea what I'm talking about, do you?"

"Cults," she said promptly.

"I suppose," he said, and led her out-of-doors.

They walked again, out into the jungle that had once been the formal gardens of an estate. Twice they went through green walls that she would have considered impenetrable, but Jonas knew just where to push his way, and they continued.

And he talked. She was well on her way to establishing herself as his *soror mystica,* she thought, but she had begun to feel a deep sympathy for Sami Dooley. When she got caught on a branch as he was telling her about the life of Arnold of Villanova, he merely reached back and hauled her bodily through the gouging, scraping branches. She tried to raise her spirits by the thought of what a fascinating study she would someday write of this whole episode, but the humor was halfhearted and the pain too sharp, and more immediate was the knowledge that she was being led off into the lonely woods by a man who made her feel as if she were carrying a rattlesnake in her coat pocket.

Focus! she ordered fiercely. Think, you stupid woman. Listen to what he's saying, this modern alchemist who believes, with all the power of his stunted emotions and considerable intellect, that the very nature of matter can be transformed by the application of a precise set of changes, forces, circumstances. Listen to his words, pick out his key images and the central ideas that drive him; use them to nudge him toward where you want him to be. Yes, he's a goddamn genius, but even the brightest minds have their blind spots, and you are about to become his. You can do this. You have to.

The path had cleared somewhat, and Ana walked just behind Jonas, her hands clasped behind her back, her head bent to catch his words, the perfect disciple. He was talking again about the stages of transformation that the *prima materia* goes through on its path to perfection into gold. She waited until he came to a resting point, and then she asked him a question.

"I do see that is like the rising of the *Kundalini* through the *chakras*. Don't the Chinese call them *chis*?"

That set him off on the topic of nerve centers and the rising of energies, sexual and otherwise, and the Indian/Chinese ties throughout history. Ana walked quietly, listening to his remarkably explicit descriptions of the frankly erotic discipline of *Tantra,* and then asked him, struggling to keep the question matter-of-fact, "To what extent do you think the alchemists saw the *Kundalini* as a metaphorical idea rather than actual, physical *Tantra* yoga?"

She might have been asking about rocks for all the overtones his answer held. "The alchemist always speaks on several levels at once: literal, then metaphorical, and then on the plane where the literal and the metaphorical are one. He who has ears to hear, let him hear." He then went on to speak about the role of the *soror mystica,* the mystical sister, during the course of which he left Ana in no doubt about the distinctly non-sisterly actions that Sami had performed for him, and in great doubt about why she had possibly thought of him as an asexual being. He seemed unconscious that she might be feeling any discomfort, but she was distinctly relieved when he finally abandoned the topic of the metaphysical energies aroused by various sexual positions and wandered on to discuss the nature of the "pure dew" that some medieval recipes specified was to be gathered for the process—was it actual on-the-leaves morning dew or, rather, a virgin's urine?—and then shifted into the esoteric objects used in various alchemical recipes. That kept him busy for a while, but eventually he mentioned, for the third time since they had met, the problem he was having with the current Work, and Ana knew she had to seize her opportunity. She summoned every scrap of sincerity and innocence that she could find and put it into her voice.

"Um, Jonas? When you talk about the need of the alchemist to be in balance, both with the external universe and with the microcosm within the alembic, and also about the duality of the Stone, I just wondered if you'd ever considered pairing up for your Work with one of the high-ranking women initiates in Change, to give you the balance of duality? It's just a thought."

There it was, presented to him by the tentative, always helpful, never threatening Ana Wakefield. With any luck, he would soon believe that he had thought of the solution himself.

Just then, however, he had something else on his mind. They had been walking in a rough circle and were now headed back toward the house and into the sunset, when the thick growth abruptly stopped, as it had that morning at the grotto. This open space, though, seemed somehow less restored than it did reserved, as if nothing but green grass had ever grown in a wide rectangular space around the low, crumbling walls of what had once been a sizable building. It was quiet there, but it was not the utter silence of lifelessness and strangulation; what she heard was the hush of content and respect.

"Abby," said Jonas, to Ana's confusion and shock. When she did not answer, he turned and saw her strange expression, and frowned.

"The abbey," he repeated. "This was a Benedictine abbey until the Dissolution of Henry the Eighth. This particular part of the estate is a historical preserve, or else I might have been tempted to do more restoration work. I'm glad I didn't: It took me years to discover that this is the energy center of the land around, and a line drawn from here to the house precisely bisects, at right angles, the line between Stonehenge and Glastonbury. Can't you feel the energy?"

Ana nodded obediently, a bit too distracted to feel the subtle ley lines under her feet. It was, however, a very lovely spot, and she felt that she would like to return there under different circumstances.

She walked forward into the cruciform ruins, entering at what had been the front doors of the building. In some places the stones of the nave walls were missing completely, and in others the grass and wildflowers grew up over the tumbled stonework to waist height. The remnants of the walls were taller at the end of the building where the altar had been; they rose past Ana's head, and the base of one of the windows could be seen, its decorative carving long weathered into soft shapelessness. Small ferns and wallflowers had rooted themselves among the cracks.

Once away from the walls, the entire floor of the

abbey was a smooth carpet of green turf set with tiny white wildflowers, but for one massive rectangular stone which, judging by its location, marked where the altar had stood. Someone had taken care to keep its surface clear of grass, trimming the edges back—in fact, the entire stone looked renewed, as if it had been lifted and relaid to keep it from sinking into the earth and disappearing entirely. It did not even have much moss on it. Jonas may have decided that this point marked his ley line, which would be an ironic variation on the ancient Christian tradition of building a church on the holy ground of its predecessors: The New Age reclaims a Christian site for its primal energy potentials. Ana stood with her toes nearly touching the revealed stone, looking up, trying to conjure up the ghostly outlines of the church that had once formed the center of this lively monastic community.

When Jonas's hands came down on her shoulders she nearly leapt out of her skin. He heard her gasp and slid his grip down to her upper arms. He squeezed once, and then moved around to the other side of the altar stone, taking care not to step on the stone itself. She lifted her eyes to his, and could not pull them away as he began to speak.

"The Philosopher's Stone, the object of alchemical labors that provides immortality and turns base metal to gold, is also called The Hermaphrodite. It is the union of all opposites. Male and female, hot and cool," he said, his words like a chant. "The dry and the wet, the wise and the innocent, the red of the sulfur and the silver of mercury, the generative power of the sun and the reflective forces of the moon. Alchemical drawings depict this union as a king and a queen lying together in the coffin of their alembic. The Absolute, the Brahman, the Stone, the Tincture, is a union of Shiva and Shakti, destruction and nurturing, the seed and the blood, the male and the female. It is the stage beyond the gold, and it renders the participants immortal.

"Since the first blacksmith discovered iron, man has been applying fire to dull stone and creating miracles. The unrefined human being, rocklike and dumb, is no different from gold-bearing ore. It takes only the right technique—the right knowledge—the proper manipulation of forces, to transmute a mere man into something greater, something miraculous. My Parsi master took me to meet immortals, men who could pierce themselves and not bleed, be bitten by cobras and not die. My teacher himself is three hundred and twelve years old, and looks to be sixty. Immortality and the power to heal, those are the characteristics of the human Philosopher's Stones I have met.

"It is also what my entire life has been leading to. I learned to walk on burning coals without feeling pain, that I might become a Master of Fire. That was one of the titles the alchemists used of themselves, did you know that, Ana? Master of Fire. The next step, my transmutation into a human Philosopher's Stone, a walking tincture, also involves, as you yourself interpreted from my vision, a walk not over fire, but through it. Amusing to think that I have spent twelve years of my life studying the patterns of transformation in this laboratory of mine, and you should come here and tell me something that is plain before my eyes. Your hidden talent, indeed, to see what is needed. I must remember to thank Steven." He chuckled, a rumble deep in his chest that reminded Ana of a waking bear.

His gaze held her, locked her to the turf, quaking to her bones. The most terrifying thing was the man's complete rationality, the impression he gave that what he believed and what he proposed—whatever it was he was proposing—was utterly reasonable. Ana tried to speak, cleared her throat, and tried again in a strangled voice.

"What do you want me to do?"

He smiled at her engagingly, even sweetly, and with complete patience and confidence in her. "That's the beauty of it. You don't need to do anything, not until the very last part of the process. You just need to be yourself, the cool, wet, innocent moon-woman, as male and female join together in the furnace and conjoin into immortality."

If Jonas had moved so much as a muscle in her direction, Ana would have broken and fled shrieking into the green woods. Instead, he looked down at the altar stone at their feet, studying its roughness as if deciphering some secret text carved into its surface. He dropped to his heels and tickled his blunt fingertips delicately back and forth over the scrubbed stone, a thoughtful, sensuous gesture that Ana felt as a caress up her spine. She flushed at the disturbing ghostly sensation, and Jonas smiled to himself, patted the stone as if it were an old friend, and then in an abrupt and characteristic return to the prosaic, he stood up, glanced at the lowering sun, and said, "We're going to miss dinner if we don't hurry." He clambered over a low place in the wall, dislodging several stones in the process, and made off in the direction of the house.

She was sorely tempted to let him go, even if it meant spending the night on the altar stone. She might easily have remained behind, frozen there among the abbey ruins, had it not been for the knowledge that Jonas was moving back toward the house where Jason and Dulcie were sheltering. She could not leave them alone with him. With infinite reluctance she took a step in the direction he had gone, and then another.

She who has ears to hear, let her hear.

And Ana heard. Another woman might have picked up the nuances of spirituality in his words and been pleased with her understanding, but Ana had seen, had literally been witness to, the extreme behavior that people were capable of in the pursuit of religious truth, and her ears told her that this was no metaphor. Whatever it was Jonas did in his alchemical laboratory, he had convinced himself and Steven and all the others that he and they could change matter into gold. But it did not stop with the walls of the actual laboratory, not for a man with Jonas Seraph's massive intellect and self-absorption. The estate itself, bought with his inheritance, had become in his mind his laboratory, from the grotto where his curiosity about fire's purification had been thwarted to the current inhabitants and their peculiarities and characteristics. Jonas thought of this place as his workroom, where he might observe the principles of Change functioning. Which made Ana and everyone else here, in effect, his personal *prima materia*.

That kind of godlike vision of the world, ironically, depends on the adoration of others, to bring the venerated one food and carry out his wishes. Samantha Dooley had gotten tired of it and passed on, only to have her shoes filled by a born personal assistant to this small universe's CEO. Marc Bennett could strut and crow and order people about to his heart's desire, and Jonas would continue to treat him as a piece of furniture, because in Jonas's mind, that was what all people were.

Ana pulled her coat around her, feeling the cold as the sun went down and as the sudden thought hit her that perhaps Sami Dooley had not tired of her role; perhaps she had been pushed too far.

When was that large amount of nitrate fertilizer bought? She couldn't remember, but she was certain it had been for Britain, not Boston. Was it purchased shortly before the arguments started between Jonas and Sami? The two things might have nothing to do with each other, but she could feel the disquieting possibility of that fertilizer's purpose nibbling at the edges of her mind.

She knew Jonas had to have a human-sized alembic in the cellars, behind one of those three locked doors. What else could he use as his "power nexus" for the conjoining with his moon-woman? What concerned her more, though, was the question of how he intended to apply the necessary heat. Would it be from six small brick furnaces such as those that had kept Jason warm during his solitary trial under Steven? Or was Jonas insane enough to think of something bigger, something more suited to the dramatic transformation of a man into a Philosopher's Stone? Something as explosive on the outside of the alembic as what was due to go on in the inside?

It was insane, sure, but Ana could not keep from wondering: Just how big a fire would it take to transmute a man into an immortal?

She had been right her first night here, terribly close to the truth: This really was Texas revisited, and Utah. Here she was again, with two young hostages in the hands of her enemy and the responsibility for the entire community on her shoulders; the difference was, this time she knew it. In Texas another woman, a far different Ana, had selfishly walked away from the only people who mattered to her, so engrossed in her own problems that she was blind to the signs, deaf to the warning bells, dangerously, murderously ignorant.

No more. She could see this man playing with his vision, turning it over in his big, hard hands, changing and shaping it until it matched his idea of perfection. A moment's fear, a sudden conviction that "they" had infiltrated to his bosom and were about to take his Work away from him, and he would move instantly to set the final Transformation in motion. She could all but smell the danger, and her ears rang with the ghostly echo of gunfire, her nostrils twitched with the remembered stink of fresh blood and old death.

Her only hope was to keep her wits about her and to get help.

On her own, she could do little more than seize Jason and Dulcie and flee, evading the camouflage-clad guard and hoping to make it as far as the main road and the arms of the constabulary. But what then, when their abrupt departure was discovered and Jonas realized that his chance for immortality was slipping away from him? Would he reach out for another and set off on his ultimate quest? And if so, who would be Ana's substitute? The innocent Sara? Or perhaps young, blond Deirdre? And what would it do to Jason and Dulcie when they eventually found out what their salvation had cost? What does it profit a man, that he gain his life and lose the world?

Ana could not both protect the two children and keep an eye on Jonas, not for long. She had to have help. She could try to break into the phone system, call Glen—but had he even received her last letter yet? And how long would it take him to set up a response in a foreign country? A long time, knowing governments; longer even than it would take her, a private citizen of a foreign country, to work her way through the local authorities until she found someone. Too long. Furthermore, although she longed to hear Glen's cold and competent voice, craved his presence with a lust stronger than sex, a single man on a white horse was not about to make much difference.

Once, long long ago, she had thought that fear was the energy that kept her persona together, a potential resource like pain or desperation that with acceptance and rigid concentration could be shaped and used. Not this kind of fear. This fear was too deep to be grasped, too slippery to be handled, too disorienting to be accepted; it left her utterly alone and directionless, wishing she could crumple into a corner and weep like a child.

That was not possible. She just had to pull herself together—the ghosts of murders past were getting in her way, obscuring her vision of what was and what she must do. Her only option was the same one she had been following since she arrived here, that of watch and wait. This was no time to lose control, and the all-too-obvious fact that she had no business being here, that she was no longer capable of doing this work, could not be helped. She would just have to shove her panic back into its box and do her best: There was no one else.

And think about it: Jonas wanted her voluntarily, which meant that he either had no wish to drag her into the alembic with him or, more likely, he could not envision the necessity. She needed to see the basement, to examine the alembic itself and to see if there was any sign of a nitrate bomb. She would have to convince him of her need to see his workshop, just as she had convinced him that he needed her as the key to his great Transformation. Work herself in to his side, hope he left his telephone open or—better—that modemed computer, and get a message to Glen.

Yes, she had to have help. Agreed, there was no way she could do this alone for more than another few days. The best way for obtaining that help was the same way she always had: Write a journal entry for Glen.

Only this time she'd have to make damned certain that nobody found it, because there would be no pretty subterfuge here. Write down the truth, in all its detail, and then she would either get herself a map of the estate and sneak off to a mailbox, or feed the pages through

Jonas's scanner and slap the result into an e-mail to Glen. That would take less time than Jonas had been gone to urinate.

Buy time, call for help, act normal.

And the hardest of these is normality.

CHAPTER 29

proposed article on theological synthesis
>   titles: Dream Logic
>   Signs and Portents
>   The Apocalyptic Mind

Intro: One of the ~~searier~~ more frightening sides of religious synthesis is the apparent lack of rational thought, the willingness of the participants to embrace wildly disparate ideas and images and then to make great leaps in interpretation and meaning. To the apocalyptic mind, signs and portents abound, messages wait in the most obscure places, and the whole of creation pulsates with Meaning, for the one who can truly See. There is no coincidence, no casual link in the universe: everything is connected.

>   (Examples: --Judaism & the minutiae of kashrut rules--holiness is in
>   the details
>   --Post-resurrection Christianity, sifting the life of Jesus for
>   symbols and unseen prophecies
>   --Modern examples--Heaven's Gate, etc.)
>   To the apocalyptist, who literally awaits the Great Uncovering, all
coincidence is synchronicity, all accident revelation.

>   (note: intro ideas of archetypal/depth psych?? Examples in
>   therapeutic situations, or Biblical dream interp???))

... It is the same logic one finds in the interpretation of dreams, where all events are related, where enlightenment comes with the understanding of links and the symbols thrust up from the unconscious.

>   What would seem to most of us a coincidence of minor importance, to the searching mind becomes a road sign to holiness. The unpredictability of these minds makes it very difficult to forecast where Meaning will be found.

>   If we wish to understand, we must contrive to stand over this person and look over his (her) shoulder, listening to his inner dialogue and duplicating his close scrutiny of his surroundings, before we can even begin to predict his interpretation of events, his understanding of portents. Like the chemist who knows what reagent will set off a certain reaction in his beaker-- and even then, the being human individuals rather than simple chemicals, the variables are great, and it is easy to be very wrong.

From the notes of Professor Anne Waverly

The smell of food in the dining hall filled Ana with nausea, but she craved something hot to drink. She took a mug and filled it from the big urn, added sugar, and took it to her corner, where she cupped her hands around it as if the tiny heat it gave off would drive away the coldness of her bones. Three mugs later her thirst was slaked but she was still shivering in the warmth of the dining hall.

Then she looked up and saw Dulcie, and one glance at the child's expression cut her shivering off. Dulcie needed her; there was no time for weakness.

"Hello, Dulcinea," she said gently. "How's my squire this evening?"

The child shrugged, a motion so like her brother that Ana wanted to reach out and pull Dulcie to her, burying that sad, remote little face in her embrace. Instead, she put her mug down on the table and stood up, casually holding out her hand to the girl.

"Why don't you show me your room, Dulcie? Then I'll show you where mine is. Sorry my hand's so rough and covered with Band-Aids—I spent the afternoon digging and I got a bunch of blisters. I shouldn't call them Band-Aids, though, should I? Here they're sticking plasters. I wonder why they call them plasters? Plaster is that white stuff they cover walls with, that turns really hard and you can paint it. You remember that gray mud that Tom and Danny were using back in Arizona, that would get big blobs in their hair and when they came to meals they'd look really funny? Oh my little sweetheart, what's the matter?"

Dulcie had drifted to a halt halfway up the stairs and was now just standing, one hand limp in Ana's, her shoulders drooping and her head down. She was crying. Ana sat down on the upper step and pulled Dulcie to her. The child was pliable but unresponsive, weeping as if she were too tired and dispirited to do anything else. Ana crooned wordlessly and rocked her, oblivious to the people coming and going on the stairway, aware only of the small, warm head of hair tucked under her chin, and the slack hopelessness of this young body, and eventually the shuddering intake of breath as the tears tapered off. When the tears ended, some of Ana's own hopelessness seemed to have worked itself out as well.

"Where is your room, Dulcie?" she asked. The child stood without speaking, and they continued up the stairs and down the hallway, Ana's hand resting on the back of Dulcie's neck. Dulcie chose a door and Ana followed her in. She picked up the child and sat her down on the bed with the teddy bear from the pillow, and then sat next to her. Dulcie leaned into Ana's arm.

"What's wrong?" she asked the child again.

"I want to go home."

"Home to Arizona? To where Steven is? Or home—?" Where was the child's home, anyway?

"To Steven."

"Why are you unhappy here? Jason's here."

"No."

"He isn't?" Ana looked quickly around the room: shoes in the corner, a familiar plaid shirt over a chair, books and papers on the desk—all reassuring signs that a teenager lived there.

"He's always doing things. Talking to Her, or That Man."

"Jonas, you mean? And who's 'Her'?"

"The girl." Dulcie's voice vibrated with disgust.

Ah. "Do you mean Deirdre?" Dulcie nodded. "Dulcie, listen to me. Jason loves you. He's just excited to be in a new place, and it's hard for him to keep his mind on things. I'll have a talk with him, okay? Ask him to settle down a little?"

Dulcie nodded, then said, "But I still want to go home."

Ana thought for a minute and decided it was best not to bring That Man into it at all, but, rather, to dwell on the positive side. "There are some nice things here. Have you seen the barn with the horses? And there's lots of kids."

"I can't understand them."

"Their accents, you mean?"

"They talk funny. Like on TV."

"You know, I'll bet they think you talk funny like TV, too. There's a lot of American shows on English television." Not that the Change kids saw much TV, come to think of it, but never mind. "Come on, let's go see the horses go to bed."

Ana spent the next hour coaxing and amusing the child out of her feeling of abandonment. Dulcie found the horses beautiful, the lambs amusing, the cats still at the kitchen door, and the voices around her not quite as unintelligible as she had thought. At the end of their tour they went to see Ana's room. Ana let her look around, bounce on her bed, and paw through her meager belongings, and then told the child that she could come to visit anytime she wanted.

They talked for a while about church mice and other important matters, and then Ana took Dulcie down a set of stairs and along the long corridor and around a corner to the room the child shared with her brother. Jason leapt out of his chair at their entrance, looking worried and angry, but before he could berate Dulcie for disappearing, Ana broke in.

"Oh, Jason, there you are. Sorry I didn't leave you a note to tell you I'd taken Dulcie down to see the animals in the barn, I should have realized you'd wonder where she was. Dulcie, maybe you should pop in and have a bath after petting all those horses and playing with the cats. Need a hand?"

After the child was dispatched to the bathroom down the hall, Ana lingered to talk with Jason about school and work and how he had spent his day. His dark eyes were alive with enthusiasm and she enjoyed the rare— the formerly rare—sight of Jason Delgado smiling, twice. His animation and willingness to talk to her at length about ordinary things were disorienting but steadying, and as enormously comforting as the physical contact with his sister had been earlier.

"You know," she told him gently when he paused to draw breath, "Dulcie seemed kind of lonely and a little upset tonight. You've been busy, and she was feeling left out. Though I'm glad you're enjoying it here."

"It's all right," he said, adding, "I like some of the people."

"You're going to miss the basketball," she said.

"Season's over anyway."

"Tomorrow after lunch, let's get together and look at what you and the others need to do to finish the school year. Dov and I brought the final exams with us" (a thousand years ago, it seemed) "so maybe you could take them early and have the summer ahead of you."

"You don't think we'll be going home before school's out, then?"

"Doesn't sound like it to me. Why, did Steven say you were?"

"Nobody said anything," he said with a wry grimace. "Just 'get on the plane.' I didn't even know we had passports."

She did not tell him that it was standard procedure at Change for new members to apply for passports, or whenever possible for minors to have the application made for them. International experiences (carefully monitored, of course) were used as a selling point by the school.

"Well, I hope you get to see something of the country while you're here." Dulcie was making final splashing noises down the hall. "Tomorrow is our half day, you know that?" Once a week, in addition to Sundays, the Change residents had an afternoon free. Thursday was theirs. "After the school meeting, assuming I'm free, I'd like to take you two for a walk. I have a little surprise for you. You personally, I mean."

Jason nodded, concealing his interest well, and went to supervise the nightgowning of his sister. Ana waited to give Dulcie a good-night kiss, and then she returned to her room. She had intended to join the evening meditation, now that Jonas had acknowledged her existence, but she felt weary and distant, and when she had to make an effort to exchange a few simple words with her next-door neighbor, she knew she could not bear the entire gathered community. She closed her door, jammed the chair under the knob, tugged the curtains as closed as they would go, and sat on the hard bed, her skin crawling with tiredness and a cold that did not come from the soft night. Too tired even for sleep, twitching with the day's tensions, she took out her diary and got to work.

She sat on her narrow bed with the covers pulled up to her chest, and she wrote. It began as a straightforward report like any of those she had submitted to Glen in the past, detailed and analytical, complete with maps and diagrams, but within a page or two it began to get away from her. Speculations began to intrude: Her personal reactions became a necessary part of the explanations. There was, in truth, very little about this case that was straightforward, and the attempt to reduce it to analysis and point out the logical progress of her thoughts only served to make the lack of logic more obvious and her own position more tenuous, even desperate. As she wrote, she was aware of how personal she was becoming, how she was revealing not her competence as a trained investigator, but her feelings—claustrophobia and grinding anxiety, the upwelling of fears and memories, the sensation of impotence. (*What is the female equivalent of impotence, Glen?* she found herself writing. *Hysteria? Well, I am both impotent and hysterical.*) What she wrote was like nothing she had ever given Glen before, presenting details of her self and her life that she had never given anyone, not since Aaron had died, but here she was, her hand shaping letters that described just what Abby's face had looked like in death and how that vision kept intruding itself on her current choices and decisions. Even while she wrote, she was appalled at the intimacy of the document, fully aware that Glen would have no choice but to set it before countless others, but unable to stop herself from writing. The sensation of open communication was a lifeline to sanity, the words a catharsis that reached down to her bones. She told herself that she would destroy it when she finished, that she could write a second, expurgated version for Glen, but she knew she would not.

Lights-out came and an officious passerby tapped at her door, so she turned out her lamp and opened the curtains to write by the light of the compound floodlights. She wrote until she had it all down, up to the point of what she planned to do next, and as she was thinking about that she fell asleep.

She woke some hours later, her diary jabbing her cheek and the floodlight shining in her eyes. Her bladder was also protesting at the number of cups of tea she had drunk, so she removed the chair from under the doorknob and went down the hall to use the toilet and brush her teeth. When she got back to her room, she saw the diary lying openly on the pillow, and she closed the door and cautiously tore out the incriminating pages. The only place she could think to hide them was inside the sole of her Chinese slippers; she folded the pages over and over and pushed the long rectangle in between the cloth lining and the sole. Not ideal, but as a temporary hiding place, as good as she could do.

She put her head back onto the pillow, and was asleep.

Ana's day began two hours later, long before the birds had begun their dawn chorus, when her bedroom door was flung open and a man's voice began talking at her. She went from deep sleep to heart-pounding panic in a split second, whirling around in the tangling covers and bruising her elbow on the wall before she was upright and blinking at the door. It was Jonas.

"What?" she croaked.

"What is wrong with you? I said I'm not going to need you during the day, I'm working on some calculations, but I may want you tonight. Be available. Listen for my call. You know how to get there?"

She sat up more fully, scratched her scalp to encourage brain activity, and said, her sarcasm half swallowed up by a yawn, "I think I can find it again, Jonas."

He stepped back and was gone. After a minute she climbed out of bed and closed the door. The sarcasm that she had let slip was not a good sign, but she was, after all, fast asleep, and it was annoying to be credited with barely enough brains to walk downstairs to the Bear's den.

Her eyes went to the diary on the bedside table. After a moment, she took it up and turned to a clean page.

Glen—

I fully intend to watch my step, take care, and all the rest. For the first time in many long years I can honestly say that I do not want to die. Realistically, though, things happen. You and I both know that. We've known it since the day you planted your finger on the doorbell of my apartment fifteen years ago.

I should have died eighteen years ago with my husband and daughter. I did not. I have finally come to accept that, thanks in no small part to you, and to think that maybe the years between my should-have-been death and my actual one have been good for something. God's will is not a phrase I care to use, but there is a fate, Glen—a divinity, as Shakespeare calls it —and it does shape our ends.

My fate was to meet Jason and Dulcie. If it brings my end, if a thing happens to me in the next week or two, it will have been worth it. All I ask is that they be kept safe.

I ask it of God, and I ask it of you. I've never asked you for anything, Glen, not even an explanation. I am asking this. Keep those two children safe for me.

　　　　　　　　　　　　　　　　　　　—Anne

She tore out the page and folded it up, and was beginning to slip it into the shoe, when she paused to run a hand over the rubbery skin of her face, then smoothed out the page and took up her pen again.

P.S. Sorry about the maudlin sentiments—I haven't slept much recently and my brain is a bit fried. If I can't e-mail this to you in the next two days, I'll find the village post office or a nice friendly helmeted constable riding his wide-tired bicycle down a country lane

and send it to you that way. Not to carp, Glen, but you
had better hurry. There's not a lot of time here.
P.P.S. Oh, and Glen? I hope you're planning to in-
vite me to your wedding. If you don't, I plan to turn
up anyway and really embarrass you.

—A

She smiled as she folded the page into the slipper. As
she set off in the direction of the early-morning coffeepot, she detoured to take her revenge on Jonas's followers by yanking the pull chain on the antique and
incredibly noisy toilet.

She spent the morning happily and mindlessly scrubbing
floors, and after lunch joined Jason and two other American students for a brief but productive meeting with
Dov and one of the other teachers. Jason, blasé as he had
been, found it difficult to take his eyes off the lumpy sack
she had brought into the room.

After the meeting they gathered up Dulcie from the
kindergarten room (where she sat listening carefully to a
wildly chattering friend), and Ana led them out through
the kitchen and across the yard to a flat, paved area that
was used to park the farm tractor during the rainy season. She had spent the hour before breakfast sweeping
away the dirt and hanging up a circle she wove from a
roll of baling wire. Jason stood with his hands on his
hips, puzzling out the odd markings, and when he
turned and Ana bounced the ball off the rough concrete
and into his hands, a look of pure, uncontained pleasure
lit up his face. He dribbled the ball a few times to get the
feel of the surface, then circled around, took three fast
steps, and shot it neatly through the lopsided hoop.

"I thought they didn't play basketball here," he said.

"Does that look like a regulation hoop? They don't—well, not many of them. I brought the ball with me."

That stopped him short. "You brought the ball in your—oh. Duh. You let the air out first."

"I thought I was going to have to blow it up with my mouth like a balloon. Sara found me an old pump in the tool shed."

So she and Jason and little Dulcie played basketball, undisturbed and undistracted by the adults and children who came to investigate the odd noises. She blocked him, he dodged her, and Dulcie ran after them both, shrieking in joy. Twice Jason lifted his sister up so she could dunk the ball down through the makeshift and increasingly asymmetrical hoop. The third time Dulcie dunked it, the hoop came down. Dulcie felt terrible, but Jason only laughed.

Ana retrieved the mashed hoop. "I think this design needs some work," she said, putting it into the sack with the ball. "But now, I want to take you two for a walk."

She took a smaller sack out of the lumpy one, threaded the handles up over her shoulder, plunked obedient hats on all three heads, and led the two children down the road to the east of the house. The sparkling air was rich with the fragrances of mint (from Dulcie, whose class had worked in the herb garden) and roses, lavender and cut grass, and the clean smell of sweat from the boy at her side.

The abbey was not quite as impressive when approached from the direction of cultivated land, but it was still a place of calm loveliness, even to a six-year-old girl and a fourteen-year-old boy.

"It used to be a church," she told them. "Four hundred years ago it was part of a monastery; you can see the outline of the walls. That lumpy ground over there was probably the monastery itself, where the monks lived and worked."

They walked up and down, investigating the vague shapes beneath the turf, and then went into the space between the abbey walls and up to where the altar stone peeped out of the grass. There she laid out her picnic of cheese sandwiches and juice and three large and somewhat travel-worn cellophane-wrapped chocolate chip cookies that she had bought at the airport in Phoenix. She gave them each a packet of broken pieces, keeping for herself the one that had been completely pulverized.

They ate their open-air meal, and after they had finished she lay back on her elbows, watching surreptitiously as the two children explored the crumbling walls and ran their fingers over the time-softened carvings. It was a new sensation for Jason to be valued, she decided, first by Steven and now by Jonas. The approval of the two male authority figures and the complete change in setting had continued to work their magic on him. He looked younger and more nearly content than she had seen him, and it was like a knife in her heart to know that if she had anything to say in the matter, it would not last. Jonas would be revealed as a dangerous lunatic, Deirdre would go back home with her parents, Steven's school would be smashed, and these two children, who in a few short weeks had taken control of her thoughts and her affections, would be farmed out again to the chance protection of foster homes.

And all that only if she was very lucky.

The sun grew low in the sky, and eventually she stirred and began to gather up the papers and bread crusts. "Thank you," she told them. "I can't remember when I had a nicer afternoon."

"Thanks for the basketball," Jason said. "That was cool."

"Even though I broke the hoop," said Dulcie.

"It can be fixed," Ana said.

On the way back to the house Dulcie alternately

lagged behind and raced ahead. On one of these surges Ana drew a breath and let it out slowly.

"Jason," she said, "there's a couple of things I need you to know and then forget unless you need them. And I have to ask you not to say anything about either of them to anyone, not for, oh, maybe two or three months. It is extremely important to me that you particularly not tell Jonas what I'm about to say. I realize this isn't fair to you, keeping a secret from someone like that, but if he or Steven found out, I could be in big trouble. I'm asking you to trust me. Will you?"

After a while he said, "Okay."

"Promise?"

"I said I would," he said testily.

"Thank you. Two things. If anything happens here, if there's a raid or someone appears with a gun or we have an earthquake—no, come to think of it, they don't have earthquakes in England. Anything major and confusing anyway, I want you to promise me you'll grab Dulcie and get her away from the house. Take her to the abbey, or the woods. Don't try to find me or Jonas or your friend Deirdre or anyone, just grab Dulcie and run."

"What's the other thing?"

She again took a deep breath and let it out. "I have a friend, an old friend, who works for the FBI. Yes I know, it seems unlikely, doesn't it? Anyway, his name is Glen McCarthy. If you're ever in real need of a friend yourself—years from now, even—get in touch with Glen. He owes me big. Mention my name and he'll help you."

Jason studied the trees for a minute. "I thought you were a friend."

"I am, of course I am. But things happen, and I'm sometimes hard to find. With Glen, every small town in the United States has an FBI branch office, practically, and a lot of other places as well, like London in this country. And who knows," she added under her breath, "you might even like him."

"Glen McCarthy and take Dulcie into the woods. And I'll forget them both unless the roof falls in."

"Thank you, Jason." She stopped and turned to study his young-old face, the hawk nose and dark eyes and shorn hair. She noticed suddenly to her surprise that his was not actually a handsome face, just compelling. She reached up impulsively and rested her palm for a moment on his cheek. "I wish—" She stopped, and looked down past the crook of her elbow to see Dulcie gazing up at her.

"What are you wishing, Ana?"

Ana removed her hand and bent down to look Dulcie in the face. "I was wishing that I could take you both right this minute to an ice cream parlor I know in Portland, Oregon, where they make their own ice cream and serve it in giant bowls with paper umbrellas on top, and we'd order pizza ice cream for dinner and green pea sherbet for our vegetables and chocolate pistachio cream pie ice cream for dessert."

Dulcie giggled. "*Pizza* ice cream? Yuck."

"Where's your sense of adventure?" Ana chided. "Sancho Panza would eat pizza ice cream. Even Don Quixote might."

As they walked back to the house through the shimmering afternoon, Ana allowed herself to open up to the pleasure of their companionship and to treasure the small, glittering gift of their affection. We do not deserve to come to this thy table, Lord, she thought. The tender mercy of communion with these two may have been undeserved, fragile, and based entirely on her own deception, but it was nonetheless real, and none the less warming.

•   •   •

The sensation of comfort did not survive three steps beyond the kitchen door. The entire household appeared to be gathered there, all of them shouting at one another. Ana stopped abruptly and escorted her two countrymen back outside.

"It looks like dinner's going to be late," she told them. "Why don't you guys go in the side door and get some schoolwork done."

Jason had no objection to being spared the turmoil that lay inside, but Ana watched them start around the house with a fervent wish that she could join them. Instead, she walked back into the kitchen, where she found near the door a distraught-looking Vicky, the woman who had met them at the airport.

"What on earth has happened?" she asked. Vicky stared at her as if she'd just inquired what was going on at Pearl Harbor.

"They're taking our kids!"

"What, *all* of them?"

"No, of course not," she said sharply. "Though they're going to try, you watch."

"Who's 'they'?"

"Social Services," Vicky spat out, and it all began to make an awful sense.

Back in Arizona, Ana had heard of a custody battle between one of the Change members and her ex-husband who was trying to remove their son from the community. Now, it seemed, another battle was brewing, over nearly identical circumstances, only this time there were four children involved, the eldest of whom was actually a stepson, but adopted by the man when he married the boy's mother seven years before. Now he wanted them all out of Change, and that afternoon, while Ana was sitting in the sunshine admiring the abbey ruins, a social worker had arrived clutching Emergency Assessment Orders for all four children, with a brace of large constables to enforce them. The kids were removed for the compulsory seventy-two-hour observation period, the mother packed a bag and followed them, and Change was in an uproar.

Ana studied all the faces in the room, one at a time, looking for the too-familiar signs of desperation and outright panic such an event could set off. She saw a lot of anger, a universal sense of frustration, some misery and fear, but the only face she saw that was white and pinched with distress was that of a young woman whom she knew to be under such a threat herself, a single mother barely out of her teens whose parents were trying to pry their grandchild loose from Change. Ana began to breathe again, for what seemed to be the first time since entering the room. What had happened was bad but not catastrophic. Nothing was going to happen to Change tonight because of it.

The same thought seemed to occur to the others as well. One by one they turned away from their collective outrage to resume their life. One woman shot a glance at the clock and turned, tight-lipped, to drag a clattering armful of pans from a cupboard, while two others simultaneously opened refrigerator and onion bin. Two men set off into the house, still hashing it over at the tops of their voices, while another yanked open a corner drawer and snatched up a long white plastic apron and a wickedly sharp knife. Ana eyed him nervously as he started for the door, but Cali, the woman at the stove, called out, "Peter, you don't have to do that now. Leave it for the morning."

"Got to eat," he grumbled, and marched off. Ana, reassured that he was not about to turn the blade on himself or others, quickly washed her hands and began chopping vegetables for an improvised raw salad to go with the rice and the beans that had been started before the Social Services invasion had thrown the kitchen into a state of confusion.

Twenty terse minutes later the rice was cooked, the salad assembled, and Ana was starting through the kitchen with a full tureen of red beans and sausage in her hands when the air was split by the bloodcurdling shriek of a soul in mortal terror. Deirdre dropped a glass into the sink and Cali jerked and sliced open her finger, but on Ana the effect was disastrous. A gallon of half-liquid beans hit the floor and erupted in a spicy shower over every surface. Beans spattered the ceiling, scalded exposed flesh, dripped down the walls, and covered the floor; in the midst of the carnage stood Ana, hands out, gaze far away, her body gone rigid as stone.

"She's having a fit," said a voice.

"Don't let her swallow her tongue," someone else contributed, but Ana did not hear them. She was not there. She was eight years distant and ten thousand miles away, standing in *another kitchen with gingham checks on the windows and the hot Utah sun beating down outside, with the squeal ringing in her ears of a terrified blond teenager named Claudia being dragged through the dust by an enraged spiritual leader, knowing that she was about to be locked into the stifling padded closet he used for the purpose of enforcing discipline. It was this sound that crystallized Anita Wells's decision to get out, now; this sound that led to her key in Rocinante's ignition, her foot on the accelerator, her quick glance in the side mirror to see Calvin the cook through the billowing dust, raising his automatic pistol at her; this same shocking, high human shriek of pro-test and pain that set into motion the events that ended in Calvin's gun and the incomprehensible violation of her own pain, and two miles down the road the slow, inevitable collision with the jumble of boulders that rose up before her, all set off by the* loud series of furious animal squeals that were coming from the Change barnyard.

Ana looked down at her feet, where the pieces of the crockery tureen were still rocking, and she began to shake. Deirdre, pretty young Deirdre with the golden hair like young Claudia's, began to gather up the pieces. Someone else—Vicky?—was speaking in an urgent and worried voice right in Ana's ear. Ana pushed the voice away and bolted for the small washroom just inside the back door, where Vicky found her retching violently into the toilet.

When nothing was left for her body to get rid of, Ana sat back on her heels, gasping and shivering.

"Are you okay?" Vicky asked for the tenth time. This time Ana responded.

"I'll be fine. What the hell was that noise?"

"Terrible, wasn't it? Peter's usually pretty good at sneaking up on the animals so they don't know what's happening, but I guess the pig saw him coming. Pigs aren't stupid."

"A pig. Christ."

"It doesn't happen very often, honestly it doesn't," Vicky told her earnestly. "Almost never."

"I could see why you wouldn't want that every day. The kids must be freaking out." At least the room shared by Dulcie and Jason was on the far side of the house. They might even have missed it entirely. She gave a last shudder and got to her feet, which reassured her attendant into stepping back and leaving her alone.

She splashed her face, rinsed her mouth out, and stood with her head bowed over the small hand basin for a minute, waiting for equilibrium to set in. She took a few slow breaths and raised her face to the mirror, and then she did lose control, well and truly.

Her face was the only clean thing in the mirror. Her hair was a red-brown cap plastered against her head.

Her once-yellow T-shirt was mostly the same brown color, dotted with individual kidney beans, bits of green pepper, and one slice of sausage lodged in a fold. Her legs were brown, her feet indistinguishable from her sandals, and her skin felt as if she had a sunburn beneath a drying mud pack. She was a sight.

The women in the kitchen looked up at her entrance, alarmed at the snorting noises she was emitting. Ana checked for a moment at the appearance of the room, but then she caught sight of three beans nestling on the top of Deirdre's head, and she doubled over in uncontrollable hilarity.

The giggles spread, until the kitchen and a rapidly growing audience were deep in half-hysterical laughter, gales of it that were renewed at each new discovery of the scope of the disaster. Ana finally had to leave, staggering brown and sticky upstairs toward the bath. She did not know if she wanted to share her colorful state with Dulcie and Jason or to hide it from them, but the choice did not come up, and she was soon safely locked in the bathroom with the water running.

After dinner, she joined the group meditation for the first time. She found it strangely disappointing, a colorless round of chanting and silence followed by a flat sermonette by Marc Bennett. The brittle edginess of the community was neither increased nor dispersed by the hour spent in the hall, but it lay under their actions and was resumed at the door when they left.

Ana spotted Sara coming out and went over to talk to her. After asking about the condition of the baby cabbages and confirming what Sara had heard about the disaster in the kitchen earlier, she tipped her head back toward the meditation hall and commented, "I'd have thought that Jonas would lead the meditations."

"He used to a lot, but not in the last few months. Which is fine," Sara admitted, lowering her voice, "because his meditations were getting a little . . . confusing. He's too lifted up for my little brain to follow. How are things going with you?"

"Fine," Ana told her. "Just fine."

She made her way upstairs and found Dulcie still awake, so she settled down with her and they read the remainder of the church mice story, as well as one of Ana's personal favorites, a book she had bought Dulcie in Sedona and which was already looking worn, the story of Ferdinand, the least-testosterone-burdened bull in all of Spain. Ana then went back down to the kitchen to spend an hour scrubbing the cabinet fronts with a toothbrush and to drink a cup of tea, and then she exchanged good-nights with the others and went back upstairs.

It was not until she was brushing her teeth that she remembered her midnight visit from Jonas. *I'll come for you,* he had said; *be ready.*

The last thing on earth she wanted was another session with the Bear, but there was not much she could do to avoid it. She sat in her room and tried to read the Jung book through drooping eyelids, until lights-out came and she decided that either Jonas had forgotten her in the heat of his calculations or he had been distracted and would send his summons when he damn well pleased. She might as well go to bed.

Still, she dressed for bed in clothes that could as easily serve as actual daywear, in case he crashed through her door again at two in the morning. She pulled on her better, light gray sweatpants in place of the dark blue ones with the hole in the knee, and a white T-shirt with the banana-slug logo of U.C. Santa Cruz on the place where the breast pocket would have been, and got into bed. After a while, she got up again and removed the folded diary pages from her slippers, putting them instead under the inner sole of her running shoes. Then she climbed under the covers and slid away into sleep.

CHAPTER 30

CONIVNCTIO SIVE
Coitus.

From the journal of Anne Waverly (aka Ana Wakefield);
reproduction of the *coniunctio* stage of the alchemical process
from the *Rosarium Philosophorum*, Frankfurt, 1550

Jonas did not come crashing through her door.

Instead, she dreamed.

What came to her that night was not one of her usual innocuous dreams with emotional overtones, but a true nightmare, rare and vivid, and causing the flesh to creep. It was as if her mind were reminding her that the flashback she had experienced had not been healed by the laughter, only hidden.

She dreamed she was driving in a car with Abby, going home, and she decided to take a different route from the one they usually took. After all, what good was it to have a Land Rover if you couldn't take a muddy dirt road occasionally?

So they turned off the main road onto the mud track deeply surrounded by trees, and drove with the branches pressing close on the windows. Then they were walking, with that seamlessness of dream logic, still going home, heading down a stone passageway with a backpack resting between her shoulder blades and hiking boots on her feet, with Abby in front of her and other people behind, all of them everyday commuters like herself, going home. The walls of the passageway grew closer, the ceiling lower and lower, until the tunnel was nothing more than a low horizontal gap in the stone.

Ana knew it was passable—not only for Abby, who had already vanished through the crack and gone before her, but everyone behind her seemed so matter-of-fact, she knew this must be a normal occurrence for them, just another part of the commute.

So she lay down onto her back, the pack cushioning the rock, and scooted along, feetfirst, into the gap. There was a distinct slope that made forward progress not only possible, but unavoidable, so she lay in the position of a luge racer, except with her arms stretched up over her head because of the low roof, and let herself slide down after Abby.

Only she did not come through the other side. Her boots caught on the roof of the gap, and she was stuck. There was no space above her body to allow her to turn her hips, so her knees could not bend and find purchase for her boots; there was no way to bring her arms down to push herself back up the slope, because the sides were too narrow. Her fingers could find nothing to grab onto above her head: She was trapped in the rock with no way to push or pull herself back up the slope, and she could hear the man behind her preparing to launch himself after her, but when she tried to draw a deep breath to call for help, the rock pushed down on her chest, and she could feel the horror of being enveloped rising up in her and—

She jolted awake, drenched in sweat, the implacable pressure of the rock face pressing against her trapped boots, and tingling up the front of her helpless legs. It was one of the most gruesome dreams she had ever experienced, and she had to get up and walk up and down, rubbing at the front of her legs before the sensation of entrapment left her.

There would be no sleep after that.

What she badly needed was either a long walk or a trashy novel, but she could not go out and she would have bet that such a thing did not exist under this roof. Instead, she sat down on her hard chair and opened her diary by the light of the floods, and forced herself to concentrate on an elaborate drawing of the abbey ruins.

After three botched efforts, the immediacy of the dream faded a little, and the drawing became easier. Eventually she turned to draw a boojum tree, and although it occurred to her that the mysterious snark might well live in a low gash in a rock tunnel, the image did not come to life, and she continued to draw lizards and rocks and even, thinking of Jason, a cat.

She was deep into her pointless labors when a small sound knocked her out of her artistic reverie, a noise both unfamiliar and disconcertingly reminiscent of some evil experience. She strained to hear over the sudden pounding in her ears, and waited for it to come again.

When the sound was repeated, she knew instantly why it had acted like a cattle prod on her distracted mind. She covered the distance to the door in two steps, yanked it open, and looked down at Dulcie, in pink-flowered nightgown and bare feet. She had her teddy bear in her arms, and she didn't look cold; other than that, it was all terribly familiar. She pulled the child inside and closed the door.

"What's the matter, Dulcie?" she said in a low voice.

"They took Jason again," the child whimpered. "He told me to be a big girl and go back to sleep, but I can't."

Ana shushed her rising voice and gave her a brisk hug. "That's fine, Dulcie. I told you to come here anytime, and I'm glad you did. Now, why don't you hop into my bed and see if you can follow Jason's advice?"

"Not Jason," the child said, obediently climbing up into Ana's bed.

"Jason didn't tell you to go back to sleep, you mean? Then who was it?"

"That Man."

"Jonas? You mean Jonas came to get your brother?"

"With the loud man." Ana identified this second person without difficulty as Marc Bennett.

"That's okay," she said, though she feared it would not be. "We'll settle it like we did before. Now, night-night."

"But where are you going to sleep?" Dulcie asked.

Ana looked at the hard wooden chair and the hard wooden floor, and in the end she pulled up the blankets and got in next to Dulcie. The child curled up and snuggled into Ana with a grunt of contentment. Slowly, deliberately, Ana brought her arm up and wrapped it around the thin, warm body next to her.

"Ana?"

"Yes, Dulcie."

"I'm scared."

"What, because of Jason?" The wild mop of black hair nodded beneath Ana's chin. "Don't be, sweetheart. It's like before, he's gone to do some work, only this time it's with Jonas instead of Steven. Big boys have work to do."

"He was scared, too."

"Jason was?" Surprising, how normal her voice sounded, how little concerned, when her gut was clenched around a block of ice.

"He pretended he wasn't, but he was. I can tell."

"I'll bet you can."

"He was scared before, when Thomas and Danny came and got him," the child continued inexorably, the words pushed out of her by fear for her brother. "He was scared, and when he came back he wouldn't tell me what happened, but it made him have bad dreams, and Jason doesn't usually have bad dreams, not like me. And now they took him away again and he was even more scared than he was before."

She lay in Ana's embrace, waiting desperately for adult reassurance that it was going to be all right, and Ana struggled to find an answer to give her. She never lied to a child if she could possibly avoid it, and she did not want to lie to Dulcie now. For one thing, she knew how good children were at picking up unspoken messages, and she doubted that giving Dulcie any more reassuring words crossed with the pheromones of dread would help matters at all. On the other hand, it was cruel to burden a young person with adult weakness and doubt just when strength was needed most.

In the end, she gave Dulcie a squeeze and told her, "Dulcinea, I don't know what's going on either, but as soon as people are up and around, I'll find out. I'm with you, Dulcie. You're not alone."

That seemed to be the right approach, or at least one adequate enough to allow the child eventually to relax back into the safety of sleep.

Not the adult, though. There were no words reassuring enough to quiet the bone-deep trembling Ana could feel inside. Spiritual hypothermia, she diagnosed, striving for humorous detachment; optimal treatment to include a familiar woodstove, two dogs, and the warm company of friends. Although at this point she would settle even for Glen's icy presence—anything but to be there alone with deadly decisions before her.

She was jamming herself down between a rock and a hard place, to be sure, but she was also standing on a high wire, balancing over two abysses.

On the one side was Jason, who was a part of her in ways she could not begin to understand, and who at that moment, while Ana lay with the limp figure of his sister clasped to her, might well be staring at the dim interior of a second metal alembic—this time under the far-from-gentle protection of Marc Bennett and Jonas Seraph.

On the other side lay the massive responsibility she had for this community. The physician's oath to Do no harm was paramount in every aspect of the work she did with Glen. It infused her daily life while in the communities she investigated with the urgent need to tread lightly, to slip into a preset role and slip out again, leaving no trace. Her work for Glen had always been based on the idea that the long-term effect was the only goal, the larger good more important than the individual. In earlier cases, her heart had occasionally ached at the mistreatment, as she saw it, of the community's children or one of the adults who found himself to be a round peg faced with a square doctrinal hole, but she had rarely succumbed to the temptation to interfere, knowing that in the long run, Glen and his agency would sort it out. Uncomfortable and uncertain as she might be about Glen, when it came down to it, she trusted him. He would do what was needed.

Now the question was turned around on her. Jason's welfare was at stake here, and it appeared to demand an immediate and aggressive action that Glen was not there to provide. But, could she trust her own judgment? The persistent intrusion of Anne Waverly's past and personality into the body and actions of Ana Wakefield, the increasing incursions of memory that had come to a head in yesterday's devastatingly real flashback, were confusing her. She was aware of a constant jittery anxiety focused on the two children, and she worried that Anne's frantic concern for the boy was severely hindering Ana's ability to remain the passive, open-minded individual she desperately needed to be. It was obvious to the rational side of her mind that she was well and truly losing it, hagridden by the specters of her past just at the time she most needed to be clearheaded and objective.

Long, long ago, when a thirty-year-old Anne Waverly entered the university graduate program eighteen years before, she had begun by building a persona on the wreckage of her former life. She had paved over the rubble, sealed up the debris of catastrophe with the clear, hard shell of academic discipline. When that cracked a bare three years after it had been laid down, when the snapshot of Abby had rumbled through her and pitched her into the darker corners of her mind, what had dragged her out again was Glen, who happened along to use her and bully her and incidentally show her the way to survival: to split herself into two persons, one rooted in either side of the events of Texas, two individuals whose only point of joining was the bridge crossing into an investigation, and later leaving it.

Now that bridge was disintegrating, cracked in a hundred places, and the events of the past were welling up out of the dark abyss beneath her. Marla Makepeace, no doubt, would be jubilant, considering it a healing and whole-making event; to Ana it felt like being overtaken by birth pangs in a collapsing building. She had to control the process, just for long enough to get out and into safety. She simply could not afford it now. Jason and Dulcie could not afford it.

She must have tightened her grip on the child, because Dulcie stirred briefly, then subsided.

So, could she trust herself in this state? Her mind was urging caution and rationality, forcing her to admit that the individual threats she had seen here did not necessarily add up to the sort of desperate scenario her inner eye was putting together: An antagonistic attitude toward the authorities, a man in the woods carrying a shotgun, a titular leader who was thinly connected with reality, and a de facto leader who was overly full of himself. That was it. Everything else came from her and her strange ties to two children, and all of it was tainted by her own past. Dulcie reminded her of Abby—that was where the cracks had begun. And then Bennett looked like Martin Cranmer, and the woods made her nervous, and by the time the pantry and the communal phobia about outsiders entered into the equation, she was so sensitized to parallels that a particular brand of pencil would take on an ominous significance. She had no business being there, no right to jeopardize everything by making decisions that could be based only on irrationality. The best thing for everyone would be if she were to stand up and walk away from the compound.

Leaving behind Jason in his alembic.

Abandoning Dulcie to strangers.

They would survive, her mind insisted. They would be fine.

But her gut, her heart, her every instinct cried out that here and now, the rational decision would be the wrong one, that the long-term goal was just too far away. There were times when the expedient solution was not the right one, when only faith justified an action— educated and open-eyed faith if possible, but if that failed, blind faith would have to do.

There was, in truth, no choice to be made.

The deep trembling had subsided while she wrestled with her demon, and with that final realization, that a decision had made itself, she actually drifted into sleep for a while, free at last of the tension of being of two minds. When she woke, the harsh blue glare of the floodlights pressing at her curtains had given way to the gentle rose light of dawn, and she was not the same person who had lain down on this bed the night before.

"My name is Anne Waverly," she whispered into the room. For better or for worse, Ana was gone, and when she went to the toilet down the hallway and moved to the sink to wash her hands, she half expected to see a woman with hair curling onto her shoulders. Instead, the same crop-haired woman looked back at her, although her eyes were calm and her face seemed older. She looked . . . satisfied.

Back in her room, Anne exchanged her sweatpants for jeans, took out a plain T-shirt for the upper half, and then thrust that back into the drawer and took out the small buckskin medicine pouch she had been forbidden to wear. She dropped it defiantly over her neck, and then pulled on a high-collared polo shirt to conceal the cord.

The sound of the drawer closing woke Dulcie, who sat up, blinking.

"Ana, are you going to find Jason?"

"We're going to get you dressed, and then we'll have breakfast, and then you're going to the schoolroom—no, today is Saturday, isn't it? Well, we'll find something for you to do, and after that yes, I'll go and see if anyone knows about Jason. But, sweetie, I think it would be best if you didn't say anything about Jason to anyone else for a little while. Some of the work that people do is kind of private, and they might not think it was a good idea if I tried to find out what Jason is doing. Okay?"

Dulcie nodded solemnly. One thing her past had taught her was the importance of not blabbing to adults.

Dressed and scrub-faced and downstairs with their bowls of muesli, Anne spotted Sara and led Dulcie over to her table. Introductions were made and the topic of the weather disposed of, and then Anne asked Sara about her plans for the day. The dining room was noisy and Anne, sitting next to Sara, pitched her voice low. Dulcie, concentrating on slicing a banana for her cereal, did not even look up.

"I'll be working in the runner beans most of the day," Sara told her. "You know, down near the stream?"

Anne nodded; the field was at the far end of the clear area from the house, an ideal place for Dulcie today. Keeping her voice low, she said to Sara, "I wonder if you'd mind having a small helper for the morning? I have to do some Work, but I should be finished by lunch." *One way or another,* a quiet voice in the back of her head added. "She's a good little girl and I'm sure she wouldn't be any trouble."

"Sure, no problem. I'd be happy to have someone help me weed. Dulcie," she said across the table, "do you know the difference between a baby bean plant and a weed?" Dulcie shook her head doubtfully and Sara laughed. "That's quite all right, dear. It's a skill many adults haven't mastered either, but something tells me you'll catch on in a flash. Finish your breakfast, my dear, and then we're off to rescue the runner beans from the weeds. See you at lunch, Ana."

To Anne's relief, Dulcie went with neither protest nor question, swept up in Sara's energetic program. The child was as safe as Anne could make her for the next few hours. Now for her brother.

Anne loaded up a tray of dishes. Deirdre was on kitchen duty this morning, and after Anne had deposited her contribution in the lineup to the right of the sink and exchanged a few cheerful phrases about the never-ending nature of washing-up, their mutual preference for bean-free clothing, and the beauty of the morning, she left Deirdre and the others to their labors.

At the door she paused, hovering on the edge of saying something, of issuing a vague warning, or at least of urging Deirdre to take herself down to the bean field with Sara for the day, anything but staying in this brick monstrosity where anything might happen. Deirdre glanced up and frowned vaguely at her, and the words died on her lips. What was there to say, after all? I'm going to go and bait the bear in his den, perhaps? Or, I plan to go help Jason with his Work, so beware the explosion from the laboratory? She turned and left the kitchen.

Outside the insignificant door that led to Jonas's subterranean world (and, she prayed, Jason Delgado), Anne knelt to tie her shoelace four or five times until the hallway was clear of people. When she was alone, she stepped quickly forward, wrenched open the door, and closed it behind her as silently as she could.

The landing and the stairway it gave onto were as cramped and unadorned as they had been when the Victorian builder had created them for the use of the servants. The only essential change was the string of bare electrical bulbs where once a solitary gas flame would have hissed and sputtered.

Anne stood still, on the threshold dividing two worlds. Outside the door were voices and movement, the rattle of dishes in the kitchen and a snatch of song. She heard a vacuum cleaner start up in a distant room, and a woman's voice asking Cali if she thought the flour would last until Tuesday. From below came nothing. Silence crept up the stairway, as palpable as the odor of damp stone.

Anne was a woman well accustomed to the textures of silence. She lived alone in a house with no neighbors and she rarely listened to recorded music or the television set. She knew silences that were uncomfortable, or pointed, or suggestive, but silence for her was generally more a matter of potential than of absence.

The silence coming up the stairs at her was the same silence she had felt out in the jungle with Jonas, thick and alive and with a distinct trace of malevolence. A person from Sedona might declare that bad things had happened here, to disturb the building's aura. A Victorian might say there was a ghost. Anne knew it to be a projection from her own mind onto the blank screen of the disappearing staircase, but it hardly mattered; they all amounted to the same thing.

She started down the stairway, leaving the upstairs noises behind.

The stone of the walls was dry and cool, and whispers from her clothing ran up and down the stairwell. The ceiling seemed to become lower as she approached the bottom, although she could not be certain that it was not just an intrusion of her nightmare.

At the bottom, she was again faced with the three

blank doors with their sturdy locks, the damp tiles of the floor, and behind her, Jonas's lair. The only sounds were from upstairs, and even those were more the sense of movement than actual noises. It was a sturdy building. Anne stepped softly around the stairs to Jonas's room, and found that, too, empty of life. She was alone, with the outside world there at the touch of an electronic finger. She would not get a second chance.

The whine the computer made when she switched it on seemed loud enough to be heard in the kitchen, and the click of the scanner was not far behind. She looked at the door as if expecting Jonas to lumber through with his paws outstretched, then took a deep breath and committed herself.

She called up the computer's e-mail program without opening up the line, and with excruciating slowness transferred the written journal pages from the sole of her shoe into the electronic file, laying two pages at a time on the scanner's glass screen. She wished she had written smaller, wished Jonas had updated his hardware in the last two years and gone for speed, even wished she had rallied her students on that long-ago afternoon in the lecture hall and let them throw Glen out the doors.

Her polo shirt was wet by the time the last page had been read, and she rapidly created an attachment of the scanned pages, typed in Uncle Abner's e-mail address, and hit the SEND button. The screen blinked and it was gone.

She then had to remove it from the records, so Jonas wouldn't happen across this curious document, a process that took more time on this unfamiliar setup than sending it had. At last she had to assume it was as deleted as she could make it. She turned off both machines, checked again to be sure she had not forgotten any sheets of paper on the scanner, rolled the pages back up, and feverishly stuffed them back into her shoe, which she then jammed onto her foot and tied.

She dropped into Jonas's big leather chair and stared at the dark screen in astonishment. She had actually done it. God, how rare it was, the sense of completion that hitting the SEND bar had given her. She could not know that Glen would be too preoccupied to check the Abner e-mail until it was too late to make a difference, but that did not matter. She had done her job, she had finally fulfilled her duty to Glen. That small movement of her finger had somehow cleared all past debts. She was free to deal on her own with the problem of a courageous, loyal, great-hearted, quixotic boy too old for his years who had, she knew in her bones, submitted for the second time to the alembic of a Change leader. Glen would never approve, but she no longer belonged to Glen. Now her only responsibility was to Jason Delgado and his curly-headed sister.

She scooted the chair back a few inches and began to open the desk drawers, looking for keys. The locks on the three doors outside Jonas's study were all new enough to retain their brass shine, and she thought it highly unlikely that an amateur like her could pick all three without being discovered. She didn't even know if English locks differed from the American brands she had learned on. She had a brief image of herself reduced to battering down the doors with a fire ax, and shook her head. Another thing Glen had left her unprepared for.

Instead, she searched for a key. Possibly a set of keys, but since all three locks looked identical from the outside, there was a good chance Jonas would have asked for one key rather than fumbling to choose the right one.

In the bottom left drawer she found a wooden cigar box containing a rich cache of keys; unfortunately, most of them were of the long-shanked skeleton type gone black with age, obviously original to the building. There were half a dozen newer keys, but when she went to look at the doors, none of the keys matched the brand names on the locks. She pulled out two or three likely candidates, but none of them fit.

They were all labeled, cardboard circles with metal edges tied on with loops of string, but the words written down bore no resemblance to locations. The one in her hand, for example, had a Greek phrase written in a neat hand that she thought might be that of Jonas Seraph. She puzzled over it for a moment and decided it said, "All men have one entrance into life," which she thought was from the Apocrypha—given the language, probably from the *Wisdom of Solomon.* Then she realized what the key was for: the front door. A similar key bore simply the word "anus," which seemed peculiar until she came up with its euphemism of "back passage": This would be the key to the outside door near the kitchen. Jonas had his own sense of humor, inconvenient and juvenile, but clever.

She put the keys back and closed the desk drawer on them. It was, of course, all too possible that he had only one key and he kept it with him at all times, in which case this entire enterprise was about to trickle off into farce. Still, she was not finished yet. She pushed herself away from the desk, returning the chair to its original position, and turned to the shelves.

A painstaking half-circuit of the room, beginning with the door and working her way along the left side of the room, left her with filthy hands, a heightened respect for the man's depth of scholarship, and no key. She sorted through the wild assortment of objects covering the windows—the only windows in this level of the house, she had discovered—but there was no key, even though it would have been his style. She did find, hanging among the display of dry bones that covered the third window, a silver necklace, a worn lump of silver similar to the golden shape Steven wore, only slightly elongated and curved inward at the ends. It looked, actually, a bit like a crescent moon, and she thumbed it, wondering briefly whose Work this had been, before her growing apprehension and sense of time running out drove her back to the room's entrance to start the sweep of the other half of the room.

Three shelves down from the top, at fingertip reach for a man of six feet four but needing a ladder for her, a title jumped out at her: Mary Baker Eddy's book that formed the basis for Christian Science interpretation of the Bible. Its name was *The Key to the Scriptures,* and Anne knew instantly why it was there among a group of geology textbooks. She carried over the library ladder, pulled down the book, and opened it at the red ribbon: a key.

She slid the book back, put the ladder away, and took the beribboned key into the hallway. The house had fallen silent above her, which meant only that it was not yet time to begin the preparations for lunch. No time to waste.

She began with the left-hand door. The key turned, but the door did not open. Her heart sank, then speeded up. If her key did not open it, that was not because it did not work; there must be another lock, turned from the inside. Someone was behind this door. Very gently, she rotated the key the other way to remove it, and when she withdrew her hand from the knob, it turned, and the door came open. She stumbled backward, and then felt like smacking herself on the forehead: The door had been unlocked to begin with.

Looking inside, she could see why. This was Jonas's private rest room, and the only reason he might lock it at all was the extensive collection of oversized books on erotica that took up most of one wall. She closed the door and tried the other two knobs. Both of those were locked.

The right-hand door proved to be a closet, with nothing more exciting than an elderly computer sitting among the reams of paper and printer cartridges. She locked the door without even entering the small room, and turned to the middle door, where she found a web of scratches around the keyhole. The key turned, the door opened, she put her head inside, and for the first time she heard noises—a slow, rhythmic thump punctuated by the indistinguishable rumble of male voices. She contemplated the sounds for a minute, and then she withdrew her head, went back to the study, and replaced the key inside Mary Baker Eddy. This time when she came out she walked directly over to the middle door and went through, closing it behind her but not turning the latch. I found it open, Jonas, she would say innocently. You must have forgotten to lock it, she would add with a blink of her big blue eyes.

She was in a dim subterranean passage, stone walls again to support the brick structure above. It was long and straight, its only features the doors that faced each other every ten feet or so, most of which were heavy, old, and locked. Two of them were massive, strapped with bolted iron and set with elaborate black locks that looked considerably more ancient than the building over her head. Arnold Schwarzenegger might be able to pick those mechanisms, but Anne hoped she wouldn't be called on to try.

The rhythmic noise increased as she walked down the passageway. A stone barrier blocked the end, but when she reached it she found not another pair of doors, but a T-junction, with the passageway splitting at right angles in either direction. She had chosen the left both in the study and then with the three doors, neither of which had been very helpful, but she decided to give the direction one more chance, and walked softly down the narrow corridor to the left toward the sound of machinery, the steady hiss of air, and the ever-clearer voices.

The stone walls went for thirty feet and then took another ninety-degree turn, this time to the right. The sound of her rubber-soled shoes on the grit was lost now, and she could hear, unmistakably, the deep voice of Jonas Seraph in an uninterrupted monologue. The walls turned another corner to the right, but she seemed to be nearly on top of the sounds, so instead of stepping out into whatever space lay beyond, she knelt, putting herself below eye level, and peered around the wall.

Opposite her, perhaps fifty feet away, a stone archway opened up—the right-hand half of the split corridor, which together with the one she had followed formed a squared Y around the central room. The wall between her and the archway had two doors, both shut. She eased herself forward, more and more of the room coming into view, until she saw a man seated on a high stool, his back to her. It looked like Marc Bennett; he seemed to be just sitting and gazing at something on a long, heavy, beat-up workbench. If she had chosen the right-hand passage, he would now be looking straight at her.

Keeping her body well back from the room's line of sight, she edged her gaze farther out into the room. Next she saw Jonas himself, also on a stool and directly facing her, although what she had thought to be monologue was actually him reading aloud from a heavy volume in archaic English on the Peacock stage of the alchemical process, and he did not look up. His voice rose and fell, infusing the nonsense with considerably more drama and meaning than it possessed.

The hiss and thump continued without faltering, and Anne braced herself for what else the room would contain. She was soon looking clear to the end wall, but what she saw was not a metallic pear-shaped object the height of a tall man emitting muffled cries of distress, but a small brick furnace topped by a pear-shaped glass object, the flames blown white-hot by a large bellows worked by Jason Delgado, stripped to the waist, with sweat coming off his back in runnels and his hair down in his face. His back muscles bunched and moved, and she could tell at a glance that every part of him burned with tiredness, yet his left arm kept a steady beat with the bellows handle. His right hand came up and dashed the sweat from his eyes, and then he shifted his position and transferred the handle over to his other hand.

She sat back against the wall with a thud. It took a moment for her mind to get around this image of Jason, it was so absolutely unexpected. She had been operating since the early hours under the assumption that for the second time in three weeks, Jason was trapped, sweltering and alone, inside a Change alembic. She had struggled and come to the decision that she had no choice but to sacrifice herself, Glen's investigation, and very possibly the lives of everyone here in the drive to free him, when all the time he was sweating not inside an alembic, but over one. She rested her head back against the stone wall and laughed silently until the tears ran down her face. Here she was, tiptoeing around like a criminal, pumped full of adrenaline, preparing to offer herself up for Jason's salvation, only to find him laboring away like an obedient young idiot over a fraudulent transmutation of matter. The sense of anticlimax would have been devastating had it not been so hopelessly funny.

Still, she reflected more soberly, Jason did not look very happy, and Dulcie would be waiting. Perhaps she could still save Jason some anguish and break up the uneven little triad in the next room. She got to her feet to go back down the corridor and upstairs to the kitchen, where like any good British housewife she prepared a tray with a pot of tea and a bowl of cookies—biscuits, she corrected herself, very nearly humming under her breath. One of the men came in while she was filling a jug with milk. He nodded at her, and ran more water into the kettle. She nodded in return and picked up the tray, walking openly through the door to the cellars. Three people saw her; no one stopped her. At the foot of the stairs she pulled open the middle door and walked in. She followed the right-hand passage this time, and without pausing she strode straight into the laboratory.

"Anyone fancy a cup of tea?" she said brightly.

Marc Bennett leaped backward at her sudden appearance, sending the stool flying until it tangled with his feet and brought him down with a crash and an oath. Jonas's reading was interrupted at the phrase "spiritual fire"; he yanked off his half-glasses and glared at her with thunder gathering on his brows. Jason broke off his work at the bellows, tried to straighten up, and instead went down on one knee with a brief cry that was instantly clamped back inside his lips. Anne took one glance at the agony on his face as the extent of his pain made itself felt, and then she swept in, set the tea tray down on the scarred, cluttered wood of the laboratory table between an astrolabe and a tall object draped in a pristine white cloth, and prepared to pour the tea.

"What the fuck are you doing here?" Bennett shouted at her, extricating himself furiously from the long-legged stool. "How the hell did you get in?"

Anne faltered, the teapot in one hand and a saucer in the other. "I thought you'd like a cup of tea," she repeated, sounding confused. "Dulcie told me that Jason was doing his 'Work,' so I figured you'd be down here somewhere, and the door was open, so I just came in. Why? Shouldn't I have?"

"I locked that door," Bennett declared angrily.

"Well, someone left it open."

"I locked it!" This time he looked to Jonas in appeal, but the big man just shrugged. "I did!"

"All right, so you locked it," Anne said, sounding like a mother soothing a petulant child. "But it unlocked itself and when I tried the knob it opened. Now, do you want some tea?"

"But you can't interrupt a Work!" he protested. He sounded as if he was about to stamp his feet in frustration.

"Oh, I'm sorry. You mean you don't take any breaks at all?"

"You know the rules."

She set the teapot down with a bang and turned on him indignantly. "Well, actually, no, I don't know the rules. I've been with Change for more than six weeks, and the only things I know about the Work of Transformation are what I've figured out by myself. Now, shall I take this back? You may have been sitting on your stool all morning, but the boy looks nearly done in."

"Maybe she'd like to work the flames for a time, Marc," suggested a deep voice from behind her. "If she's so concerned for the boy's welfare."

"But that's not—"

"I know," Jonas said. "But nothing else about Ana is usual; why should this be? Jason, show Ana what to do."

The boy peeled himself off the wall and bent to his task with a groan between his teeth. She left the men to their refreshments and went over to the stifling heat of the furnace.

"How long have you been at it?" she asked him.

Jonas answered. "He has been at his Work for six hours, and he will manage another six, with your help."

Anne bit her lip and studied the process, which involved the slow, steady depression and lifting of the handle of a large fixed bellows, its nozzle aimed at the low brick furnace filled with charcoal. The alembic in the top was about eighteen inches high and had some unidentifiable blackened mass inside. The tube that ran through its stopper ended in a container of water, where it bubbled occasionally with escaping gases. She waited until she had the rhythm right, and then she stepped up next to Jason and put her hand over his on the bellows handle. He kept his grip for two beats and then he pulled his sweat-soaked body away and let her work.

It was a hellish position, stooped and slow. In ten minutes her arm was numb, after twenty her side burned from scalp to hip. She shifted arms, worked for another quarter hour, and then Jason took over again.

It was a long, long day. Jonas resumed his reading aloud, Marc perched on a replacement stool and climbed down from time to time to add charcoal to the fire or make minute adjustments to the alembic, the contents of which seemed to change not at all. Jason's unspoken and guilty gratitude each time she took over was all that kept her going. Even with his youth, his muscles had to be screaming every bit as much as hers. The phrase "sweat meditation" floated into her mind, though she could not remember where it came from, and she would probably have continued with the pointless, hypnotic labor until she collapsed into the fire had Jonas not suddenly stood up, slapped his book shut, and declared, "The stage of calcination is at an end, and our material must rest before the Work is resumed. You have done well."

He moved to the workbench and snatched up the white cloth, revealing a tall, elegant glass pitcher and a matching glass. He filled the glass with water from the pitcher, picked up one of the teacups and dashed its dregs to the floor, then poured water into that, too. He carried cup and glass over to where Jason stood bent over and Anne sat against the wall, and presented her with the cup and Jason with the glass. When they had drunk the water, he took back the two vessels and put them next to the pitcher, and draped the cloth back to cover them. Marc Bennett had come around the table and was whispering furiously in his ear, but Jonas waved Bennett away and came back to stand over them, saying ceremonially, "It is time to cleanse ourselves and to take food again, and to practice the discipline of silence to those who have not seen our Work. Ours is a secret Work, about which nothing is revealed. You have done well," he repeated, and that seemed to be the end of the liturgical blessing, because Bennett leapt in again and insisted, "But she hasn't been cleansed and she hasn't taken her vows. You can't just turn her loose."

Anne narrowed her eyes, not liking the sound of that, but Jonas just threw up his hands.

"All right, Marc, do what you have to. But remember, I told you, Ana isn't following the usual Work here."

Which statement did not please Marc one bit. Still, it did seem that they were to be allowed upstairs once she had taken whatever vows were required; poor Dulcie would be overjoyed.

They followed Jonas down the stone passageway to the outer door with Bennett bringing up the rear. They paused to watch him lock the door, and when he straightened and looked meaningfully at Jonas, Anne braced herself. Bennett marched over to the door of Jonas's washroom, drew it open dramatically, and told her to go in.

"What? No, I'm not going to—"

"Ana," said Jonas. "Go."

She looked from one man to the other, but could read no threat in either of them. Bennett might be looking forward to teaching her a spiteful lesson, but it would not go beyond that, and Jonas, inscrutable as always, nonetheless seemed to be on her side. She did not want to be locked in that small space, but she had to admit that her nervousness did not justify frightening the boy by making him witness a doubtless futile struggle. She dredged up a smile. "Don't worry, Jason," she told him. "I seem to have gone about things backward, so I can't go upstairs until I've been through the starting rituals. It'll be okay. Go and find Dulcie—she'll be biting the carpets, wondering where we both are."

To save him from having to protest, she stepped forward into the small bathroom, then heard the key turn in the lock. Footsteps and voices faded as she examined the close space; with her luck lately, she thought in disgust, they'd forget all about her until Jonas needed to pee. And no doubt the ceremony was something that couldn't begin until midnight.

Still, there was plenty of water to quench her raging thirst, and a toilet, and she had gone without meals before. The water in the tap even ran nice and hot, and she set about cleansing her body, if not ritually then certainly in fact. In exploring the cupboards, she was pleased to find a bottle of aspirin with codeine, which made movement of her stiffening shoulders more bearable, and a cache of thick towels to cushion the floor.

She should have been so exhausted that she would welcome sleep, even in the cramped setting, but sleep would not come. Her muscles refused to relax, her mind leapt and skittered at every small noise, her eyes would not focus on the books of erotica even when the print was large enough to read without glasses. Her body wanted to throw itself noisily at the door, kicking and screaming, and her fingernails itched to peel away at the crack until they could insinuate themselves into the opening. Her lungs even tried to insist that they were low on air, that she was dizzy with lack of oxygen, although she knew it could not be so. More than anything, she longed to pace like a caged beast, but she could take no more than two steps before being trapped by the shelves or the toilet. It was all a part of their absurd alchemical ritual, she told herself again and again. Once she had expressed the proper awe and submitted herself to their masculine authority, they would be satisfied and let her go.

Long hours crept by. The noises of dinner built up overhead, feet slow and quick, heavy tread and the light patter of children. She found herself salivating like one of Pavlov's dogs when the sounds paused for the evening meal, and then the feet sounds resumed for the after-dinner chores. There was another pause during evening meditation, a lesser buildup of noise when that was finished, and finally all the noises faded away. The house quieted. Water, hot or cold, did nothing to satisfy hunger. The muscles of her shoulders and back burned in any position, and even the volumes of erotica lost their ability to distract after the first half-dozen. She found herself eyeing the delicate Japanese pictures of couples (and more) coupling, wondering if the pictures were printed on edible rice paper.

She hadn't heard a footstep overhead for at least half an hour, which put it close to midnight, when a noise came from outside the door. Struggling stiffly to pull herself upright from her nest of towels, she waited, her heart racing. A single pair of heavy feet descended the wooden stairs; half a minute later a key scraped in the lock. The door opened. Jonas stepped back, allowing her to emerge.

His dark eyes studied her, looked in at the small room, and came back to her face. "Did you enjoy my library?" he asked her.

She gaped at him. "Did I—? Well, no, to tell you the truth. Not under the circumstances. I didn't even have my reading glasses."

He nodded as if that were the only consideration, then asked, "Did you wash yourself?"

"Not very well, but—"

"That should do it, then."

"What?"

"Good night, Ana." He reached forward then, immobilized her head between his powerful hands, and bent to kiss her mouth, briefly but with a thoroughness so reminiscent of Aaron that it made Anne's scalp tingle. Before she could react, before she knew whether the tingle was lust or revulsion, the bearded mouth left hers. Then she felt his thick fingers enter the neck of her polo shirt to draw out the buckskin pouch and pull it over her head.

He picked open the drawstring top with surprisingly delicate fingernails and shook the contents onto the palm of his hand, turning them over curiously with one thick finger. The bead, tufts of fur from the dogs, stones, and bee pollen he funneled back into the pouch, but he took the silver crescent that she had bought in Sedona between two fingers and turned it back and forth, watching the light play across the low indentations of its beaten surface.

"The moon revels in the reflected glory of the sun," he mused. "In alchemical allegory, Luna reaches the height of her existence in her conjoining with the sun." He turned the pendant around again, and said, "Come."

She followed him reluctantly past the stairs that led to open air and back into his study. He went over to the strange collection of bones and objects at the third window, detached one item from the rest, and brought it back to her, displayed on his palm, its leather cord dangling down the back of his hand. It was the rough moon-shaped object she had noticed earlier, an elongated, worn silver nugget threaded onto a thong. He smiled to himself, the same private smile she had seen as he caressed the altar stone in the abbey ruins with his fingertips, and then he curled the thong around the moon shape and pushed it into the buckskin pouch and drew the bag shut.

"I'd like you to take that," he said. "It is . . . appropriate that you should have it."

Anne studied him, and asked slowly, "Why? Whose necklace is that?"

"It belonged to Samantha Dooley, who is no longer with us," he told her. "She did not, shall we say, live up to expectations."

Still smiling to himself, he tied the pouch snugly shut and dropped the cord back around her neck. He tucked the medicine bag inside her shirt and then tugged her collar up to hide it, a gesture that was somehow even more intimate than the kiss he had given her. "You may wear it," he said.

And then he walked out of his study and disappeared through the door to the laboratory.

Anne stood rubbing her hands across her mouth and scalp, trying to wipe away the tingle, to scrub away the taste of Aaron that Jonas had left behind, shocking, unexpected, and just too damn much, on top of everything else. She felt punch-drunk, and not only because of the painkillers she had swallowed. The past few days had been one long, deep plunge into the terror of her past ending with the abrupt euphoria of anticlimax, sleepless nights thinking she was balanced precariously over a bottomless abyss only to discover that it was all a fake, constructed by tricksters and fed by her own dark imagination. All in all, it was more than she could deal with. She felt like a jigsaw-puzzle person scattered across the landscape, and she craved only to have Marla Makepeace standing over her, gathering up the pieces one by one and putting her together again. She wanted to go after Jonas and draw his mouth down onto hers. She wanted to vomit at the idea. She thought about dashing her head against the stone wall until she lost consciousness. She felt as if she would never be rational again. She felt as if she had just faced death and walked away again.

She felt . . . she felt monstrously hungry, and would have killed for a cup of English tea.

She raided the refrigerator and gulped down a bowl of cold red stuff that looked like spaghetti sauce and tasted like Swedish meatballs, and followed it with a cup of scalding, strong tea. In the dim kitchen of the silent house, life seeped back. She palmed a couple more pain-killers from the bottle in her pocket and swallowed them gratefully. She might even manage to sleep tonight.

She went upstairs, aware of the silence and of the simple well-being that food brought, conscious of the blessed goodness of life in spite of everything. The urge to walk away from it all was powerful, but she held the two children before her like a talisman, her still center in a maelstrom of threat and desire and confusion. Jason and Dulcie would be asleep, but she decided to take the long way around and lay the palm of her hand on their door in passing, a silent good night. Snores came from a few of the rooms, most were still, but when she got to the children's door, to her surprise she heard low voices coming from within. She tapped very lightly, and the room went instantly silent. She tapped again, and heard movement inside, and then the door cracked a couple of inches.

She started to put her mouth to the opening and say that she just wanted to wish them a good night, when the door flew back and Jason—taciturn, undemonstrative, cool and aloof Jason Delgado—lunged out and flung his arms around her. She grunted at the pain and he immediately let her go, but Dulcie squeaked, "Ana!" and they hushed her and scurried inside the room, closing the door behind them.

In the end all three of them huddled together on one of the beds, Dulcie tucked in between them and fading fast.

"Are your shoulders as sore as mine are?" Anne asked him when Dulcie was limp.

"It's my back that kills me, when I bend over."

"Here, take one of these," she said, and tapped out a couple of the pills from the bottle. "If it doesn't help in an hour or so, take the other."

"Thanks." He reached for the half-glass of water next to Dulcie's bed, and winced at the movement. She put a third tablet down next to the one she had left on the table, just in case.

"So what did you think of all that?" she asked, very casually.

"I don't know. I mean, they're good people, but I've got to say, I don't understand half of what they're saying. And that alchemy stuff—it's weird shit."

Her heart sang even as he apologized for his language, and she reached over and squeezed his hand. "It's okay, Jason. We'll figure it out. Just give me a couple of days. Now, you get some sleep."

She stood up and moved to the door, where she paused for a moment to look down at Dulcie nestled in her bed and at Jason sitting on the edge of the other bed, bending stiffly to take off his socks. This might be the last time she was alone with them for days, weeks even. If she brought in the authorities (as she intended to do) and if they broke Change up (which they would), the truth of who she was and what she was doing here would be revealed to these two, and the trust of their relationship with her would be shattered.

Jason looked up, and frowned at the expression on her face. "What is it?"

"Nothing," she told him. "My dear Jason, it's nothing at all. Sleep well. We'll talk tomorrow." She left the room and closed the door on the two children, blessedly unaware that there would be no tomorrow.

CHAPTER 31

Change: Are you sure you're okay, Jonas?

Seraph: I told you I was fine. Stop harassing me, Steven.

Change: Okay, okay. You just sound troubled, is all. Are you sure the Social Services thing is off your neck? I could come over and--

Seraph [shouting]: Steven! Enough!

[a silence]

Change: I'm sorry, Jonas. You know best, of course.

Seraph: And before you ask me, no the work has not progressed. But I think it shall, very soon. I think I've seen the problem. Your friend Ana showed me it, in fact.

Change: Oh, that's really great news, Jonas. I don't suppose you want a hand with keeping the fire hot? Like the old days?

Seraph [laughing]: No, Steven, I don't think that will be a problem.

Change: She'll be helping you, I suppose. Ana. The boy can't be that far along yet.

Seraph [laughing]: Ana Wakefield will indeed help me in the great work.

Change: The great work? Jonas, what are you going to do?

Seraph: I am going to perform a transformation, Steven.

Change: But what kind, Jonas? Jonas, what do you have planned?

Seraph: You're not listening to me, Steven. I told you. Transformation.

Change: Jonas, listen. You're not--

Seraph: I have to go now, Steven.

Change: Jonas, Look--I was thinking today that maybe it's time to go on that trip to Bombay we were talking about. I could phone...you know, and see if he could see us.

Seraph: Good bye, Steven.

Change: Jonas, wait! Don't hang up. I need to-- [connection cut]. Damn.

[end of transcription]

Excerpt from the transcription of a telephone conversation between Steven Change and Jonas Fairweather (aka Jonas Seraph), 1:34 A.M. GMT, May 24, 199_

Anne Waverly continued upstairs to her own room, and to bed, and she drifted away into the first easy sleep she had found since getting on the plane. It was such a vast, earth-shaking relief, to know that she was just plain nuts, to know that her poor twisted imagination had simply carried her away, to know at last that everyone was safe. Not least of all was the half-humorous satisfaction of knowing that after the mess she'd made of understanding Change, Glen McCarthy would never ask her to do another job for him, ever again.

She had thought Jonas Seraph capable of insane violence. However, now it appeared that the most violent act the Bear was interested in was a sort of Tantric union with her. His primary goal seemed to be convincing another generation of followers that they, too, could make gold. She had thought Jason locked inside an alembic; instead, he had been set the task of a medieval apprentice. She had even believed that Jason was converting to Change doctrine, but now—the joy of his phrase "weird shit" rang in her ears, and she slipped into sleep with a smile on her lips, allowing herself to wonder what the two Delgado children would make of Anne Waverly's silent cabin in the woods.

She slept, and the house slept, unaware that below in the depths, the signs and portents of the last day were coming together in the mind of Jonas Seraph, freeing the fiery serpents from their mortal bondage. He gloried in this Woman, in what she had brought him and what she would do for him, and he labored hard to finish the preparations for this last and greatest Work of his lifetime. After so many trials and failures, after the disastrous mistake of thinking Sami would be the moon to his sun, the silver to his gold, after so many petty deceptions of gullible minds for the sake of perpetuating the whole, all the years of seeing one Work after another go dead and dry, at last it was upon him. Sami had been a mistake. Her energies in the end proved insufficient, her dedication no match for his own. That last Work with her had nearly robbed him of his confidence, reduced him to a thing as dead as she. Not this time. Soon, very soon, the final Transformation would be his. Every so often he paused to look up through the narrow windows, until at last he saw what he knew would be there, waiting for him: a delicate crescent, the first night of the new moon. And it was good.

The house slept, the moon rose and faded, and then at two o'clock in the morning, the peaceful, dignified Victorian mansion seemed to exhale sharply. The heavy cough jolted the building from one wing to the other; it startled the birds from their nests, set the dogs to barking, and reached down through the thick layers of fatigue and drugs to jerk Anne Waverly upright. She did not know what had woken her, but she heard the dogs and after a minute became aware of a strange vibration in the air, a distant roar almost too low to register as noise. She thrust her bare feet into her shoes and opened her door. Down the hall she saw movement as another person stepped out of a door on the opposite side.

"Did you smell smoke?" the woman said tentatively.

"Oh, God," Anne cried in despair. "Call 911," she ordered, starting down the hall in the other direction. "I'll wake the kids."

"Nine one one?"

"The fire department," Anne shouted over her shoulder, and then drew a deep breath to bellow into the night the alarm of "Fire!"

She flew along the corridor and down the stairs, making as much noise as she could, banging on doors, shouting continuously. Others had heard or smelled the danger and were doing the same. Screams built, one door after another flew open, the occupants rushing toward the stairs and safety.

When she reached Jason and Dulcie's room, the hallway was filled with running adults and children and the door to their room was standing open. She wasted agonized seconds looking under the beds and checking the bath down the hall, but they were gone. She could only pray with her very bones they had heard the alarm and run outside with everyone else.

The old house was going up like the stack of tinder it was. No need for a bomb made of fuel oil and nitrate fertilizer when one had a century-and-a-half-old house kept dry by its radiators, Anne thought in a brief bolt of rationality before she returned to the impossible task of checking the rooms.

She found one child sitting upright and rigid with terror as the flames broke through at the end of the corridor and roared full-throated at them. Anne snatched up the girl and fled down the back stairs, feeling the house trying to come down on her head.

The night air was thick with ashes and smuts and the fire leapt and swallowed with nothing to stand in its way. Beneath the noise of the blast furnace, adults shouted and cried out, children wailed, dogs barked and howled wildly, and the horses in the field screamed out their terror. Anne thought once she heard a siren in the distance, but nothing came near, and none of the residents caught shivering in the dancing light had any way of knowing that some of the popping glass they heard was actually gunfire, as Change guards in camouflage suits, unaware of what was happening, took potshots at the emergency vehicles gathering at the gates.

Anne was more interested in the absence of the only two people who meant anything to her. She pushed her way frantically up and down through panicked clusters of people, demanding if anyone had seen the two American kids. She found Sara, who looked at her uncomprehendingly from beneath a bloody scalp wound, and Deirdre, who was herself unscathed, although the woman she was with, probably her mother, was curled on the ground clutching her leg, white-faced with pain. Neither had seen Jason and Dulcie. Some of the adults were gathering the children together at a distance from the buildings. Two women ran up with an armload of first aid kits they had retrieved from the Change vehicles, dodging three white-eyed horses that pounded through the yard and vanished, freed with the other animals from the burning barns. Men and women staggered up to the place of refuge laden with horse blankets, buckets of water, and a couple of highly unnecessary kerosene lanterns, but their paltry attempts at organization amid the maelstrom of heat and the battering confusion of noise and panic was like a nest of ants working dumbly to restore order as the ground was being uprooted around their heads.

Anne dodged through the chaos of running adults in nightwear, past clusters of terrified children, around strange heaps of possessions that had been rescued and then abandoned—a sofa, three closed suitcases, a bedsheet wrapped around a tangle of clothing and framed photographs—looking for Dulcie and Jason. The cacophony of noise beat at her, the heat was a blaring, monstrous force, the bright, leaping illumination alternating with black, stretched-out shadows created a surrealist vision from hell, and Anne would have given five years of her life for a single deep breath of cool, smoke-free air.

And still she could find no sign of them. She stood for a moment in the lee of a wide, scorched-smelling oak tree and tried to gather her thoughts. Other than the house, which possibility Anne's mind refused to consider, there was only one place they could be. She wiped the edge of her white T-shirt across her filthy face and prepared to turn her back on the moaning adults and the screaming children—only to be grabbed by the shoulders and shaken furiously by a maddened figure shouting and spitting in her face. It took a moment to see Marc Bennett beneath the soot and the distorting terror and fury, and to interpret his words as a demand to know where Jonas was.

Her own fury flared to meet his. She shook off his grasping hands and slapped him hard, and when he took a surprised step backward she leaned into him, ten inches shorter and ready to tear him to pieces.

"You stupid piece of shit," she spat at him. "Your beloved tin-pot god went nuts. He went and sat in your alembic and set the place on fire around him, to see if he could make himself immortal."

"What are you talking about? What alembic?"

"The steel alembic you have in your basement. The one you use to lock boys in when they misbehave." God, she didn't have time for this. She tried to push past him, but he grabbed her right shoulder again and pulled her back to face him.

"You're the mad one here, you bloody woman. That's Steven's alembic you're thinking of. Now, where the hell is Jonas?"

Anne gaped at him, and her own hand came out to grasp his upper arm. The two of them stood as if they were hanging on to each other for support in the flaring, feverish light of the fire.

"Are you telling me you don't have an alembic?" she demanded.

"You think you know the first thing about us, all the high secrets, don't you? You don't know shit. We don't have an alembic for initiates. We don't need one. The whole place is an alembic." He freed his hand to gesture at the house, and she followed his fingers to see the stepped-up pear-shaped wall of the front of the house, now devoured in flames, and the chimneys at the top gathered together like a stem—or like a plug at the neck of a vessel. As she watched, one of the chimneys teetered, then fell away into the flames.

She swung her gaze back to his face, and when he saw her eyes, he tried to retreat. Her fingers dug in and held him.

"Where would Jonas go?" she demanded.

"What do you mean?"

"His 'power nexus'—where is it?"

But she knew. Before Bennett opened his mouth, she knew.

"The abbey," he said. "But how—"

She seized him by the lapels of his striped pajamas and pulled his head down until his face was almost touching hers, all the fury and fear of the last weeks lying naked in her face. "If you go there, if you so much as stir from this place, I will rip off your balls and feed them to you."

She saw her string of brutal monosyllables hit home, saw the fear in his eyes telling her that he did not doubt that she was perfectly capable of carrying out her threat. Then she turned and ran, stumbling in the uncertain light and cursing the branches and thorns that caught at her, plucking at her clothes, tearing her skin and slowing her down. Away from the glare of the fire, the sky was growing light, and when she fought her way out of the woods and into the abbey clearing, the day was already there.

So were Jason and Dulcie. They were not alone.

Anne stood, gasping for breath and fighting for calm with streams of black ash and bloodred sweat running down her face, her once-light-gray running pants filthy and torn, her heart pounding from exertion. Seeing Jonas seated on the altar stone, one distant corner of her mind abruptly knew, with the sure revelation of a light going on, that Samantha Dooley had never left Change, that she had given her life to Jonas Seraph's search for Transformation, that her remains now lay beneath the stone that Jonas had patted so affectionately when he first showed his new partner this place.

She was barely aware of the knowledge. The whole of her vision was taken over by the sight of Jonas Seraph, sitting on the newly settled stone, a shotgun resting across his folded knees, its barrels pointed directly to where Jason sat, half turned away from Jonas, his arms wrapped protectively around Dulcie. Anne walked forward slowly, and Jonas saw her.

"You are late!" he shouted furiously. "The fire must be nearly out—I called for you an hour ago."

Anne tore her eyes away from the two frozen children, and continued up the grassy aisle toward Jonas with her hands out at her sides, fingers splayed and palms down in the gesture of peace.

"I'm here now, Jonas, so you can let the children go."

He did not seem to be listening; instead, he had begun to stare at her with what looked like reverence. "My vision," he breathed. "A woman in white with the sweat of many colors on her face, giving birth to the golden-haired man."

"Let the children go, Jonas," she repeated. "They'll just be in the way."

His focus shifted to her face. "Innocence is needed."

"*Two* are needed, not four. I am the innocent here, and all the sacrifice you need."

"I don't . . ." he wavered.

Anne took another step forward, talking calmly. "Jonas, the fire is past its peak. You must have the female for your male, the moon for your sun, the mercury for your sulfur. You need me, Jonas. Now or never."

She reached down for the hem of her T-shirt and pulled it over her head. She wore nothing underneath it but the lumpy buckskin medicine pouch between her breasts.

She kicked off her shoes and moved across the cool grass to stand directly in front of Jonas. Without hesitating, she shoved her thumbs into the waistband of her sweatpants, peeled them off, and dropped them onto the turf. Turning her head slightly to meet Jason's astonished eyes, she said, "Take Dulcie and run," and then she threw herself at Jonas.

Anne's final awareness was of gratitude. Jason ran, with Dulcie in his arms: It was not all in vain.

7.
TRANSFORMATIO

transform *(vb)* to change in composition or structure; to change in character or condition; cf. CONVERT.

Procede we now to the Chapter of *Exaltacion,*
Of whych truly thou must have knowledge pure . . .
For when the Cold hath overcome the Heat,
Then into Water the Air shall turned be,
And so two contraries together shall meet,
Till either with other right well agree.

CHAPTER 32

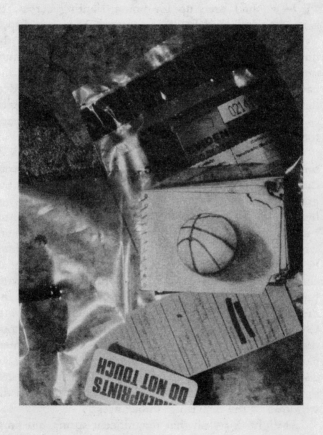

**From FBI documents relating to the Change case, Somerset
compound. Evidence photograph showing sketchbook
belonging to Jason Delgado.**

At eight-thirty on that May morning the sun had been up for hours, slanting across the hills and fields of southern England, dispelling the dew from the rich grass and the flourishing hedgerows. The air was still, the leaves motionless, and neighboring farmers in their fields and barns only now began to pause and sniff the air, wondering if the slow-moving haze in the air might not be connected to those distant sirens that had awakened them during the night.

The trees around the brick shell that had been a Victorian manor house were scorched and withered from the heat. Those farther away were no longer green but gray, laden down with the dirty snow of ash. The air was heavy with the stink of burning things, timber and foam rubber, plastics and fuel oil, leather and flesh—although whether the flesh was human, animal, or both would not be known for many hours. And now a great number of combustion engines made their contribution, spewing fumes into the sweet May morning, all the petrol and diesel motors that had first trickled, then surged into Change as soon as the camouflaged guards had stood down. Police and fire personnel, ambulances and emergency communication vans, NCIS investigators with Social Services hard on their tail, and the media left slavering at the gates to snatch photographs through the windows of the departing ambulances.

At eight-thirty on that magnificent spring morning, two more children came stumbling out of the woods. The boy wore a pair of running shorts, a once-white T-shirt, and one high-topped athletic shoe; the small girl had on a long flannel nightgown, filthy and torn, and her black hair was a wild mat of leaves and twigs. Both were shocked and footsore, badly scratched and caked in mud from their long, circuitous battle through the English jungle. They stopped at the edge of the clear ground, gaping at the incomprehensible sight before them. The girl whimpered, and the boy gathered her up into his arms and stood for a minute, studying the strangers.

Jason knew a cop when he saw one, even an English cop wearing a tweed suit, and although this was the first time in his life he had actually sought a policeman out, once he had chosen his man he did not hesitate. He adjusted Dulcie's weight in his aching arms and carried her up the drive toward the man, waiting at the tweed elbow until the man finished giving instructions to a pair of uniformed police constables.

"The bastard in the car, Bennett, knows where he is, but he's not telling. So have your men spread out, and for God's sake, be careful—he may be armed, too." When the two uniforms had trotted away, the man looked down at Dulcie and then quickly at Jason. "Is she hurt, lad? You need to take her over to that tent by the big tree, you see?"

"She's not hurt. Not much," he corrected himself at Dulcie's protest, and went on firmly. "There's a man with the FBI in the United States named Glen McCarthy. I really need someone to help me get in touch with him."

The man looked puzzled, and then to Jason's amazement he said, "I wish that was the hardest thing I had to do today." He raised his head and shouted across the yard, "Hey, McCarthy. There's one of your countrymen here, wants to talk to you."

Jason watched the approach of this mysteriously conjured figure of ultimate authority with a mixture of suspicion and awe.

"You wanted me?" the man asked in his American accent, and then took a closer look at the girl. "Dulcie?"

"Mr. York!" Dulcie cried. "What are you doing here?"

"You're Glen McCarthy?" Jason asked incredulously. "With the FBI?"

"That's me."

"Ana told me that if I—"

"Where is she?" McCarthy demanded.

"She's in the abbey."

"She's naked," Dulcie said, and let out a high-pitched giggle. Glen stared at her briefly before turning to Jason.

"Show me," he demanded.

Jason refused to move, just shook his head violently and cast a significant glance down at Dulcie.

"Oh my God," Glen murmured, and turned away with his hand across his mouth.

Jason looked around and spotted Benjamin and his mother. He led Dulcie over to them, dropped to his knees, and told her that she would have to stay with Benjie for a few minutes while he took Glen McCarthy to find Ana. Dulcie's lip trembled, but she allowed her brother to transfer her hand to that of Benjamin's mother, who picked up a blanket and wrapped it around Dulcie's shoulders. Jason went back to Glen.

"Okay," Glen said grimly. "Let's go." He looked around for the first policeman, and called, "Paul! Okay if we borrow a car?"

The tweed-covered arm waved its permission, but Jason said, "I don't think you can get there in a car."

The Land Rover took them most of the way, leaving them a five-minute walk to the abbey ruins. Glen strode across the uneven ground, torn between the habitual need to hurry toward the scene of any disaster and the deep knowledge that he really did not want to lay eyes on Anne Waverly's dead body.

She was there, naked, as Dulcie had said. She lay in a welter of blood across the still figure of a big, bearded man who appeared to have taken the main brunt of the shotgun blast that had downed them both. There had been a struggle, the boy Jason started to explain. His young voice broke, loosing tears of despair and self-loathing to run down his scratched and filthy face. Ana had tried to get the gun away from Jonas, and it went off. He should have stayed; he could have helped her. He should have put Dulcie down in the woods and come back to Ana, but the gun went off then, and they ran for help and got lost, and it was his fault, all his fault.

Glen knelt down next to Anne Waverly, less aware of the boy's words than he was of the cropped hair on Anne's head, the worn brace on her knee, and the unutterable tragedy of her pale nakedness. Some of the blood that covered her upper body was still bright red and wet. He settled his fingers automatically over her pulse, brushing aside a cord she had around her neck, knowing the search for life would be futile. He was so busy trying not to see her that it was a full twenty seconds before his fingers gave him the message: She still had a pulse. It was thready, but it was there, and in that moment Glen's hands felt a faint movement as the naked, bloodied woman drew a tiny breath.

Glen shouted aloud and stumbled to his feet, fumbling for his cell phone with shaking hands. Anne Waverly was alive.

Thus here the *Tract of Alchemy* doth
end,
Which (Tract) was by George Ripley
Canon penn'd;
It was composed, writ, and sign'd
his owne,
In Anno twice Sev'n hundred
sev'nty one:
Reader! Assist him, make it thy
desire,
That after Life he may have gentle
Fire.
Amen.

ABOUT THE AUTHOR

LAURIE R. KING lives with her family in the hills above Monterey Bay in northern California. Her background includes such diverse interests as Old Testament theology and construction work, and she has been writing crime fiction since 1987. The winner of the Edgar, the Nero, and the John Creasey awards, her most recent novel is *Justice Hall*.

Visit her website at www.laurierking.com.

"Rousing . . . riveting . . . suspenseful."
—*Chicago Tribune* on *The Beekeeper's Apprentice*

"Prickling with excitement."
—*Booklist* on *A Grave Talent*

"A lively adventure in the very best of
intellectual company."
—*The New York Times Book Review* on
A Letter of Mary

Enter the spellbinding world of
LAURIE R. KING

The thrill of the chase . . . literate, harrowing
suspense . . . There's nothing elementary about the
mysteries of Laurie R. King!

Since 1993, Laurie R. King has been tantalizing readers
with her award-winning, internationally acclaimed
novels of mystery and suspense. Turn the page for a
special look at Laurie R. King's books, along with
excerpts from the more recent novels. Each is available
now wherever Bantam Books are sold.

A GRAVE TALENT

A Kate Martinelli Mystery

WINNER OF THE EDGAR AND JOHN CREASEY AWARDS FOR BEST FIRST NOVEL

*The unthinkable has happened in a small community out-
side of San Francisco. A series of shocking murders has
occurred, each victim a child. For Detective Kate Martinelli, just promoted to Homicide and paired with a seasoned
cop who's less than thrilled to be handed a green partner,
it's a difficult case that just keeps getting harder.*

THE SECOND CHILD was found six weeks later, fifteen
miles away as the crow flies, and in considerably fresher
condition. The couple who found her had nothing in
common with Tommy Chesler other than the profound
wish afterwards that they had done something else on that
particular day. It had been a gorgeous morning, a brilliant
day following a week of rain, and they had awakened to
an impulsive decision to call in sick from their jobs, throw
some Brie, sourdough, and Riesling into the insulated bag,
and drive down the coast. Impulse had again called to
them from the beach where Tyler's Creek met the ocean,
and following their picnic they decided to look for some
privacy up the creekside trail. Instead, they found
Amanda Bloom.

Amanda, too, was from over the hill in the Bay Area,
though her home was across the water from Tina's. There
were a number of similarities in the two girls: Both of
them were in kindergarten, both were white girls with
brown hair, both were from upper-middle-class families.
And both of them had walked home from their schools.

The Beekeeper's Apprentice

A Mary Russell and Sherlock Holmes Mystery

In 1915, long since retired from his observations of criminal humanity, Sherlock Holmes is engaged in a reclusive study of honeybee behavior on the Sussex Downs. Never did he think to meet an intellect to match his own—until his acquaintance with Miss Mary Russell, a very modern fifteen-year-old whose mental acuity is equaled only by her audacity, tenacity, and penchant for trousers and cloth caps, unthinkable in any young lady of Holmes's own generation. . . .

I WAS FIFTEEN when I first met Sherlock Holmes, fifteen years old with my nose in a book as I walked the Sussex Downs, and nearly stepped on him. In my defence I must say it was an engrossing book, and it was very rare to come across another person in that particular part of the world in that war year of 1915. In my seven weeks of peripatetic reading amongst the sheep (which tended to move out of my way) and the gorse bushes (to which I had painfully developed an instinctive awareness), I had never before stepped on a person.

It was a cool, sunny day in early April, and the book was by Virgil. I had set out at dawn from the silent farmhouse, chosen a different direction from my usual, and spent the intervening hours wrestling with Latin verbs, climbing unconsciously over stone walls and unthinkingly circling hedgerows, and would probably not have noticed the sea until I stepped off one of the chalk cliffs into it.

As it was, my first awareness that there was another soul in the universe was when a male throat cleared itself loudly not four feet from me. The Latin text flew into the air, followed closely by an Anglo-Saxon oath. Heart pounding, I hastily pulled together what dignity I could and glared down through my spectacles at this figure hunched up at my feet: a gaunt, greying man in his fifties wearing a cloth cap, ancient tweed greatcoat, and decent shoes, with a threadbare Army rucksack on the ground beside him. A tramp perhaps, who had left the rest of his possessions stashed beneath a bush. Or an Eccentric. Certainly no shepherd. . . .

To Play the Fool

A Kate Martinelli Mystery

When a band of homeless people cremate a beloved dog in San Francisco's Golden Gate Park, the authorities are willing to overlook a few broken regulations. But three weeks later, when the dog's owner gets the same fiery send-off, the SFPD has a real headache on its hands. The autopsy suggests homicide, but Inspector Kate Martinelli and her partner have little else to go on. They have a homeless victim without a positive ID, a group of witnesses who have little love for the cops, and a possible suspect, known only as Brother Erasmus, whose history leads Kate along a twisting road to a disbanded cult, long-buried secrets, the thirst for spirituality, and the hunger for bloody vengeance.

HIS BREATH huffing in clouds and the news announcer still jabbering against his unemployed ears, the currently unemployed former Bank of America vice presidential assistant was slogging his disconsolate way alongside Kennedy Drive in the park when, to his instant and unreasoning fury, he was attacked for a second time by a branch-wielding bearded man from the shrubbery. Three weeks of ego deflation blew up like a rage-powered air bag. He instantly took four rapid steps forward and clobbered the unkempt head with the only thing he carried, which happened to be a Walkman stereo. Fortunately for both men, the case collapsed the moment it made contact with the wool cap, but the maddened former bank assistant stood over the terrified and hungover former real estate broker and pummeled away with his crumbling handful of plastic shards and electronic components. A passing commuter saw them, snatched up her car telephone, and dialed 911.

Three minutes later, the eyes of the two responding police officers were greeted by the sight of a pair of men seated side by side on the frost-rimed grass: One was shocked, bleeding into his shaggy beard, and even at twenty feet stank of cheap wine and old sweat; the other was clean-shaven, clean-clothed, and wore a pair of two-hundred-dollar running shoes on his feet.

The two officers never were absolutely certain about what had happened, but they filled out their forms and saw the two partners in adversity safely tucked into the ambulance. Just before the door closed, the female officer thought to ask why the homeless man had been dragging branches out of the woods in the first place.

By the time the two officers pounded up the pathway into the baseball clearing, the second funeral pyre had caught and flames were roaring up to the gray sky in great billows of sparks and burning leaves. It was a much larger pile of wood than had been under the small dog Theophilus three weeks earlier, but then, it had to be.

On the top of this pyre lay the body of a man.

A Monstrous Regiment of Women

A Mary Russell and Sherlock Holmes Mystery

The dawn of 1921 finds Mary Russell, Sherlock Holmes's brilliant young apprentice, about to come into a considerable inheritance. Nevertheless, she still enjoys her nighttime prowls in disguise through London's grimy streets, where one night she encounters an old friend, now a charity worker among the poor. Veronica Beaconsfield introduces Russell to the New Temple of God, a curious amalgam of church and feminist movement, led by the enigmatic, electrifying Margery Childe. Part suffragette, part mystic, she lives quite well for a woman of God from supposedly humble origins. Despite herself, Russell is drawn ever deeper into Childe's circle . . . far closer to heaven than Mary Russell would like. . . .

THE DOOR CLOSED behind Veronica, and I was half-aware of her voice calling out to Marie and then fading down the corridor as I sat and allowed myself to be scrutinised, slowly, thoroughly, impassively. When the blonde woman finally turned away and kicked her shoes off under a low table, I let out the breath I hadn't realised I was holding and offered up thanks to Holmes's tutoring, badgering, and endless criticism that had brought me to the place where I might endure such scrutiny without flinching—at least not outwardly.

She padded silently across the thick carpet to the disorder of bottles and chose a glass, some ice, a large dollop from a gin bottle, and a generous splash of tonic. She half-turned to me with a question in her eyebrows, accepted my negative shake without comment, went to a drawer, took out a cigarette case and matching enamelled matchbox, gathered up an ashtray, and came back to her chair, moving all the while with an unconscious feline grace—that of a small domestic tabby rather than anything more exotic or angular. She tucked her feet under her in the chair precisely like the cat in Mrs. Hudson's kitchen, lit her cigarette, dropped the spent match into the ashtray balanced on the arm of the chair, and filled her lungs deeply before letting the smoke drift slowly from nose and mouth. The first swallow from the glass was equally savoured, and she shut her eyes for a long moment.

When she opened them, the magic had gone out of her, and she was just a small, tired, dishevelled woman in an expensive dress, with a much-needed drink and cigarette to hand. I revised my estimate of her age upward a few years, to nearly forty, and wondered if I ought to leave.

"Why are you here, Mary Russell?"

"King has a gift for the rich, decisive detail and the narrative crispness that distinguished Conan Doyle's writing." —*The Washington Post Book World*

With Child

A Kate Martinelli Mystery

Adrift in mist-shrouded San Francisco mornings and alcohol-fogged nights, homicide detective Kate Martinelli can't escape the void left by her departed lover, who has gone off to rethink their relationship. But when twelve-year-old Jules Cameron comes to Kate for a professional consultation, Kate's not sure she's that desperate for distraction. Jules is worried about her friend Dio, a homeless boy she met in a park. Dio has disappeared without a word of farewell, and Jules wants Kate to find him. Reluctant as she is, Kate can't say no—and soon finds herself forming a friendship with the bright, quirky girl. But the search for Dio will prove to be much more than either bargained for. . . .

AND STILL, ALL THAT FALL, she looked for Dio. Once a week, she made the rounds of the homeless, asking about him. Always she asked among her network of informants, the dealers and hookers and petty thieves, and invariably received a shake of the head. Twice she heard rumors of him, once at a house for runaway teenagers, where one of the current residents had a friend who had met a boy of his description; and a second time, when one of her informants told her there was a boy-toy of that name in a house used by pederasts over near the marina. She phoned a couple of old friends in the Berkeley and Oakland departments to ask them to keep an ear out, and she arranged to be in on the raid of the marina house, but neither came up with anything more substantial than the ghost she already had. She doubted he was in the Bay Area, and told Jules that, but she also kept looking.

That autumn, in one of those flukes that even the statistician will admit happens occasionally, it seemed for a while that every case the Homicide Department handled involved kids. A two-year-old with old scars on his back and broken bones in various states of mending died in an emergency room from having been shaken violently by his eighteen-year-old mother. Three boys aged sixteen to twenty died from gunshot wounds. Four bright seventeen-year-old students in a private school did a research project on explosives, using the public library, and sent a very effective pipe bomb to a hated teacher. It failed, but only because the man was as paranoid as he was infuriating. A seven-year-old in a pirate costume was separated from his friends on Halloween; he was found the next morning, raped and bludgeoned to death. Kate saw two of her colleagues in tears within ten days, one of them a tough, experienced beat cop who had seen everything but still couldn't bring himself to look again at the baby in the cot. The detectives on the fourth floor of the Department of Justice made morbid jokes about it being the Year of the Child, and they either answered the phone gingerly or with a snarl, according to their personalities. . . .

"Like a slow-burning fire, the story makes you hurt deeply for King's characters before you realize what's happening to you." —*Kirkus Reviews* (starred)

A Letter of Mary

A Mary Russell and Sherlock Holmes Mystery

Late in the summer of 1923, Mary Russell Holmes and her husband, the illustrious Sherlock Holmes, are ensconced in their home on the Sussex Downs, giving themselves over to their studies: Russell to her theology, and Holmes to his malodorous chemical experiments. Interrupting the idyllic scene, amateur archaeologist Miss Dorothy Ruskin visits with a startling puzzle. Working in the Holy Land, she has unearthed a tattered roll of papyrus with a message from Mary Magdalene. Miss Ruskin wants Russell to safeguard the letter. But when Miss Ruskin is killed in a traffic acci-

dent, Russell and Holmes find themselves on the trail of a fiendishly clever murderer.

THE NEXT DAY, *The Times* arrived at one o'clock in the afternoon. It still lay folded when I turned off the lights and went upstairs, and it had not moved when I came back through the house on Friday for an early cup of tea. Two hours later, Holmes came down for breakfast and picked it up absently as he passed. So it was that nearly forty hours had elapsed between the time I saw Miss Ruskin off on the train and the time Holmes gave a cry of surprise and sat up straight over the paper, his cup of tea forgotten in one hand.

"What is it? Holmes?" I stood up and went to see what had caught his attention so dramatically. It was a police notice, a small leaded box, inserted awkwardly into a middle page, no doubt just as the paper was going to press.

IDENTITY SOUGHT OF LONDON ACCIDENT VICTIM

Police are asking for the assistance of any person who might identify a woman killed in a traffic accident late yesterday evening. . . .

I sat down heavily next to Holmes.

"No. Oh surely not. Dear God. What night would that have been? Wednesday? She had a dinner engagement at nine o'clock."

In answer, Holmes put his cup absently into his toast and went to the telephone. After much waiting and shouting over the bad connexion, he established that the woman had not yet been identified. The voice at the other end squawked at him as he hung up the earpiece. I took my eyes from Miss Ruskin's wooden box, which inexplicably seemed to have followed me downstairs, and got to my feet, feeling very cold. My voice seemed to come from elsewhere.

"A wonderful book, simultaneously inventive, charming, witty, and suspenseful. I loved it." —Elizabeth George

The Moor

A Mary Russell and Sherlock Holmes Mystery

Though theirs is a marriage of true equals, when Sherlock Holmes summons his wife and partner, Mary Russell, to the eerie scene of his most celebrated case, she abandons her Oxford studies to aid his investigation. But this time, on Dartmoor, there is more to the matter than a phantom hound. Sightings of a spectral coach carrying a long-dead noblewoman over the moonlit moor have heralded a mysterious death, the corpse surrounded by oversize paw prints. . . .

THE TELEGRAM in my hand read:
RUSSELL NEED YOU IN DEVONSHIRE. IF FREE TAKE EAR-LIEST TRAIN CORYTON. IF NOT FREE COME ANYWAY. BRING COMPASS.

HOLMES

To say I was irritated would be an understatement. We had only just pulled ourselves from the mire of a difficult and emotionally draining case and now, less than a month later, with my mind firmly turned to the work awaiting me in this, my spiritual home, Oxford, my husband and long-time partner Sherlock Holmes proposed with this peremptory telegram to haul me away into his world once more. With an effort, I gave my landlady's housemaid a smile, told her there was no reply (Holmes had neglected to send the address for a response—no accident on his part), and shut the door. I refused to speculate on why he wanted me, what purpose a compass would serve, or indeed what he was doing in Devon at all, since when last I had heard he was setting off to look into an interesting little case of burglary from an impregnable vault in Berlin. I squelched all impulse to curiosity, and returned to my desk.

Two hours later the girl interrupted my reading again, with another flimsy envelope. This one read:

ALSO SIX INCH MAPS EXETER TAVISTOCK OKEHAMPTON, CLOSE YOUR BOOKS. LEAVE NOW.

                                                    HOLMES

Damn the man, he knew me far too well.

"The great marvel of King's series is that she's managed to preserve the integrity of Holmes's character and yet somehow conjure up a woman astute, edgy, and compelling enough to be the partner of his mind as well as his heart." —*The Washington Post Book World*

O Jerusalem

A Mary Russell and Sherlock Holmes Mystery

At the close of the year 1918, Russell and Holmes enter British-occupied Palestine under the auspices of Holmes's enigmatic brother, Mycroft, and find themselves at the service of two travel-grimed Arab figures who receive them in the orange groves fringing the Holy Land. A recent rash of murders seems unrelated to the growing tensions between Jew, Moslem, and Christian, yet Holmes is adamant that he must reconstruct the most recent one in the desert gully where it occurred. His singular findings will lead him and Russell through labyrinthine bazaars, verminous inns, cliff-hung monasteries—and into mortal danger.

THE SKIFF WAS BLACK, its gunwales scant inches above the waves. Like my two companions, I was dressed in dark clothing, my face smeared with lamp-black. The rowlocks were wrapped and muffled; the loudest sounds in all the night were the light slap of water on wood and the rhythmic rustle of Steven's clothing as he pulled at the oars.

Holmes stiffened first, then Steven's oars went still, and finally I too heard it: a distant deep thrum of engines off the starboard side. It was not the boat we had come on, but it was approaching fast, much too fast to outrun. Steven shipped the oars without a sound, and the three of us folded up into the bottom of the skiff.

The engines grew, and grew, until they filled the night and seemed to be right upon us, and still they grew, until I began to doubt the wisdom of this enterprise before it had even begun. Holmes and I kept our faces pressed against the boards and stared up at the outline that was Steven, his head raised slightly above the boat. He turned to us, and I could see the faint gleam of his teeth as he spoke.

"They're coming this way, might not see us if they don't put their searchlights on. If they're going to hit us, I'll give you ten seconds' warning. Fill your lungs, dive off to the stern as far as you can, and swim like the living hell. Best take your shoes off now."

Holmes and I wrestled with each other's laces and tugged, then lay again waiting. The heavy churn seemed just feet away, but Steven said nothing. We remained frozen. The thud of the ship's engines became my heartbeat, and then terrifyingly a huge wall loomed above us and dim lights flew past our heads. Without warning the skiff dropped and then leapt into the air, spinning about in time to hit the next wave broadside, drenching us and coming within a hairsbreadth of overturning before we were slapped back into place by the following one. Down and up and down and around we were tossed until eventually, wet through and dizzy as a child's top, we bobbled on the sea like the piece of flotsam we were and listened to the engines fade.

"Welcome to Palestine," Steven whispered, grinning ferociously.